A Divorce in Salem

Laurie S. Pittman

A Divorce in Salem

Laurie S. Pittman

Woodhall Press | Norwalk, CT

Woodhall Press, Norwalk, CT 06855
WoodhallPress.com
Copyright © 2025 Laurie S. Pittman

All rights reserved. No part of this book may be reproduced in any form or by any electronic or mechanical means, including information storage and retrieval systems, without written permission from the publisher, except by a reviewer who may quote passages for review.

Cover design: LJ Mucci
Layout artist: LJ Mucci

Library of Congress Cataloging-in-Publication Data available

ISBN 978-1-960456-19-9   (paper: alk paper)
ISBN 978-1-960456-20-5   (electronic)

First Edition
Distributed by Independent Publishers Group
(800) 888-4741

Printed in the United States of America

This is a work of fiction. Names, characters, business, events and incidents are the products of the author's imagination. Any resemblance to actual persons, living or dead, or actual events is purely coincidental.

WARNING

THIS NOVEL EXPLORES ASPECTS OF PSYCHOLOGY AND MENTAL HEALTH AND CONTAINS A DEPICTION OF PRIOR ALCOHOL ABUSE, AND SUICIDE.

PLEASE READ WITH CARE. IF YOU ARE FEELING SUICIDAL OR YOU ARE HAVING SUICIDAL THOUGHTS, CALL 988 AND A QUALIFIED REPRESENTATIVE WILL ASSIST YOU.

Dedication

This story is dedicated to my children, because they taught me how divorce impacts children of different ages. My first marriage of twenty-three years never prepared my three daughters for how to weather their parents' divorce. Each suffered unique traumas, including separations from a parent and vast distances from other siblings. Throughout the separation and divorce process, each daughter found unique ways to cope. At times, her chosen pathway confused the rest of us.

Despite their mother's mistakes (they have no qualms pointing such errors out to me, and they do so each time we gather), yet after the errors are acknowledged with sincere resolve to do better, their laughter and tears never fail to peal from the rafters. Despite upheaval, they bloomed into independent, strong, and keenly intelligent women. Their metamorphoses are a credit to their own tenacity, their ability to forage for what each needed at the time, and for their unusual comedic talents. I breathe their light and gulp their love, and yet, my thirst for more is never quenched.

Ladies, your support means everything. In fact, at my lowest, it was your support I most feared losing. But, because we were all brave enough to insist on honest and open communication, even when words and sharing felt painful, it always brought forth new awareness and perception. We bonded even more deeply than any of us could have predicted.

I cannot wait to see what each of you will do next, what miracles will emerge from your creativity.

But, while I'm waiting, will one of you please let the dog out?

Contents

Chapter 1:	Hope Springs Eternal Disappointment	1
Chapter 2:	The Sit-Down	11
Chapter 3:	Parting Ways	19
Chapter 4:	We're Not in Kansas Anymore	23
Chapter 5:	Guess How Many People Live Here?	28
Chapter 6:	Talk Is Cheap	38
Chapter 7:	Broadway—Bound?	43
Chapter 8:	The Family Who Carves Together, Stays Together	55
Chapter 9:	Do You Hear What I Hear?	68
Chapter 10:	Mirror, Mirror, On the Wall	71
Chapter 11:	There Are No Small Roles	81
Chapter 12:	Bearing Good Tidings of Great Upheaval	89
Chapter 13:	A Voice Is a Powerful Tool	95
Chapter 14:	I Spy… an Actress	102
Chapter 15:	Marriage Closure	110
Chapter 16:	Duck! Duck! Goose!	130
Chapter 17:	The Ides of March Offers the Omen of Fowl Weather	147
Chapter 18:	Odor Most Fowl	155
Chapter 19:	A Stitch in Time?	163
Chapter 20:	The Wolf Comes to Blow Your House Down	168
Chapter 21:	Veterinary House Call	174
Chapter 22:	A New Way of Thinking	180
Chapter 23:	Best—Laid Plans	188
Chapter 24:	What Is a Friend?	192
Chapter 25:	You Can't Make Someone Love You	199
Chapter 26:	'Cause Ya Gotta Have Friends	205
Chapter 27:	Another Win for Michaela	212
Chapter 28:	The Walls Are Closing In	223
Chapter 29:	She'll Either Ignore You, or She'll Bite	227

Chapter 30:	Feeling Trapped	234
Chapter 31:	The Need for a Plan	247
Chapter 32:	The Princess Is Your Sister	251
Chapter 33:	Timing Is Everything	262
Chapter 34:	Getting There Is Easy, Staying There Is …	267
Chapter 35:	Rationing	271
Chapter 36:	Here's Your Misstep	274
Chapter 37:	There's No Place Like Home	277
Chapter 38:	I Think I Can! I Think I Can!	282
Chapter 39:	The Holy Grail Is Not Meant to Be Found!	286
Chapter 40:	How The Mind Wanders When Death Is Near	288
Chapter 41:	Jonah Exits the Whale!	290
Chapter 42:	There's No Place Like… a Hospital?	297
Acknowledgments		309
About the Author		311

1

Hope Springs Eternal Disappointment

At fourteen, Haylee didn't know why she scarfed her father's wedding ring from the kitchen counter. All she knew was she relished the use of a word like '*scarfed.*' The word transformed from wolfing down food into a new definition. *Scarfed* described both the stealth needed to not be discovered in the act as well as the exhilaration she experienced, an actual fluttering in her belly, from taking an object that did not belong to her. For Haylee, word usage could feel alchemic. Manipulation of a simple word could now seduce all five of her senses.

She dropped the wedding band in the pocket of her stone-colored barn coat and closed the front door behind her with as little noise as possible. Her fingers curled around the ring in secret, repeatedly. Haylee continued to twirl the ring inside her pocket. At the same time, she wondered why one small band of gold could make otherwise rational people believe that, worn daily, somehow the symbol meant two adults melded into one organism.

The day started as a raw March Monday. Sheets of icy drizzle coated the pavement of her sleepy community, tucked away in the southwest corridor of Chicago. The neighborhood nestled along the towns of Beverly, Morgan Park, and Blue Island and juxtaposed beneath the east side of the snowcapped Blue Island Glacial Ridge. From where she stood, Haylee scanned the rolling hills as their dusty colors speckled the horizon.

"No school for Haylee today," she declared on the front lawn. A painful memory intruded her peace. She remembered a time when kids at school laughed at her when she referred to herself in the third person during a science presentation. Confused by the flashback as well as the previous week's warmer temperatures, Haylee felt as vulnerable as the spring buds peeking through the last of the snow from two days prior.

Reaching into her other pocket, Haylee fingered for the money she'd need for her secret trip to the city.

"Oh, no!"

Haylee scurried back into the house, quietly turning the doorknob and closing the door just as stealthily behind her. A noise from upstairs prompted her to tuck her boots and barn coat back into the hall closet in case she couldn't escape without notice. Clambering upstairs, she rushed to retrieve the forgotten money.

Safely inside her room once more, Haylee lifted a small ceramic box from her dresser and opened its lid to count the money inside. Unlike her sister, who favored spending, Haylee saved every dollar—a twenty from her grandmother in Massachusetts, two fives from aunts on her father's side, a twenty from her father's mother, a ten from her last birthday, and a five for tidying up the basement.

Haylee knew her dad would scold her for skipping school, but she felt certain he would calm down once he realized she wanted to treat him to lunch. After all, he often said he wished he could spend more time with his family.

Connecting with her father was so much easier for her older sister Michaela. The two of them liked the same things—listening to music, watching television shows, and going to football games. He even coached Michaela's field hockey team. In the car, they would sing along to Freddie Mercury, the Goo Goo Dolls, and Toto. Whatever pastime they chose, even though Haylee might be right there, too, their comfort with each other made Haylee feel like the third member of a duo.

While Haylee knew her father loved her, she also knew her Dad wasn't as comfortable in her company as he was in Michaela's. Haylee liked to tinker—tearing apart radios, watches, appliances. On one occasion, she dismantled her sister's hair dryer. The tinkering infuriated both Michaela and her dad.

Even worse was Haylee's curiosity over his priceless stained-glass panel, as it sat atop an intricately carved teak coffee table in the living room. For Haylee, its colors and design created an irresistible compulsion. Why couldn't he understand she was just trying to be interested in something he loved?

So, Haylee figured out a way to sit near her dad without upsetting his penchant for order and stillness. Instead, she withdrew into her own artwork. The new habit allowed her to sketch the surrounding scenery. Sometimes, she even created entirely different worlds by depicting futuristic cities, oddly posed aliens, and mischievous elves.

But Dad didn't particularly like her art supplies spread out on the table, either. Just yesterday, after warning her three times, he threw away her favorite piece of charcoal. Haylee's response had been to fidget, fiddle, and shred paper. She even chewed a few pen caps. Of course, this made Dad even more upset with her, seeing her reaction to his sense of discipline.

Surely a visit to his dental office would be the perfect way to reconnect. Haylee enjoyed clacking the denture molds he used to illustrate proper brushing. And she loved the way his receptionist greeted her with a toothy grin.

Haylee tucked the treasured cash in her pocket, bounced down the staircase, and accidentally crashed into her mother's prized fern. She grabbed the teetering Asian urn just before it fell, then slid down the banister and plummeted to the kitchen floor.

Luckily, her mother did not notice. She was pouring coffee into a mug that declared her the 'WORLD'S BEST MOTHER.' Her long black hair sat high in the back of her head with a hair clip offering a sleek ponytail.

Haylee tiptoed from the oak banister just as her mom said, "Morning, Haylee." Those all-seeing blue eyes were already surveying Haylee's outfit for appropriateness.

Moments later, Haylee's dad lumbered down the staircase, commanding attention in his emerald cashmere sweater and business slacks with well-defined creases. He grabbed his 'DENTISTS EAT VAMPIRES FOR THE PERFECT BITE' mug from the cabinet, poured his coffee, and grabbed a single-serving yogurt from the refrigerator.

As soon as he sat down at the breakfast counter, his cell phone buzzed. He grabbed it and quickly replied to a text message.

"Liz," he said flatly, "Marcia added a five o'clock appointment with the Mendenhall boy. Seems he lost a filling."

His thumbs continued to fly across the phone.

Haylee's mother slammed down her newspaper. "Not tonight, Dan. You know we have parent-teacher conferences at five-thirty."

"Can't be helped, hon," he said, sipping his coffee and spooning yogurt from its cup. "Besides, Michaela's a great student. Conferences about her are no big deal."

He rose and walked to the sink, rinsed his mug, and shoved it into the dishwasher. With a quick flick of his wrist, he threw the yogurt container in the trash. Out of habit, he washed and rinsed his hands.

"Well, work calls! Bye, Haylee! Bye, Liz!" he said, as he grabbed his winter coat from the hook in the hallway.

Tension lingered thick as a heavy fog. Unable to sneak out now, Haylee sauntered over to the trash can, retrieved her father's discarded yogurt container, and threw it in the recycle bin under the sink. Then she grabbed a bowl, a box of cereal, and a spoon. Because she hated milk of any kind, she poured cereal in the bowl and sat on the stool next to her mother. The order in eating meant Haylee enjoyed the largest, intact rectangular pieces first, then and only after the larger rectangles were digested, did Haylee proceed to the smaller frayed pieces of cereal.

"I hope your homework's done," her mother said.

Nodding, Haylee kept on chewing.

Her sister Michaela marched into the kitchen wearing a navy-blue corduroy skirt and yellow angora sweater with diamond shapes around the collar. She took one look at Haylee and blurted, "Mom, you really need to teach Haylee manners. She eats as though she was raised in the wild!"

Mom either did not hear or chose to ignore Michaela's comment. Scoffing after a sip of her coffee, Elizabeth declared, "Leave it to your father. Marcia scheduled an emergency appointment at five. Now, your dad won't be able to attend parent-teacher conferences tonight."

"That's why they pay him the big bucks," offered Michaela, as if her father's no-show did not matter.

No wonder Michaela and Dad get along so well.

But their mother's irritation still festered. After each sip of coffee, she banged her mug on the granite counter.

"Well, *I* need to catch the bus," said Haylee as she slipped off the stool and went to the sink with her bowl and spoon. "Unlike *Miss Popular* who has a boyfriend with a car."

Her mother raised an eyebrow and veered to study Michael's reaction. Haylee snatched the cereal box and shoved it in the cabinet.

Then she kissed her mother's cheek, grabbed her backpack, and trotted to the foyer to get her coat from the hall closet.

"Bye!" Haylee called, slamming the front door behind her.

Outside, she felt free, unleashed, like a runaway dog. Stepping gingerly onto the horseshoe-shaped driveway, so as not to slip on the ice, Haylee headed toward the bus stop. No point going in the opposite direction and causing a neighbor to call her mother.

She tilted her head up and opened her mouth to swallow some of the drizzle. Haylee loved how rain made it possible to hear sounds undetected when the sun shone. Shuffled leaves, chirping birds, and even human footsteps echoed in a way no one else would notice. She savored the dampened world by herself.

Alone, but not lonely.

As soon as the kids at the bus stop came into view, Haylee remembered a New Age book her mother had purchased. The book explained how a person could assume the role of a wolf and using intense visualization, become so focused as to render the image camouflaged. The wolf was able to hide in plain sight amidst trees. While blending into the environment of trees and brush, the wolf could rush undetected to catch its prey. Now visible, a person could stand amid the crowd and yet no one would know they were there.

Trudging on, Haylee visualized herself as a wolf. She imagined being camouflaged, able to hide from the other kids at the bus stop. In her mind, Haylee sported pointy ears and grew large, brown eyes that could zoom in and out, ever alert and ready. Haylee pictured herself growing strong limbs for running, and of course, she swished a long bushy tail.

Haylee knew if she crossed the street in front of her classmates, someone would shout, "Hey, Neurodivergent! Where do you think you're going?"

How she hated the label, *neurodivergent*, the school psychologist had given her. Her mother had cried when the evaluation came back with the label. Haylee knew Michaela, in turn, had blabbed the results to her friends. News traveled fast at Reagan Middle School, especially when Haylee's peers had older siblings who shared classes with Michaela.

It's not fair. It was my secret, not hers.

To avoid being hollered at, Haylee approached the bus stop from behind and blended among the cliques of twos and threes. To be sure they continued to ignore her, she remained at the back of the pack. For a moment or two she waited, listening to the others debate about football.

Now, before the bus arrives!

With a casual style that belied her eagerness, Haylee walked away and turned the corner. She kept glancing back to see if anyone had noticed. Finally, convinced no one had, she sped toward the avenue. To avoid the icy sidewalks, and for better traction, she moved into the street and increased her pace.

She went six blocks on LeMond, then veered onto Coates Street. Ten more blocks and she'd reached the Metra line. The entire way, she paid attention to her breath, enjoying the wisps of each exhale. Her fast pace made the cold bearable.

At last, she stood in line for a boarding pass on the Metra.

"Cicero Street," she told the ticket clerk.

On the train, Haylee relished the vibration of the rails as well as the speed of the ride. Gazing out the window reminded her of a picture in an art gallery she'd once explored. In the lithograph, cars sped past the photographer. The camera seized the flashing colors without any definition of the vehicle's outline. Instead, the cars blurred into horizontal shafts of neon.

Slowing, the train came to a complete stop. Backpack secure, Haylee weaved her way through the other commuters to get to the outside world. She chuckled, as she imagined her fellow travelers as cows bumbling single file along an enclosed cattle chute.

A Divorce in Salem

Haylee strolled through heavy, white sleet, shifting her barn coat to keep from getting soaked by the icy rain. She veered left and stopped at the brownstone that held her Dad's dental practice, 2012 Cicero Street.

Where should I take Dad to lunch?

She guessed he'd want to go to Theo's Pizza. It was only a block away.

Entering the elevator, Haylee cried, "Fifth, please!" She assumed the woman who stood in front of the controls would press her father's floor.

While the elevator slowly moved, Haylee checked her reflection in the metal panels.

I look as good as I do on any other day.

Once the doors opened, she strolled down the hallway toward her father's practice. Intentionally, she walked past the main entrance. She wanted to avoid the receptionist who would undoubtedly yell, "Hey, Haylee!" which would spoil her surprise.

Instead, she crept down the hall to an unmarked door most people probably assumed was a utility closet. She turned the knob slowly, then closed the door behind her without a sound. The only noise came from water dispensing into cups and the buzz of drills from interior offices. Her wolf ears picked up everything clearly.

One more door to walk past. On her way, she practiced grinning. When her dad saw her, she wanted her smile to be as wide as Lake Michigan. She would catch the gleam in his eyes and bellow, "Surprise!"

1, 2, 3 here goes!

Haylee took the final step and pushed the door just enough to peek into his office.

Her wolf eyes and ears shut down. Time stopped.

Dad wasn't drilling. In fact, he didn't have a patient with him. Yet, he wasn't alone, either.

Haylee's eyes rested on her father and his dental hygienist folded in an embrace. She longed to look away, but stood frozen, rigid, almost paralyzed. Her father lingered over Tiffany, the hygienist, as he kissed her.

Staring at her father, all Haylee could think was that he and Tiffany didn't look anything like what she remembered from the sex education film she'd watched in last year's health class. Even though she understood there was more to it, the health class film had sex seem like a chore adults did when the latest Netflix series ended.

What her father and Tiffany were doing, didn't look clinical, or unpleasant. She watched Tiffany sink more deeply into her father's arms. She watched her dad smooth Tiffany's hair from her neckline, her eyes widened as she witnessed her dad run his index finger down her spine. Glued to the scene, Haylee wondered if Tiffany was the hunter or the prey?

White-hot tears clouded Haylee's eyes. Her knees wobbled. And suddenly it felt like she had taken flight, like she hovered across the ceiling. Looking down upon the whole horrid scene, she imagined she were a crop duster spraying pesticide on a field below. Hand inside her pocket, Haylee's fingers plucked at her father's wedding ring.

Suddenly, she ran. Without caring if she made any noise, she yanked the back entrance open and let the door slam behind her. Not waiting for the elevator, she scrambled down the side stairway and out into the street. Her chest heaving with sobs, she ignored passersby who stared at her as she ran. *Rotted fruit.*

That's what the image felt like in her brain.

Who could she tell? Certainly not Mom. And Michaela wouldn't believe her. Her sister would just snitch on her for ditching school.

Haylee wanted to rewind, to go back to earlier that morning, where she was waiting at the bus stop. If she could do it all over again, she'd choose school instead. What a haven school would have been, compared to this.

Her thighs burned as she ran on, and now a stitch stuck under her rib cage. Icy sheets of rain soaked through her clothes, making them heavy. Her breath came in rapid pants. Still, she ran on. The only thing she could think to do was focus on the mathematical formula for the area of a rectangle. *Yes, geometric truth*. Its beauty relied on exactness, purity, and ultimate fact. Un-messy. Balanced.

She didn't know how she made it on the train and got all the way home, but suddenly, there she was, standing in the horseshoe-shaped driveway, looking at her house. Never again would she think of that awful brownstone building as Dad's dental office. Instead, she would forever refer to it as '2012 Cicero Street.'

Sliding in through the front door, Haylee wiped her boots on the oriental rug in the foyer. Her mother must have heard her because she poked her head out from the kitchen.

"I'm sick," Haylee fibbed. "The school nurse drove me home."

Her mom stared at her for a moment, then offered, "Take off your wet clothes and get into bed. I'll bring you some soup in a little bit."

Haylee was relieved. Her Mom must have interpreted her reddened face as proof of illness and not of crying.

She climbed the stairs, threw her barn coat on the floor, and crawled into bed. She didn't care in the slightest that her father's wedding band was no longer in her coat pocket having disappeared somewhere between the city and home.

2

The Sit-Down

Four months later, Haylee saw sautéed salmon and asparagus for dinner. Haviland Limoges china. Cloth napkins.

Not a good sign.

Haylee knew the last time they'd had a fancy family dinner like this was when her mother announced that Grandpa had suffered heart failure and died.

After another nice summer evening of romping and drawing, this was the last thing Haylee wanted to endure, a dinner under the guise of delivering bad news. She cringed at the silence enveloping the dining room and shoveled a piece of salmon into her mouth. Rather than chewing, Haylee took a swig of water and swallowed the bite of salmon whole. She hated the texture of fish, and texture meant everything. Creamy peanut butter-*In*. Flaky, fatty salmon-*Out*.

Hoping to lighten the somber atmosphere, Haylee tapped a knife against her water glass. She'd seen it done on TV sit-coms preceding big family announcements.

Michaela wrinkled her nose and glared. Her father stopped pushing bits of salmon around his plate and looked up. Her mother reached across the table and grabbed Haylee's hand midair. But nobody shouted.

*Not good. **Not good at all.***

As soon as Mom let go of her hand, Haylee cut up her asparagus in small pieces, then followed the same swallowing routine to eat it, preventing herself from having to taste the the wild weed. Finished with the required three-bites rule, Haylee fiddled with the cloth napkin on her lap.

Maybe Grandma died this time.

The dinner scene reminded Haylee of stories her mom talked about when she referred to her mother's teenage years, of coming home from a date to find Grandma—Mom's mother—barely dressed in her nightgown, spraying window cleaner across the storm door on a snowy winter night and reeking of beer. Mom said her date—this was before she met Dad—peeled out of the driveway without even walking Mom to the door. On a different occasion, Grandma flirted with another of Mom's boyfriends, a star quarterback.

Grandma was no Mother of the Year.

Haylee glanced at her family. No one spoke. No eye contact, either. The only thing left to do was to focus on her dinner roll by pulling it apart, bit by bit, until it was no longer recognizable as a piece of bread. Silence hovered over the dining room like an over-loaded rain cloud. Lips pursed; Haylee's mother spoke.

"Girls, gather the dishes, please. Rinse them well before you put them in the dishwasher. Your father and I will meet you in the living room when you're done." Standing, her mother snuffed out the tapered candles on either side of the begonia centerpiece.

Haylee gathered the china and silverware while Michaela brought the glasses and serving bowls to the kitchen sink. Both huddled, side by side.

"What do you think Mom's going to say?" Haylee whispered.

Michaela smirked. "Did you get into trouble at school again?"

Why does it always have to be MY fault?

"As if my getting into trouble at school would require you to participate in a family meeting!" Haylee retorted.

"All I know is, we haven't won the lottery. They'd be a little more cheerful," reasoned Michaela.

Dishwasher loaded, Haylee watched as her sister put detergent goop in the designated trays and gave a firm tap to start the machine. Then, using an open palm, she ushered Haylee into the living room.

Their mother sat on the peacock-blue chair, arms folded, legs crossed, the one on top swinging mechanically. She stared at the ceiling. Their father's arms were splayed across the back of the white sofa.

Haylee made a beeline for the stained glass on the coffee table. She couldn't help it. She just had to fiddle with it.

In an instant, her father jerked forward. "Haylee, leave my Frank Lloyd Wright panel *alone!*"

Good thing a sketchpad and some colored pencils lay nearby. Haylee settled on the floor by the coffee table and started to draw the logo of one of her favorite bands.

"Well, Elizabeth, do you wish to start?" Haylee's father asked.

Michaela had flopped down beside him on the sofa, where she snuggled in, resting her head on his shoulder.

I never do anything like that with Dad.

Haylee's mother uncrossed her legs and placed her hands on her knees. She cleared her throat.

"Girls, your father and I love you very much." She paused and reached out to grab a tissue from the box on the end table. Then she blurted, "Your father and I have been talking, and, well ... we've decided to get a divorce."

Haylee put down her pencil.

"A divorce!" Michaela screeched, shooting up from her comfy slouch.

Dad took her hand and stroked it. "I know this is hard, Michaela," he said, then added as if it were an afterthought, "and Haylee." He paused for a moment. "Your mother and I are no longer happy together. We think it will be better for you girls if you don't have to listen to us arguing all the time. We just want what's best for you."

Haylee still couldn't look up. Not yet.

"What about marriage counseling? You haven't even tried that!" Michaela spouted. "There's even a daytime TV show to help couples like you and Mom!"

Dad leaned over and yanked tissues from the box to hand to Michaela, who was crying now.

Elizabeth, as if she'd suddenly grown weary, slipped from the edge of the chair to the floor, where she put the soles of her feet together, as if they were hands clasped in prayer.

"Honey," she said, "some marriages are not meant to be. Your father and I can't seem to agree on anything anymore, and our fighting isn't healthy for you girls." She put a hand on Michaela's knee, who sobbed and hung onto Dad.

Dad cleared his throat, and Haylee noticed his eyes glistened, too.

The fantasy she'd constructed of that long-ago March Monday now four months in the rearview mirror of time crumbled around her like grains of sand escaping a gripping palm. Though she'd known all along that she hadn't made up the kiss, it was easier to believe she had.

She stared at the sketchpad in front of her as she gathered courage to ask, "Are you getting a divorce because of Tiffany?"

Her father's face reddened. Wrenching his arm away from Michaela, he pointed violently at Mom. "Elizabeth, you promised!" he hissed.

Elizabeth rose off the floor and standing with arms crossed, stared him down. "For your information, Dan, I did not tell our girls anything about Tiffany! You don't know me at all! I would never hurt them with this kind of ... *sordid* information!"

"Well, then, Haylee must have overheard you whining to one of your *friends*, or worse yet, your loose-lipped mother!"

Haylee wanted to take flight, just as she had on that icy Monday, but instead she raised her chin and looked directly at her father.

"I saw you kissing Tiffany at your office."

Mom gasped. Michaela's eyes grew wide.

"You couldn't have!" Dan bellowed as he wrenched away from Michaela and stood up. "You haven't been to my office in two years!"

Haylee closed her eyes and kept them closed while she spoke.

"Mom, do you remember the day I said the school nurse brought me home because I was sick? I never went to school that day. I took the money I'd saved up and got a train ticket, and I went to Dad's office. I wanted to do something different from boring lectures at school, so I decided to take Dad to lunch."

She paused to catch her breath, which was suddenly wheezy.

"I ... I tiptoed to the rear door, 'cause I wanted to surprise you, Dad. But I didn't alert you 'cause I saw you kissing Tiffany. You were using your finger to glide up and down the zipper of her dress."

"Oh, Haylee, you're making this up!" her father snapped.

"I hoped she was kissing you because you'd given her a raise," Haylee murmured.

Michaela guffawed, and her laugh forced a giggle from Haylee.

Dan's hands now balled into fists, and he looked furious.

"Michaela, do not laugh at your father," Elizabeth scolded.

"I wasn't laughing at *him*." Michaela was still chuckling. "I was laughing at how dumb Haylee was for thinking there would be a kiss because of a raise in salary."

"You might as well know the rest," Haylee mumbled.

"Oh, dear God, there's more?" her father said.

A Divorce in Salem

"Yeah," Haylee admitted. "It's my fault you're getting divorced, cause I'm the one who lost your wedding ring, Dad."

Standing, breathless, Elizabeth cried, "Haylee, your father and I argued about that ring for months!"

"Yes, you assumed I chose not to wear it!" Dan barked.

Michaela stood up and swept her long black hair off her shoulders. She wasn't crying anymore. She wasn't laughing, either.

"Well, now that we know your plans, may we be excused?" she asked coldly.

"Not so fast," Mom said. "You need to hear the rest."

"Great!" Michaela sighed, plopping back down on the sofa.

Dan said, "Your mother decided to move to your grandfather's house in Salem, Massachusetts and you girls are going with her."

"*Mom!*" Michaela wailed. "I don't want to move to that hick town. Dad told us it's full of witches and warlocks!"

Haylee remembered their father saying those things about Salem. She knew that's where her mother grew up, but Mom had never returned to Salem once she and Dad had relocated to Chicago. Accepting her parents' divorce was one thing, but the idea of moving to a new town where she'd have to meet new kids, go to a new school, felt overwhelming.

Michaela will spread rumors about my Neurodivergence/Spectrum just like here, and a whole new set of people will make fun of me and call me, Neurodivergent, or say that I'm an alien.

Haylee bit her lip as a flood of tears gushed from her eyes like an angry river breaking through a dam.

"Notice that when your father is disrespected, I support him!" Mom muttered, chewing the inside of her cheek. "But when I need backing, I get none. I get none."

Chewing her cheek meant screaming would follow. Only this time, Haylee's mother didn't scream. Instead, she said quietly, "Your dad and I agree on this. If the three of us move to the house your grandfather willed to me in Salem, there will be more money for you girls, for clothes and other things you want, as well as for your activities, and later, for college."

Haylee didn't want to be upset with her mother; she wanted to feel bad for her. But Haylee couldn't stop the anger roaring to a boil inside. By moving them away from Chicago, Mom was going to spoil everything!

Michaela cleared her throat. "Have you two considered who's going to teach me to drive?" Michaela swung around for emphasis. "It can't be Mom. We'll kill each other if she tries to teach me."

Neither parent responded to this inquiry of an upcoming milestone. Oddly enough, Haylee suddenly felt the urge to giggle. She pictured Michaela and Mom in a heated argument about which way to turn or something. Unfocused, due to the image of their bickering, Haylee could see her sister veering off into a ditch.

Michaela stomped off.

Focusing on her sketchpad once more, Haylee started to draw the trunk of a tree. "I don't suppose the house in Salem has a pool, does it?" Haylee wondered aloud.

"No," Elizabeth said. "But it's a charming, two-story home with lovely gardens in the backyard. Did you know it was built in 1822? And it's painted yellow, so I think you'll like it."

Haylee couldn't imagine how an old house, even if it were yellow, could make up for not having a pool.

Quickly adding, Elizabeth suggested, "I applied for a bookkeeping position at McClure, Packer and Bourke, and I start on Monday."

"*Monday!*" Michaela thundered back into the living room. She obviously hadn't gone far "That means we won't even have time to say good-bye to our friends!"

"You won't have to say good-bye to them, sweetie," Dad said. "Think about social media. You'll be able to stay in contact with your old friends, yet you'll make lots of new ones in Salem, too."

Before Haylee knew what was happening, her arm was grabbed by Michaela who yanked her toward Michaela's torso. Michaela bellowed, "C'mon, Haylee. Let's leave our parents to do what they do best—make our lives miserable!"

Michaela stomped loudly up the stairs, so Haylee did, too.

At the top, Michaela whispered, "Wanna sleep in my room?"

Wow. I'm usually not even allowed to go near her room, let alone sit on her bed.

Once in her room, Michaela asked with eyes bored into Haylee's, "Are you scared?"

Nodding and tearing up, Haylee acknowledged, "You got that right!"

3

Parting Ways

Haylee popped the cream-cheese bagel between her teeth and grabbed the handle of the plaid suitcase containing most of her clothing. Eyeing the living room of the only home she'd ever known, Haylee flinched, as her stomach knotted into a tight ball.

She realized she wouldn't see the eggshell chair hung by a chain in the corner of the living room anymore. She wouldn't sit nestled inside the Morris chair in the opposite corner, a gift her father had received after doing pro bono dental work for a soldier returning from Afghanistan. This furniture she'd climbed over, laid her head on, and on which she'd eaten forbidden snacks, no longer belonged to Haylee.

Haylee felt like her father had earned sole custody of every comfort Haylee held dear, while relinquishing any connection to her. Could that happen? Could Haylee lose all rights to a relationship with her father?

Will I wake up tomorrow and no longer belong to him?

While grinding her teeth made her jaw ache, the new habit kept her tears from sight.

Last night, she'd wasted precious sleep time by dreading today's long car ride. Once again, she ran through all the states they'd cross—Illinois, Indiana, Ohio, Pennsylvania, New York, and finally, Massachusetts.

Invariably, Michaela would claim the front passenger seat and expect to do so without argument. As the family learned years ago, Michaela had a way of making everyone miserable if she were relegated to the back of the car. Haylee, on the other hand, had adapted. She'd even learned to enjoy the solitude of the forgotten backseat. Since the journey would take days, a pillow would be necessary, to make sitting for long periods more comfortable, and to help her survive her mother's anxious driving, so she grabbed one.

Pillow under one arm, suitcase dangling from her other hand, Haylee stepped outside. Slate—gray clouds sprinkled drizzle.

Fitting. Even the Chicago weather is sad.

Haylee neared the SUV, watching her mother shove a laundry basket filled with linens and bedding into the trunk.

"Michaela, get out here now!" she hollered.

Silence.

Haylee slowed her own pace to see how her mother would react.

"I know you can hear me! We need to leave *now!*"

A moment later, Michaela stormed through the door, and it slammed behind her.

Haylee caught their father peering through the living room window. A moment later, he stepped out onto the porch.

"Elizabeth, let me say good-bye," he pleaded.

Sighing, Haylee's mother waved a dismissive hand.

Michaela stomped back up to the porch, and Haylee followed. Grabbing their arms, Dan pulled them back into the foyer, under the crystal chandelier. He started to sob as Michaela wrapped her arms around his waist.

"Oh, Daddy!" she wept.

Haylee shifted her weight from one leg to the next. She still carried her pillow and suitcase. The intensity of the moment made her itch with discomfort, so she glued her eyes to the marble and crystal chandelier that hung from the foyer ceiling.

"We can video—call, and you can text me whenever you want," Dad offered. Rubbing Michaela's back, he said, "And I'll come there to Salem, to see you both once Marcia clears my schedule."

"I don't see why we have to move away from you, Daddy! Mom is so cruel!" Michaela wailed.

Dad put his hands on Michaela's shoulders, "No, Michaela, your mother and I agreed." Then he reached over and cupped Haylee's chin in his palm. "I didn't like the idea of your moving so far away either. But after going over our finances, we realized it would be better for you if we didn't have to handle two mortgages. I know this is hard to understand because you're young, but it's for the best." he said firmly.

He disentangled himself from Michaela and pivoted to pick up two small boxes from the foyer table. "I was going to give you these when you turned eighteen," he said, "but in light of the separation, I thought maybe I should give them to you now."

He held out the long slender box to Michaela. Haylee set her suitcase and pillow down to take the square one he handed to her.

Michaela opened hers and gasped, as she picked up a strand of pearls. "Oh, Daddy, they're gorgeous. Thank you!" She threw her arms around his neck and kissed him on the cheek.

Haylee delicately lifted a pearl bracelet with a diamond clasp from her box.

"Wow," she murmured.

In truth, she didn't know how to react. Michaela was much more skilled at demonstrating appreciation. Showing gratitude made Haylee feel exposed, vulnerable.

She returned the bracelet to its box, then stuffed it in the side pocket of her suitcase.

Her father cleared his throat and yanked a Kleenex from his pocket. He gave it to Michaela and then just stood there, staring into her teary eyes.

Haylee felt like an intruder.

"Okay, now, your mother's waiting," he said. "I'll walk you to the car."

He opened the front door for them, and Michaela kept her arm around his waist as they stepped onto the porch and walked down the short walkway to the car. Haylee traipsed behind.

Mom started the car, and despite the drizzle, stuck sunglasses on her nose. Haylee noticed how her mother firmly planted both hands on the steering wheel and stared straight ahead.

Dad gave Michaela a squeeze, and then he hugged Haylee, too. To them both, he said, "I love you. Mind your mother."

Haylee stuffed her pillow and suitcase into the backseat and climbed in after them. She wondered how her father would eat, take care of the house, keep up the yard and manage his dental practice, all at the same time. The idea made her weep with empathetic overwhelm.

She looked out the window, as tears, in catalogue, scaled down her cheeks.

Her Dad slammed the car door and sprinted back into the house.

Dad's looking forward to a home without us! That's why he's running away from Michaela and me. He thinks Tiffany is the better deal!

Haylee scrubbed away her tears. She'd find a way to make him pay, even if she didn't know what making him pay looked like, yet.

4

We're Not in Kansas Anymore

The August sunset hovered above Route 1—A. Haylee donned sunglasses and asked Mom why she'd chosen this path from Boston, since the GPS had suggested another, faster way to Salem.

"This way is more picturesque," Mom said. "You'll love the charming coves, isolated beaches, and quaint shops of all sorts."

But instead of gushing over the view, Mom groaned the whole way about traffic and cursed the idea of urban sprawl. Cars, smaller trucks, and bicyclists used up every inch of the road which meant their progress was slow with a lot of stop-and-go engine and brake lunging.

"Don't they know how to build proper roadways out here?" Michaela scoffed, fiddling with her cell phone.

"I know you girls will love Salem as much as I did when I was your age," Mom said. Haylee caught her glance in the rearview mirror. "When I was a teenager, my friends and I walked everywhere. We used to swim in the quarry, and then go to town for ice cream. In the fall, we collected Cat-o'-Nine—tails."

In the mirror Haylee saw her mother's wistful smile and noticed how her grip on the steering wheel had loosened.

Michaela, of course, remained glued to her phone.

"You can go sledding on the hill above the cemetery when it snows," Mom continued. "And Haylee, you'll love meandering around Salem Common. Michaela, you'll adore the shops on Pickering Wharf."

Mom reached over and patted Michaela's knee, to no effect. "Haylee, there are all sorts of sandy coves to explore. "My friends and I loved to wander where we knew adults weren't likely to follow."

Haylee stared down at the sketchpad in her lap. Her latest drawing depicted the sun hovering over a calm ocean. Just as she grabbed the right—colored pencil to add glistening light to the water, both hers and Michaela's phones dinged. A generic text from Dad.

I miss you girls!

Let me know when you reach Salem.

Love you.

How dare he send a text like that, after making a beeline into the house when we left. He didn't even wave good-bye!

Haylee turned off her phone without replying, but Michaela was typing feverishly.

Through the window, Haylee saw an obese man stoop to pick up something he'd dropped by a parking meter on the sidewalk.

Michaela's clicking stopped. "Eat another donut!" she shouted.

"Michaela!" Mom chided. She pressed the gas, and the car lurched forward. "The window is open! How do you know he's not diabetic, or that he doesn't have a thyroid disorder! You should be ashamed of yourself."

Michaela ignored the reprimand. "This place is a *dive*," she sneered. Grabbing a shank of her silky hair, she pulled it over her shoulder to inspect for split ends.

Haylee rolled her eyes and focused once more on her sketch.

"You spend more time drawing than you do on actually living," Michaela scoffed over her shoulder.

Haylee ignored her. Instead, she concentrated on the seagull she'd drawn, soaring above a cresting wave.

A short time later, Mom declared, "Girls, Look! We're here! Finally, after two days of driving, we've made it to Salem."

Her mother's cheerful tone made Haylee realize she must have really missed her hometown. For her sake, Haylee tried to pay attention to the small town's winding roads and old buildings.

"Your father never understood my love for this place," Mom remarked. "I left my home for him, to put him through dental school, so I was the employed one. I worked as a bookkeeper, and now, have come full circle."

In the rearview mirror, Haylee observed the lines around her mother's mouth and noticed how her thought deepened the wrinkles.

She's pissed at Dad, too.

"Hey, there's a satanic Church! Where have you taken us?" gasped Michaela.

"North Street," Mom said, chuckling.

Haylee didn't think that comment warranted laughter. Goosebumps traveled down her forearms.

"Chicago has satanic churches, too," Mom said. "You just didn't know about them, because your father and I saw no purpose in pointing them out to you."

The car glided down a narrow street, and Mom explained that up ahead was Salem Common. She pointed at a bronze statue, "That's Roger Conant in front of the witches' dungeon, facing the Hawthorne Hotel. That's a favorite museum for tourists interested in the Mass Hysteria."

Haylee flipped to the next blank page in her sketchpad, and drew Roger Conant, with his billowing cape and Pilgrim hat. She shuddered at the scowl she'd drawn on his face. He looked menacing, harsh, as if following the Pilgrim bible meant enduring lifelong punishment.

"Who was he exactly, Mom?" Haylee asked.

"Roger Conant led the first Pilgrim settlement. In fact, he fought against the Puritans who came soon after, and in so doing and winning, became the first governor of Salem."

With furious strokes, Haylee scribbled over her drawing. Her heavy strokes moved effortlessly, as Haylee captured every wrinkle, every sunbaked crease that depicted a life of insecure piety.

Haylee spent the next leg of their journey wondering what Salem looked like before the settlers had erected their homes, churches, and barns. She imagined deep snow drifts several feet high thinking there wouldn't have been any factories to alter the climate and landscape. Haylee knew snow and ice could be cruel to those trying to keep live stock sheltered from the bitter winds.

How dark was the sky when multitudes of geese flew overhead? After all, birds would have flown undisturbed, since few hunters existed to limit their numbers. What flowers and reeds grew wild in the days when Native American tribes farmed Salem's landscape?

One page after the next, Haylee sketched what she saw in her mind. Through art, Haylee found herself awakening to what Salem had to offer—magic, excitement, and exploration. In sharp contrast, she felt trapped in the car. She wearied from riding in the backseat of the SUV and felt as shackled as a Pilgrim in pillory. Wriggling back and forth in her seat, Hayley borrowed from the way she molded sand to fit her body on the beach. The effort still resulted in discomfort. Haylee pleaded, "Mom, how much farther?"

"We're almost there. Just another turn, here, down Essex Street, and the house will be just ahead," Mom declared brightly. "I hope you girls love the place as much I did."

As Haylee examined the passing Colonial and Victorian architecture, more ideas bloomed. She dreamed of scaling hills and fording streams, embracing what the outdoors would offer all five of her senses. Haylee liked to live free. She drank sunshine. She gulped misty rain.

"At last, we're here! 128 Essex Street!" Mom announced.

Michaela huffed, sounding disgusted, but Haylee's eyes widened at the sight of the clapboard house. It had black shutters and was painted a bright buttercup yellow.

"I get the bigger bedroom!" claimed Michaela.

Haylee couldn't have cared less about the size of her room. All she needed was a private space that was hers and hers alone.

"We have a lot of unpacking to do, so I need both of you to help," Mom said. "No grumbling either."

Mom opened the door of the SUV and climbed out. For a moment she just stood there, staring at the house. Then she marched to the back of the car and opened the trunk.

Hauling everything from the vehicle to the house was tedious, and Haylee's arms began to hurt after the second trip, but she didn't really mind. The house seemed nice enough, she supposed, though it wasn't nearly as big or as finely decorated as their home in Chicago. Her room was much smaller, too, but it was okay.

The interior of the house wasn't what pulled Haylee. The backyard was what enticed Haylee to explore her new habitat of treasure.

As soon as Mom felt satisfied that everything had been unloaded, Haylee slipped through the kitchen door to the outside world. The yard itself was a vertical rectangle, and its trees were taller than the Japanese maples in Chicago. A garden of flowers and shrubs lined the edges of the emerald, green lawn, and at the rear of the yard was a separate building—a small garage.

Haylee felt chills running down her arms and legs like someone was staring at her. But no one was in sight. The only sound came from a lawn mower buzzing in the next yard.

It's likely no one really cared that they were moving into this house ... so who could be watching?

5

Guess How Many People Live Here?

Haylee watched her mom grab the orange juice from the refrigerator and pour it into two glasses.

"Is your sister coming down for breakfast?" she asked.

"I'm not her messenger, Mom," Haylee muttered.

Mom's nostrils flared as she yelled, "Michaela, get down here. Now!"

Haylee grabbed her Cocoa Puffs. Unlike Michaela, she answered her mother's initial summons, and with good reason. The cove in Gloucester that sat underneath the Massachusetts Bay Colony Rock awaited. Haylee looked forward to dodging the tedium of school, and the incessant bullying from Mack Giles, who never failed to remind her that she was weird. Haylee learned in I.E.P. meetings that taking flight was a common attribute for those who were Neurodivergent. For Haylee, she viewed exploring not as a trait but as a way of resetting after experiencing over-stimulation.

Gliding into the kitchen, Michaela flipped her smooth hair from beneath her collar. With a sigh, Haylee noted the resemblance between Michaela and their mother—slender frame and sleek, blue-black tresses. How Haylee envied their high cheekbones and manageable hair.

By contrast, Haylee's face was round, and her chestnut-colored hair offered wild and bushy waves of curls. Haylee believed her hair had its own personality, so years ago she'd named it, "The Beast." Often, Haylee' hair seemed to enter a room five minutes prior to Haylee's entrance. It was that big.

"Must you gobble, Haylee? It's gross! Mom, can't you do your job and make Haylee chew like a normal person?"

"Can't I do my *job?*" their mom repeated, one eyebrow cocked. "I would never have said such a thing to my mother."

"Haylee eats like a pig, Mom! Make her stop!" Michaela stomped her foot.

Inhaling another handful of Cocoa Puffs, Haylee chomped as loudly as she could and grinned at her sister.

"Honestly, girls, I'm about to scream!" Mom growled. "I don't need this. I have a pile of accounts waiting on my desk to be logged and balanced, and I must get it done by the end of the day!"

Mom slammed the drawer on the kitchen island, took a measured breath, and stared at the ceiling. Probably counting to ten, Haylee guessed. She did that sometimes. This time she added, "Haylee, don't forget to feed and walk your new dog, Barney, when you get home from school. Remember, you can ..."

"I know, I know!" Haylee interrupted, then recited, "I can only have a dog if I feed him, walk him, and give him love and attention."

"That's right," Mom chimed, as she grabbed her hound's tooth corset coat from the back of a chair and slipped her arms through the sleeves.

"Michaela, swallow that bagel and get your science fair display loaded in the car. Don't make me be late!"

"Did you get that coat at the consignment shop?" Michaela sniggered. "Where women like you pretend, you're still wealthy?"

Haylee waited for the storm of ranting to follow. Fortunately, today Mom ignored Michaela's insults. Michaela swallowed another bite of bagel and swiped a spot of cream cheese from her bottom lip.

"Don't worry, Mom. I'm always on time, unlike *some* people in this room."

Haylee followed her mother's example and ignored Michaela.

As she continued shoveling cereal into her mouth, Haylee felt something heavy and warm settle on her thigh—Barney's chin. Barney was Salem's Humane Society's Best black Labrador Retriever. He was a gift both parents agreed to give the girls to make moving more inviting and to give the girls comfort as they navigated new schools and making new friends. Haylee smiles when she thinks of the day, they all selected Barney. They chose a Saturday to visit the organization. Wagging his tail, but not barking voraciously like his cohorts, Barney's soft brown eyes captured their hearts. Michaela spoke about how pretty he was, but it was Haylee who favored caring for Barney. Now, the black Lab whined while staring up at Hayley, so even though she wasn't supposed to, she slipped him a Coca Puff or two. The dog's jowls flapped happily as he seized and swallowed the treat.

Michaela finished her bagel, grabbed a jacket that matched her skirt, and maneuvered her backpack straps over her shoulders. Then she hoisted in her arms the bulky science display.

"Somebody's hoping Jason, who's a SENIOR will notice her," taunted Haylee. For added effect, she feigned swooning with an arm over her forehead.

The tease offered irony, since Michaela's charm exuded the air that all she cared about was her looks and her grades. She lived for compliments from her teachers and peers whenever either noticed a new outfit or praised her for her papers and scores on tests.

Haylee couldn't understand why anyone would care so much about grades.

"Maybe if you win the science fair, Jason will congratulate you again."

Michaela spun on her heel. She glared at Haylee, but quickly smiled a toothy grin.

"Maybe he will. At least I get good grades. We've lived here for two and half months, and you still blame your bad grades on adjusting to a new school."

"Haylee, make sure you have all your homework, and don't be late for the bus," Mom warned. "Michaela, let's *go!*" Mom grabbed her briefcase and flung the door open.

Haylee waved to her mother and snickered as she watched Michaela struggle maneuvering the front door with the giant display.

After the front door closed, Haylee relished the silence of being alone. Except for Barney, of course. She put the cereal away and embraced the quiet. "We're not lonesome, are we, Barney?"

The dog woofed, and Haylee patted his silky head.

The ensuing stillness reminded her of their last family dinner. *The last supper*, she'd dubbed it. Though she'd hated listening to her parents argue all the time, and she knew her mother was upset about Dad's affair, Haylee felt certain that if she'd been more compliant, or a better student, her parents might have stayed together or at least stayed married until she and her sister had graduated from high school.

These days, Mom and Dad rarely spoke on the phone. The first week after the move, Haylee had overheard her mother shouting into her receiver on her phone, *"You and your whore!"* Since then, Dad only called when he knew Mom wouldn't be home.

Haylee's way of coping had been to spew her thoughts out into her journal. Ironically, jotting her thoughts each day enabled her to connect with Salem more easily than Michaela. Her sister had demanded a whole new wardrobe, saying the kids at John Proctor

A Divorce in Salem

High School dressed differently than the ones in Chicago. Haylee hadn't noticed. And she didn't think the new clothes made a difference in helping Michaela fit in. Of course, Michaela blamed this failure on the clothes because they'd been bought from thrift stores and not upscale Chicago shops.

Haylee, on the other hand, didn't worry about fitting in. What mattered to her was her new routine of ditching school every couple of weeks. On these wonderful days—she'd had a couple of them so far—she spent her time roaming around Salem. Once, she'd used her allowance money to travel by bus to Gloucester to explore Stage Fort Park, the most wonderful place in the world. Gloucester was her destination today. She had more than enough saved to cover the bus fare.

Before leaving the house, Haylee did everything she was supposed to, including taking Barney out for a short walk. Soon she was boarding the bus to Gloucester, and a short time later, Haylee arrived at the park entrance and headed toward the Massachusetts Bay Colony Rock.

Trekking over the enormous boulder, Haylee realized the acme of the boulder was where Miles Standish had ordered the Pilgrims to agree to a contract: if they wanted to eat, they needed to work. If they refused to work or feigned illness, no food would be provided.

Haylee looked out upon the cove that sported cannons from the Civil War. She sketched the entire scene, carefully inserting the dump truck with its wheels in the water and blending the colors to depict the beach as accurately as possible. Switching to muted hues, she penciled a swooping crane lunging for fish under a wave. For the sky, she used a bird's—egg blue with a touch of lavender. For the color of the ocean, she mixed hues with her spit to create a murky gray.

When satisfied she'd captured the scene, she packed up her stuff and lumbered down from the Colony Rock. She was ambling around the cove when she spotted something fantastic—*a cave!*

Haylee tiptoed into the darkened, cool atmosphere, noticing numerous bats sleeping on the cave ceiling. She set down her backpack and touched the cold, jagged walls. The sides glimmered with ribbons of graphite interwoven throughout the slate gray. Fingering the unique texture of the walls as she stepped cautiously, Haylee meandered deeper into the womb of the cave.

In history class, she'd learned about privateers hired by the government for piracy in colonial days. She could imagine the very same pirates here, using the cave to store their treasures. Pirates and chests of gold were just the beginning of the many fantasies she conjured. Haylee became so engrossed in her musings, she didn't realize how much time passed, or how far into the cave she'd gone.

Grabbing the ridges sticking out of the cave wall, Haylee made her way back to where she'd dropped her backpack. While breathing in the deep earthy and sulfur cent of decaying earth, Haylee made a private pact of her own: This cave would be her very own secret place. She would share it with no one.

Next time, I'll bring a headlamp, so I can explore further and farther. And maybe some sort of mesh to keep the bats out of my hair.

When Haylee sat on the bus to head home, she spied a woman midway down the aisle, red spectacles perched on the woman's angular nose. Knitting needles twirled quickly in her hands. Figuring anyone who knitted couldn't be harmful, Haylee settled in the seat beside her. The bus wheels turned, and the woman's needles clacked along in perfect rhythm.

Without missing a stitch, the woman explained, "I'm making my tenth blanket for one of my grandchildren. I try to pick different colors for each one, but there've been so many, I fear I've lost track of what colors I've already used."

Haylee smiled. "My grandmother's not as talented as you. She doesn't knit. She drinks." The words came out of her mouth before Haylee could stop them.

A Divorce in Salem

"Terrible disease," the knitting lady said, "You know, when I was your age, I loved to hike. I walked everywhere and could eat anything I wanted. Nowadays, you, young people, spend too much time on your phones, and playing those silly video games!" She tsked disapprovingly.

Haylee wasn't guilty of such frivolity, but she felt the need to defend herself anyway. "I don't like video games, and the only person who calls me on my cell is my dad. But that's only once a week or so."

Why am I telling her this? She's a complete stranger.

When they arrived at the last bus stop, Haylee was relieved to leave the knitting lady behind. Descending the bus steps, Haylee walked toward the Roger Conant statue. The monument still seemed creepy to her. Even though she'd walked by it numerous times since they had moved here, she still didn't like the imposing figure. She felt certain Roger still existed inside the bronze structure, daring her to pass. The wind rustled up leaves by the curb, so Haylee scampered down the sidewalk, until Roger was well behind her.

Soon enough, she was unlatching the shiny, black wrought—iron gate on Essex Street and walking through the front door.

"Haylee Carmichael Higgins" Mom's head popped out from the kitchen. "Where have you been? I've been worried sick!"

"Just walking," Haylee replied, as innocently as she could.

"Don't *ever* do that again! Do you *hear* me?"

"What? I only went for a walk. What's wrong with that?" Haylee dropped to the floor.

"You skipped school," Mom accused.

"Haylee, you're such a dweeb!" Michaela said as she slinked by their mother. "Only dimwits think they can get away with not showing up for class!"

Mom sighed. "Michaela, need I remind you that I am the mother and not you?" Grabbing Haylee's hands, her mother made eye contact that she knew Haylee disliked, and explained, "Honey, when you skip school, I don't know whether you're safe or in trouble. How would

I know if you were just wandering around town or if you'd been hit by a car? Or even worse, were abducted?" Straightening her knees to stand, her mother reminded Haylee, "We have your IEP meeting next week. I'll make certain your teachers know how to prevent you from skipping school again." The lines around Mom's mouth softened. "Both of you, set the table for dinner. We're having meatloaf."

Haylee groaned. She didn't like meatloaf. She also hated her Individualized Education Program – a death sentence for any kid's creativity.

"Please, Haylee, don't start," Mom said. "You're lucky I'm not the kind of mother who sends her children to bed without supper. Remember, I tolerate your dislike of salmon, asparagus, milk, you name the texture, you can't stand. There are Mothers out there who'd insist you chew each bite and that you'd eat each bite. Why my mother insisted I eat the entire dinner, and she was no cook when she was drinking!"

Obediently, but with rolling eyes, Haylee pulled the placemats from the dining hutch and collected the silverware, while Michaela gathered plates and glasses.

Initially, dinner was a silent affair. The sound of their utensils clinking on the china was amplified in Haylee's ears, yet another Neurodivergent trait. She tried to ignore the sounds by taking small bites and swallowing them whole. She had to eat like this anyway, as it was the only way she could tolerate the meatloaf's texture.

"Chew your food, Haylee!" reprimanded Michaela.

Haylee glared at her sister.

"Girls," Mom said, clearing her throat. "I have some news. Grandma is coming to stay with us. She has a sponsor now and has started her twelve-step program at Caron. That's what she told me, at any rate." Their mother's tone implied grave doubt about Grandma's latest recovery. Michaela glanced at Haylee to gauge whether she shared her displeasure over such news.

"Who's Karen?" asked Haylee, pushing peas around on her plate to form a rectangle.

Mom chuckled. "No, sweetie, C-A-R-O-N. It's one of the best rehab centers for alcoholics in the country. I just hope she means what she says. I've heard it many times before." She sighed. Swallowing a bite of baked potato, Mom added, "In any event, Grandma promises she'll help us with housework as well as taking care of you girls."

"You mean she's going to *live* with us?" Michaela balked. "Where will she sleep?"

Like you'd ever share your bedroom.

"She'll sleep in the office where the computer is. Her bed's being delivered tomorrow." Their mother smiled, but her expression looked forced. "As for you, Haylee," she reached over and put her hand on Haylee's arm, "The office secretary at John Proctor sent a list of the work you missed today, as well as your homework for tonight. So, no excuses. Get upstairs, and I don't want to see you come down until you're finished. Skedaddle!"

Not amused, Haylee rolled her eyes.

Truthfully, Haylee didn't mind the homework. She wrote out the essay for biology and enjoyed coming up with ways to weave in the science vocabulary. Next, she opened her social studies book—Colonial history—and answered the questions at the end of the chapter. Finally, she worked on math, the one subject she resented. For Haylee, she wanted to understand the *why* of it all rather than to simply plug numbers into ready-made formulas. Tonight, she learned about Euclid's geometry and answered the problems with dutiful, but reluctant compliance.

Finished, Haylee stuffed all the work into the designated folders and shoved everything into her backpack.

Although she'd sped through the homework, it had taken longer than expected. Bedtime already.

Haylee knew she wouldn't sleep well unless she said good night to her mother, so she bounced down the stairs to the living room. Mom stood near the TV with the remote in hand.

"Good night, Mom," Haylee said.

"Come here." Mom opened her arms for a hug, and Haylee let herself be folded into them. "All I want is for my girls to grow up straight and strong. Please don't run away again. Promise me," Mom whispered, and kissed the top of Haylee's head.

"Salem looks so different on weekdays without the tourists. I was just trying to get to know everything better. I wasn't doing anything bad."

Cupping Haylee's chin in her palm, Mom explained, "Sometimes you're too impulsive. You don't realize there are people who'd take advantage of a wayfaring teenager. What would your father say if he knew you ran away today? Now, do you promise never to do it again, Haylee Carmichael Higgins?"

Haylee met her mother's forehead with her own.

"I promise," she whispered, but averted her eyes.

6

Talk Is Cheap

Michaela was beaming as she opened the front door for the old lady standing on the stoop. Years had passed since their last visit, but Haylee thought Grandma looked the same as she remembered.

Grandma barreled over the threshold and scooped Michaela in her arms. At the same time, she grabbed Haylee's elbow, and then swooped back and forth, repeatedly kissing each of them on the head.

"It's so good to see you girls! My, how you've grown!" She pushed them to arm's length and chuckled. "You're so lovely to look at. Oh, we'll have such adventures! Just you wait!"

Michaela shook her head emphatically, and then picked up their grandmother's suitcase by its gold handle and carried it to the living room. Grandma and Haylee followed. Their mother was already sitting on the sofa, waiting.

"This sure is a different setup than your house in Chicago," Grandma remarked.

Haylee looked up from the gold handle, so sparkly, in time to see her mother wince. Mom clearly took Grandma's comment as an insult. Whether Grandma meant it that way, Haylee wasn't sure.

Grandma clapped and raved on, "But it's just lovely, isn't it, girls? The furniture may not be brand—new, but antique furniture like this has its own special appeal. It was your grandfather who favored antiques of all kinds." She clasped her hands for emphasis.

"Why don't you take your coat off, Grandma?" Michaela suggested.

Grandma slipped out of the sleeves and handed the bulky garment to Michaela. Her eyes twinkled. "Go ahead and look in the pockets. You'll find something there for both of you."

Haylee ran over, but of course, Michaela got to them sooner.

"Girls! Show some manners, please." Elizabeth scolded.

Too late, Grandma's pockets held necklaces, one for each of them. Michaela's necklace gleamed with her topaz birthstone, and Haylee's, in contrast, was made of intertwined leather and silver.

"Thanks, Grandma!" Michaela said. "I love it!"

"You know, Mom," Mom said, "Michaela's birthday is just three weeks away."

"I know." Grandma's eyes still twinkled. "Don't worry, I would never forget my granddaughter's birthday."

"But if you spoil her now, what will she expect then?" Mom asked with a shaking forefinger. "Mom, let me show you to your room: Girls, Grandma and I need a few minutes to talk about some things." Grandma picked up the suitcase by its shiny handle and followed Mom up the stairs and down the hall to the office at the rear of the second floor. Haylee liked that room. It had sunny yellow curtains with blue cornflowers sprinkled throughout the fabric. Grandma's bed had arrived earlier that day, and Mom had made it up with sheets and blankets, adding matching yellow and blue pillows.

Even though Mom had requested privacy, Haylee trailed after them anyway. She tiptoed discreetly enough that neither of them noticed her presence, reaching the room just after Mom had pulled the door shut. In yet another I.E.P. meeting, Haylee recalled the school psychologist informing Haylee's parents how those who are neurodivergent struggle with boundaries as well as social cues. Haylee thought the information insulted her. From Haylee's perspective, she figured out how some people in her life spoke of her very differently to her face as opposed to when they were unaware of her presence. So, Haylee learned to glean more accurate impressions from others by eavesdropping whenever she felt insecure about how they viewed her.

So, Haylee wasn't about to leave. With her hand cupped between her ear and the door, she listened, as best she could.

"If you need anything—extra blankets or pillows for the bed—let me know. Or you could get them yourself from the linen closet in the hallway," Mom said.

"Thank you, dear, I'm sure I'll be fine." Grandma sighed. "You've done a wonderful job, Lizzie. I know things haven't been easy. I've been through divorce, too. I remember how terrible it was."

Mom didn't say anything, but Haylee could imagine her pursed lips. Her mother did that a lot when she struggled with several emotions at the same time.

Edging toward the door now ajar, Haylee saw Grandma entwining her fingers between her daughter's hand. "I'm glad you agreed to let me come help you, especially after my latest relapse. I understood our not talking afterward." Grandma bored her slate gray eyes into Mom's. "My drinking is my greatest shame. It's hurt everyone I love, especially you."

Feeling a nudge in her back, Haylee recognized Michaela had shoved in beside her.

"I wasn't there for you when your marriage started to fall apart," Grandma said, clearing her throat. "Not that I could have prevented your divorce, but I could have supported you better. I know the feelings of fear, hurt, and my best friend, anger. I've felt them all, Lizzie, so I know what you're going through."

Grandma paused staring out the window draped in blue cornflowers and yellow birds. "You know what's funny? Feeling powerless to take away your pain has been the nudge I needed to embrace sponsorship this time around in my recovery. I know I can stay sober this time." She veered her head to look her daughter in the eye without hesitation. "Because, this time, I have the support necessary to navigate my own emotions while I try to help you. It's time I started taking better care of myself, you and those precious girls."

Mom was quiet for a moment, before blurting out, "Mom, Dan wants to come here to visit." Haylee's chest thumped. She wondered if Michaela shared in the physical gut wrench.

Smiling a toothy grin that belied deadpan eye contact, Grandma suggested, "That's a good thing, isn't it?"

"No. What if he brings that ... *that whore into my home?*" Mom hissed. "I can't prevent him from having a relationship with that woman, but does he have to flaunt the situation where I'm trying to adapt to his desire for a divorce? I don't want her to step into our home, or the girls' school. I don't want her meeting *my* girls' new friends."

Michaela put her arm around Haylee's shoulders. They waited together, silently, to hear what would come next. Haylee bristled automatically. She hoped Michaela didn't notice her spine clenching, becoming rigid. Whenever Haylee received affection or touch of any kind, her body reacted automatically. She knew others assumed she was cold. That wasn't it. Haylee felt powerless over her own nerves. She resented what others could enjoy, and how her sensitivity of nervous system stacked against her other need for separateness, precious autonomy.

Cupping Mom's chin in Grandma's long, slender, blue-veined hands, she reasoned, "Honey, the man is lost. Maybe with time and distance, you'll learn that he did you a favor."

"A favor?" Mom's voice rose. "Is that what you call being humiliated and forced to move a thousand miles away? A *favor?*"

Releasing her hold, Grandma thumbed the stitching of the quilt to focus on her thought. She then raised her right hand, shaking it when the words emerged. "The truth is, honey," Grandma continued, "if he wasn't happy in the marriage, *you* weren't either. It was the same for me when it came to the relationship I had with your father. Just make sure you don't talk negatively about Dan in front of the girls. I bitterly regret the terrible things I said in front of you when your father left me."

Mom spun her teary face from Grandma, "Nice, Mom. You always have to make everything about you!"

Grandma stood right behind her daughter who now struggled to leave. "It took years for me to realize, Elizabeth, that it wasn't your father's leaving that scarred you. It was my venom toward him that wounded you the most," Grandma said.

"So, you're saying *I'm* the one screwing up my daughters' lives?" Elizabeth looked down at her enlaced hands.

Haylee recognized Mom's tone. It meant Mom was going to look for a way to escape.

Hearing heavy footsteps, Haylee surmised her sister must have also recognized Mom's tone, because she shoved Haylee. They both took flight in opposite directions to avoid being caught eavesdropping.

Behind her, Haylee heard the rattle of the doorknob as Mom shouted, "I can never talk to you again!"

The door slammed so hard it shook the newly hung family pictures in the hallway.

7

Broadway-Bound?

Haylee awoke, as usual, floating somewhere toward the ceiling caught between dreaming and awareness. While savoring the blurry boundary, she questioned which world was better.

Reality intruded and bumped the dream world out of Haylee's mind. Rubbing grit from her eyes, she tumbled out from under the covers.

Remembering her newfound passion for the cave at Stage Fort Park, and feeling determined, Haylee decided she would shop at Casselman's Hardware on North Street to buy some supplies, including rope and a headlamp. The items would make exploring possible. She could intrude another world, one only she knew existed.

While shifting the sheets and duvet on her bed to feign the appearance of a well-made bed, Haylee considered when would be just the right moment to steal a blanket from the linen closet. After all, research informed her the cave was a littoral one, formed from thousands of years of lapping, turbulent sea water. So, rehearsing before the biggest excursion of spelunking would be much cooler now that autumn had fully set in. Luckily, she already had good boots and barn coat to keep her warm.

As Haylee slipped her bare feet into sheepskin slippers, she suddenly remembered Misty, a new classmate, had insisted they audition for the class play together. Auditions were to be held after school today.

Even though Haylee hoped to get some small role, her intense shyness dictated retreat. She hated it when others stared at her, especially like the time she was forced to read her book report aloud. Whenever Haylee stood to speak in front of people, overwhelming panic gripped her. What if she farted? Or threw up all over herself? Or worse, her tongue swelled, making it impossible to pronounce consonants? *"Maloraw borofay lahssflay* — she pictured herself voicing such gibberish prior to going into a seizure, or worse, throwing up on someone else, and then seizing.

Haylee realized her perfect older sister would criticize her the most if she dared to audition. In fact, she'd probably fill her head with the many reasons she couldn't possibly nail a role, even if there was a part playing a tree in the background while leads garnered focus from the audience.

But Haylee knew the after-school tryouts would give her the ideal excuse; it would even allow her enough time to swing by Casselman's on the way home.

I'll just tell Mom I want to sign up as stage manager for the play. Both Mom and Michaela would be satisfied if she said she was taking on a behind-the-scenes-role.

Shuffling toward the bathroom, Haylee stopped midway. As usual, Michaela was holding court before the bathroom mirror. Deciding otherwise, Haylee descended the stairs to join her mother in the kitchen.

"Mom," she said, "Michaela's hogging the bathroom, so I can't shower yet, but I have something to tell you."

Her mother continued to scour the sink without looking up. "I don't want to hear any excuses about why you haven't finished your homework."

"No, Mom, I did it all. I'm up to date in every class." Haylee handed her mother a coffee cup she forgot to put in the dishwasher.

Her mother re-tied the belt of her silk kimono and stared with her lie-detector blue eyes. "So, what's so important that it trumps being annoyed with your sister?"

"Well, we have auditions for the school play today and I want to be stage manager, so I'll be late coming home. Will you sign my permission slip?"

Without waiting for an answer, Haylee rushed back to her room, retrieved the paper, and returned to the kitchen. She pushed the slip across the kitchen counter.

Mom raised an eyebrow but smiled as reached for a pen to sign the form. "I'm pleased you want to do this, Haylee. You must be feeling more comfortable here."

Haylee nodded as she put the slip in her backpack, just as Grandma appeared. Unsure what would happen between them given last night's eavesdrop, Haylee bit her tongue and waited.

Mom broke the silence first. "Good morning."

"Good morning to you both!" Grandma grinned. "I thought I'd go to an AA meeting today and then spend some time getting the lay of the land again." She looked for her coffee mug previously on the kitchen island, shrugged and pulled another from the hook beside the window and poured herself a cup of coffee. "I want to find places to walk around. I need the exercise, and Salem is lovely this time of year, especially with all the foliage, the mums, nasturtiums, and asters everybody purchased for their front porch steps." She lifted the mug to her nose and inhaled before sipping. "I forgot how much fall in New England lifts the mood," she said standing with her back to the counter and shifting her weight onto her left leg. With a burst of energy, she offered, "Hey! We should carve pumpkins! Wouldn't that be fun?"

Mom exhaled, which wasn't a good sign, but then she considered for a moment. "Actually, that sounds like fun."

"I'll pick some up on my way home," Grandma said. "And mums. And asters. And some hay bales. Maybe a cornstalk or two. I just love the look of pumpkins and fall flowers together," she said winking at Haylee.

Michaela strolled in and, without a word, grabbed a protein bar. She drank the orange juice she poured for herself in one gulp, then grabbed her backpack and bellowed, "Gotta go!"

Calling after her, Mom instructed, "Michaela, dinner will be later than usual, because your sister's signing up for stage manager in the school play."

Michaela mumbled something Haylee couldn't hear and slammed the door behind her.

"I should head out, too, or I'll be late for my meeting," Grandma said. "Oh, I was thinking I could make spaghetti for dinner. Do we have any hamburger meat?"

"In the freezer," Mom answered. "We also have garlic bread."

"Perfect!" said Grandma. "See you girls later." She gave Barney a pat and raced out the door.

As Mom was donning on her coat, she said, "Haylee, I'm proud of you for wanting to be stage manager. I think it's a great sign. You're bonding with a group of kids, and you're not sulking over the move anymore. Now hurry up, or you'll miss the bus." She waved her hands to usher herself out the door.

With that, Mom kissed Haylee on the cheek and vanished, too.

As always, Haylee loved the rare moments of quiet when she was alone in the house. She loved being able to let her mind wander without interruption. Today, however, she couldn't afford to waste time. She had a mission to plan.

First, she mentally reviewed the list of items she wanted from the hardware store. Next, she collected her savings from her jewelry box. She'd made quite a lot of sacrifices to accrue $72. Her only worry was whether it would be enough to buy everything on her list. If not, she'd have to save more, and that meant more packed lunches and more warm juice boxes.

At last, she grabbed her copy of the script for the school play. The play was a fractured fairy tale, and she'd read it so many times she'd practically memorized every line.

If she actually did find the courage to try out, would she get a role? Would the director give the 'new girl' a chance to prove herself?

As if sensing her jitters, Barney cocked his head sideways.

Haylee patted him, cooing, "Sorry, boy, No dogs in this script."

Barney barked in protest.

Haylee saw right away that several other students were already in huddles mingling at the bus stop. She was relieved to see Misty was one of them, so Haylee hurried over to wait for the bus with her.

"Hey!" she greeted. "I think my mom is more excited than I am about the play."

"Mine, too," Misty grinned.

Brandon, a boy with dark hair and glasses, poked Misty in the back with his umbrella.

"Cut it out!" Misty snapped.

But Brandon poked her again. "Oh, hail the superstar!" he bowed with a snigger. Literally, he got down on one knee and stretched his arms upward, his umbrella raised like a sword.

"You're mental" Misty scoffed.

Both Brandon and Josh—Brandon's minion—busted out laughing. They even looked alike, sort of. Except Josh didn't wear glasses, and his hair was russet—colored with strawberry—blond streaks highlighting every few strands.

Thankfully, the bus arrived. Misty located a seat toward the back, and Haylee plopped down beside her. Brandon and Josh lumbered past and, of course, sat in the seat directly behind them.

Still thinking of the auditions, Haylee said, "The teachers like you, Misty. You'll be a shoo-in."

Haylee's heart deflated like a punctured tire when Misty didn't return any comment about Haylee's possibility for a role. Josh stuck his head over the seat and said, "I have been here for less than two weeks. I have been starved out, felt up, teased, stalked, threatened, and called Taylor Swift."

They all laughed at Josh's reference to the character Piper in Orange Is the New Black.

Misty raised her own umbrella to bop him on the head. She swung too far, though and accidently clocked Brandon.

Chuckling, Brandon mocked, "First, we're quoting Piper from Orange is the New Black, and now, I've been zapped by a star. I'll never wash my forehead again!" He pretended to faint.

Haylee giggled. She couldn't help it. Josh laughed, too.

Picking up a gum wrapper from the seat, Josh stuffed it down the collar of Haylee's coat. Haylee shifted and flailed to get the little piece of foil to fall out by the hem of her shirt. Turning her head toward Misty, Haylee declared, "I'm proud our school affords all children the right to an education—no matter the disability."

Both girls burst out laughing.

Misty turned to peer over the seat, "Are either of you auditioning for the play? Someone besides Tyler needs to get the lead. He's been the star in every show since second grade."

Shaking his head, Josh replied, "My Dad would have conniptions if I tried out for a play. He thinks it's bad enough I play the saxophone."

Putting his thumb on his index and middle finger pads, Brandon declared with a French accent, "*Mais oui*, your music gives you *sax appeal!*"

Josh smacked Brandon across the chest.

Haylee thought maybe Josh struck a hard button or the zipper on Brandon's coat, because he winced when he pulled his hand back.

"Luckily, my dad doesn't know my mom signed the permission slip. Brandon, buddy, I know your mom signed yours, too, 'cause she told mine on the phone last night."

Glaring at Josh, Brandon's cheeks flushed a scarlet red from embarrassment by Josh's revelation that their mothers still babied them.

Haylee understood. She didn't like it when other people shared her secrets, either.

"Let's make a bet," Misty suggested. "You guys try out, and if you both get parts, Haylee and I will do your homework for a week. If you don't make it, you have to sing to us at lunch." She and Haylee fist—bumped.

Then, because neither of the boys said anything, Misty goaded, "What are you? Scared?"

"What if we both audition, but only one of us makes it?" Josh asked staring out the window on Haylee's side.

"Do you seriously believe the teachers would split you up? That'd be like buying only one sock!" Misty said, laughing.

Brandon and Josh looked at each other, and Josh sighed, "You're on," he said.

Suddenly, the bus veered around a curve, hurling Josh out of his seat and into the aisle.

Misty chortled. "Well, he has his exit down!"

Both Brandon and Misty laughed. Haylee giggled, too, but she stopped when she saw Josh's face turn red.

Throughout the morning in school, Haylee's thoughts drifted to her private inner world. She managed to turn in her homework, and she made eye contact with furtive glances to fool her teachers into assuming she was on task.

Haylee dreaded lunch the most. In the cafeteria, she chose a table where she sat alone, waiting for Misty to get through the long line. Haylee opened the lunch bag her mom packed for her—yogurt, crackers and cheese, and grapes. She then busied herself by reading the script again.

Misty sashayed to the long metal table and set down her tray. "Do you think Brandon and Josh will actually audition?" she asked.

"Sure," Haylee replied. "They can't pass up our dare."

Misty looked around the cafeteria, seeking them out, but they weren't anywhere her eyes perused. "Do you think they're talking about it?" she asked.

Haylee swallowed a grape and shook her head.

"Girls talk about this kind of stuff, not guys. They'll go to the auditorium and act surprised that their legs brought them there."

Afternoon classes moved as slowly as a dental visit. At last, the final bell of the day rang, and the school hallways became alive with noise and bodies. Most students raced to the buses. Others headed to the locker rooms to get ready for football and other sports' practices. Haylee met up with Misty, and together, they headed to the auditorium.

At the door, Haylee's palms became sweaty, her stomach heaved, and her tongue swelled.

Why did I think I could do this? I should just sign up for stage manager, like I told Mom.

Once inside, all the noise from the bustle of kids running for their buses evaporated like the mirage Hayley saw when her mother drove on a steaming, muggy day. Misty scanned the seats below the stage for the judges' table. Haylee's jaw clenched. Dozens of kids were trying out. No Brandon. No Josh.

"If they like you, they'll ask you to try different roles, or do the same role several times," Misty instructed, as she headed to the third row back from the stage and motioned for Haylee to sit. "At least, that's what I've heard from other kids."

A student passed out forms to each attendee, while the director, Mrs. Esty, explained that the forms needed to be turned in before auditions could begin.

Skimming the page, Haylee balked, "They want to know my prior experience. I've never been in a play before."

Two older students—popular, pretty girls –Danielle and Carly— sat in the row ahead of them. Haylee overheard Danielle brag, "I can't even name all the plays I've been in. There aren't enough lines on the form!"

"I should just leave now," Haylee muttered.

"You're not leaving me here alone," Misty murmured back. "Think back. What about church? Were you ever in a church pageant?"

"I was a lamb," Haylee countered. "I didn't speak. I baaed!"

Misty grinned. "The judges won't know that, so put it down." Pointing to the side door, Misty nudged Haylee's elbow. "Look who's here."

Josh and Brandon shuffled in like elderly patients from a nursing home. The student who was handing out the forms gave them some, and the boys, sauntered up the aisle. Brandon took the forms reluctantly, but he gave Josh one. They grabbed seats near the back.

Mrs. Esty clapped her hands for attention and launched into an introductory speech. Taking her seat behind a large table, she planted herself dead center in front of the stage.

Haylee's panic returned in full swing. The room seemed to sway and circle like water pulled into a drain.

Misty leaned close and whispered, "You'll be fine. Just remember to speak to the back of the room, so everyone can hear you. It's called projection.

"Calling Misty, Danielle, another girl, and two boys to the stage, Mrs. Esty commanded, "Act three, scene three, page twenty-nine. Misty, you're the Princess, and Danielle, you're her Lady in Waiting. Robert, you're Rumpelstiltskin. Tyler and Michelle, you two are elves."

Danielle sneered. Haylee assumed she was mad at not being asked to read for the role of Princess.

Scrunching forward in her seat, Haylee kept her gaze riveted on the kids who stood on stage. She wanted to figure out what made some performances better than others, to determine what she could do to improve her own.

Misty enunciated carefully and projected her voice. Awed by Misty's poise, Hayley saw how comfortable she was on stage. Thinking her friend's performance sparkled, Haylee knew her own confidence wilted.

In contrast, Danielle uttered lines in a halfhearted manner. Robert, on the other hand, portrayed Rumpelstiltskin exactly like himself—nerdy and awkward. When Tyler and Michelle screeched in high-pitched voices to mimic elves, everyone in the auditorium, except Mrs. Esty, broke out in giggles.

As soon as they'd finished the scene, Mrs. Esty said, "Thank you. Very nice."

Misty returned to her seat beside Haylee, as another group ambled to the stage.

"You were wonderful!" Haylee whispered to her friend. She could tell Misty was pleased with her own performance.

Haylee didn't think the next girl who recited the part of the Princess did nearly as well as Misty. Neither did the next, or the next.

Thinking the auditions were over, Haylee assumed Mrs. Esty had overlooked her application, but finally she announced, "Brandon,

Carly, Matt, and Haylee, you're up. Act two, scene five. Carly will be the Princess, Haylee, the Witch. Brandon will be Hansel, and Matt, you're the troll."

Haylee climbed the steps, and though she knew she was moving, she couldn't feel the steps under her feet at all. It was as if she were watching herself from outside her body.

Smiling, Mrs. Esty said, "Page thirty-two, Haylee, you have the first line."

Haylee took a deep breath, inhaling through her nose, and willed her hands to stop shaking. They did, but the tremors simply moved down to her knees. Hayley figured a witch should sound odd—a little bit jolly, but also kind of mean, so she channeled her body's reaction: clearing her throat, she forced a cackle.

"Eat up, kiddie," she gargled, offering Brandon, who was acting as Hansel, a handful of gingerbread. Brandon, in turn, grabbed it nervously. Haylee poked a crooked finger into his ribs. "You're too *skinny*."

Several students guffawed. Using her script as a visor across her eyes, Haylee peered outward.

Why did I do this? I knew they were gonna laugh at me.

Matt, playing the part of the troll, bellowed from where he stood by the footbridge.

When the scene ended, Haylee felt glad it was over. She started for the steps, ready to run as fast as she could right out of that auditorium, but Mrs. Esty ordered, "Stay there, please. Girls, I'd like you to switch roles and do the scene again. Boys, keep your parts."

In the role of the Princess, Haylee tried to act like Michaela by preening in the mirror over her hair and clothes. She held her chin up, oblivious to those around her. She complained and ridiculed without thought for another's feelings. "Honestly, Hansel," she sneered. "Didn't anyone ever teach you manners? Don't talk with your mouth full," she ordered.

Once she'd returned to her seat, Haylee put her head into her knees to hide her embarrassment.

Mrs. Esty thanked all the students and reminded them that cast and crew lists would be posted on Friday at 3pm. Departing together, Haylee and Misty whispered as they recapped who'd given their all and whose performance disappointed.

Outside, Misty's mother beeped at them from her silver sedan.

"How did it go, girls?" Mrs. Bishop asked as soon as they opened the car door.

"I think I nailed it, Mom," Misty replied, beaming.

Haylee shrugged and slouched more deeply into the backseat.

"There's always next year, Haylee," Mrs. Bishop said consolingly. To Misty, she said, "We'll have to rearrange your piano lessons. I'll call Maestro Didier tomorrow."

"Can you drop me off on North Street?" Haylee asked quietly. "I have to buy a new calculator."

"Your mother will be worried about you," Mrs. Bishop warned.

"Oh, she already knows," Haylee lied.

"Three whole days till Friday," Misty moaned. "How are we supposed to wait that long to find out who got what parts?"

The image of her father popped into her mind. Haylee hoped he would be informed too close to the play performances, so that he could use the time crunch as an excuse to not attend, especially if she were made the stage manager.

8

The Family Who Cares Together, Stays Together

Haylee exited the hardware store with her purchases: "*What am I going to do with this bag?*"

She couldn't just waltz into the house with them. Mom would wonder why she hadn't come straight home from the audition. Even worse, she'd also insist on seeing what she bought and then ask a million questions.

Haylee bit her lower lip and looked around the yard. Instead of walking through the front door, Haylee traipsed along the narrow brick—and—cobblestone walkway adorning the side of the house where it led to the backyard.

"*No place to stash it here*," she fretted under her breath.

At the gate, Barney greeted her with a subdued: "*Woof.*"

Kneeling to put her face close to his, she pled, "Please don't give me away!"

A moment later, Haylee scampered to the Beech tree where a bench circled the tree. Remembering the bench seat also served as a storage area underneath where her mother kept her gardening gloves, crocs and trowels of different sizes, Haylee gingerly lifted the lid and stuck her bag inside. She then tiptoed back around the house and entered through the front door—Barney trailed behind her, wagging his tail the entire way.

Barney sashayed in front with an announcement of a bark, "Woof!" signaling Hayley and he were home. The strong scent of gutted pumpkin permeated the living room and front entrance. Walking into the dining room, Haylee saw scattered seeds, pieces of cut-out pumpkin and knives atop the dining room table that was now covered with butcher paper.

Grandma sat with her eyes peering over her spectacles. Using a marker, and with careful precision, she drew a face on her pumpkin victim.

Michaela lay sprawled across the couch in the living room, thumbs drumming in texts.

"Haylee," Mom called from the kitchen, "come take a plate of this spaghetti Grandma made. It's her special recipe, and it's wonderful. We ate without you because we weren't sure when you'd be home. When you're done eating, you can carve a pumpkin, too."

Shucking her coat on an unused chair, Haylee made a beeline for the kitchen, where Haylee scooped pasta on her plate, followed by a ladle full of Grandma's meaty sauce on top of her noodles. As usual, she shook her head in defiance of the parmesan cheese sitting on the counter.

The plainer, the better!

Because the dining table was so full of impending pumpkin art, the only place to eat was by the kitchen island, so Haylee settled on a stool. Using her fork and spoon, she wound the spaghetti tightly until she felt satisfied with the roll, then took what she considered was the perfect bite.

"Mmm!" she murmured. "Grandma, this is delicious!"

Ambling in to receive the compliment, Grandma instructed, "The secret ingredient is molasses," as she joined Haylee at the counter. "It adds sweetness and balance to the acidic tomatoes. I'm pleased you approve." She brushed the back of Haylee's neck. "Ooh, you're chilly from being outside. I'll light the candles in the dining room. That should help warm up the room. And you, too."

"How many kids tried out for the play today?" Mom asked from the dining room. "Did anyone else ask for the stage manager job?"

Haylee thought quickly.

"I think maybe a hundred students showed up. Misty did a great job trying out for the Princess role. I hope she gets the part and not Danielle. Misty will do a better job. Mrs. Bishop thinks so, too." As soon as she said this, Haylee grimaced. She wished she hadn't mentioned Misty's mother.

Mom chuckled. "So, Mrs. Bishop is a typical stage mom? But you didn't say whether you got the stage manager position?"

"Well ... ." Haylee hemmed and hawed. "Nobody said I couldn't be, and I didn't hear anybody else asking for the position. So, I think I am." Although the lie nagged at her, she thought she needed to buy as much time as possible, and who knows, stage manager may be the only role she could garner.

"That's great, Haylee," Mom said. "I'm proud of you."

Haylee scooped up the remnants of sauce from her plate with the last bite of garlic bread.

"Come on, girls," Mom called. "Let's carve these pumpkins!"

Haylee obeyed, but Michaela didn't move from the couch, where she was still drumming her thumbs intensely. Motioning her index finger to her lips to keep Mom from calling out a second time, Grandma tiptoed toward the living room. At the entrance, she peered in and yelled, "Boo!"

Michaela's phone hurtled into the air, and she let out a loud shriek.

"Give me a heart attack, why don't you, Grandma? You could have just told me you were ready. It's not as though the pumpkins will spoil or anything!" Michaela rolled her eyes and retrieved her precious phone.

"Your mother did call you." Grandma chided as she fluffed a pillow on the couch. You just didn't hear." Peering over her spectacles, she held out her hand, and dutifully, Michaela reluctantly took it.

Haylee flipped through the patterns that came with the carving kit Grandma had purchased and chose one of a cat with an arched back sitting on a wooden fence in front of a tree. The pattern indicated it was for *advanced* carvers.

Grandma picked a moon with a skeleton's face. She said it reminded her of wrinkle cream commercials. Selecting a haunted house, Mom's pattern was meant for *intermediates*. Michaela opted for an RIP gravestone, a beginner's showcase. Of course, her cell phone sat close by, so she'd notice if it vibrated.

"Michaela, why are you so glued to that phone today?" Mom asked. Usually, you can go five to ten minutes without it."

"Jason asked me out," Michaela said, "for this Saturday. Can I go?"

"Jason? Is that the guy Haylee was teasing you about? Haven't you been interested in him since the beginning of the school year?" asked Mom.

Michaela scowled.

"Liz, if it's all right with you, I can take Michaela shopping for a new dress," offered Grandma, as she put the final supper dishes into the dishwasher. "There's a nice consignment shop two blocks from here. I'm sure we could find some great deals. You'll need shoes too, Michaela."

Despite being a secondhand store, Michaela's eyes lit up.

"If I say yes, will you take your eyes off that device?" Mom bargained.

"I just have to text Jason and let him know," Michaela said jumping up. "He'll be so psyched, Mom. Thank you, and thank you, Grandma!" Michaela wrapped her arms around her grandmother's neck.

Haylee focused on pinning her cat scene to her pumpkin, making sure to place the pins strategically so there would be no unnecessary gaps.

Grandma squinted through her glasses as she poked pins in her pumpkin. "I saw the cutest thing in the park today," she remarked conversationally. "A duck in the pond. The poor creature had only one wing! Can you imagine?"

"Oh, we've seen that duck before, haven't we, girls?" Mom asked.

Haylee and Michaela nodded.

"I felt so sorry for her," Grandma mused. "The other ducks swam together, but she stayed by herself. Even so, the missing wing didn't seem to stop her from enjoying herself. I watched her for a while. She kept putting her beak under the water and lifting it out to shoot a fountain of water droplets above her head. She quacked and sputtered for quite some time. Quite entertaining. It made me think the lonesome duck wasn't lonely after all. She's figured out how to be her own best friend."

"That duck is a 'he,' Grandma," Haylee instructed. "You can tell by his bright plumage, and the tale-tell sign, a curled feather near his butt. Females don't have the curled feather. I heard he got his wing caught in a boat rudder. That's how he lost it. People tried to catch him, to help him, but he evades the nets."

"Well," Grandma sighed, "what will become of him when the rest of the ducks fly south for the winter?"

Michaela looked up from her carving and asked curiously, "Why can't he just stay on the pond?"

Haylee started slicing her fence tableau and chimed in, "If the pond freezes over during the winter, he won't be able to stay warm, and he won't be able to get to the grains and insects to eat. He'll die."

"That's what I'm worried about," Grandma agreed.

"If you're concerned, why not ask Dr. Raintree?" Mom suggested. "He's the vet who checked Barney out. He might be able to figure out a way to protect the duck, or at least suggest something helpful."

"I'm done!" declared Michaela. She undid her pins and turned her pumpkin around, so they could all see.

Haylee took one glance at Michaela's finished design and then pretended she'd dropped a pin and stooped to get under the table, hoping her sister wouldn't notice her silent laughter. Her back shuddered in giggles.

Michaela spun the pumpkin around again to eye her own artwork. In dismay, she said, "I drew a Halloween ....," turning the pumpkin toward her, she landed on the word, "Oblong." Even her RIP scrambled away from the pins.

"I suspect Michaela would have fared better if we'd asked her to design a pumpkin with Jason's face as Dracula!" Grandma chortled.

Undoing the pins on her own pumpkin, Grandma placed it at arm's length. "Not half-bad," she said and turned it around for them to see.

"Ooooh," Haylee said, "That looks neat, Grandma."

Mom nodded in agreement and said, "Well done, Mom."

Haylee ran to her grandmother, tentatively wrapped her arms around the older woman's neck, and whispered, "I love you, Grandma. I'm so glad you're here with us."

Grandma kissed Haylee on the cheek. "Me, too, kiddo. Me, too!" Grandma knew how rare it was for Haylee to express affection, and so, her hug registered how far Grandma hit the target of Haylee's heart.

The next person to unveil her carving was Mom. Pulling out her pins, she yanked the pattern off, but kept her eyes closed. Without looking at it herself, she turned it to face everyone else. Only then did she open one eye.

"That's great, Mom!" declared Haylee.

Grandma clapped her hands and bellowed, "Lovely!"

Michaela didn't say anything, still busy sulking over hers. "Haylee, are you finished? Let's see yours," Mom said. "The pattern you picked looked complicated."

Haylee raised her head and discovered Michaela was glaring at her. Worried that Haylee's pumpkin would outshine hers—Haylee could not fathom any reason for her sister's insistence there be a competition; Instead, Haylee had the reverse concern. After all, she despised being the center of attention. Bravely, she undid her pins, then scampered away, though not too far, just enough that she couldn't see their expressions, and they couldn't see hers. She could only hear clearly.

"Remarkable! Look what she did in so short of time!" her mother said.

Michaela snapped, "It's perfect, isn't it?" and she stormed up the stairs.

"Michaela's would be better if she'd just put some effort into it," Grandma remarked.

Not long thereafter, Haylee peeked from her hiding place to see her mother carefully inserting candles into each pumpkin. When each pumpkin held a candle, Mom carried the jack-o-lanterns outside and set them on the porch. The pumpkins brought a Halloween cheer as they graced the descending steps, ready to be lit the following evening.

When she came back in, Mom placed her hand on Grandma's shoulder. "This was a great idea, Mom. Don't let the girls' attitudes throw you. I know I had fun, and I can't remember the last time we carved pumpkins. The spaghetti was excellent, too!" She kissed her mother on the cheek.

Wiping a tear from her eye, Grandma said, as she reeled around to gaze in her daughter's face, "I think sometimes I have an image in my head of how enjoyable an evening like this will be, only to feel disappointed when my expectations don't pan out."

"It was more wonderful than what you imagined," said Mom. "You just don't remember how teenage girls can react."

Grandma kissed Mom's cheek, so then Mom headed upstairs.

Sneaking past Grandma, Haylee followed her mother, waiting in the hall until the bedroom door closed. Then she tiptoed close to listen through the panel.

Haylee loved her mother's room. The bed was situated opposite the fireplace. Mom never lit a fire in there, because she feared birds would nest on the chimney and fall into the flames. So, she put a basket full of dried periwinkle hydrangeas and yellow asters in the fireplace alcove. An Asian screen accented the left side while a bronze statue of a Pilgrim offered balance the right. Above the mantel hung a painting of a Renaissance girl lying by a stream. The rich tones of burgundy, gold, and cobalt blue complemented the hues of the flowers inside the fireplace.

Haylee overheard her mother tapping on her cell phone. Slowly, she turned the knob of the door and edged it open just an inch. Haylee saw her mother swipe hair from her left ear.

"Dan? It's Elizabeth. I wanted to let you know some exciting news. Michaela has a *boyfriend*." She offered the last line as if it were a song.

Silence.

Haylee wondered if the call had ended. Immediately, Haylee heard irritation in her mother's voice.

"No, Dan, I didn't call about money. I called because I thought you might want to know that your older daughter is dating!"

Haylee slid the door open a tad more, just enough to see better.

Her mother unhooked an earring from her left ear, switched the cell to the other side, and then undid the right earring, too. She placed both in her jewelry box, and shouted into the phone, "No, Dan, I do *not* think that's a good idea. I can't believe you!" Her mother almost turned toward the door, so Haylee slid back further into the hallway.

"You're not going to bring that barely-out-of-the-awkward-teen-years mistress with you to share a milestone of your children's development!" Disconnecting the call, Haylee's mother threw her phone across the bed and burst into tears.

Hearing her mother scream at her phone, Haylee also listened as her mother yelled, "I hate you, Dan Higgins, and I loathe the day I met you! A tap on Haylee's shoulder made her jump.

Grandma!

How she'd come up the steps without Haylee hearing, she had no idea.

Grandma's pursed lips told Haylee she wasn't happy to catch her eavesdropping, so Haylee made a beeline for her own bedroom. Bursting into Mom's room, Grandma neglected to fully close the door behind her. Creeping out of her room again, Haylee leaned on the far wall, just at the right angle, to see both women in Mom's room.

Laying on the bed, Mom sobbed. Haylee was glad Grandma was there, since Haylee knew not how to soothe her mom. Grandma joined her daughter on the bed, and using a soft tone, while rubbing Mom's back, she cooed, "Elizabeth, when your father left, I was *angry*. I didn't have a single kind word to say about him. In hindsight, what I most resented was his *passivity*. See, I wanted him to fight for us, for our family. It never dawned on me, the more I shouted, cajoled, and put him down, the more he retreated."

Mom hiccupped into her pillow.

"Honey, I love you," Grandma soothed. "What I've learned in my recovery is that I become blind when I'm self-righteous. I'm unable to see how my own behavior affects others when I'm so certain I'm right."

Grandma sat up, continuing, "You have done remarkably well with this nasty card you've been dealt, Elizabeth. But now you need to let the shattered grief go. Dan will either notice you're no longer bitter, and he will make better choices; or he'll remain oblivious."

Grandma stroked Mom's sleek black hair.

"It hurts when you believe you're supposed to set him on a straight course. You can't, or he would have heeded your advice long ago. You only hurt yourself when you think you have the magic words to make him behave or react a certain way, or that you can force him to make a better choice. You don't have that kind of power."

She leaned over and kissed Mom's forehead.

"And Elizabeth, I worry about the girls, and what they overhear. They can't relate to your frustration. Their not-yet-mature outlook is to assume you are the one who's wrong, and to them that means their father must be right. They haven't experienced enough of life to understand how complicated relationships are."

Haylee wanted to interrupt. She wanted to tell both, Grandma was wrong. She *did* understand.

But Haylee knew she couldn't step in. Not without being caught again. Tears trickled from the corners of her eyes.

"Mom?" Haylee's mother asked. "Do you know a good therapist who could help Dan and me navigate through all of this? Not for us, but for the girls?"

Haylee had seen and heard enough. She crept the rest of the way down the hallway, down the stairs, and to the kitchen, where Barney was snuggled in his crate. He raised his snout and wagged his tail.

Haylee put a finger to her lips, then opened his crate. Soon she and Barney were slinking out the kitchen door to the back porch.

Haylee saw they weren't the only ones who needed to get away.

"You couldn't sleep either?" Haylee asked as she sat next to Michaela on the stoop.

"I hate when Mom and Dad fight," Michaela murmured. Barney circled several times, then slumped into lying beside Haylee with his snout on her thigh.

Unlike Haylee, Michaela already was wearing pajamas—the emerald, green silky ones. Everything Michaela wore was perfectly coordinated, even her nightclothes.

For several minutes, they sat together in silence. Haylee looked at the distant, waxy moon and contemplated what else could be out there, floating in space.

"Do you ever think about Dad?" Michaela asked.

"All the time," Haylee admitted, as she sat down on the step with her sister.

An owl hooted in the Red Sunset Maple tree.

Gathering her knees to her chest, Michaela wondered, "Why do they still fight so much even now that they're apart?"

Sighing, Haylee reasoned, "I think Mom argues with Dad because of Tiffany. Dad likes Tiffany because she doesn't argue. Dad, on the other hand, argues with Mom because he thinks Mom has the upper hand after she learned about his affair with Tiffany."

"I hate Tiffany!" Michaela said fiercely. She buried her face in her knees, and she pulled them close to her chest.

"Well, I have news for you. Dad wants to bring Tiffany when he comes to see us."

"I know," Michaela said. "I heard the whole thing. Mom doesn't know I can hear what she says in her room through the vent."

Haylee giggled.

"I don't want him to come," Michaela declared as she hurled an acorn toward the bench surrounding the Beech tree.

"Because of Tiffany?" Haylee asked.

"Yeah." With her eyes focused upward, Haylee changed the topic. "Look at the sky," she said. "The stars make me think how small and irrelevant we are. We think our problems are monumental, but when you compare them to the vast sky above, I think our problems are so miniscule they just don't matter."

"You're weird," Michaela said flatly.

"And your pumpkin was terrible," Haylee countered. She butted her knees into Michaela's thighs. Barney sighed and curled into a ball.

"Thanks a lot." Michaela's disdain was evident, but then, with her head tilted toward Haylee, she said, "You're lucky. Everything you touch turns out well. You have so much talent."

"I can't put together an outfit, or style my hair like you do," said Haylee. "You have talent, too. You're just too busy being social to use it."

Michaela bumped Haylee's shoulder with her own. "Yeah. Well, you're too busy being talented to be social. Come on, let's go inside. It's freezing."

Michaela stood up and opened the back door.

"You go ahead. I'm gonna stay here and gaze at the stars a little longer." Alone again—except for Barney—Haylee looked at the looming shadow of the Beech tree. The swaying of the shadow reminded her of her hardware store purchases. She wondered how long it would be before she could visit the cave again. It wasn't just any cave. It was her own special hideaway, free of crowds and noise and arguing. No expectations, no comparisons, no divorce. Just a womb of bliss.

Unable to resist, she sauntered over to the tree. For a moment, she ran her fingers over the bark, imagining centuries' worth of growth that resulted in what she was now touching. It was overwhelming to think of all this tree had witnessed throughout its long life. It cradled history, secrets unshared with anyone.

Raising the bench seat, Haylee peered inside. It was hard to see, but she could make out the bag she'd placed in there.

And something else.

Right on top of the bag, placed in the very center, was a heart-shaped rose quartz crystal.

"*Somebody must have seen me put the bag in here*," she whispered. "Then they came and put the crystal on top."

Haylee spun around, peering in every direction, but no one was in sight. An odd shadow—her yard and the neighbors'—briefly drew her focus, but it had been like that for several days. Nothing amiss there.

Barney wasn't on high alert, and he wasn't acting strange at all. Even so, the sudden eeriness—and the distinct sensation she was being watched—caused goose bumps to form on the back of Haylee's neck.

She grabbed the crystal, shoved it in her pocket, and let the lid drop on the bench seat. She tore back to the house without looking back.

9

Do You Hear What I Hear?

Haylee lay in the back of her mother's SUV. Mom didn't know she was there, because she'd scooched down between the seats and lay covered up with the blanket used to protect the upholstery from Barney.

Haylee knew her mother wanted to find a therapist, because she'd overheard her mother and Grandma talking about it. She wanted to know who her mom would pick to be the co-parenting therapist.

Better be a good one and not some quack.

Haylee almost giggled aloud, picturing the one-winged duck as a therapist.

For more than an hour, she'd been burrowed in like this, waiting for Mom to finish her appointment with the therapist. She contemplated how on earth a Salem shrink could teach Mom to co-parent, especially considering the other half of the "co"—her dad—lived a thousand miles away.

Haylee moved around, trying to find a more comfortable way to stretch her legs, when the car door opened. The door slammed shut and Mom murmured aloud, "Better get this over with." A second later, the Bluetooth system kicked in, and Haylee heard the pulse of a cell phone ringing.

"Don't hang up, Dan," Mom said as she put the call on speaker to enable her to situate the phone on the dashboard holder. "This is a red-letter day, so set down the laughing gas and the Novocain."

Haylee reined in the urge to uncover her head, so she could hear more clearly.

"What do you want, Liz?" Dad didn't sound pleased.

"After our last call, when I screamed at you, I decided to find a therapist. Yes, I know it's a shock."

"Great, Liz. *You have a therapist now. I'm happy you're getting help.*" He didn't sound happy. He sounded annoyed.

"The therapist—Dr. Warren—is for both of us, to give us advice on how to help our girls through this mess. Today she said that in cases like ours, divorced parents can communicate by passing a notebook between them. That way, information gets shared without risking the kids overhearing us when we talk—or even yell 'AT EACH OTHER.' Since we can't pass a notebook back and forth, she suggested we use e-mail or texting to communicate."

"That's fine, Liz. Whatever you want."

Haylee's mother shifted in the seat.

"Dr. Warren also says neither of us should say negative things about the other in front of the girls." Her mother sighed. "That means I won't say anything about Tiffany, your affair, or your parents. Lord knows I could go on."

Mom peered at her hair in the rear-view mirror.

"Yeah, right, Liz. Do you really expect me to believe that? I'm sure you've already given the girls an earful, telling them how rotten I am."

Haylee could tell by the way her mother was breathing that she was on the verge of sobbing. She wondered if her dad could tell.

Grabbing a tissue, Mom pleaded, "I'm trying, here, Dan. Our girls are worth it, don't you think?"

"So, what exactly do you want me to do?" Dad said flatly. "I'm not traveling all the way to Salem just to meet with your Dr. Warren."

"Haven't you been listening? All I'm asking is that our correspondence from now on be done via e-mail. You still have my email address, don't you?"

"I have it."

Placing her elbow on the steering wheel, Mom added, "Okay, fine. From now on, I'll e-mail you with news about the girls." Then she added, as if it was an afterthought, "Of course, if it's an emergency, I'll call."

"I should hope so," Dad huffed. "I wouldn't appreciate finding out through e-mail that Michaela's in the hospital."

Figures he'd be more concerned about Michaela than me.

Tears welled in Haylee's eyes.

"Dr. Warren also suggested I find a hobby," Mom said. "Something to distract me from wanting to scream at you all the time."

"Are we done here?" Dad asked, followed by a curt "Good-bye, Liz."

The Bluetooth system beeped off. Without making a sound, Haylee tucked herself more deeply under the blanket and tried to ignore the sound of her mother crying.

Her mother turned around to move the blanket before backing out of the parking space.

"Haylee Carmichael Higgins!" she gasped! "What are you doing here?"

10

Mirror, Mirror, on the Wall

Six days later, Grandma had made pot roast for dinner. When Haylee returned from a long day at school, she enjoyed it when the house was filled with the aroma of beef stock, paprika, and tubers. Although Haylee didn't like Grandma's pot roast as much as her to-die-for spaghetti, she had to admit that it tasted better than their weekly meatloaf.

Haylee helped her sister set the table without prompting, after which she settled in her favorite dining room chair, the one that afforded clear views of all entrances and exits. Such a line of sight was keenly important to Haylee, as she hated feeling trapped, especially if such confinement required conversation, or worse, attention.

During dinner, Haylee noticed that Michaela was refusing to speak to her. Under normal circumstances, Haylee would be thrilled, but she felt concern when she realized Michaela hadn't said two words since they'd gotten home from school. Across the table, Michaela's glare was as wicked as Roger Conant's statue stare.

Haylee thought about what possible sin she might have committed to upset her sister so.

Using her blow dryer?

No. Haylee had used her mother's ever since the fateful day Haylee had taken apart her sister's appliance and couldn't put the necessary parts back in place.

Haylee concentrated.

Had she disturbed Michaela's layout of eye shadow palette and lip gloss on her vanity? No. Haylee had no use for such supplies. Haylee knew no matter how many layers of goo she'd attempt to apply, she'd end up looking like John Wayne Gacey in his clown makeup. Why upset children already doomed to school attendance?

Haylee had no idea what Michaela was up in arms about, and she had no interest in being ambushed during dinner. All she wanted to do was finish her meat, then chow down on the caramelized carrots that should not (and would not) ever touch her portion of pot roast, and then the final glory, savoring the russet potatoes for the feast's finish. After she'd eaten, she planned to go to her room where she could lie on her bed and luxuriate in being alone. In peace.

But she wasn't going to be that lucky! Haylee could feel Michaela's death stare. She knew the *High Noon* confrontation was coming. Unlike in the Old West, her sister didn't need a pistol. Michaela's words could level any cowboy, clear any saloon. Why, even tumbleweeds would scurry to hide. Haylee tried to ignore her sister by staring at the lithograph of maple trees gracing a rural lane that hung above Elizabeth's head.

"Are you feeling okay, Michaela?" Mom asked. Michaela took a sip of water. "I have something important to tell you, but I'll wait until after dinner." Michaela never looked at her mother. Instead, she landed an icy glare on Haylee.

Grandma blurted, "Did Jason break up with you, dear? Boys can be fickle creatures," she said tsking.

Grandma passed a basket of rolls to Haylee.

Haylee wasn't paying attention, so Grandma took a roll and set the basket on the table.

Michaela slowly turned her glower on Grandma, as she smiled the most gruesome, chilling, sneering grin. "No, Jason didn't break up with me," Michaela said and flipped her hair behind her right shoulder. Under her breath, Michaela muttered, "At least, not yet."

Mom prodded. "Is it your grades? A problem with one of your classes?" Elizabeth sounded compassionate and concerned.

"My grades are fine. Let's just drop this until after we eat." Michaela said scraping her plate with her fork. Michaela knew Haylee despised the sound of a fork screeching against any dish. With this gesture, Haylee knew beyond a doubt that Michaela was furious with Haylee. But why? *This makes no sense!*

"Okay," Mom said, then smiled cheekily, "I actually have some news. I met someone today."

Haylee looked up, noticing that all their gazes were trained on Mom. *Is she going to tell everyone about her therapist?*

Mom's eyes twinkled.

"I made some deposits for the company today. The bank manager expressed an interest in my accounts."

"I'm sure he did," Grandma said, chuckling. "And I'll bet he wasn't wearing a wedding ring."

Michaela rolled her eyes.

Because she didn't know what to say, Haylee grabbed the serving dish and scooped two more chunks of meat onto her plate. Only one piece remained in the dish.

"Haylee!" Michaela snarled. "You should ask if anyone else wants seconds before you take the last piece."

Haylee shoved an overly large forkful into her mouth, chewed with gusto, and rinsed with a big gulp of water.

A Divorce in Salem

"May I be excused to do my homework? I have an English test tomorrow." Haylee spoke rapidly, hoping to hear an automatic *yes*.

"No!" Michaela barked. "What I have to say after dinner concerns you."

"All right, Michaela," Mom said resignedly. "What is so important that you have to bite your sister's head off?"

Michaela cleared her throat. "At school today, all anybody could talk about was the play, and the auditions. I have it on good authority that our Haylee is *not* going to be the stage manager. In fact, Haylee — never even asked about that job." Michaela folded her arms as though she were an attorney resting her case before a judge.

Uh—oh.

Mom looked concerned, and Grandma, curious.

But Michaela wasn't finished. Slamming her palm on the table, Michaela added, "You're never going to believe this, Mom. Haylee auditioned for an actual role. A *speaking* role." Michaela looked at each person around the table, ending with Haylee. "I would like to know— what possessed you to consider doing such a preposterous thing?"

Turning her head, Mom asked, "Haylee, is this true? You actually auditioned for a part?" She leaned over and put her hand on Haylee's arm.

Pulling away, Haylee stared at the remnants on her plate. She couldn't look up. Not able to speak, Haylee nodded in response. She felt small, yet somehow, swollen, too. She disliked feeling exposed, as though something inside her demanded that she blends in with the furniture. If she was noticed, it felt like her immune system would become inflamed. Maybe she was a chameleon in a former life.

Standing up and pacing, Michaela ranted some more.

"You should have warned us! After all, we're your family, and the things you do impact us!"

Haylee knew Michaela was standing now because she insisted on a position of authority. Michaela wanted to hold ultimate power, even over their mother and grandmother.

Clearing her throat, where her saliva felt thick and stagnant, Haylee murmured, "All I did was read for a stupid part. And for your information, whatever intel you heard, I didn't kill anyone. Oh, and I didn't burp, or throw up. In fact, I didn't even fart!" For the first time, Haylee felt empowered enough to look her mother, Grandma, and sister in their eyes. "I don't think I embarrassed the family at all," Haylee concluded, throwing her napkin on the table.

"Well," Michaela said, "Tomorrow, you need to inform the director you've changed your mind. You can't be in the play." Michaela stared at her sister, then swung her head toward her mother for affirmation.

"Michaela!" Mom chided. "Aren't you being harsh? How do you know she didn't read well at the audition? At any rate, why does this even matter to you?" Elizabeth sounded uncertain and looked to her mother for further guidance.

"Mom," Michaela cried. "Don't you see? All day long, all I heard was that Haylee Higgins had tried out for the play. The other kids—Ryan and Pamela and Kiersten, made fun of her! She already sticks out enough. Kids mock her all the time. She reads *Anti Gonee*, for Pete's sake!"

"Is that one word or two?" Grandma interjected casually, reaching for her mug.

Clearly disconcerted, Michaela growled, "I don't know! It's some dumb Greek play, and proof that Haylee's weird!" Michaela had sat back on the dining room chair, both legs draped over the armrest. Grandma clasped her hands in recognition.

"Oh, you mean *Antigone*. The play by Sophocles!" Grandma winked at Haylee. "Wise choice, kiddo. Filling your head with classic literature will open doors you never thought possible."

Mom pushed her chair back. "Haylee, honey, why don't you go ahead and do your homework. Grandma and I need to talk to Michaela."

Haylee complied, or at least she made them believe she did. She started up the stairs but didn't go all the way into the upstairs hall. From where she remained, she could still hear their conversation.

Gathering dishes, Elizabeth scolded, "Michaela, what is wrong with you? There is nothing your sister wouldn't do for you. All she cares about is your approval, and yet you cut her down, like this? I can't believe you!" Elizabeth shook her head.

"You just don't understand, Mom," Michaela pouted and gathered flatware for the dishwasher. "Haylee doesn't dress like other kids. Her interests—books, drawings, *everything* she does—makes her stick out! She's bullied enough, and this play is only going to make it worse!"

Can't argue with that.

Haylee slouched down and positioned her head between two balusters in the stairway.

Grandma picked up a ladle and spatula to take to the kitchen.

"Sometimes, if a person *is* different, they'll fare better when observed by a group rather than individually," Grandma chimed in. "Van Gogh was a great example. Do you know who he was?"

Michaela must have shaken her head, because Mom said, "Does the painting *Starry Night* ring any bells?"

"Oh," Michaela said in acknowledgement.

"Van Gogh's brother, Theo, was often frustrated and annoyed with him. And look what Van Gogh accomplished!" Grandma said while maneuvering flatware and kitchen utensils from the dining room to the dishwasher. Then, her voice softening, she added, "Do you really believe Haylee doesn't know she's different? You think she doesn't notice the stares and hear the comments made about her? I think being brave enough to audition in front of other kids is admirable. I'm proud of Haylee, and you should be, too." Grandma pat Michaela on her shoulder and nodded at Elizabeth.

Haylee wasn't sure what Grandma meant, about it being more likely to be accepted by a group than individually, but something about that statement resonated.

"You don't understand either, Grandma!" Michaela spouted. "This is not just about Haylee. It's about the whole family. I work hard to be normal. I had to change just to fit in here. You don't know how important it is to have the right clothes and the right interests. And Haylee *won't* change! Now, by auditioning for this play, she'll ruin us!"

"Michaela," Mom said. Her voice was quiet, but that couldn't hide the thinly veiled anger. She shoved the dining room chair into the table and added, "Do you know why I supported you when you insisted on changing your wardrobe? Do you know why I took you shopping?"

If Michaela answered, Haylee didn't hear it.

Mom said, "I took you shopping because I knew it would help you feel better about yourself. The new clothes would help you feel as though you could 'fit' in with new peers."

Haylee struggled with her desire to set all of them straight. She wanted to scream but thought it better to continue to listen to how all of them thought about her unusual choice to audition.

"But Haylee isn't like you." Mom added. "Imagine how confused she would have been if I had insisted, she change her wardrobe? She would have assumed something was wrong with her clothes, because getting new ones wasn't her idea, wasn't something she even cared about."

Slamming her fist on the kitchen island, Michaela wiped tears from her red-hot cheeks. "Why are adults so out of touch?" she wailed. "You just don't get it. This isn't about clothes! If Haylee gets a part in the big spring play, she'll be made fun of even more than she is already. And because of her, our whole family will be a joke! I'll become a laughingstock!" She dropped her head on the dining room table.

Mom clucked, a sign her temper was about to boil over.

"Michaela, you are a beautiful, intelligent young woman," Mom said. "What I don't understand is why, when you have so much going for you, you'd believe that comments made about your sister would have anything to do with you?" Shaking her head, Elizabeth sighed. "I'm truly sorry for you, Michaela, if being judged by your peers is more important to you than your own sister. I wonder if it's even dawned on you to stick up for Haylee when you hear other kids making fun of her? Have you ever?"

Haylee used her butt to lower two stairs, so that she could see and hear her mother and Michaela.

Looking her mother in the eye, Michaela snapped, "Aren't you the one who decorated the house in Chicago to please Dad and not yourself?" Michaela asked pointedly, her eyes boring into her mother's steel—blue ones. "I've been told my whole life that I'm just like you."

Inserting herself between Michaela and Elizabeth, Grandma bellowed, "Girls! That's enough!"

It was good that Grandma cut in, because Michaela's last comment had all but propelled Mom over the edge. Haylee knew words could hurt; that's why, she feared them, better not to speak.

Grandma had moved closer to Michaela and was smoothing her sleek hair. "Michaela, did anyone at school say *how* your sister performed at the audition?" Grandma asked calmly. "I think the fact that they didn't speaks volumes. Perhaps your sister has a talent no one was aware of. Would that give you some relief?" Grandma paused for a moment. "I was a big sister, too, you know. When my sister and I were in school, I was always telling her what to wear and how to act. Do you know what all that wasted energy got me? She went on to become the vice president of a bank, and I became an alcoholic."

Grandma and Michaela guffawed.

"Mother!" Mom exclaimed.

Grandma put out her hand, speckled with liver spots. "Forgive me, dear. I'm not saying Michaela will become a drunk. What I'm telling you is, my love, that I tried to turn my sister into a rose when she was already a beautiful orchid."

This time when Michaela spoke, her voice betrayed her. She was already emotional.

"You both think I don't care about Haylee, but I do. I'm just trying to keep her—and us—from being mocked more than we already are. I don't like it when Haylee gets bullied. She's, my sister!" Michaela wiped tears from her cheeks.

Mom spoke next, and this time she didn't sound angry. She sounded resigned.

"Michaela, you and Haylee, have weathered so much change these last few months. I need to apologize to you both. My own stress blinded me. Now, as for this play, we don't know yet if Haylee got a part. But if she has, I will not ask her to bow out. I will support her no matter what. So will Grandma. And so should you."

Grandma pointed her finger upstairs. "Why don't you go up and take a good long soak in the tub. Put your earbuds in and listen to your crazy music. Perhaps tomorrow you'll feel differently about all of this."

Haylee could tell by the sounds of chair legs scraping the floor that Michaela re-straightened the dining room chairs, signaling the end of cleanup after dinner. So that she wouldn't be caught on the stairs, Haylee high-tailed it up to her room. There, she waited, listening until her sister's door closed.

Then, as stealthily as she'd left the dining room, Haylee made her way back down the stairs. She'd missed some of Mom and Grandma's discussion, but not all of it.

"... and what if Michaela's right? What if Haylee *is* facing further ridicule? Would it be better for her if I stopped her from doing the play?"

Throwing a kitchen towel over her shoulder, Grandma nodded, "Maybe kids will make fun of her — But Elizabeth, there comes a time when parents must limit how much control they exert over their children. An important part of growing up is learning how to cope, learning how the child comes across to peers. Deciding whether she wants to be in the play must be Haylee's choice. Not yours." She chuckled mildly and added, "If you'll recall, you had plenty of your own stubborn, willful moments. And look how you turned out? Pretty darn great, if you ask me."

Mom handed rinsed plates to Grandma who stacked them into the dishwasher on the lower wrack. She said wryly, "When I was Michaela's age, I was just like her. Trying to fit in. I didn't take risks like I should have. And I regret it. Maybe that's why this damn divorce has brought me to my knees."

She sighed, lost in her thoughts, then continued. "You know what my first thought was when I learned of Dan's affair? I worried that people would say I was an incompetent wife. It didn't even occur to me to question whether *I* was happy in my marriage."

They talked more, but the topic moved away from Dad. Nothing more was said about Michaela, or Haylee, or the play.

Haylee found herself tuning them out. Her mind was too cluttered with the facts she'd just learned.

Back in her room, she jotted three main points in her journal:

Grandma may be an alcoholic, but she's smarter than the knitting lady on the Gloucester bus.

Mom still loves Dad.

Michaela doesn't care about anyone but Michaela. Especially when it comes to me.

11
There Are No Small Roles

At breakfast the next morning, Haylee questioned the silent collusion of her sister, mother, and grandmother in ignoring last night's heated discussion of—her audition. Even so, she sighed with relief when the rest of her family left for work, school, shopping, and an AA meeting.

She still had some time before leaving for school, so she released Barney from his crate and escorted him to the backyard. Normally, the silly dog romped around until he'd found the perfect spot to do his business, but today he didn't romp. He just stood there, looking up as if he saw something overhead. And then he barked. And barked some more.

Following his line of sight, she could see nothing that would warrant a bark, let alone a series of them. Though the temperature felt mild, Haylee shivered. "What's wrong, Barney? Who are you barking at?" she asked, stroking down his raised hackles.

And that's when she saw it—another heart-shaped rose quartz. It was identical to the one she'd found in the bench under the Beech tree. Except this one lay in the middle of the yard, so Barney must have sensed a person depositing the crystal. But who could it be and why?

Standing around wondering who'd dropped it in the backyard seemed futile, so she grabbed the smooth stone with one hand and Barney's collar with the other and she and the dog ran back inside.

She closed and locked the kitchen door and soothed Barney, saying, "You'll be all right, Barney. Serial killers don't leave heart-shaped stones."

Barney wagged his tail and woofed.

Haylee didn't want to step foot outside again, not while her chest was pounding. But she had to leave. School beckoned.

Reasoning that whoever had left the stone had done so by traipsing through the backyard and not the front, Haylee calmed down enough to say good-bye to Barney and headed out the front door.

Nearing the bus stop, she was relieved to see Josh and Brandon there waiting for the bus to arrive.

Brandon smiled and said, "Hey."

Haylee froze. She didn't know how to reply to a *hey*. After all, Brandon typically didn't acknowledge her. Actually, no one ever did.

Josh didn't say anything. Instead, he scuffed his sneaker across the gravel.

"Josh is nervous about seeing the casting list," Brandon explained. "Are you nervous, too?"

"How can I be nervous when I know I didn't get a part?" she said shifting her weight to feel grounded.

"Yeah, I feel the same," Brandon said. "I figure I'll check out the posting anyway, just in case."

Misty came bounding over. Her house was in the opposite direction from Haylee's.

"Hi guys!" she hailed. "Are you talking about the casting list? Mrs. Esty said it will be posted at two o'clock today. I can't wait to see if any of us got parts." Whenever Misty felt shy, the corners of her mouth turned upward. While others assumed she was confident, Haylee knew better. Since it looked like she was smiling, Haylee knew the expression often masked Haylee's nerves, especially when she was near a boy she liked.

Josh continued to shovel gravel with his foot.

Trying to think of something to say, Brandon asked, "Want to meet outside the auditorium at two? We can check out the list together. There's solace in numbers!" He glanced at Josh, but Josh was looking at cars passing by.

At last, Josh spoke. Staring at the Cape Cod house across the street, he said, "I hope I didn't get in. My father would die if I did. The only place where he wants to see me perform is inside a football stadium."

"Yeah, but he probably won't see you there, either" Brandon joked giving Josh a playful shove.

"I'll be happy so long as Danielle and Tyler don't get the leads," Misty said as she shifted the weight of her backpack. "I'm sick of them and their I'm-so-perfect attitudes."

When the school bus rolled to the curb, Haylee lumbered aboard first and plopped down into a seat.

Misty sat beside her, but Haylee paid her no mind. She was engrossed by the frost coating the bus window. Using the sleeve of her jacket, Haylee wiped it enough to make a small circle. Peering through, she observed leaves on the sugar maples dancing like quivering arrows. The vivid hues of plum, scarlet, and burnt orange floated and fluttered like feathers as several tumbled to the ground. The quivering motion of the leaves and their colors created a brilliant canvas. Haylee was enchanted. She could have stared at the scene for hours, but the bus lurched forward.

Turning to Misty, Haylee asked, "Have you ever seen any crystals around your house?"

"What are you talking about?" Mysty veered her head toward Haylee.

"I found two heart-shaped quartz crystals in my backyard," Haylee told her. She pulled one out of her backpack and showed it to her friend.

"Oooh," Misty's eyes flashed. "You have a secret admirer!"

"I seriously doubt that." Haylee said wryly. "This morning when I took Barney out, he kept looking up and barking, as though he sensed who the intruder was. It was strange 'cause Barney doesn't usually bark. But then I saw this thing on the ground, and it gave me the willies. I found another one in our bench around the Beech tree, exactly the same."

Misty shifted, so she faced Haylee. "That's creepy. I mean it, you need to tell your mom or your grandmother," Misty advised. Changing the subject, Misty said, "I'm so anxious about the cast list. I don't know how I'll get through the day."

When the bus reached school, Haylee followed Misty down the aisle. Hoisting her backpack so it was positioned more securely on her shoulder, she descended the steps, and started up the sidewalk toward the school entrance.

A voice suddenly called out "Hey, Haylee!"

The bellowing call stunned Haylee. A tall boy with honey—brown hair dodged around and through other kids, making a beeline for her.

Misty tugged on her sleeve and whispered, "Oh my god! That's Nathaniel! He's a sophomore, and, like, the hottest guy in the whole school!"

Misty didn't have time to say more.

"Your name is Haylee, right?" Nathaniel asked. "I saw you audition for the play and wanted to tell you; you were really good." He grinned. "See ya "round." And with that, Nathaniel sauntered off.

Misty grabbed Haylee's arm. "I can't believe you just talked to Nathaniel Dimond! He's like the star football player on our team, and he also plays drums. I heard him in the talent show last year. He's amazing!"

"I didn't actually talk to him," Haylee mumbled. "I didn't say a word."

Behind them, Brandon swooned into Josh, batted his eyelashes, and in an overdone falsetto said, "Do you really think he likes me? Do you think he looked me up on Instagram? Does my backpack make my butt look big?"

Josh laughed and shoved Brandon away.

Misty glared at them. "Shut up! You're both dorks!"

To keep Misty from hollering anything more, Haylee quickly said, "Do you want to meet in front of Mr. Quincy's classroom at two o'clock? It's right next to the auditorium."

"Good idea," Misty agreed, but she glared at Brandon and Josh again. "Let's make a pact that we'll all be kind to each other, whether we make it or not."

"Deal," Brandon said.

Haylee looked at Josh, wondering if he'd agree. A beam of sunlight glinted off his hair, turning it from russet to fiery, blood red orange. Something in Haylee's stomach flip-flopped, but she didn't understand why.

Swiping his hair from his eyes, Josh asked, "If I make it, will you guys come over and be there when I tell my parents? Seriously, I don't want to tell my mom without my dad being there, 'cause then she'll blab to him, and he'll confront me when Mom isn't around. If you guys are with me, I could tell them both at the same time. You could tell them I was just lucky, and then say something like, "Acting doesn't mean he chose a career."

Although Josh's tone sounded casual, Haylee could sense his fear. Josh was afraid of his dad. She couldn't imagine fearing hers, just feeling deeply disappointed. It made her feel sorry for Josh.

"I think that's a great idea," Misty said. "Not just for Josh, but for all of us. We can go to each other's houses together and tell all our parents." She put her hands in the pockets of her pea coat.

Josh fears his dad, and Misty's scared of her mom.

Haylee felt she wouldn't have as much trouble waiting for two o'clock to come, but somehow it turned into the slowest school day ever. In every class, it was all she could do to sit still until the bell rang.

Gym, the last class of the day, seemed to go on forever.

When it was over, Haylee quickly showered and dressed, then hastened through the busy hallway to Mr. Quincy's classroom.

She was the first one there, but it wasn't long before Misty showed up.

"Any sign of Brandon or Josh?" Misty asked.

"Not yet," Haylee said, eyeing the hallway full of kids. The cacophony of laughter and voices was deafening.

As she shifted from one leg to another, Haylee wished for the old days of naptime and Fig Newtons, monkey bars and swing sets. Those days when she was still a little girl were the best.

"I see them!" cried Misty.

Josh and Brandon were making their way toward them. Haylee recalled the way they'd spoken to her earlier that morning, like she was one of them. She'd never really belonged anywhere before. Thinking further, she hadn't contemplated belonging ever before.

"Are you guys ready?" Brandon said, as soon as they ambled up. "I think the rest of us should wait here while Misty looks, for all of us."

Even though he said he wasn't, Brandon's nervous, too.

Josh nodded, and Misty said, "Okay. I'll go."

Misty disappeared around the corner, and again Haylee felt stupid. She didn't know what to say to the boys. It didn't help that it seemed like Misty was taking an inordinately long time.

Josh joked, "Maybe she got lost?"

Suddenly, around the corner, Danielle came running. She ran all the way down the hall and through the school doors, tears streaming down her cheeks.

"Looks like the queen of John Proctor High has lost her title," Brandon smirked.

"If Danielle didn't get a part, then probably none of us did, either." Josh reasoned.

Haylee assumed he would be relieved, because he wouldn't have to tell his dad, but he didn't sound relieved. Instead, he sounded upset.

Misty came barreling around the corner, almost as fast as Danielle, except she wasn't crying. She was grinning and panting with excitement. Pulling herself together, Misty shrugged, as if nothing important was at stake.

Haylee saw right through the feigned nonchalance.

"Come on, Misty," Josh prompted. "We've been waiting long enough."

Misty's lips curled and her eyes gleamed.

"You'll never believe who got the part of the prince. *Josh!* You got the male lead!"

"No way," Josh muttered. His shoulders slumped so much so his backpack slid off and landed with a thump on the floor.

Misty continued, "Brandon, you're so lucky, 'cause you got Rumpelstiltskin, the most hilarious part of all! And I'm the Wicked Witch! That means I get to be mean to everybody." She cackled with her new witchy, sneering laugh. "You'll never believe where Mrs. Esty put Danielle," Misty uttered breathlessly. Paused for full effect. "She's an elf!" Doubling over, Misty guffawed. That means I can be mean to her, too!" Misty cackled again.

Haylee bit her lip.

Don't cry! Not now. Not in front of Brandon and Josh.

To keep the thickness in her throat from ballooning, she chewed the inside of her cheek, the way her mother did when she wished to hide a flow of tears. Longing to congratulate Misty, Josh, and Brandon, she resented how she couldn't make any words erupt.

"Don't worry, Haylee," Josh murmured. "There'll be other plays."

"What do you mean, *other plays*?" Misty chortled. "You didn't let me finish. Haylee, you rocked it! You got the female lead! Girl, you're the *Princess!*"

Haylee looked around, as the hallway swirled like the amusement ride in Chicago.

Misty hooted, "We all made it! We're gonna have such a blast! And we get to taunt Danielle the entire time—is that divine justice or what?"

Having difficulty believing what she'd just heard, Haylee quietly asked, "Are you sure, Misty?" Her voice cracked. "You're not just joking?"

Nodding and pushing Haylee forward, Misty urged, "Go see for yourself if you don't believe me."

Haylee didn't need to see for herself.

"Wow," she gulped. "The lead. I'm the Princess."

Michaela's going to be as thrilled as Josh's dad.

12

Bearing Good Tidings of Great Upheaval

Haylee felt like they were Dorothy, the Tin Man, the Scarecrow, and the Cowardly Lion, each standing in Misty's front yard, staring at the house ahead of them.

The four friends decided to deliver their news to Misty's mother first, for no reason other than the fact her house was closest to the bus stop. Misty's home was also one of the newest and nicest in the eclectic neighborhood. Her mother had adorned the outside with Indian corn, gourds, and asters on the windowsills and porch.

Picture Perfect.

Unlike the neighbors, Misty's mother decorated each and every windowsill such the sides as well as the backyard of the home appointed with all the favorites of Autumn. The attention to detail struck Haylee. It dawned on Haylee; she felt a connection to Misty's Mother. She, too, poured similar attention to detail in her own drawings.

Observing the surrounding homes, Haylee noticed they too favored Autumn reminders, but their decor limited designated objects associated with FALL. Not true of Misty's Mother, as it mattered not to her whether a neighbor could view her meticulous care. Misty's Mother paid homage to the season such even an aerial view could attest to her love for decorating. On the six stairs, leading up to the front porch, sat yellow and orange mums, asters, and nasturtiums on top of small bales of hay underneath looming cornstalks. Canary-yellow, brown, and orange garlands flanked the front door. Even though it wasn't fully dark yet, candles glowed in the center of each window. Haylee wondered if Mysty fully appreciated her mother's skill and her ability to entrap the eyes away from neighbors.

On the other hand, Haylee knew Misty's father disdained her mother's love for decorating, as she overheard her parents argue about the money Misty's mother had been spent on decorations. On one occasion, Haylee recalled her mother shouting in return that whatever money was spent was dwarfed by how much Misty's father spent on 'booze.' On that occasion, Haylee came up with an excuse to go home.

The tension in the ensuing silence made her stomach lurch and plummet with a finale of hiccups. The hate could not leave Haylee. It felt like a slimy cobweb entwining her thoughts afterward. Only sleep provided refuge.

The inside of Misty's home was just as cleverly seasonal. Directly ahead, a grand staircase glistened like it had just been dusted with furniture polish. The burgundy runner on the stair defied any speck of dirt. The banister featured garlands of mums, asters, assorted greenery as well as small, shapely gourds. Pumpkins of all shapes and sizes, both orange and white, ornamented the foyer. Haylee didn't miss the standing candelabra at the rear of the front hall.

Josh cleared his throat and whispered, "Should we take off our shoes?"

Haylee thought he looked uncomfortable, like he didn't belong in such a posh place, as if he'd feared breaking something just by breathing.

Overhearing Josh's question, Misty explained, "Of course not," as she flung her jacket onto the cherry umbrella stand while dumping her backpack on the floor next to it.

The others followed suit, perhaps with a little more decorum than Misty's obvious comfort.

Without a greeting, Misty's father grunted and swiped at a a drooping garland out of his eyesight. Grunting inaudible words, he headed toward what Haylee knew was his den. He used the room not only for work, but also to escape Misty's mother's ongoing requests to communicate. Coming out from the kitchen, Misty's mother stepped confidently, but stopped short upon seeing the teenagers. She stared for a beat, then smiled a toothy grin.

"Well, this is a nice surprise! You kids have perfect timing. I just took brownies out of the oven." Not needing to alert, scents of melted milk chocolate exuded the foyer. "Thanks, Mrs. Bishop. I could go for some," Brandon said.

"Come to the kitchen, all of you," Mrs. Bishop said. "Misty, come help me pour the almond milk. Brownies aren't nearly as good without it."

"Mom, I wanted to take my friends to the basement," Misty whined.

"Oh, okay," her mother said. "Tell you what, I'll bring some down to you."

"Thanks, Mom," said Misty. "And, oh yeah, we have some news!" Misty said while she twirled a curl around her index finger.

As Misty bounded toward the door leading to the basement, the rest of them followed.

Haylee took a keen interest in the family photographs in gilded frames that graced the walls on the ground floor as well as the basement.

Once at the bottom of the basement stairs, Misty hollered upward, "Mom, when you bring the brownies, I'll share the news." She held up crossed fingers for her friends to see. She then raced up the steps. Soon, the four friends were relaxing in the finished rec room, complete with a wide-screen television and a fireplace. True to the front and backyard, Haylee saw the mantel of the fireplace in the basement was as ornately decorated as the one upstairs.

Misty plopped down on the sofa while Brandon settled in the recliner. Haylee plunked down in one of the burgundy wingback chairs, but Josh didn't sit. He meandered over to the billiards table and ran his finger along its green felt edge.

"Josh," Misty said, "You have to be the one to tell my mom when she comes down with the brownies."

He didn't reply right away. Finally, he mumbled, "Sure."

To keep busy while they waited, Misty dug matches out of a decorative porcelain container on the coffee table and walked around lighting each of the many candles.

As soon as they heard Mrs. Bishop's footsteps on the stairs, Josh hastened over from the pool table and sat stiffly on the wingback next to Haylee.

Misty's mother set the tray she'd brought on the coffee table. Along with the brownies were four glasses of milk and a short stack of autumn-themed napkins. She sat on the sofa next to Misty and said, "Help yourselves, everyone." She glanced around each teen and blurted, "Don't keep me in suspense. What's the news?"

Josh didn't say anything.

Misty glared at him and whispered his name under her breath.

"Oh," he mumbled. "Sorry. I ...I mean, we ... we all tried out for the play, and well, the good news is, we all made it."

"Fantastic!" Misty's mother beamed. "Young man—I'm sorry, I don't know your name, but what part did you get? And Haylee, dear, what about you?"

"I'm the Prince," Josh said quickly, "and Haylee's the Princess. Misty got a great role as the Wicked Witch, and Brandon is Rumpelstiltskin."

Haylee thought Mrs. Bishop looked like she was about to have a meltdown, a near temper tantrum, kind of like Michaela sometimes did. Either that or she was about to cry. Her chin crinkled and her lips trembled. She turned her head away.

"Mom," Misty blurted, "Please don't be mad. I love the idea of being the Wicked Witch. I get to torture Danielle through the whole production."

Mrs. Bishop stood and smiled, though Haylee could tell the expression was forced, as her smile looked smeared on her face. "Well," she said stiffly, "I'm sure Haylee will make a fine Princess. Congratulations, Josh and Brandon. Enjoy the brownies." Without another word, she hurried up the stairs.

"Whoa," Brandon murmured. "Misty, you weren't kidding when you said she'd be upset. Geez!"

"Don't worry, my dad will be worse," Josh muttered.

"No sense letting these go to waste," Brandon said. He took a big bite of a brownie and went on with his mouth full. "Misty, your mom may be pissed off, but she makes awesome brownies! Dude, you gotta try one."

Josh did take one, but unlike Brandon, he took a napkin first.

"Hey, what's that book?" Brandon asked, pointing to the antique-looking, leather-bound tome on the coffee table. "Looks cool."

"That's our family genealogy." Misty rolled her eyes. "Mom thinks genealogy is everything. She's forever researching our ancestors. I think she's trying to trace our history back to Adam and Eve. My Dad, on the other hand, says genealogy is for narcissists."

Brandon asked, "Can I look at it?"

"I wouldn't," Josh said. "What if you accidentally get chocolate on it, or worse, rip a page or something? Misty's mom is already upset over our reporting of roles for the play." Wiping his hands on the colorful napkin, Josh threw the used paper in the trashcan with the liner.

"Dude, chill out." Brandon said, as he wiped his hands on the napkin, tossing it into the same trashcan. He then leaned over the coffee table. Rather than picking up the book, he opened it right where it was. "Check this out. It's pretty cool."

Haylee slipped from the chair to the floor for a better look.

A Divorce in Salem

Inside the yellowed pages were rows upon rows of names. Beside each name was listed birth, marriage, and death dates, as well as places. As Brandon turned the pages, she noticed other facts—professions and accomplishments.

"Any serial killers in your family tree?" Brandon asked, stifling a burp from the milk he consumed in one gulp.

"Nothing that exciting," said Misty. "The juiciest story I know is about my great, great, great, great, great, great-grandmother. She was a midwife. People back then didn't understand how midwives, otherwise known as Doula's, learned their techniques. They accused her of witchcraft, so they hanged her during Salem's Mass Hysteria." Lowering her voice to a whisper, Misty whispered, "I think she's the one who haunts this house."

"Your house is haunted?" asked Josh. He yanked his head around the basement.

Misty's eyes flashed, and she nodded fiercely. "Sometimes our doors close on their own, even when there's no breeze. And at night, I hear moaning. Mom says it's just the ventilation system, but I think she's wrong."

"That's creepy," said Josh.

"I think it's cool," said Brandon. "Guess we can't stay here all-day eating brownies. Three more houses to hit."

"Haylee's next. She needs to let her dog out," Misty said.

They followed Misty up the stairs. At the top, she stopped them with a finger to her lips, whispering, "Mom's on her cell, probably telling Aunt Sharon what an awful daughter I am for not getting the lead. Perfect time to sneak out!"

Haylee knew Mrs. Bishop was upset, and somehow, it seemed all of Misty's Mother's upset was Haylee's fault. If she hadn't auditioned, she would not have gotten the lead. Instead, the part of Princess would have gone to Misty, for sure. *I poison everything I touch!*

13

A Voice Is a Powerful Tool

The four fellow travelers left Misty's house and strolled down Essex Street. After stopping at Haylee's, so that Barney could go out, the four paraded passed Cauldron Court to Josh's white-and-black trimmed Cape Cod. The house was much smaller than Misty's and needed a bit of love. A couple of the clapboards were weathered, and the white paint gracing the clapboard siding looked more like Earl Grey.

But the driveway at Josh's stopped everyone. He stood in front of them, scratching his right calf with his left knee bent, the way a stork defies gravity.

"Okay, let's get our plan straight," he said. "First, we'll chitchat with my mom, but we can't say anything about the auditions until my dad is around. Then Brandon will announce the news. Haylee and Misty, you act like Brandon just informed us that he won the lottery." Then, with much seriousness, he declared, "When my dad grabs the bottle of whiskey, we all run."

Tentatively, Brandon inquired, "Why do *I* have to deliver the news? Why don't you just do it, Josh?"

Brandon fears Josh's Dad, too.

Misty explained, "Josh's dad can't get mad at you the way he would if Josh said it."

Patting Josh's shoulder, Hailey nervously suggested, "I think we should just go in and get it over with."

The four started up the driveway. Unlike the girls' homes, Josh's didn't have a garage. The boards holding the roof slanted, questioning how sturdy the carport was.

With hand trembling, Josh turned the doorknob and led the group through a side door into a narrow kitchen.

The first thing Haylee noticed was a strong aroma of coffee that exuded coziness, yet the rest of the atmosphere wasn't anything like Misty's kitchen, or even her own. The space felt cramped, the appliances looked old, and though the floor wasn't dirty, scuff marks made it appear to be.

But Haylee liked the country-style curtains on the single small window overlooking the carport, and the way the windowsill was lined with tiny pots of purple violets and cooking herbs of all sorts.

Josh's mother was wiping the kitchen counter beside the sink. When Josh's mother heard the kids come in, she turned around and gave them a smile that ransomed her vivid green eyes.

"Hi, honey," she said, still grinning. Focusing on Josh's best friend, she asked, "Brandon, how are you? Oh, and Josh, are you going to introduce me to your other friends?"

Josh's face turned red, but he stammered, "This is M-M-Misty, and this, well, this is Haylee. You guys, this is my mom."

Haylee stifled a giggle as she could feel Josh's tension.

Beaming over each one, his mother gushed, "I'm so pleased to meet you, girls," she said. Smoothing her hands on her apron, she shook hands, first with Misty, then with Haylee. Her gaze lingered a bit as she held Haylee's hand. Rubbing his hand behind his neck, Josh asked, "Is Dad around?"

"He's in the basement with your brother," she said.

Josh led the way and motioned for the rest of them to follow.

Unlike at Misty's house, Josh's stairs creaked with every step and some steps were loose, making navigation of the boards tentative. And the basement didn't contain a finished rec room. Instead, it was cold and gray with the walls of typical, basement cinder blocks.

After navigating the creaking stairs, the friends entered the cellar. All eyes took in how each wall was covered in pegboards, obvious organizational tool for a workshop. Josh's father and brother were stooped over a metal table, and they were staring at a piece of machinery.

Brandon and Misty knew Josh's brother from years of freelance tag football and yard games of Border Patrol, Tag, and Mother May I. Haylee knew Josh's younger brother from the bus stop.

"Hey, Pop," Josh greeted. "These are my friends. You know Brandon, but these are also friends, Misty, and over here is Haylee."

Josh's father grunted. He didn't look up.

"Hey, guys," Mark said grinning.

Josh loved his brother Mark, and Haylee saw how much he cared for his younger brother when he asked Mark what he and his dad were building. "Is this your science project?" Josh wondered as he circled their table with a torn apart engine on the table's surface.

"Yeah!" Mark said in shallow breaths. "I'm making an engine."

"That's cool, dude," Brandon said, and he stepped closer to get a better look.

Haylee grinned as Josh gave Brandon the same glare Misty had given Josh when they were at her house. They'd rehearsed their plan, but Brandon seemed too distracted to remember. Brandon looked up and added, "What?"

Josh coughed, and his face reddened, this time from the neck up, like a rapid, rip-tide lapping at the shoreline.

Brandon nodded, and said casually, "Here, I'll help hold the engine so you can screw that thing in. Oh, by the way, did you folks hear the news, yet? I bet Josh didn't have time to tell you. We all made it into the school play. I get to be Rumpelstiltskin and Misty here gets to be herself, the Wicked Witch."

"Very funny," Misty said.

Mark giggled, and Haylee covered her mouth to hold back her laughter.

"What part did you get, Haylee?" Mark asked.

"Haylee is the Princess, and Josh gets to be her Prince! Isn't that awesome? We're all so psyched!" Brandon knew as soon as he added the 'so,' he'd gone too far to be believable in trying to sound spontaneous.

The girls chimed in according to their rehearsal, but after a few moments, there was nothing but silence. The tension hovered, making it hard to breathe. Even Mark put his head down, as if suddenly concerned over part of his engine.

Josh's father completely ignored them.

Speaking first, Misty made no attempt to hide her irritation. "Well, we're sorry to have bothered you. We still have to tell Haylee's mom and Brandon's parents, so we'll be on our way."

With that, Misty spun around, almost slamming headfirst into Josh's mom. Haylee was sure they should have heard her coming down—all those creepy steps—but everyone seemed as surprised to see Mrs. Mullin as Misty was.

"I think it's terrific news," Josh's mom said, without missing a beat. "I have such wonderful memories of the school plays I was in, and I know you will, too, Josh," she gushed.

Turning to all of them, Mrs. Mullin grinned, "Gosh, I'm so happy for all of you! And did I hear correctly, Haylee—you're the Princess, and Josh is the Prince? Those are the lead roles, right?" She nudged Josh, and immediately he bloomed bright red once again.

Brandon and Misty nodded. Josh lowered his chin.

Haylee froze.

"Imagine!" Josh's mom went on. "The lead parts! I'll have to call your grandparents, Josh. I'm sure they'll want to come see it."

Another moment of silence passed.

Irritated, Josh's mom snapped, "John, say something. Aren't you proud of these kids?"

"Sure, Emily, it's great news, just great." His voice boomed as he declared, "But right now, your *other* son and I are doing something important, learning a skill that he can use in *real* life. So, I'm sure you'll excuse me for not fawning all over Joshua and his the-a-ter."

Josh's father dropped the screwdriver he was holding, and it landed on the metal table with a stark, sharp clank.

Haylee cringed. Misty shook her head in disgust.

"You kids, these days!" Mr. Mullin said, trying to appear calmer, more in control. "You know, when I was in ninth grade, I was busy with a paper route, saving Coke bottles for rebates, mowing neighbors' lawns in summer and shoveling their walks in winter. I didn't have time to play Prince Charming in the *thee-ay-ter*."

Haylee gulped and squeezed her eyes shut. "*Poor Josh*." She longed to get out of there as fast as possible, but she remained in place, frozen.

Despite her heart pounding, Haylee spoke, "Mr. Mullin, I believe all the hard work you did as a boy is the reason both of your sons have the privilege to study subjects your generation couldn't. Very little thanks are given to the miner, the bricklayer, the road paver."

Haylee focused on Misty because she trusted her friend would encourage Haylee to share her thoughts. Haylee pressed forward by acting as though she was speaking only to Misty.

"I know I take the privileges I have for granted, assuming I have the right to study whatever interests me. In fact, even though I couldn't afford a college education if I had to pay for it myself, many people in prior generations fought for legislation and programs that make it possible for me to get student loans. Perhaps our generation has been remiss." She handed Josh's brother the socket wrench he was groping for. "We haven't thanked our parents and grandparents who worked jobs they disliked, so that we could have the opportunities and privileges we have today, including the right to explore theater arts."

Josh's father took a hanky from his pocket and blew his nose. Eyeing Haylee and looking back at Josh, he stated, "If this young lady is in the play with you, I guess it'll be okay. But don't expect me to believe it's not a waste of time." At first, Haylee didn't realize the atmosphere had altered, becoming lighter and cheerier. But then she saw Josh trying to hide a smile.

Slapping Brandon on the back, Josh said, "Come on, let's go! We still have to get to Haylee's and Brandon's. I won't be late for dinner, Mom, I promise. Umm, bye, Dad."

The four friends scampered up the stairs and burst through the kitchen door. As soon as they were outside, Josh spread his arms wide and swung around. "Oh, my gosh! Oh, my gosh!" he chanted. And then, shocking them all, he grabbed Haylee and kissed her. Right on the mouth.

Haylee stepped back from Josh's embrace, her eyes as big as saucers. Josh looked almost as stunned as she felt. Peripherally, she noticed both Brandon and Misty nudging one another.

Josh blinked and stuttered, "I ... I'm sorry. I shouldn't have done that. It's just that you—well— you got my dad to say it was okay. I couldn't believe it!" His eyes lowered and he whispered, "You're ... you're, like, magic."

Haylee stared at Josh, at his russet, sometimes fiery red hair, at his expressive brown eyes, at the mouth that had just brushed against hers, and she wanted many things, most of which she couldn't define. The one thing she *did* know was that she wanted to feel his lips on hers again. She couldn't believe Josh had done and said she was magic. He was wrong, of course. She wasn't magic. He was. His kiss blended a sense of knowing her, yet his kiss offered mystery, too.

Josh knew her.

For the first time, Haylee realized she hadn't been understood. But Josh understood her. She wanted to explore that and Josh further.

Straightening his back, Josh turned to Misty and Brandon.

"Thanks, guys, you were awesome. You were all awesome." His eyes landed on Haylee's.

No going back.

"I think we should go to Haylee's next," Misty said, giggling a little, "so we can let her family know." Haylee kept her thoughts to herself about how Michaela would react.

14

I Spy...an Actress

The four friends returned to Haylee's house on Essex Street. Ushering them into the foyer, she unzipped her jacket and hung it on one of the hooks. The others followed suit. Grandma was the first to notice their unexpected arrivals. She came out of the kitchen, drying her hands on a dish towel.

"Oh, Haylee, sweetheart, we were wondering when you'd be home. I'm so pleased you brought your friends."

"You know Misty, Grandma. And this is Josh and Brandon."

The boys said, "Hey," in unison.

From the kitchen, Haylee's mother hollered, "Is that you, Haylee? Why didn't you call to tell me where you were?"

She came around the corner, saw the four of them, and they made the round of introductions again. "Mom, my friends came with me because we have some news."

"Great," Mom said. "Why don't we all go in the living room?"

Michaela, already there, had her face buried in her phone, her thumbs whipping rapidly.

In her desire to get the announcement over with, Haylee waited just long enough for everybody to sit, then blurted, "We all made it into the play. Brandon is Rumpelstiltskin, Josh is the Prince, Misty is the Wicked Witch, and I … well, I'm the Princess."

Michaela, who had failed to acknowledge them at all, suddenly dropped her phone on the floor and started coughing. Not just once, but several times. Haylee realized she'd never seen her sister's face that shade of eggplant purple.

Grandma was grinning with all her teeth showing. Haylee thought she'd be excellent in a denture commercial.

Haylee's mom plopped down on the sofa. "Oh, Haylee! Oh, my goodness! I'm so … Gosh, I don't even know what to say. That's the lead role, isn't it? Oh, my goodness …"

Haylee wasn't sure what to make of the sheen in her mother's eyes. She couldn't tell if her mother was upset or pleased.

"I think it's fabulous!" Grandma gushed. "What fantastic news, for all of you. This is just wonderful! So, tell me, when do rehearsals start?"

"Tomorrow," Brandon said. He was sitting in the peacock-blue chair with his hands clasped behind his head. "Just once a week after school on Thursday's, until winter break."

Grabbing a cookie from the coffee table, he bit into it and then added, in between swallows, "After New Year's, we'll rehearse three to four times a week. And then the two weeks prior to the performance, we'll practice every single day."

Brandon shook his head. He couldn't really see himself doing anything on a daily basis, much less rehearsing for a play.

Standing, Michaela looked furious. Her brown eyes bored into Haylee's.

"Did it ever dawn on you, Haylee, that you might have gotten the part because they felt sorry for you? Or worse, because they wanted another excuse to mock you?" She licked her lips with pleasure over her cruelty.

"Michaela, go to your room," Mom barked. "Now!"

But Michaela didn't go. Instead, she railed, "You don't get it either, Mom. Kids make fun of her all the time. You don't know because you don't have to hear it. But I do! Every day. This is like *Carrie*, all over again!"

With that, she grabbed her phone and started to leave the room. "No," Josh cut in. "*You* don't know." Although Josh stayed seated, his voice was firm and commanded attention.

Haylee looked over to see him leaning forward in his chair, in a power position, clenching and unclenching his fists repeatedly. His eyes, sharp like rapiers, were focused directly on Michaela.

"Your sister has talent," said Joshua. Her audition was spot—on. Better than you could ever do. So, if you think she's weird and want to make fun of her, go right ahead. You can think I'm weird and make fun of me, too."

"Same with me," Brandon spouted.

"Me, too," Misty chimed in.

Desperate to melt into the floor, Haylee's body registered the heat under her skin. She knew her face was scarlet red and covered in beads of sweat. It was impossible for her to look directly at any of them, but most of all, Josh. All the gumption she had mustered earlier at his house had evaporated. She wanted to run, so she did—all the way up to her room.

She didn't stay there long, however, only long enough to hear Michaela's door slam shut. Carefully, so no one would notice the hinges creaking, Haylee peered out into the hallway. Although she couldn't see what was happening downstairs, with the door open, she could hear.

Misty's voice was the first Haylee heard. "Umm, thank you, Mrs. Higgins, I mean Ms. Tierney, but I think we should go."

The next thing Haylee heard was Grandma saying good-bye as the front door closed. Haylee's friends were gone.

Silence inflated the tension, now another character in the household. Haylee listened to Grandma, who said, "Lizzie, I know this is hard, but you need to remember that both of your girls are in pain. Be careful of your tongue. Your goal is not to rebuke, but rather to help them learn to appreciate each other, so they can feel closer."

"Which one should I go to first?" Mom asked.

"The one you have the most difficulty understanding," advised Grandma.

Haylee knew what that meant.

Quickly, she ran to her room, closed her door and made a beeline to sit at her desk. She waited, but the knock that resounded in the hallway wasn't at her door.

For the longest time, Haylee remained in her chair, unsure what to do. Her curiosity wouldn't allow her to stay where she was. She sneaked out of her room and crept down the hallway to listen outside Michaela's room.

"Haylee admires you, Michaela," Mom was saying. "She sees what I see—a young woman who knows how to carry herself and be accepted by her peers. But honey, sometimes in your desire to be accepted, you create the environment you wish to see, and you assume others are wrong if they don't think or see it as you do." Pausing, her mother explained, "You think Haylee is wrong because she doesn't copy you."

"Mom, it wouldn't be that hard for Haylee to care more about her appearance." Michaela scoffed. "She just needs to look in the mirror once a day."

I do. I just don't like what I see.

"You're missing the point, honey. In this case, Haylee *did* listen to you. She saw that her peers were excited about trying out for this play, and she took your advice. She decided that no matter how scary it was, she was going to join them. She would never have auditioned in the first place if she hadn't heard you talk about 'fitting in.'" Mom paused, then added, "Michaela, your sister got the lead. My gosh, honey, do you have any idea what a huge accomplishment that is, especially for Haylee?"

"What'll I do when kids say she's embarrassing?" Michaela asked. "Or when they tell me she's ruining the play, because she's so oblivious to what's going on around her? You know how she spaces out." Michaela fell backward on her bed.

"This is where your logic is skewed, Michaela. Your peers aren't the ones who picked Haylee for the role. It was the director. She made the choice, along with other teachers who weighed in on whether Haylee could pull it off. Think about it," Mom said as she put her hand on Michaela's forearm. "They would never purposely subject a student to ridicule." Lowering her voice to be more soothing, Mom added, "I know you believe other kids will make fun of her. If that happens, why can't you counter their comments by telling them to say whatever they have to say to Haylee directly?"

I don't need Michaela to defend me. She never has before, why should she start now?

There was a brief silence before Mom continued.

"Imagine if the opposite occurs, and Haylee ends up being fabulous in her role. What if kids come up to you and say, 'Haylee is amazing! She's the perfect person to play the Princess!' How will you feel then? Will you be okay with the compliments, or will you be *jealous* of your sister?"

Haylee could tell by the hiccups and sniffles that Michaela was crying.

"Mom," Michaela murmured, "am I a mean person?"

"No, darling, you're human," Mom said with a sigh. "We all get bitten by the green-eyed monster every now and then. Right now, I'm merely asking you to explore your motivation and your intent. If you know what those are, you can protect both yourself and your sister."

"I know Haylee has talent," Michaela sniffled. "She can draw, and she understands math and science better than I do. That's why I get so mad when she doesn't even try and yet still manages to pass." Michaela huffed in disgust. "I have to work so hard and study way more than she does. It really bugs me when I think of how much better she could do if she would just make a serious effort. But she never does. Ever."

"This is what I mean," said Mom. "You're seeing Haylee through your own lens and concentrating on what you think she doesn't know about herself. It doesn't serve you well, honey. One, you can't make her see what you see, and two, what you're focusing on is your idea that she is flawed. But that thought only makes *you* hurt more."

Elizabeth paused.

"Instead, why don't you try to see Haylee through Haylee's world. She knows what she needs to do to get a passing grade, and she does it, just enough. Why? Because it allows her more time for doing the things she really enjoys, like drawing or walking around town. She doesn't think of mediocre grades as shortchanging her efforts. She thinks of it as maximizing her free time." "Okay, Mom," Michaela said. She wasn't sniffling any longer. "I'll lay off. And if any kids say something negative, I'll tell them to say whatever it is directly to Haylee, and to leave me out of it. And I'll tell Haylee, I'm sorry for being so mean."

Haylee could tell her mom was hugging Michaela. "I know Grandma offered to take you shopping, but how 'bout I take you tomorrow, after I get home from work?"

"Sure, Mom, that would be great," Michaela said. "And thanks."

This was Haylee's cue to rush back to her room. She was careful to close the door without making a sound before sitting back into her desk chair.

A knock came a moment later.

A Divorce in Salem

"Come in," she said. Mom entered tentatively, smiling, but Haylee refused to look up from the drawing pad in front of her. She was drawing a dark cave and a girl with thick, curly hair wearing a headlamp.

"Spooky," Mom commented. "Are those bats hanging from the icicles?"

"Yeah," Haylee murmured. "Did you need something, Mom?"

Her mom had moved over to the bed, where she positioned herself near the headboard, shuffling a few pillows for comfort.

"I just wondered how you were doing after your sister's explosion." Her mom said. "You raced upstairs so fast, I wanted to make sure you're okay."

Haylee didn't look up from the sketch.

"Michaela thinks I'll make a fool of myself. She's worried she'll be embarrassed because of me." Haylee swung around to look at her mother. "Mom, tell me, honestly. Do you think I'm making a fool of myself? Do you think I made a mistake by auditioning?" Tears were pooling in Halee's eyes.

Shaking her head, Elizabeth emphatically said, "No, I don't. I already know you can do anything you put your mind to." Mom said. "What's important, sweetheart, is that you believe it, too. Do *you* think you made a mistake?"

"At first I didn't think I could do it, but then," Haylee curled her knees to her chest, "When I was up on stage, Mom, it was like I could *taste* the part. I knew exactly what mannerisms to use, how to make my voice sound. I observed myself from across the auditorium. And it was fun." Haylee swallowed. "People laughed, and I thought they were laughing *at* me. I didn't realize until I overheard people talking later, that they were laughing because they thought I performed like a comedian. That I was funny, hilarious, even."

"Awww, honey ..." Mom murmured.

"I still didn't think I'd get the part," Haylee said. "I thought maybe I'd be a tree, or at most, one of the elves or something. When I saw my name on the cast list, I couldn't believe it, Mom." Her voice cracked. "I know I can do it. So no, I don't think I made a mistake."

"I'm so proud of you," Mom said. She smiled and brushed away tears of her own. "I'm sorry Michaela reacted the way she did. I'm sorry for the things she said."

"It's hard changing people's opinions, isn't it, Mom?" Haylee asked. The revelation made her think about her parents and their fights.

"Yes, it is," Mom agreed. "We get comfortable assuming we know what others are going to do or say, and what their talents and abilities are." Giggling, she admitted, "But we don't like it when they pigeonhole *us*. Remember, honey, even when she says things that hurt, Michaela still loves you. She still sees herself as wanting to protect you, like a big sister should."

"I know," Haylee sighed looking down at her creation—the cave, the bats, the stalactites hanging from the ceiling, and the lone girl standing among them. "Don't worry, Mom, I can take care of myself."

Elizabeth gave Haylee's leg a pat, "When you're a mom, I want you to remember what you just said to me," Mom chuckled. "A mother *always* worries." Then she stood up. "You know what I'm looking forward to?"

"What?" asked Haylee, looking up at her mother.

"Helping you learn your lines. I know Grandma will want to help, too. Boy, she'll have a blast. I'll bet we can even get your sister to join in."

Haylee rolled her eyes at the latter.

"Give me a hug, kiddo, so I know you're okay," Elizabeth urged.

"I'm okay, Mom," Haylee said giving her mother a big hug. "I promise."

After her mother departed, Haylee mulled over her plan. "I'm okay, because I don't need Dad's house or this one. My home is what I discovered, the cave!" Haylee turned down her bed and eagerly awaited for precious sleep.

15

Marriage Closure

Even though Haylee was relieved auditions were over and she'd landed the lead, the reality of her situation also brought new, looming anxieties that plagued her at night. Lying in bed, arms splayed over her head, she reflected on how much her life had changed since they'd moved from Chicago. She never could have predicted what a life in Salem would look like.

Haylee recalled how scared she'd felt as they'd taken their long road trip to Salem. Awake and aware she missed the fast-paced lifestyle of Chicago with its avenues dotted with museums of art and science, major financial institutions, and, of course, Wrigley Park. Haylee acknowledged she'd picked up on some of her dad's snobbery and had put Salem down without ever having visited her mother's hometown. She had assumed Salem was limited to all things' witchcraft. Now, she was learning more in history class, about how, Salem represented the dangers of groupthink. It frightened Haylee to know that innocent people were hanged because of ridiculous bickering over land as well as people's suspicions that neighbors weren't as pious as they should be.

Haylee realized that her father had only scoffed at Salem, rather than embracing important lessons that prompted journalists in the future to question rumoring until they could assert such with factual proof.

That wasn't the case in Salem during the 1690's when the town council had believed in "Spectral Evidence," meaning that if one of Salem's farmers reported they'd seen a ghost of someone—even a figment of a living person—that such reporting would be accepted as proof that someone in Salem was guilty of aligning with the Devil.

Haylee shivered, pulling up another blanket at the base of her bed and pulled it over her quilt.

As Haylee lay there, sleepless, she was making connections between what was later known as Mass Hysteria and her parents' divorce. Connecting the dots made Haylee sit up in bed.

An owl screeched in the big oak tree outside her bedroom window. Rubbing her eyes, Haylee swore she could see the bird in the oak tree.

Turning on the lamp beside her bed, Haylee retrieved her journal from the bedstand's drawer. She grabbed a pen and scribbled, "I think I've accused Tiffany of causing my parents' divorce. Isn't that as unfair as Ann Putnam accusing Rebecca Nurse of causing her multiple stillbirths in 1692?" Haylee held the pen under her chin and thought further.

Having read that Rebecca Nurse had enjoyed a stellar reputation up until her accusation that she was a witch caused bewilderment in Haylee. In fact, Rebecca was known throughout Salem for helping neighbors near and far, no matter the weather and no matter the time of day. The pious woman offered prayers, food and clothing she made, ever sacrificing for those in need.

Okay, that certainly doesn't hold true for Tiffany. She never sacrificed anything or gave to others except her father.

A Divorce in Salem

Rebecca had been blessed with eight children. Perhaps Ann Putnam had envied Rebecca Nurse, since she herself had suffered multiple stillbirths. Back then, Puritans believed God would show favor in outward appearances or deliver punishment by manifesting death, crop diseases, any such loss or disaster. So a pilgrim had to worry daily if God were pleased or not.

So, when Ann Putnam had not one, but several, stillbirths, rumors were rampant that perhaps the Putnam household had sinned behind closed doors. The evidence of such rumoring? Why, the stillbirths, of course, they were the proof of God's harsh judgment on the Putnam couple.

Haylee knew well that envy could evoke the ugliest of reactions. After all, Haylee absorbed the weight of her father's affair for months. All the while Haylee's secret harbored not only her own pain, but her mother's denial that anything was amiss, too.

In fact, Haylee remembered how she had incurred her mother's wrath after the discovery of Tiffany's existence. How her mother would scream at her, whether she'd spilled a glass of milk, or her colored charcoals had melted in the backseat of her mother's SUV! Haylee knew the screaming meant much more than Haylee's mistakes. Instead, she surmised the outbursts declared meant her mother wasn't feeling free to leave. Haylee concluded she was an impediment to options for her mother. In essence, Haylee was a human cage, one that prevented her mother's happiness. All because of Haylee. Nothing to do with Tiffany

If Haylee were older, her mother could demand more from her. She could grow as distant as Haylee's father, maybe even take up an affair for herself. Haylee imagined her mother as a cougar, romancing a younger man, poolside as she sipped on a slushy alcoholic drink in fancy glassware.

Thinking back, her mother's displays of rage only served to push her father further into Tiffany's embrace. In contrast, Tiffany seemed safe, calm, and oh, so pretty.

Yet, Haylee tapped into a deeper conclusion. When she thought about her parents' marriage, Tiffany was not at the heart of their problems. She remembered her parents living very separate lives long before Tiffany became her father's dental hygienist. In fact, Haylee remembered that when she and Michaela were younger, her mother would gather them up and take them to visit their dad's dental practice, just to say, "Hello, we're your family!"

But, as time went on, and the girls would beg their mother for a pop-in visit, she would dismiss their requests. Even on weekends, their father spent a great deal of time at his practice. If he was at home, he was often holed up in his den, watching a game. So there really wasn't much interaction as a family for years, and certainly no conversation or sharing of ideas.

Instead, weekends meant their mother would drag Haylee to go watch her sister in an activity like field hockey, lacrosse, or soccer, or they all would go shopping for sneakers or electronics. There was no family time, unless you counted the time spent bickering or slamming doors.

So, Haylee realized Tiffany wasn't the real crucible that undid her parents' marriage. Instead, Tiffany was another form of Spectral Evidence, a made-up excuse for declaring that a marriage had flatlined, even though the love in question had died a long time before Tiffany had ever appeared on the scene.

Haylee rolled over and sighed.

Adults sure are complicated.

Still, she couldn't fall asleep. Now she was thinking about the constant texting between Michaela and their dad.

Haylee knew Michaela felt special when their father texted Michaela first with updates on what he was doing or offering his plans for custodial time. But, Haley also knew it hurt her sister when he informed Michaela he was using an app to learn Italian prior to a trip to Tuscany he'd booked—of course, with Tiffany. Haylee was often ignored in these texts, or she was just an afterthought, as in, "Oh, tell Haylee, her pop says, 'hello!"

If Haylee spoke up about this, Michaela would always defend him. "Haylee, he doesn't know if you're in rehearsal—he just doesn't want to interrupt!"

"I think it's a sure bet I'm not rehearsing at ten o'clock at night," Haylee would quip. Most of the time, Haylee observed their mom would bite her lip and just give into whatever request their dad made, unless he was using Michaela as a messenger without having cleared a request with their mom. Honestly, Haylee felt conflicted over hearing about their dad's communications indirectly. While she realized she didn't like talking on the phone or texting, she still resented the fact that all his messages went through Michaela first. And using her sister as his mouthpiece certainly made their mother angry and annoyed Haylee.

How could Michaela act surprised when he let Michaela act as the Town Crier of news? At other times, Haylee enjoyed affording her mother to be the vicarious funnel for upsets Haylee felt, even though what upset their mom rarely upset Haylee. In fact, Haylee had been glad to learn their father was coming to Salem for Christmas. Haylee expected it. The dreaded moment of announcing the plan drummed frequently in the back of her mind, but as the months went by and her mother failed to mention any details of his flight or visit, Haylee assumed their father had chosen another date for custodial time. Haylee had forgotten how much both parents delighted in the biggest Christian holiday of the year. But divorce and new interests change more than the couple ship. They change rituals Haylee was used to counting on.

The last time Haylee had seen her dad was the day they'd left Chicago for Salem. Haylee couldn't forget the way, her father had sprinted back to the house, barely saying good-bye. That one action seemed to declare he wouldn't miss them, and even more stinging, how much he was looking forward to his new life. A life without her and her sister.

Haylee felt like she could never forgive him. While Haylee stayed alert for phone calls between her parents, there hadn't been any recently, just as Mom's therapist had suggested.

So, Haylee had continued with her snooping, and through eavesdropping and such, she had learned her dad would becoming this very day. First, he would meet her mom at Sophia's Bistro at one o'clock.

Haylee arrived at the restaurant at precisely 12:40pm, just in case either of them showed up early. She had taken great pains to travel incognito, putting her bushy hair into a low ponytail and wearing an old brown hoodie she'd borrowed from Misty. The last piece of her disguise: sunglasses purchased at the drugstore, three doors down from Sophia's. Haylee was sure she wouldn't be noticed.

She didn't have to wait long. Through the large window draped with ferns, Haylee spied her mother's black SUV edging into a space at the curb right out front. A minute later, her mother slipped into Sophia's, smoothing her sleek, black hair from the nape of her neck.

Haylee yanked the bulky poinsettia from where it stood by the salt and pepper shakers to the center of the table and slinked down low into the cushioned booth. Using the technique found in her mother's New Age book, Haylee visualized herself with pointy ears, a bushy tail, and the keen eyes of a wolf slyly peeking around the poinsettia toward her prey. Suddenly, her father appeared, just inside the door by the coat rack. Haylee's stomach soured, her palms grew sweaty, and her breathing shallowed.

Dad didn't look the same!

Something about his face distorted what she remembered of his facial features. His cheeks weren't the way she remembered. They seemed flatter, sunken-looking, and even from a distance, she could see his cheekbones protruding. She didn't remember his chin jutting so distinctly, either.

Her father took his coat off and shook some snow off his collar. It looked like he'd bought clothes way too big for him, except Haylee remembered the shirt and slacks he wore, so they couldn't have been new. Now, the shirt that used to fit snugly, hung loose off his shoulders and fell around his waist. Haylee didn't remember her dad's stomach being so flat, or ever seeing his belt cinched so tightly. Even the pants draped loose around his legs.

Tiffany must not be a very good cook

"Hi, Liz," he said to Haylee's mom. "I hope you weren't waiting long."

"No, not too long," Mom answered. "Shall we find a booth?"

Sophie's wasn't crowded. In fact, several tables were available. Her parents walked up the narrow aisle, heading straight toward Haylee. She turned her head to look out the window and hoped they wouldn't look past the poinsettia. Haylee couldn't believe it—her mother slid into the booth directly in front of her, with her back to Haylee. Dad sat opposite, and neither of them glanced her way.

"Thanks for suggesting this, Liz," Dad said, running his fingers through his hair. "I agree that it's a good idea for the two of us to talk first, before I see the girls." Dad looked down at the menu, "I'm embarrassed to admit it, but I'm nervous about seeing the girls."

"Well, the therapist recommended that we talk, to make certain we don't fight in front of the girls. That's the real reason I insisted."

Haylee caught her mother rubbing her right temple, something she did prior to the onset of a migraine.

Dad smiled, "So you started therapy to help you bash me to the girls?"

Haylee thought Dad was trying to make a joke, but Mom didn't take it that way.

"No, Dan," Mom snapped. "The sessions aren't about you." She paused and pursed her lips.

Mom looked Dad directly in the eyes, a new sign of confidence for her.

"Actually, the sessions are helping me to come to terms with how you and I lost control over our marriage. "In fact, I've been looking back, and I realize how much we were just co-existing. We didn't share any time together. We rarely set any mutual goals or plans, even seasonal ones like working in the garden or going on vacations. Through therapy, I'm learning more about what co-parenting looks like after divorce."

Mom shifted back into the booth, so that she sat in front of the plate before her. She whispered, "Dan, each hour I am in therapy gives me greater, grander ideas of what a future without us as a couple can look like for the girls!" Leaning in and grasping Dan's arm in a tender way, she added, "I am using the therapist to learn effective co-parenting tools. The tools offer us a frame to organize our time and energy mindfully so we keep the focus on parenting our girls.

As we practice, we'll get better at not fighting." Mom picked out a paper napkin from the dispenser and dabbed her lips. Gulping all her water, Mom motioned to the waitress, and signaled that she needed more water in her glass. The waitress came over with pitcher in hand and topped off both glasses.

"Dan, the framework my therapist offers would ensure us that our wonderful, beautiful girls could grow and face teendom, because they will have good boundaries that you and I set firmly. If we agree to do discussions first, away from the girls, we can be assured we are on the same page. This way, our girls could be shielded from our impasses. Therapy is teaching me more about what our future could look like." Mom gulped more water from her glass. "So, even though we are divorced, we're still co-parents, and we owe it to the girls to figure this stuff out. These sessions are really helping me learn how to rebuild our identity from married, trapped people to interdependent, individuals who can remind our girls, we are still their parents."

Wiping a crumb from the table, she confided, "Dan, I not only participate in co-parenting counseling, but," and she gestured playfully in a drum roll on the edge of the table, "I am also in individual therapy to identify who am I now that I am no longer a dentist's wife." Tears streamed down her cheeks apparently, because Dad handed her another napkin from the dispensary for Mom to dry her tears. "Seriously, it scares me how easily I deluded myself that we were okay, that we were just in a rut as a married couple." She paused to see if Dad was still listening.

It seemed to Haylee that her dad didn't know how to respond to her mother's disclosure. To buy time, he sipped some water from his glass. After a few moments of silence, her father said, "I'm sorry. I need to learn how to be less defensive, so we can work these things out together." Smiling at Mom, he offered the rest of his water for Mom, since she seemed to be so parched.

"To be honest, Dan, I continue to have other things to work on, too." Mom said softly. She shifted in her seat, "I have vented about your affair within our daughters' hearing, and Dan, I am utterly ashamed. But, I am finding in therapy, much of the vitriol was the inner child in me mimicking what I heard my mom do when my dad left." Mom put her head in her hands for a minute before she regained composure.

Hayley nodded. She knew a lot of Mom's history and could empathize why her mom would be so easily triggered to say and react to Dad's affair the way her mother had when her grandfather said he wanted to divorce. Hayley feigned looking at the lithograph on the wall to distract her father from noticing her nod.

"My therapist claims guilt is only useful when it fosters authentic change in behavior. Otherwise, guilt is useless and a waste of valuable energy."

"That makes sense," Dad said, nodding slowly. He wasn't looking at Mom when he added, "I hate that my daughters live five states away. I just ... hate it. To be honest, it takes me back to when my parents moved us from Scranton, Pennsylvania to Chicago, Illinois. I see now, although we agreed that your move to Salem would save boatloads of money that would have gone to attorneys and court fees, the move was a gut punch."

Haylee hoped her mom would stand up for Michaela and her, if only she would ask, "Don't you think that on the day your daughters lost the only home they'd ever known, their school, and all their friends, activities, and everything they'd ever love, you could have at least stayed to see them leave?"

Mom didn't have a chance to respond because right then, the waitress came to take their orders. Mom ordered tea, and Dad, coffee.

The waitress added, "Our specials today include ham and broccoli quiche as well as cherry or blueberry scones," she said.

Mom suggested she'd like a blueberry scone and more peppermint tea.

Dad grunted, "The quiche sounds fine with more coffee, please, and cream and sugar."

Haylee sensed the waitress would ask if Haylee wanted anything. Quickly thinking, she shook her head, looked down and lifted her water glass for additional water. Mom wouldn't have noticed anything, because her back was to Haylee, but Dad might have. Luckily, he seemed focused on Mom.

Not wasting any more time, Mom offered, "I wrote down what the therapist suggested," as she picked through her purse for the sheet of instructions from the therapist. Mom donned her reading glasses and held up a dog-eared sheet of paper.

Dad chuckled, "I feel like I'm on a quiz show. I'll take Affairs for $250, or better yet, how 'bout child support for $1800?"

Mom sighed, "Dan ..."

"I'm kidding, Liz," Dad anticipated. He sounded resigned to Mom's procedure, "I regret the jibe. I'm just nervous, I guess." The waitress returned with their orders and hot drinks. As the waitress moved toward Haylee's booth, Haylee mimed with her hands, 'See no evil, Hear no evil, and Speak no evil.' The waitress shrugged and sauntered toward the bakery to put in additional orders. For a moment, neither parent spoke. They remained fixated on their tea and coffee.

Fiddling with his cup, Dad said, "I know this isn't exactly in line with the exercise we're supposed to be doing, but there's something I want to say to you, Liz," Dad said. Splaying his fingers on the edge of the table, he cleared his throat and admitted, "When we first got married, Liz, you tried so hard to foster a relationship with my parents, and I didn't get it. In fact, I viewed your efforts as meddling into business that was not your affair or anything that had to do with us. I realize now that you were just trying to be a good spouse. You wanted to combine our families into one big family. I regret I couldn't see what you were trying to do."

As usual, Dad put creamer and sugar in his coffee, while Mom doctored her tea with a minimal dose of honey. Hearing him apologize now made Haylee's blood boil. Anger oozed from her pores. She wanted to jump up from her seat and yell, "How dare you! You made us miserable! And for what? Your need for Control?" But of course she couldn't yell at him without giving herself away.

"Thank you for that, Dan," Mom murmured. "That means a lot."

Breaking the silence, Mom read, "Identify three things the other partner did that you appreciated during the marriage."

"Whoa," Dad murmured, "something positive?"

Haylee couldn't imagine either one of her parents saying something positive about the other. Her pointy wolf ears perked.

With a sigh, Elizabeth offered, "I'll start," A smile belied a memory surfacing across her thoughts, almost like a film reel showing previous recap of an episode.

"Do remember when Michaela was a baby, and it was my birthday, but I got the flu?" She flushed red, as she placed her manicured acrylic nails on her breast, "Dan, you took the entire day off from dental school, walked me back to bed, and then tended to Michaela, so I could sleep, a deep sleep." Expressing surprise by how smoothly he sacrificed all he had planned, Elizabeth continued, "Seriously, I slept all day. All day. When I woke up there were flowers by the bed. You apparently packed up Michaela, put her in the car seat, and took her to the florist." Wiping a tear from her cheek, Mom declared, "Dan, it was the nicest gesture."

Of course, Mom's good memory moment had to have Michaela in it.

Setting down his coffee cup, Dan nodded. "You were so sick. I never knew someone so petite could exude that much mucous," Dad chuckled. "I felt so inept. I didn't know what to do for you."

The waiter brought Mom's scones and Dad's quiche. This time he didn't bother looking at Haylee, and Haylee exhaled with relief.

Now, feeling competitive, Dan challenged, "Okay. I have one," Dad said.

Shifting in the booth, he explained, "When I first met you, you used a shampoo that smelled like cucumbers. I loved the way your hair smelled. Even now, all these years later, any time I'm in a grocery store and I see cucumbers, I have an urge to inhale their scent, and I think of your hair." He paused, lowered his voice and added, "I think of you." His eyes landed on her steel blue ones that seemed to soften under Dan's gaze. Was that more of a royal blue, now? Hayley surmised her dad couldn't be sure.

Nodding as she stirred the honey addition to her tea, Elizabeth mused, "I remember that shampoo," she said wistfully. "It came in a dark green bottle."

Haylee couldn't see her mother's face, but she could tell Mom was smiling.

Tossing his spoon and napkin down, Dan sighed. Initially, he rubbed his eyes, as though he were shutting off his own misperception from a discarded history. Now, Dan rubbed his entire face so that he could see unobstructed. Patting her arm,

Dan suggested, "I realize now, you were just trying to be a good spouse. A warm, loving spouse who wanted to combine our respective families and create one wonderful larger family. I'm sorry I was so self-focused back then." Dad cleared his throat, then blew his nose on his napkin.

Haylee remembered the things her mother used to do for her grandparents. Mom always invited them over, or suggested they go out to dinner. Countless times, when Grandpa was at their house, Mom made them all watch *Patton* because it was Grandpa's favorite movie. Mom even used to get tickets to the symphony, and she'd coordinate a babysitter so the four of them; Mom, Dad, Grandma and Grandpa, could go together for an evening of enjoyment. But Haylee knew her Dad resented how close her mom could get to his parents, especially Haylee's Grandmother when all Haylee's father wanted was distance that only alone time could afford.

Often, Haylee knew bitter, low-belt vitriol would color the rest of the day whenever Dan's parents left to go back to their home. No matter how cheerful the goodbyes between Haylee's mom and dad's Mom, or how sincere the 'Talk-to-you-later, son,' Haylee knew that hours of arguing would escalate after Dad's parents left.

Soon after the third or fourth occurrence of predicted ugliness, Haylee was diagnosed with ulcerative colitis. Funny, her parents stayed in what looked like a fine fettle of health, but Haylee now never knew when stomach cramping would curb any semblance of spontaneity that she used to be able to take for granted. Now, Haylee's backpack was a storage of various nausea patches, calming oils, and just in case, another set of underpants, skirt or, more likely, pair of pants in case she soiled during school.

Dad consistently would yell, *"I wish you'd just stop meddling, Liz. They're my parents. Not yours! Just stop it!"*

To offer another example, Elizabeth folded her arms across the table and considered. Suddenly, the lines around her eyes increased as her grin spread across her face!

"I so appreciated your culinary skills while you were in dental school, Dan, and I knew you were studying hard, while I was working. You know," she chuckled, "to this day, I can't replicate your chicken marsala."

"Ha!" Dad laughed. "I will never disclose my secret ingredient."

"I'm serious," Mom said stealing a bite of Dan's quiche. "All day long, I used to daydream about what you'd serve for dinner when I got home."

Dad shuffled a scone across his plate. He'd been doing that ever since the food had been served. Apparently, Mom just noticed. Mom giggled, and Haylee thought she sounded like a child getting away with a prank.

"Okay," Mom said, all serious again. She held up her dog-eared paper. "I think we should move on to the next exercise. We're supposed to declare to the other what we wish to say goodbye to."

"Oh, geez!" Dad muttered. He set down his fork and took another sip of coffee.

"Now don't fret," Mom soothed. "My therapist urges that we not to use the word 'you' in our sentences, and she cautions we're supposed to say goodbye to reactions we ourselves made that didn't help either of us, or the marriage."

Like the time you threw a plate at the dining room wall, Mom?

"How can we possibly avoid the word 'you' if we're saying goodbye?" asked Dad. "Sounds like a bunch of psychobabble." Dan thought this exercise was one he felt determined to pre-judge a dislike.

"She says if we say things like, 'When I heard' or 'When I saw' or 'When I experienced' and then describe our own behavior or identify the action to avoid the word 'you,' we'll avoid defensiveness." Elizabeth sat up like a teacher's pet.

"This sounds complicated," Dad said shaking his head. He moved another piece of scone over to Elizabeth's plate.

Mom took a sip of her tea and paused for a moment. She grabbed a tissue from her purse and dabbed her eyes.

Holding down the brim of her cap, Haylee prayed, "Don't fold, Mom! He's just bluffing you with his oily charm!"

Instead, Mom sniffed, put her tissue back in her purse and declared, "Well, I guess it's my turn!" "Dan, why aren't you eating?" Mom asked. "I can tell you've lost a lot of weight. Are you ill or something?" She placed her hand on his wrist.

Dad looked up and sighed. "Truth is, anytime I try to eat these days, I can't seem to make myself swallow. It feels like the food gets stuck in my throat. And I pace a lot mostly at night. I don't sleep well anymore without you and the girls."

Ever once wonder how your daughters sleep? Guess not. It's always about you, Dad.

Nodding, Elizabeth admitted, "I don't sleep well, either. Divorce really messes with you, doesn't it? No matter which side you're on."

Dad laughed. "You can say that again."

Mom leaned forward and set her notes down. "Dan, don't you want to end this endless rancor between us, and focus on healing? Not for my sake, or yours, but for our girls?" she asked.

"Okay, but remember, I've had less practice than you. Oops, I used the word 'you.'" He gestured with his index finger and made a checkmark in the air.

Mom ignored his teasing. Splaying her fingers on the table, she inhaled and replied, "I surrendered too easily to wishes, tastes, and needs that weren't mine. I did it to prevent what I perceived as your sulking. But by doing so, I neglected my own wishes and needs, and that made me bitter and irritable. Even I couldn't stand my irritability sometimes."

Dan gasped, "Wow! That's true, Liz! I'm sorry. This is so hard. I did it again and referred to 'you.'" Gathering courage, Dan cleared his throat, "You're right. I did sulk whenever I didn't get my way. I viewed each situation as if one of us had to win and the other needed to lose, a zero-sum game. My sulking only drove a deeper wedge between us. I still struggle with the idea of letting go of control." Pausing for a moment, he added, "I hope I can break that habit going forward. If I do it as we co-parent, I want you to call it out for when I err."

"Wow!" Mom exclaimed. "Dan gives birth to change!" they both laughed.

Livid, Haylee rolled her eyes.

As if you people practice what you preach! You don't even see your own daughter in the next booth, but somehow, you're convinced you've had an epiphany!

"I've realized that I was wrong in thinking an affair could help me cope. My cheating, my betrayal, so many lies ... I know it hurt everyone, including me." He sighed. Using his discomfort, Dan confessed, "I believed a younger woman would somehow make *me* feel younger, more alive. To be honest, I felt depleted by our routine of co-existence and how well you handled everything. It never dawned on me to question whether a younger woman's motives had more to do with my income than whether she loved me for who I was ... a middle-aged dentist who struggles for attention."

Haylee sat up straighter. So did her mother.

Mom asked hesitantly, "Are you saying you're no longer with Tiffany?"

Wolf ears pricked upward and funneled like expensive speakers!

Dan nodded.

Haylee's head suddenly swam. All the drama and heartache they'd been through, and now Tiffany was gone? Did this mean Dad wanted to get back with Mom?

Staring into Mom's eyes, Dad promised, "Next time, the only way I'll feed my ego will be through building something with my partner at the practice. I won't look for anyone to buoy my self-esteem."

"Well, miracle of miracles!" Mom laughed. Sipping her tea, she said, "Seriously, Dan, your affair cut deep, but I realize that I wasn't being a good wife either. I was always angry. Frankly, I'm surprised you tolerated the marriage as long as you did." After a deafening pause, Mom declared, "I think this time together has been really positive. We just need to continue to do this exercise each time there's an issue with the girls." Continuing, Mom said, "Dan, even today, so many years later, I can still remember how bitter my parents were when they got divorced." She shook her head and wrapped a shank of her silky tresses to her right shoulder. "I don't want that same toxicity for Michaela and Haylee. I want them to be able to invite both of us to the big events in their lives, whether it's a graduation, a wedding, or the birth of a child. I don't want them worrying about tension between us, or that one of us will make a scene."

Dan spooned swirls into his coffee cup. When he looked up, he nodded, "I want the same thing, Liz. We made beautiful children together. I want us all to be able to share in our girls' lives."

Mom nodded looking away toward the coffee urn, cups, napkins, swirlers, creamers, and sugars of all types. In fact, it took a moment for her to speak. Haylee knew her mother's silence and its import. At least though, this time, Mom didn't hunt for a tissue in her purse. Nodding, emphatically, she affirmed, "Yes, we did. Absolutely!"

"More truth?" asked Haylee's father, lowering his eyes. "I know it probably doesn't mean much right now, but there's something to the saying, 'What goes around comes around.'" Hunching over his cup and plate, he offered quietly, "I understand now how you felt about my affair. I know I have no right, but I envy your Dr. Raintree. He's dating a lovely woman."

What's he talking about? Haylee gasped and put her hand to her mouth. *Mom's dating Barney's vet? How did I miss that one?*

Putting her elbows on the table, Haylee searched for clues in her memory. Suddenly, she understood her mother's "visits" to the library were excuses to see Dr. Raintree.

Haylee felt guilty all over again, since she was the one who introduced Mom to Dr. Raintree. After all, she noticed that Barney had a rough patch on his belly, so she suggested her mother take him to Dr. Raintree. Dr. Raintree suggested a biopsy and when the biopsy showed no cancer, he suggested a neck cushion for a few days to prevent Barney from licking off the steroid ointment.

It's as if I handed Barney on a silver platter for Mom to use as her excuse to see Dr. Raintree. And boy were there ever frequent trips to 'the library' AKA "Dr. Raintree."

Whispering so faintly Haylee could barely hear him, Dan said, "I'm so sorry Liz. I am ever sorry for hurting you."

"Thank you, Dan," Mom said. "That means a lot."

Waltzing to the table, the waitress interrupted with the bill.

"I've got it," Dan said, scrambling for his wallet.

"But you didn't eat anything," Mom said tenderly.

"Yeah, but I ordered it all, just the same," Dan admitted.

Haylee watched her parents scoot out of the booth and stand. From where she sat, huddled behind the poinsettia, she watched her father go to the cashier and pay.

Joining her mother at the coat rack, Haylee's father held her mom's coat for her to make donning her arms through the sleeves easier. Before they walked out, they embraced.

Confused, shocked, and irritated didn't cover all Haylee felt. For the first time, Haylee registered the feeling of loneliness. The image didn't fit like a tool that's supposed to lodge in a designated mold, but for some reason, now shows incongruence. Her parents weren't affectionate when they lived in Chicago, so why now was there tenderness? The water she had slugged down when she watched behind the poinsettia, now turned sour, leaving a metallic taste in her mouth.

A Divorce in Salem

One point Haylee understood, she never should have planned on coming to Sofia's Bistro. Haylee regretted spying on her parents, especially now that she knew her father wasn't using custodial time to see either her sister or her. She should have gone to school, or better yet, to the cave. If she had prioritized her favorite, private place, she would have been spared hearing and seeing her parents perform a kumbaya moment.

In the cave, wonder and imagination weren't false or forced. Haylee determined adulthood was messy and meant to be dreaded. Embracing the magnificence of the cave proved to her that time could offer precious revelation of True North, no matter her mood when she first stepped inside. The cave was a womb of protection, certainty, and feeling that all inside whether on the ground as shiny stones or on the ceiling of ice and salt headed into True North. Nothing fake. And best of all, no judgment.

Although Haylee had no concrete plan identified, she resolved that if her parents insisted on ruining the futures for Michaela and her, she, Haylee Carmichael Higgins, would manifest a retaliation, and that her vague image of tit-for-tat, quid pro quo, would make her parents feel as upset as she was. Dishing out the perfect plan, whatever that would look like, needed to force her parents to feel *exactly* the misery she felt.

Otherwise, if she afforded her parents to assume control as they had been, Haylee was certain, her fate would mean perpetual infliction of invisibility. Her parents' modus operandi would inflict impact of their insistent rash choices where the consequences landed onto Haylee as well as her sister upheaval, confusion, and chaos. A revolving door of romantic partners who could care less about her sister and her. No more.

The bells on Sofia's Bistro doors jingled, signaling her parents were leaving. The sound of door chimes interrupted her thoughts. Similar interruptions were typical for Haylee as they occurred all the time in school when the class bell rang, but adding injury to what felt like a mortal wound was another image she could not easily discard. Her father held open the door for her mother! Haylee could not recall any sliver of memory of her father practicing such chivalry when they lived in Chicago under the same roof. In fact, her parents walked much the same way Haylee saw ducks and geese waddle. Never did fowl walk side-by-side. Single file was comfortable and expected when her parents were together.

"Hey, it got warmer," Mom declared removing her neck scarf. "Maybe, it's a good luck sign?" Mom smiled.

Not for long, Mom, not for long!

16

Duck, Duck, Goose!

"Squawk! Squawk!"

These were unusual sounds, even for Grandma.

Calling out from the couch in the living room to the kitchen, Haylee asked, "Grandma! What gives?" Dropping her sketchpad on the coffee table, Haylee raced into the kitchen. Knowing her grandmother had prior relapses from sobriety, she wondered if the squawking was typical drunken speech for Grandma. Resenting the interruption from her art, Haylee took one last glimpse of the living room display of St. Patrick's Day decorations of green and gold garlands appointing the fireplace mantle, pots of chocolate 'coins' encased in gold wrapping on end tables, and the much-revered replica of St. Patrick's Cathedral in Dublin, Ireland.

Leaning over the double basin sinks in the kitchen, Grandma was not rinsing dirty dishes for the dishwasher as was her routine. Instead, there was a duck splashing a civil disobedient protest in which Haylee thought Grandma might lose the contest.

Using a paper towel and a dab of liquid dish detergent, Grandma, in between jerks of feathery might, tenderly wiped the frightened duck's wing.

Laughing at her own plight, Grandma urged, "Come see, Haylee! I found him at Lynn Woods Reservation on my walk this morning. I'm trying to get this—I think it may be motor oil—off his feathers. Poor, dear fellow." Cooing to calm him, Grandma encouraged, "What a good duck you are, Mr. Mallard. You are cooperating so well. And look how handsome you are."

Mr. Mallard *was* stunning, with his liquid emerald, melted milk chocolate, and stark white ribbon feathers. Under the faucet, his coloring gleamed in the morning sun descending from the kitchen window that afforded the view of the lush green backyard. The amount of greenery arose early for Salem, but warmer temperatures brought forth from the ground moss, grass as well as hyacinth, daffodils and tulips.

"See here, Haylee," Grandma showed, as she gently maneuvered the duck. "He's got a fishhook stuck in his wing. Poor thing. I've been trying, but I think I'm just hurting him more. We need to get him to Dr. Raintree."

Ambivalent, given the knowledge her mother had been secretly making 'library trysts' to see him, Haylee rolled her eyes at the idea Dr. Raintree would serve as the Knight in Shining Armor to her mother, let alone an injured duck. But Haylee could see the bird continued to react with much distress. Haylee worried Mr. Mallard's wing injury would serve as but another opportunity for her mother to date Dr. Raintree.

Why do my parents co-mingle with people in proximity? Have they not heard of dating apps where you can date someone you neither work with nor who cares for your pet? Isn't this a boundary lesson 101? The thought of her mother having a boyfriend was sparking a flare-up of her ulcerative colitis.

Still, Haylee couldn't tolerate witnessing any animal in trouble. Resigned to compassion, Haylee suggested, "we'd better take him right away."

"Squawk! Squawk!" protested Mr. Mallard, and his dark orbs for eyes pointedly searched into Haylee's hazel eyes. Creeped out, Haylee knew the bird was communicating pointedly to Haylee rather than her grandma.

Relieved Mr. Mallard's plea was being intercepted by Grandma, Haylee heard her grandma repeat, "Honey? Did you hear me? Look in my purse on the hallway stand. Can you find Dr. Raintree's number, sweetie? If you can locate the sheet of paper, you might as well add his number in my contacts after you make the call."

Mom kept a list of important numbers on the refrigerator, so Haylee easily found the number without having to rummage through the deep abyss of Grandma's purse. Repulsed and frightened by any depth where she could not see the bottom, Hayley rummaged in her grandmother's purse with as much zeal as when she was asked to gather kitchen utensils from the murky water of the kitchen sink after a big, family dinner. The opaque liquid reminded her of her fears as a toddler of some sort of monster lurking in her bedroom closet or underneath her bed. Even after her mother or her father tried to prove nothing existed in the darkest of places, Haylee continued to put blankets and comforter or quilt over her head. Why she assumed a monster couldn't get to her through the blankets wasn't the point. Haylee had to have some behavior like rubbing a rabbit's foot to feel relaxed enough to fall asleep.

Despite wanting to run to her room to avoid any more disgusting tasks, Haylee found Dr. Raintree's phone number. She felt compelled to add the phone number to Grandma's phone contacts after Grandma handed over her cell phone to Hayley while she juggled Mr. Mallard who was wrapped now in a terrycloth towel. He looked surprisingly comfortable under the crook of her elbow.

Sighing after a pause, Haylee surrendered further resistance. Frowning at Haylee, Grandma expressed fear she might let go of the bird if he'd jump or wriggle out of the dampened towel. She added concern that if a fall ensued, he might damage his wing even more. When the receptionist responded on the fifth ring, Haylee held the phone for Grandma's ear.

"Yes, hello," she said. "My name is Marjorie Tierney. I found an injured duck on Lynn Woods Reservation, but I think the mallard suffers from a broken or, I don't know, torn, maybe, wing?"

Explaining about the fishhook, Grandma also described how the duck got himself covered in motor oil, and how the slippery goo rendered the hook removal especially challenging.

Pause with no audible sound from the phone.

Grandma blurted, "I have him here in the kitchen sink with two basins. I've got most of the oil washed and rinsed. Look, I realize it's a Saturday, but the poor duck still needs Dr. Raintree's attention." She smiled a broad grin, "Yes, yes. I can do that. Thank you. I'll see you in half an hour."

Grandma sent Haylee to get another towel to envelop Mr. Mallard. Knowing Mom would have a fit if she used one of their bath towels, Haylee grabbed one of Barney's towels from the mudroom.

"Rrrrruff!" cautioned Barney. He set a boundary as best he could that the towels were his and not for avian use.

While she was helping Grandma ready the duck for a car ride, Haylee heard Michaela shuffle down the stairs, still in her pajamas. Scratching her tousled hair, Michaela asked, "What's going on? Why are you guys hovering over the sink?"

Grandma said, "Haylee's helping me with the—"

"*Squawk! Squawk!*" Mr. Mallard interrupted. He ruffled his feathers and water splattered everywhere.

Both Grandma and Haylee squealed in laughter.

With her jaw gaping, Michaela exclaimed, "Oh, my gosh! I know who that is! That's the duck or the goose, whatever he is, you mentioned a while ago during dinner one night! Do you remember?" Michaela declared the identification, as though Haylee and her grandmother might not know who he was.

Habits are tenacious.

Immediately, Michaela blamed Haylee by indicating, "Haylee what have you done? All birds are gross! They're filthy and they poop non-stop!" Dumbfounded, Michaela assumed the world' problems rested on Haylee's shoulders like a hunchback jutting out from Atlas' shoulders.

Haylee stammered, "I haven't done …" but Grandma blurted before Haylee could finish her statement.

"Yes, Michaela, it's your grandmother who discovered this little guy. Now, the poor bird's hurt, and your sister's going to help me take him to the vet. I think we've got him now, Haylee. You keep Mr. Mallard still, while I get my purse."

Haylee nodded.

When Grandma sped out the front door first, Haylee mouthed to Michaela, "Mom's dating Dr. Raintree!"

Michaela looked confused, as her mother didn't need a vet. Her mother saw a family doctor.

Haylee was about to repeat her mouthing for Michaela to lipread, when their mom entered the kitchen from the stairs. Trying to be subtle, Haylee pointed to the magnet on the refrigerator and ever slowly mouthed, "Mom is dating Dr. Raintree!"

Mom glanced at all three of them, and asked with suspicion, "what's all this fuss?"

Fast on her feet, Haylee, thought quickly, since her mother also wore pajamas as was typical for a Saturday morning. But, Michaela blabbed, "Apparently, Grandma brought home a duck for dinner."

Upset beyond words, Haylee grabbed her stomach for fear acid reflux would lurch into her esophagus.

Elizabeth glowed with delight. "Oh, I haven't had duck in ages!" Calling to her mother, Elizabeth suggested, "Since Michaela and I are shopping for her Prom dress today, we could pick up orange marmalade on the way home."

Mortified, Haylee stared in disbelief.

Michaela howled in laughter, knowing how much she upset her younger sister.

Grandma, who'd just turned around with a new towel around Mr. Mallard, scolded, "Elizabeth, really! Don't you see, the duck's alive? Haylee and I are taking him to Dr. Raintree."

"*Squawk! Squawk!*" Mr. Mallard struggled to ruffle his damp feathers.

Elizabeth cried, "Oh, Saint Francis of Assisi!" She blinked several times as if she were hallucinating. "Why, that's a living duck! Get it out of my house!"

Michaela, proud of the reactions she created, stated flatly, "I must have misunderstood. You don't want to eat him. I suppose you want to keep him as a pet, like ole Barney boy."

As if on cue, Elizabeth barked, "Oh, no, no, no, no. Absolutely not! We are not keeping that bird in this house. Heaven knows we have enough chaos here already, what with one girl having the lead in the Spring play, and the other going to Prom with a Senior. Don't even consider it for a nanosecond!"

Glowering at Michaela, Grandma retorted, "I didn't say I wanted to keep him." She lowered her voice, as she took the duck from Haylee's arms. "Really, Elizabeth, I thought I'd raised you to be more compassionate for living things of all sorts. Both you and Michaela should be ashamed of yourselves. Haylee, get your jacket, and let's go."

Haylee delighted whenever Grandma could give her mother a 'What For.' In fact, Haylee noticed the corners of her mother's mouth pursing. Any pursing of Mom's lips indicated her mother felt a tiny bit of contrition with a dash of bitterness. Michaela, on the other hand, was her normal, selfish self. Grateful to be leaving the tension, Haylee held the door open for Grandma and Grandma's new-found friend.

"We'll be sure to tell Dr. Raintree you said hello," Haylee snapped, as she slammed the front door. Haylee knew very well how much her mother could not stand for either daughter to slam a door of any kind, anywhere. Smiling, Haylee knew her mother would be irritated, on the one hand, by a duck having been in the house without her say so, but on the other hand, such insult was then compounded by a slamming door. Haylee thought it was a fabulous Saturday already.

In the car, Grandma handed Mr. Mallard to Haylee who caressed Mr. Mallard while Grandma drove. Making use of the opportunity, Haylee stroked the bird's shiny, emerald, green head. Something uncomfortable stirred within Haylee. Worry for the poor boy's fate made Haylee feel relieved Dr. Raintree's office was not far from home.

When they arrived at the refurbished Cape Cod that housed the veterinary practice, Haylee delivered Mr. Mallard back to Grandma's arms and she walked in front so she could hold the office door open for them both.

Even though it was early on a Saturday, already a German Shepherd dog panted with excitement in the waiting room. On the opposite end of the waiting room, a big English Sheepdog spotted Mr. Mallard, whimpered at Grandma and Haylee, then barked hello at the duck.

Mr. Mallard declined to greet back either canine.

"I'll check in," offered Haylee.

"Good idea," chimed Grandma. She headed to a chair equally distant from English Sheepdog and German Shepherd alike.

"Oh yes, you're the folks who called about the duck," the receptionist said. "Dr. Raintree is expecting you."

Haylee sat next to Grandma in the lobby. Before long, Dr. Raintree came out of a door next to the receptionist's area and greeted them. "So, you're the duck saviors," he said smiling. "This little man is lucky. He should have migrated south months ago. I can't believe he's lasted in this bitter cold. Follow me, ladies."

Neither dog argued with Mr. Mallard being seen ahead of them.

In the examination room, Grandma set the bird on the table with her hand carefully holding him steady. Carefully removing the towel, Dr. Raintree lifted the trembling bird to weigh him on a nearby scale.

"Two point two pounds," he said. "He's small."

Haylee had an urge to show Dr. Raintree how much research she did prior to their seeing him, so she said, "We think he's a male, because of his vivid coloring, and, even more telling, how he has the tell-tale curl under his tail," Haylee said. "Are we right?"

"*Squawk!*" cried Mr. Mallard.

Haylee noticed Mr. Mallard responded with squawks after Haylee spoke. She wondered if Mr. Mallard thought of Haylee as a peer.

Grandma's eyes peered down at Haylee through her reading glasses. "Mind your manners, young lady!" We must respect Dr. Raintree's knowledge. After all, he went to school for many years beyond high school. So, we should not express audacity by thinking we can train him!" she warned in a flattened tone.

Dr. Raintree chuckled. "Yes, you are right, young lady. Male ducks get the curled plume in the back when they're about six months old. Females, on the other hand, are a mottled brown and white, so their coloring camouflages them from enemies when they breed." He eyed Haylee with dancing brown eyes. "You must be Elizabeth's daughter," he said with an outstretched hand.

Haylee shook her head thinking, "Why, oh why, can't I dislike this man?"

The next thing Haylee knew, Dr. Raintree took Mr. Mallard's temperature. The thermometer had to be inserted into the duck's rear end. So as to not cry out in distress, Haylee offered to help Dr. Raintree hold Mr. Mallard as still as possible. It wasn't as easy as she thought it would be. Mr. Mallard flapped his feathers. He even batted his injured wing. Haylee felt relief when the ordeal was finished, and data could be entered into a dropdown box in Dr. Raintree's computer.

"Okay, little fella, let's see what we can do about this wing," Dr. Raintree soothed. He retrieved a syringe from the cabinet, filled it with fluid of Lidocaine, and explained, "This will numb him, so he won't feel as much pain when I remove the fishhook. Please hold him steady again, if you will, please, young lady."

"*Squawk!*" protested Mr. Mallard, but Haylee believed the protest was for Haylee's ears and not a panic alert like he exuded at the beginning of the appointment. In fact, when the syringe and vial went into Mr. Mallard, he didn't squirm as badly as he had with the thermometer.

Dr. Raintree carefully unfurled the mangled wing and swabbed the fishhook with what smelled like rubbing alcohol. From the cabinet, he grabbed an instrument that resembled a pair of pliers. In less than a second, the fishhook was released from the wing.

"Good job," he said. "Thank you, young lady."

While he was wrapping the duck back into the towel that Dr. Raintree nuked for 15 seconds in the microwave, Mr. Mallard relaxed in the warmth. While Mr. Mallard stayed calm, Haylee scanned the office walls of various photos of dogs, cats, and birds. In some of the photos, Dr. Raintree held the patient in his arms.

"Are all of these your patients?" Haylee asked.

Dr. Raintree nodded and smiled. "They sure are," he said. "Around here, we think of pets as family."

Haylee was impressed. She couldn't help liking Dr. Raintree. He'd been nice to Barney, and he was even better with Mr. Mallard. But that wasn't the only thing she liked about him. He had a nice smile that showed off straight, white teeth.

Dad would appreciate his teeth, too.

What a mind warp that created for Haylee. She Pictured her father and Dr. Raintree watching Animal Planet together, and the image caused giggles from Haylee that bubbled away the acid from her usually sour stomach. Even more hilarious, Haylee envisioned her dad looking for cavities in Dr. Raintree's mouth. What a hoot!

Stroking Mr. Mallard's head, Grandma said, "Haylee is worried about this fella surviving this next winter. Since he won't be able to fly, how will he migrate south?"

"That's a valid concern," Dr. Raintree said. "This duck's plumage isn't thick enough to shield him from the cold here in Massachusetts. Even if he could be transported south, the next issue would be finding other ducks that would allow him to join them. Ducks tend to be fiercely protective of their families, so would a flock consider him an outsider, especially since he's injured? Would the other males in the flock view the little guy as a threat or a jinx to their survival?"

Haylee gasped. "Does that mean you'll have to put him down?"

"Well, Dr. Raintree winked. I thought perhaps you ladies might take him home and care for him. Mallards have been known to make good pets."

Grandma sighed, as she put the back of her hand to her forehead. When the gesture failed to alleviate her anxiety, she used her hand to run her fingers through her hair. Such behavior was rare for Grandma, because her hair was carefully coiffed every morning. In desperation, Grandma looked at Haylee and forked over the unspoken dread.

"Haylee, your mother will kill us," she murmured. Then, she explained aloud for Dr. Raintree's benefit, "Elizabeth is my daughter, and Haylee's mother. But then you must've met her when she brought in our black Lab, Barney."

The vet grinned a cheshire, epic smile. "I remember Elizabeth well," he said. He then headed to his computer to input notes into several dropdown boxes for Mr. Mallard, his new patient.

A Divorce in Salem

Curiously, Haylee recognized Grandma thought Dr. Raintree was handsome. So, she too considered his looks from her wise, older woman perspective.

It's difficult for a teenager to assess adult looks whether the adult is of any gender. Adulthood morphs the body as well as facial features, that Haylee was well aware. When the adult was of female gender and the adult gave birth, Haylee observed often the woman could bounce back rather quickly to the figure she had prior to the pregnancy. What Haylee feared more were the changes from two or more pregnancies. Even a woman's neck could thicken after several births, or the top of a woman's head would lower in the back of her head. The transformations frightened Haylee, since the changes meant much more than any diet or exercise could render as 'solutions.'

But Haylee knew there was a reason 'boy bands' were considered 'hot' to pre-teens and teens in that the boys in the band seemed to offer androgyny. Often, the boys shared longer hair length than adult males, soft skin as opposed to the rough exterior of older men. And, oh my, how Haylee found hair inside a man's ear to be absolute grossness.

Her father, the dentist, assured Haylee that an adult man could care about his hair, skin and nails since his hands and face are asking patients to open wide, rinse, and say, "Ah." Haylee's dad informed Haylee he believed his patients already felt vulnerable with such intimate handling, so he wished for them to not see hairy forearms or nasal and eyebrow hair.

Haylee recalled seeing a documentary on Peter Schlesinger who, from Haylee's vantage point, looked like an unmanicured Schnauzer, and Haylee usually thought Schnauzer's were adorable. But, on this old man, his eyebrows went west all the way to Cleveland, Ohio.

In Dr. Raintree's case, Haylee considered his full head of hair that, although full, was not coarse. She put a plus sign beside his hair as an asset. He also showed a touch of gray at his temples. For Haylee, gray hair was fine if it looked controlled. She believed gray hair could be wavy as well as curly if the hair looked organized. But if the hair encouraged her to reject her hamburger through a drive-thru window for fear even a hairnet would not deter a strand from dropping into the sandwich, then she would determine the hair needed a demerit behind the category.

As an artist, Haylee followed the lines of Dr. Raintree's angular nose, cheekbones, and chin. Still, Haylee struggled with the idea her mother could date another man besides her father. But Haylee had to admit she warmed up to Dr. Raintree after seeing him take such good care of Mr. Mallard. Perhaps, if her mother absolutely had to date, Dr. Raintree was better than a stranger. And so far, Dr. Raintree was miles ahead of how Haylee felt about Tiffany.

Ironically, Tiffany looked more like a teenager than any of the adults in question. Perhaps, her resentment of Tiffany had much to do with how close of a competition Haylee felt for her dad's attention. Haylee was clear. She did not see herself as wanting to be romantically inclined toward her father at all, whatsoever. But what she most wanted, if her dad had to date, was that he fall in love with an emotionally mature woman. She wanted the woman to understand Haylee longed for one-on-one time with her father, even though no such notion ever occurred when they all lived in Chicago.

Michaela held the limelight of her father's focus. Haylee was an afterthought, an etcetera in the family line. But divorce changes all the roles in the family. After all, her mother was now a disciplinarian, and less of a nurturer. The alteration of nurturer was now filled by her grandmother.

But the news that Tiffany and her father were no longer together made the entire affair seem pointless. Weirdly, she felt relief she would not have to get to know Tiffany intimately. That was such a relief, because she could not imagine what she and Tiffany would share in common save for a cappuccino.

But she had much rancor between herself and her father for him forcing her to acknowledge her father as a sensual, sexual person. Prior to Tiffany, Haylee took pleasure in thinking Haylee and her sister were conceived through immaculate conception. But, when she visited her dad at his office, she saw vividly in a disgusting way how her father approached sex. She could not forgive him for that. He ruined the role of father, and the role had been fragile even prior to his affair with Tiffany.

In fact, prior to Tiffany entering the picture, Haylee counted on Dad letting her ride in his truck to do errands on a Saturday. Haylee loved going up and down aisles of hardware stores or garden centers. Dad would find items and create a joke or use them in a prank of some sort. She also liked when Michaela would afford Haylee's presence if the three of them went to a movie. Popcorn, candy, soda, and even salsa and chips made the cinema experience a favorite memory. After Tiffany, Haylee retreated from all such experiences even when she was encouraged to participate.

"I'm prescribing some vitamins and steroid meds," Dr. Raintree suggested before Grandma could say more. "To make certain this sweet guy ingests them, I'll provide them in liquid form, which means you'll need an eyedropper."

"We already own two, Dr. Raintree. I've made certain to stock medical kits in the hallway bathroom cabinet as well as a kit in the glove compartment of my car," Grandma said.

"Great!" he said slapping both hands on his knees, then swinging his stool back to his computer to list his recommendation in a dropdown menu option. "One dropper of vitamins just to the fill line once a day; an antibiotic to prevent infection; and two days of pain medication every six hours."

"What do we feed him?" Haylee asked.

Nodding his head, affirming Haylee's question, he suggested, "Ducks eat all kinds of insects and can be purchased at any pet store.

He'll also dive into almost any plant found on the bank of a pond. The salesclerk will know the most likely plant a mallard will think is delicious, and really, plants should be the primary source of his diet." Dr. Raintree said. "You'll want to give him a warm place to bed down, too. He's somewhat fragile at two and-a-half pounds, even though he's been amazingly resilient up until this point."

"That sounds like a lot of work," Grandma said, "but I think, between Haylee and me, we can handle it. Tell me, Dr. Raintree, do you make house calls?"

Haylee's eyes widened. She wanted to crawl under the exam table what with her grandmother's manipulation being so obvious.

"Sometimes," he said. "Actually, I was going to suggest an old-fashioned house call. I could drop over next Monday around six-thirty p.m. to check on his progress, especially with his weight."

"Wonderful!" Grandma grinned broadly. "Oh, we insist that you stay for dinner, too. Haylee and I will do our best to take care of Mr. Mallard in the meantime." Grandma pulled out a compact from her purse and checked her makeup and hair.

Talk about embarrassing.

Haylee collected her jacket and grabbed her grandmother's purse, trying to rush them out of the den of indignity.

"Your receptionist has our address," reminded Grandma. Haylee tried to describe to herself Grandma's smile, but words failed to condense how fake her grandmother's flirtation was. In the world of theater, Haylee recalled the phrase, 'chewed the scenery' for when an actor went overboard in conveying emotion. Why, it was as though her grandmother became the comic relief in a stale Vaudeville act.

Grandma scribbled anyway their address on a post it note and said, "Our home isn't far from this office. It's the yellow clapboard on Essex Street. Tell you what, I'll make beef stew. You eat meat, don't you, Doctor?" she asked and batted her eyelashes ever so briefly.

Haylee vowed right then and there to beg her sister to stop her if she ever, ever, acted so silly in front of someone of the opposite gender. Coming quickly to her senses, Haylee thought, *what difference does the gender matter? No one should act so ridiculous whatever their gender.*

Dr. Raintree chuckled and nodded. "I look forward to it," he said.

Finally, heeding Haylee's tugs on her arm, Grandma made certain Mr. Mallard nestled snuggly in his towel. Tucked under her arm, the three left the exam room, stopping at the reception desk on their way out.

Snapping a wad of gum, the receptionist said, "The bill today is $250. Just give me a minute to get the medicines Dr. Raintree prescribed."

Grandma groaned and confided in Haylee, "I think we need pet insurance. Oh dear. How will we explain any of this to your mother? She's going to be furious." Grandma put her forehead on the glass partition, as an expression of her anxiety.

Assuring her grandmother, Haylee offered, "I'll simply tell Mom that Mr. Mallard will die if we don't take care of him at least until he gains weight and heals from his injury. Plus, I'll tell her that I won't make a fuss about her dating Dr. Raintree if she lets us do this for him. She can't possibly turn him out while it's not even Spring weather, yet."

Grandma's jaw dropped. It hadn't dawned on her that Elizabeth was dating already! But as she looked around Dr. Raintree's thriving practice, she couldn't help but broaden her frown into a smile. Whispering in a low tone, Grandma admitted, "I always wanted a doctor in the family!" she said.

Haylee put her hand on Grandma's purse for emphasis. "Michaela is gonna be the harder one to convince, since she isn't even keen on Barney, and everybody loves Barney."

As soon as these words left her mouth, Haylee gasped. "Grandma, we have another problem! How will we keep Mr. Mallard safe from Barney?"

Haylee didn't wait for Grandma to reply.

"I know what we can do. We'll keep Mr. Mallard in the mudroom. It stays warm in there, especially when the washer and dryer are running, and we can take Barney out the front door when he needs to go out," she reasoned.

"Sounds like a plan," Grandma said. "I'll put today's charges on my credit card. We'll need to stop by the pet store on our way home."

The drive to the pet store didn't take long. They settled Mr. Mallard, who was still wrapped in his terry cloth towel. Haylee gently nestled him into the top rack of the shopping cart and ventured through the aisles to find insects and plant food.

Home again, luck was on their side. Mom's car wasn't in the garage.

"They must still be shopping for Michaela's prom dress," Grandma surmised.

To avoid Barney's enthusiasm upon their return, Haylee and her grandmother entered through the back door, leading to the kitchen and the mudroom. The ruse failed to fool Barney, because he heard them and smelled the unusual scent of avian fowl. Barney yelped. Barney roared. Barney pined away, yearning to see what he heard and smelled.

Haylee trudged back to the car to gather all the supplies they'd purchased from the pet store. Eerily, when she returned, Haylee couldn't hear a peep from Barney.

Heart pounding, Haylee noticed the inside door to the mudroom was wide open. Tears sprang from her eyes and streaked down her cheeks. She assumed Mr. Mallard was dead, clenched in Barney's drooling mouth, an ironic ending after all the duck had endured!

"Come here, Haylee," Grandma called, and she grabbed Haylee's limp arm. "Just look at this!" Pointing toward the floor, she quickly stared into Haylee's wet face.

When Haylee made her way around the corner, she saw Grandma proceed to sit in a kitchen dinette chair with Mr. Mallard on her lap.

Barney and the duck were nose to beak. Barney wagged his tail in approval of the new-found, fowl friend.

"Squawk! Squawk!" said Mr. Mallard. His squawk was quiet and with no hint of panic.

"Woof! Woof!" Barney replied. His tail swooshed back and forth.

Haylee wondered if this scene would repeat itself or appeared as a fluke. The unexpected reaction from canine and avian, brought Haylee back to the awareness her mother was dating. Her mother was dating the well-known local veterinarian. The new world order forced Haylee to want to retreat to the Cape Ann Stage Fort cave where no one could bother her, where no one could disappoint. Safety was solitude. Solitude was identity.

17

The Ides of March Offers the Omen of Fowl Weather

The next morning, Haylee grabs a banana for a quick breakfast and says, "Grandma, I'm going outside to collect some grass clippings and moss from Mom's compost. Slipping on her barn coat with corduroy collar and cuffs, Haylee ran outside into the backyard. The afternoon sun was peeking through heavy, late-winter, early spring clouds. For once, weather was the least of Haylee's concerns. A new being, an actual friend, forced Haylee to focus on creating a perfect bed for Mr. Mallard.

She'd almost made it to the compost heap when she spied another heart-shaped rose quartz crystal.

Haylee whirled in a dizzying rotation, certain someone lurked nearby. But, of course, there was no one in sight, and again, Barney was not yelping or alerting of an intruder.

"How did anyone know I would be going to the compost pile?" she wondered aloud.

Just then, the neighbor's iron gate slammed shut. Probably a breeze, but the consequential chill made Haylee jump anyway. Shivering from panic and not from temperature, Haylee picked up the heart-shaped crystal and put it in her coat pocket. As quickly as she could, she gathered grass clippings and moss. Haylee then ran back into the house.

She longed to tell Mom, her sister, or Grandma about the crystals, but the knot in her stomach warned her not to utter a word.

Instead, hollering, Haylee called, "I have to use the bathroom, Grandma!" Barreling through the mudroom, Haylee dropped the collected grass clippings in Mr. Mallard's box and took two steps at a time up the stairway.

Of course, she wasn't going to the bathroom. She needed to put the new quartz with the others.

While in her bedroom, Haylee made her bed, something she hadn't done earlier because of taking Mr. Mallard to see Dr. Raintree that morning. Before going back downstairs, she grabbed the script for the play from her desk.

Grabbing Haylee's arm when she came back downstairs, Grandma beamed, "Mr. Mallard loves the grass clippings, Haylee. Just look at him, all nestled in. You're such a smart girl! Now, what do you say we get some lunch downtown before your mother and sister get home from shopping. I can't wait to see the dress Michaela chose. Just think, her first dance!"

"I'm sure she'll look beautiful. She always does," Haylee said matter-of-factly, a mixture of acknowledgement and envy. Why she was irritated, she didn't really know. It wasn't as though she wanted to go to the dance, too. Sometimes, a feeling was unreachable and unexplainable like trying to explain a rough riptide in the ocean.

"Is something wrong, dear?" asked Grandma.

"I just don't understand why everybody makes such a big fuss over prom," Haylee blurted. "I don't know why girls make such a fuss over having boyfriends, either. I'll never act like I need a boyfriend. I swear girls at school do stupid things like cry if a boy doesn't pay enough attention. It's embarrassing.

Grandma grabbed her purse and smiled. "You don't need to worry about boyfriends and dances yet. I think your generation grows up too fast as it is. Don't worry, dear, your turn will come when you're ready for it."

Instead of driving to the Lyceum, one of Salem's best lunch spots, she and Grandma walked. The air was brisk and cool, but it felt good. As they walked as well as during lunch, she and grandma practiced lines for the play. They'd just finished the last page on the walk back when they turned onto Essex Street.

Grandma handed back to Haylee her script and warned, "Soon we'll have to face your mother's disapproval of Mr. Mallard."

"Michaela's, too," Haylee giggled. "But you know what? You've given Mom a reason to be angry. Usually, she has to invent one."

Grandma laughed, and Haylee joined in the ever-small conspiracy to use comedy to tamp down her mother's power.

Entering through the front door, Haylee paused so Grandma could scoop up the mail that lay on the floor by the slot in the door. Haylee pet Barney, who sat panting outside the mudroom door, while Grandma shuffled through the bills and magazines.

Haylee and Grandma heard a car in the driveway.

Grandma dropped the magazine she was holding and looked at Haylee. "Here goes nothin'," she chortled.

Michaela swooped through the door and sashayed into the kitchen, followed closely by Mom.

Setting down the dress bag and hanger on the kitchen island, Michaela said, "Wait until you see my dress! It's midnight blue with a rhinestone buckle at the waist, and the skirt has waves of chiffon. The neckline is halter—style, so we bought a matching silver scarf I can pull across my shoulders."

Michaela made an elaborate display of removing the plastic bag that covered the gown while Elizabeth watched with a broad smile.

"Oh, honey," Grandma gasped. "I've never seen anything so pretty! Do you have shoes to match?"

Michaela grabbed the box out from under her mother's arm and opened it to reveal midnight blue, pointy-toed heels, with silver rhinestones lining the edges. "Aren't they to die for?" she crowed.

"Squawk! Squawk!"

Mom's head spun around to glare first at the mudroom door, then at Grandma. "Please tell me that's not what he sounds like."

"Woof! Woof!" alerted Barney, pressing his snout against the mudroom door.

"We can show you, but we should probably put Barney in his crate before we open the door," explained Grandma with her fist inside her teeth.

Haylee grabbed Barney's collar and led him to the crate. Once inside, with the latch closed, Barney looked as if he'd been betrayed, but there was nothing Haylee could do about that except to assure him he was a good boy.

Mom, with her head tilted, edged toward the mudroom. Pausing, she glared at her mother, then opened the door.

Mr. Mallard waddled right on by Mom and into the kitchen.

"Woof! Woof!" Barney yelped from his crate.

"Mother!" Mom yelled. "Are you out of your mind?"

Grandma scooped up the duck. "Let me explain, Liz," she said in a placating tone. "Haylee and I took him to see your Dr. Raintree." Grandma paused, hoping the vet's name would lighten her daughter's mood.

No such luck. Elizabeth's expression grew even more severe. "As surprised as you, I was stunned to hear Dr. Raintree encouraging us to keep him. You see, all the other ducks have already flown south. Mr. Mallard has no family here anymore," Grandma looked toward

Mr. Mallard who looked up at the four of them with a tilted, bobbing head. Grandma was pleased, since his expression looked pitiful. Continuing, she explained, "Dr. Raintree warned us, he'll probably freeze to death if left alone the rest of the winter. Dr. Raintree said ducks make great pets."

Haylee smiled sheepishly at her mother. She made concerted effort to not look at her sister, since she knew Michaela had no sympathy for animals of any sort.

"He said that, did he?" Elizabeth asked, as she put the lid back on Michaela's shoebox.

Mom was not happy and not buying into thinking Mr. Mallard was out of options. Elizabeth faced her mother almost nose to nose and declared, "Maybe you need to take that duck right back to Dr. Raintree? Tell that man he needs to make room in *his* office, if he believes ducks make such 'great pets,'" she said with a snort as she made her fingers emphasize air quotes. "After all, it's what he does for a living." Elizabeth shot glaring eye contact at her mother, then at Haylee.

Haylee withered.

Her sister grinned over Haylee's discomfort.

"Not exactly, dear. He helps other people with their pets. He doesn't keep them for himself." Moving the kitchen stool closer to the island, she looked up into her daughter's fierce, blue eyes.

Haylee knew her grandmother was going toe-to-toe with her daughter in an ultimate power move. "The good news is he makes house calls. Dr. Raintree, that is. In fact, he's coming here Monday evening." Grandma shifted her weight so her hands could support her aching hips.

Grandma smiled and nodded at Haylee, who also smiled at Mom, weakly.

"I enticed him to stay for dinner. I thought I'd make beef stew, but then I changed my mind. Doesn't pot roast with au gratin potatoes and fresh asparagus sound fabulous?" she asked, as she straightened the coffee maker sitting on the kitchen counter.

"Need I remind you that you know nothing about taking care of ducks?" Mom replied, undeterred.

Picking up the bag of medicines beside Michaela's prom dress bag, Haylee jumped in. "Dr. Raintree sent us home with vitamins, an antibiotic, and pain medicine," she explained as she placed each bottle on the counter. "And Grandma and I stopped at the pet store for insects, worms, and leafy greens. That's what Mr. Mallard eats. Dr. Raintree told us what to buy ... " Haylee's voice trailed off.

"I'm sure he did." Mom threw up her hands. "Great. Just great!"

Grandma's head bowed contritely, but Haylee wasn't fooled. She was hiding a smirk as she set the duck back on the floor again.

"Squawk! Squawk!" said Mr. Mallard as he waddled around Grandma's ankles.

Haylee peered at her sister. Strangely, Michaela had yet to say a word. Haylee knew the silence wouldn't last long, since Mr. Mallard was making a beeline straight for her.

"Ewww!" Michaela screeched. "He's spitting at me!" She scrambled away and ducked behind Haylee.

"Don't be silly. He's not a camel," Haylee said. "He doesn't spit. He hisses!" She said as she yanked her sister's hand from her shoulder.

"Woof! Woof!" declared Barney. His snout twitched with delight as he inhaled the fowl scent.

Haylee snickered at the thought of Barney's pun, 'fowl scent.'

"Good Lord, save me" Mom grumbled, as she stared at the ceiling. "I hope Barney doesn't end up turning your pet into duck l'orange."

"Barney won't eat him, Mom," Haylee said. "They're already friends. Putting Barney in the crate was important, only to make the chaos less obvious. But they're already friends."

Mom glowered.

Grandma snickered.

"Eeeek!" Michaela wailed. "He's coming after me again!"

"Don't you think it would be better to find someone to take him who knows how to care for waterfowl? They would know his needs, know what to do for him. That seems reasonable, doesn't it? Surely, we can ask Dr. Raintree to recommend someone." Elizabeth urged.

"There is no one else, Elizabeth," Grandma said.

Mom threw up her hands and grumbled, "Prom, play, recovery, divorce, and now avian health care. Why not?" She threw her head back in disgust.

"Liz, honey, just look into Mr. Mallard's eyes. He's adorable. It will be love at first sight. I promise." Grandma grabbed her daughter's shoulders and gave her a big hug.

Michaela spouted, "Don't let that thing come near me! I'm taking my gown upstairs and posting pictures to my Instagram." With such dramatic declaration, she gathered her dress, shoes and flounced off.

Mom cleared her throat and briefly closed her eyes.

"All right. Here are the rules." Putting up her index finger, she listed, "One, he will not poop on my wood floors, so he must always remain in the mudroom, unless you take him outside for a walk. Two, I do not feed, bathe, or do anything for any fowl at any time. Three, Haylee and you, Mother, will be fully responsible for him—everything he does, everything he eats, every squawk he makes. Understood?" She stared at both in her fiercest glare.

"Squawk!" Haylee declared cheerily.

"Squawk!" Seconded Grandma.

"Oh, brother," Elizabeth uttered, but Haylee saw something else on her mother's face. Although Mom was doing her best to hide it, her lip quivered.

Mom was smiling!

That meant the battle was over. Not only had Haylee and Grandma survived, but they'd also won.

A Divorce in Salem

"You know, dear," Grandma said, "Dr. Raintree is quite a handsome man," said Grandma, as she placed her finger on her daughter's ring finger. "I was glad to see he doesn't wear a wedding ring."

Haylee coughed to hide her giggle.

That evening in her room, Haylee sketched Mr. Mallard. As the sketch came to life on the page, she wondered if he missed his duck family. She then wondered if his father duck insisted the rest of the family fly south for the winter, knowingly leaving Mr. Mallard behind.

More specifically, she wondered if Mr. Mallard still had a father, and if he both missed, yet resented him as much as she did hers.

18

Odor Most Fowl

Where are you going?" Misty asked. "Can I come with you?"

"Casselman's Hardware," Haylee told her friend.

They'd just left play rehearsal, and Haylee could tell Misty felt anxious about something. She couldn't imagine why Misty would be upset. Misty didn't have to live with a dog, a duck, and a recovering Grandma while getting used to a new town and a new school. She didn't have a sister who obsessed over prom, and she didn't have a father who'd been AWOL from her since their move to Salem. She also didn't have a mother who mooned over Dr. Raintree, the only town vet.

In Haylee's view, Misty's life was pretty perfect, especially with a mother who turned everything she touched into a *House Beautiful* showcase.

Shifting her backpack on her shoulders, Misty whispered, "My mom's all mopey lately. She used to be fixing, cleaning, or decorating something. But all she does now is look at old photo albums and sobs. Even Dad's frustrated with her. When I asked her to help me with my lines, she sobbed as if I asked her to give up her Martha Stewart subscription."

Maybe not as perfect as I thought.

Apparently, Misty's mom was still mad that Misty was the Wicked Witch and not the lead of Princess.

"I feel so guilty," Haylee admitted.

Misty grabbed Haylee's wrist. "I know what you're thinking. Haylee, for the last time, I *like* my role. I think being the Wicked Witch is the coolest role. I'm not telling you this because you got the Princess role. I'm just telling you 'cause I need my friend. It's not your fault my mom went to the dark zone. I need my best friend to listen, because she's in such a funk, she ordered take-out pizza last night. When my mom doesn't cook, you know she's in a bad way."

Haylee wondered what she could say that would be helpful. Frustrated by her own lack of wisdom, she suggested, "You could tell her what we learned in today's read-through. If not for the Wicked Witch, the characters wouldn't all be united in the end. There would be no kingdom. Without the Witch, the play would be totally boring."

Misty stopped walking. "Haylee, that's a great idea. The Wicked Witch is the great unifier for the entire play! You're amazing!"

Unable to incorporate the compliment, because she struggled so with embracing any sort of talent and coupled with the confusion as to how to respond, Haylee focused on her next task. Her goal at the hardware store was to get a portable heater for the mudroom, and she found one with metal bars around it, so Mr. Mallard wouldn't be able to get burned. It also turned off if it sensed some bump or accident. Light weight, it was easy to carry all the way to Essex Street.

When they were almost home, Haylee asked, "Do you want to have dinner at my house tonight? Dr. Raintree is coming over to check on Mr. Mallard, and I think my grandmother's making pot roast."

"Since my mom's decided not to cook these days, I'd love to," Misty said.

"Cool," said Haylee.

"Look!" exclaimed Misty when they arrived on Haylee's porch steps. Right in the center of the doormat was a heart-shaped rose quartz crystal.

Haylee picked it up and shivered. "I wish I knew who keeps leaving these. It creeps me out to think someone might be following me."

"I still think you have a secret admirer," said Misty.

Haylee giggled and opened the door.

With one whiff, Haylee's grin faded.

"Oh no!" she cried.

"*Squawk!*" But the noise didn't come from the direction of the mudroom.

"I think he's upstairs," Haylee bellowed. "Misty, you have to help me find him!"

The two girls took off up the stairs. Barney was nowhere to be seen for the moment, thank goodness.

Haylee yelped, "Follow your nose. I'll go right, you go left."

In her room, nothing seemed amiss. Haylee's next stop was her mom's room, but Mr. Mallard wasn't there, either.

Within seconds, Misty called out, "Haylee, you have a major problem!" Misty stood in Michaela's room, wearing an expression of utter horror.

Haylee sped through the door and gasped. "Oh, nooooo!"

Mr. Mallard was waddling across the carpet, looking happy as a lark. No longer protected in its plastic-wrapped glory on the back of the closet door, Michaela's prom dress lay wrinkled on the floor. A nasty, reeking mess covered much of the bottom half of the gown.

"You, sir, are one dead duck!" declared Misty.

"What am I going to do?" Haylee screeched. "Michaela is going to *kill* me!" Tears streamed like a river down her cheeks.

Kneeling by the ecological disaster, Misty ordered, "We need paper towels. Lots of paper towels. And trash bags."

Thankfully, Misty was focused on problem solving. Haylee was so beside herself; she couldn't remember where Mom kept the trash bags. It took a second for her to find them, but she finally yanked a box of them from under the kitchen sink, gathered paper towels from the counter by the coffeepot, and hightailed it back upstairs, arms loaded.

The smell in Michaela's room was horrendous. Haylee thought she might throw up. The odor ponged like a Porta-Potty mixed with pond scum. She didn't know how Misty could stand it, but she was also so grateful to have a friend like Misty with her.

Grabbing the paper towels and trash bags, Misty took charge. "You take Mr. Mallard back to the mudroom, and I'll see what I can do about this."

Haylee was grateful for the momentary respite.

Scooping up the wayward duck, she ran downstairs to put him in the mudroom. Bringing in the newly purchased space heater and plugging it in, Haylee closed the door tightly behind her.

Next, she raced back upstairs to find Misty had miraculously removed the worst of the fowl business that covered the skirt, but remnants left a visible, dark mark.

"My mom says to lift a stain out, you have to use ice-cold water, but first you need to know what kind of fabric you're dealing with. If you don't, you might ruin the dye on the material," Misty warned. "I should call my mom and ask what to do with this kind of material."

Both girls heard the front door open and close. They gasped simultaneously in fear.

"Ewww!" Michaela whined. "What stinks?"

Haylee ran to the top of the stairs. "I'm handling it. Don't worry, Michaela."

Glaring at her sister, Michaela fortunately headed into the kitchen. "I have to pee," Misty whispered. "I'll go to your mom's bathroom. That way I can take Michaela's dress with me, just in case she comes up here." With that, she scooped up the gown and took off.

"How long will it take? I can't stand it in here!" Michaela bellowed. "Never mind. I'm going to the coffee shop down the street to do my homework. When you're done fumigating, call me."

The front door opened and closed again, and Haylee drew in a big sigh of relief.

Rushing back from her mother's bedroom, Misty returned holding the dress.

"I thought for sure she was going to come up here," Haylee said.

"Me, too. She would've killed us both!"

"We still need to get the stain out," Haylee cried.

"I'll call my mom." Yanking her cell phone from her back pocket, Misty anxiously waited for her mother to pick up. At last, Misty said, "Mom, Haylee and I need your advice. We have a major problem ... "That's as far as Misty got before they heard the front door open and close again.

Haylee prayed it was Grandma.

Bursting into the bedroom, Michaela took one look at Haylee and Misty, still holding her dress, and lunged.

"What have you done?" Michaela screamed. "I'll never forgive you!"

Haylee backed away, trying to keep out of reach of her sister's swinging arms.

"I haven't done anything. Mr. Mallard got out of the mudroom. Misty and I were trying to fix it. I swear!"

"My *gown*!" Michaela shrieked and yanked the dress from Misty. "I'm going to kill that stupid bird. Now what am I going to wear? I can't go to the prom smelling like a sewer! That duck's ruined everything!"

Haylee gestured for Misty to get away.

Still on the phone with her mother, Misty skulked out into the hallway.

"Misty's calling her mom to find out how to get rid of the stain and the smell. I don't know how Mr. Mallard escaped, but maybe, Grandma accidentally left the door open. She must have taken Barney for a walk. Don't worry, though, Misty and I are here helping to clean up the mess he made."

By the time Haylee had finished talking, tears were streaming down Michaela's cheeks. She threw herself face down on her bed and wailed, "I loved that gown, and now it's ruined! What am I going to do?"

"We'll fix it, I swear, Michaela," Haylee assured her.

"Where's Mom? She's never here when I need her!" Michaela kept on screeching as if Haylee hadn't said a word. "You don't understand anything, Haylee. That was more than just a prom gown. I was finally going to stand out! Because of that dress, I was finally going to *be* somebody.

"No matter what you wear, you'll be the prettiest girl there," Haylee murmured. "You know you will be."

Misty ran back into the room. She wasn't holding the phone anymore, but she had information.

"My mom says we should put ice cubes in a bowl and fill it with club soda. Then we add a few drops of dishwashing liquid. After mixing, we dab the liquid on the stain. You have to dab it, not rub, because rubbing will push the dirt into the fibers, and it'll never come out. Mom also said we must be patient and go slowly."

"I'll get everything we need and be right back," Haylee said.

Racing to the kitchen and following Misty's mother's instructions, Haylee operated exactly as her mother instructed. Then, being careful not to spill the contents, she carried the bowl upstairs.

They laid the dress out on the floor and Haylee and Misty carefully dabbed, Haylee from one end and Misty from the other, while Michaela continued to sob face up on the bed.

They dabbed and dabbed, and though it did start to look better, the stain failed to lift completely.

Outside, a car door slammed. A minute later, they heard Barney's claws clicking on the floor and Grandma called out, "Yoohoo! Is anybody home?"

"Grandma, we have a disaster!" Michaela yelled.

"Help!" Michaela raised up on her elbows with her head shaking over the lack of progress.

Grandma climbed the stairs, though not nearly as fast as Haylee had. She came into Michaela's room and exclaimed, "What on earth happened? It sure smells in here."

"Mr. Mallard got out of the mudroom," Haylee explained. "I put him back, but it was too late."

"Oh, dear," Grandma said. "Girls, you can stop. That stain isn't going to lift out completely, and neither will the odor."

"What am I going to do?" Michaela wailed.

"Now, Michaela, all is not lost," Grandma said. "What if I alter the dress?" she asked as she eyed the dress from several angles. "Hmm, ok, see the top is fine. Only the skirt got damaged. So, I could sew a handkerchief hemline of silver and blue chiffon. I think you would be happier, and it would look so elegant."

"But Mom spent so much money on this dress. She'll be furious," Michaela sobbed.

"Hush now, dear," Grandma said soothingly. "Don't worry about your mother. I'll handle her. Haylee and I will go to the fabric store right now. The roast is in the convection oven, so dinner will be fine. While we're gone, Michaela, I want you to light as many scented candles as you can find, but make sure they're all the same scent. They'll make the house smell better."

"Grandma," Haylee asked, "can Misty stay for dinner?"

"Sure," Grandma said. "So long as her mother knows. Now, Haylee, before we go, let's trim some of the hem that has the same color as where it's clean from stain and yet located near the dirt. Then we'll take the swatch with us to make sure we find fabric that matches."

"Can Misty come, too?" Haylee asked.

"Maybe she could stay here with me," Michaela cut in. She sat up near the headboard of her bed. "It was really nice of you to call your mom to get information on how to get the stain out. I really appreciate that you went to that trouble."

"Glad to help. If that were my dress, I'd be yanking out some duck feathers right about now," Misty chuckled. "And I don't mind staying here with you, Michaela."

Haylee left the room with fists clenched. What could she say?

Michaela would steal her friend, and there was nothing she could do about it.

Michaela, I helped too! But do I get thanks? It wasn't even me who let Mr. Mallard loose.

As she and Grandma drove to the fabric store, Haylee planned a way to discredit Michaela, so Misty wouldn't like her anymore.

19
A Stitch in Time?

The car had barely stopped when Haylee undid her seatbelt and opened her door.

"Haylee," Grandma called, but she ignored the plea and raced into the house. Needing to keep Michaela from getting her hooks into her best friend, her only friend, Haylee felt determined to find a wedge between them, so that Misty would be Haylee's friend again.

Once inside, Haylee slowed down to prevent Michaela and Misty from hearing her tiptoe. Thankfully, she knew exactly where the creaks on the stairs were, so she could avoid those spots. Stopping at the top of the stairs, Haylee heard both were talking in Michaela's room. Haylee's location afforded neither to see Haylee, yet she could hear them clearly.

"Aren't they just gorgeous?" Michaela said. "And they're comfortable, too. I'll be able to dance in them, no problem." Michaela carefully set down the heels back in the shoebox.

"They are beautiful," Misty declared. Sitting upright, Misty asked with a curious grin, "Is Jason a good dancer?"

Misty rushed to position her place on the bed, as she dished, "Oh, yes. I love slow—dancing with him. I know, because last semester we spent a day together in co-ed gym." Giggling, she recalled, "Mr. Sandee insisted we learn!"

Wanting to vomit, Haylee pictured her sister and Misty sprawled across Michaela's bed with all of her sister's fancy pillows. Haylee surmised her best friend would be lying on her stomach, propped on her elbows, gazing reverently at Haylee's evil sister.

"It must be wonderful to be in love," Misty sighed. "I can't wait 'til I'm old enough to go to prom. Hopefully by then, I'll have a boyfriend, too."

Placing her arms above her head, Misty switched the topic by adding, "You know, my dad's coming? Well, not to the actual prom, of course, but he'll be here to see me all dressed up. I'm just glad he won't be bringing his dental hygienist."

Misty giggled. "Is that what you call her? His dental hygienist?" They both giggled.

"Yeah, and I hate her—even though she and my dad split up. She stayed long enough to destroy my parents' marriage, but not a minute longer," Michaela said shaking her head in disgust.

Sighing, Misty nodded, "Yeah, I don't understand grown-ups at all. It's like all they care about is what they want." Shifting her torso upright, Misty explained, "Like, my mom is obsessed with our house. Sometimes, I think she couldn't care less about my dad or me. Still, I can't imagine how awful it would be if one of my parents didn't live with me anymore. I think that's why friendships are so important. Because then we have people to talk to and to escape when we need."

Michaela affirmed, "Friends are almost more important than family. "Hey! You know, I'm glad you're staying for dinner." Michaela eyed Misty with a new perspective. Misty wasn't Haylee's friend. She was her friend, too.

"Me, too," Misty said. "I love being at your house. It's cool here—you guys are so noisy and into everybody else's business. My house isn't like that at all. It's very stiff. I feel like we're dolls in separate rooms with no conversation, no interaction."

Grandma stood at the bottom of the stairs behind Haylee and whispered harshly, "Haylee—are you eavesdropping?"

Spinning around, Haylee whispered, "Of course not, Grandma," Haylee lied.

Grandma rolled her eyes and moved past Haylee and upward on the staircase toward Michaela's room, leaving Haylee with no choice but to trail behind her grandmother.

"Michaela, dear, look what I found," Grandma said brightly, the bag of treasures from the fabric store in hand. "Michaela," she sang her name musically, "your gown is going to be even more gorgeous than before!"

Pulling out several pieces of fabric, Grandma showed off the satiny silver and royal blue chiffon, long scarves. "I'm going to attach these to the bodice, to form a new skirt. These will create what's called a handkerchief hemline. Much of it will drape to mid-calf. Every time you spin, your legs will show, and the fabric will glide with you as you move."

Grandma's explanation was so enthusiastic, each girl gave out an, "Oooh!" "Wow!" "Ahhh!"

Grandma then plucked a smaller bag from the larger one, "I found these, too—rhinestones to make patterns on the fabric as well as on your stockings. Honey, you're going to be stunning!" Inhaling deeply, she added, "I promise you, this version of your dress will be even more elegant than your original dress!"

Haylee rolled her eyes, but stopped when Misty caught her mocking her grandmother.

Michaela jumped up from the bed and gave Grandma an earnest hug.

Haylee didn't know what to say or what to do.

"Okay, girls, we need to get busy," Grandma clucked. "Dinner is behind schedule. Remember Dr. Raintree is joining us tonight. Haylee, Misty, I need your help setting the table."

Haylee was glad to have something to do, so she didn't have to talk to anyone, except to tell Misty where to find the special, elegant dishes and silverware.

While they were setting the dinner table, Haylee noticed her mom came home from work. Swooping into the kitchen, her mother was still dressed in clothes for work. Quickly, she began chopping vegetables for the salad. "Mom, remember to save scraps of vegetable peelings for Mr. Mallard," Haylee urged. "I get upset that even today people think white bread is okay for ducks to eat. Ducks cannot digest the grain, glutens, and sugar found in bread." She removed what peelings were on the clean dish towel and put them into Mr. Mallard's food dish. "By the way, Mom, you came home at the perfect time. We faced disaster after Mr. Mallard made spaghetti on Michaela's dress."

Elizabeth gasped.

Grandma shushed her soothingly and gave a wink.

Haylee offered, "Grandma fixed the mess with her plan. She is going to sew Michaela a whole new skirt for the dance, and it is going to look even more fabulous than the one you bought!"

"I'm still back at Mr. Mallard eating vegetables," Mom said in disbelief.

"He eats lots of things, Mom—seeds, insects, and vegetables. Just don't give him bread, like I said. It's really bad for ducks. The gluten messes up their digestive systems," Haylee cautioned.

While she and Misty were setting the table, she noticed her mom was staring at the centerpiece for a while. Haylee didn't believe her mom was thinking about the flowers at all. Suddenly, it dawned on Haylee, her mother was nervous. Trying to soothe her mother's nerves, Haylee suggested, "Should we put on some classical music?" For background atmosphere?"

Mom looked at Haylee but didn't answer right away. With furrowed brow, her mother gasped, "Haylee, what if Mr. Mallard's accident is an omen? What if dinner is a mistake?" She turned to Haylee for reassurance.

Haylee shrugged. "I don't think ... "

But her mother interrupted, "Music would be lovely, Haylee," without even looking at her.

At least it doesn't stink in here anymore.

Haylee concluded even if her mother was losing her mind. Just as Haylee hit the button on the stereo, the doorbell rang.

20

The Wolf comes to Blow Your House Down

Haylee ran to the door and yanked it open.

Dr. Raintree wasn't too dressed up, but he didn't dress too casually, either. He looked pretty good for an old guy, Haylee thought. Noticing again his perfect, pearl-white teeth, Haylee was struck by his nicely manicured hands, too. No hairy forearms, either. Perfect for gentle handling of all the animals he helped.

"Haylee, right?" he asked with a toothy smile.

Haylee nodded and opened the door wider, so he could walk through. Grandma ambled from the kitchen, beaming.

"Dr. Raintree, so good of you to come. This is my daughter, Elizabeth. Oh, what am I saying? Of course, you already know her, don't you? And, well you met Haylee. This is Haylee's friend Misty, and Michaela, here, is my older granddaughter. Elizabeth, why are you hiding? Come closer, for goodness' sake," she said nudging Elizabeth forward.

Dr. Raintree shook hands with Grandma, Michaela, and Misty. But when he got to Mom, he kissed her on the cheek. "It sure smells good in here," he said, grinning.

Haylee knew he meant the pot roast, but she found it funny nevertheless after everything they'd been through earlier with Mr. Mallard.

"W-w-would you like a glass of red wine, Jeremy? We have merlot," Mom said.

Jeremy, huh? No wonder Mom's nervous. Dad's name is only one syllable.

"I'd love a glass, if it's not too much trouble." Dr. Raintree showed off his brilliant, white teeth again with a wide grin.

"Elizabeth," Grandma said, "why don't you and Dr. Raintree have a seat in the living room? Haylee will bring your wine, and then the girls will help me finish up in the kitchen. We'll call you when everything's ready." Instructed Grandma.

Haylee grunted, and Michaela slapped her arm.

"Come on," Misty said. "I'll show you how my mom dresses the table. It's all about the way the food is presented. She says everything has to be done in threes."

It never dawned on Haylee that food needed to be *presented*.

"What do you mean by 'threes?'" Michaela asked.

Misty explained, "Objects—even food—look better when arranged in threes. It's a balance thing for the eye. And if the items are on different levels, then the eye relaxes further. Different levels make us view the entire setting as a whole, rather than the eyes resting on each individual piece."

"We shall defer to your expertise, Misty," Grandma said with her fists under her chin in expectation.

Haylee delivered their wine and water, while Misty and Grandma hunted for the special, china serving dishes.

Returning to the kitchen, Haylee noticed the counter was full. A large tray normally used for pillared candles was what Misty had chosen for the main course.

Misty explained, "The roast is your showpiece, so it should be elevated. Now, bring the salad and the veggies. We'll use this trivet with the other candle. We'll just balance everything with berries and flowers around the pieces to draw the eye to see the food as one organism. There! A tableau of epicurean delight!" Misty exclaimed.

After clapping over Misty's instruction, they acted as a team by carrying other foods, like the biscuits, to the table. When they were finished, Grandma winked and called out, "Elizabeth, Dr. Raintree, we're ready for you."

"Please, call me Jeremy," the vet said to Grandma as he walked toward the dining room table.

"It's lovely, girls," Mom murmured.

Michaela and Misty fist—bumped.

Haylee wanted to pummel her sister. Michaela was definitely trying to steal Misty away from her.

"Where would you like me to sit, Marjorie" Dr. Raintree asked.

Grandma took over. "Right next to me, she said, pulling out the chair beside her. Elizabeth, you sit on the other side of Dr. Raintree—I mean, Jeremy." Chuckling, Grandma eyed her daughter.

"What about us?" asked Michaela.

Grandma waved a hand in the air. "You girls sit anywhere you like."

Michaela snagged the chair next to Mom, leaving one chair beside Grandma for Misty. Haylee took the seat at the opposite head of the table.

I'm used to sitting on the right side. The whole table is way too crowded.

"So, Elizabeth, how do you feel about the new member of your household?" Dr. Raintree asked, as he passed the rolls to Grandma.

"To be honest, Jeremy, it's been a disaster. Today was the worst." She put her hand against her forehead. "That crazy duck somehow got out and waddled upstairs, and ... well, he made a mess on Michaela's just-purchased prom gown!"

Dr. Raintree coughed trying to stifle laughter, but quickly grew sober when he saw the expression on Mom's face. "I'm sorry, really. I hope the dress can be salvaged?"

"Not to worry," Grandma said. "Everything is under control." She tapped the table like a drum beat.

Quickly changing the subject for fear Michaela's anxieties would dominate conversation, she offered, "Overall, Mr. Mallard is easier to care for than I expected. We enjoy having him."

Grandma almost spit out her water. "Speak for yourself," Grandma muttered, taking a big gulp of water to wet her cough.

"You don't have to keep him indoors all the time," Dr. Raintree suggested. "He'd probably prefer to spend some time outside on warmer days."

"I'm glad you said that," Grandma said twirling her water glass. "Just yesterday I bought a small dog kennel run. I thought if I layered it with grass cuttings, he'd feel more at home. I don't think our dog Barney would intentionally hurt Mr. Mallard, but I'm afraid to leave them alone together."

"Barney is young," Dr. Raintree said. "Since he's still a pup, this is the time to acclimate him to your duck. You may find they become great friends. Older dogs are more set in their ways. Probably a little like me," he said, chuckling.

Haylee didn't think the joke was *that* funny, but Grandma laughed, and Mom did, too.

Maybe it was an old person thing.

It dawned on Haylee; adults lose the intensity of the five senses we all share. Haylee wondered if the dimming of sight, the fading of hearing, the loss of touch, smell and taste explained why her parents lost 'sight' of each other and why they often couldn't 'hear' the pleas of Haylee and her sister.

Attempting to recover from the weak joke, Dr. Raintree raved, "This pot roast is delicious! I'm afraid I don't get many home-cooked meals. And I must say, the company is excellent, too."

Grandma beamed. "Thank you! It's actually Elizabeth's recipe. I followed it to the letter while she was at work."

"How is your work going, Elizabeth?" Dr. Raintree asked.

"Pretty well, thanks. As you know, I'm a bookkeeper for a large chain of jewelry stores. I'm grateful the job affords me flexible hours. So, because of the flexibility, I can go on school field trips, as well as attend Michaela's upcoming field hockey games. I just have to make up the time, which I can do by starting earlier or leaving later. Sometimes I even go in on Saturdays."

Now, there was a lull in the conversation. It occurred to Haylee, conversation operated like musical measures. Some talking felt staccato, others more fluid and instrumental like violin strings. But often, breaks in conversation offered rest for the ear and an ability to switch the energy for other topics.

Grandma broke the awkward silence.

"Our Haylee and her friend Misty here made it into the school play. Isn't that wonderful?"

"Excellent," Dr. Raintree said. "When is the performance?"

"May the twenty-fourth," piped in Haylee.

"I'd love to see it," Dr. Raintree said. "I'll bet you didn't know I'm a fan of the theater. What's your play about?"

Misty spoke before Haylee had a chance.

"There's a kingdom with elves and legendary characters like Rumpelstiltskin. Of course, there's a Prince and Princess, too. But all is not paradise. There's a Wicked Witch who puts a curse on the kingdom, separating the Princess from her Prince. Alas," Misty throws the back of her hand over her forehead, "I can't say any more than that. You'll have to see it to find out the ending!"

"Bravo!" Dr. Raintree applauded. "Excellent synopsis."

Haylee didn't think it was worthy of that much praise, but Mom laughed, and Grandma grinned. Even Michaela smiled, for once.

"Would you like more wine?" Mom asked Dr. Raintree.

"No, thank you. I have to keep a clear head, as after dinner I want to take a look at Mr. Mallard." Relieved the topic, the praise, and all the small talk changed, Haylee asked, "If we let Mr. Mallard live outside in a kennel, what's the ideal temperature for him?"

Dr. Raintree wiped his lips with his cloth napkin and replied, "Good question. Ducks prefer a temperature of about fifty-five degrees. In winter, it will be too cold to leave him out all the time, and in summer he'll need access to cool water. But you'll know if he's too cold or too hot. If he's cold, he'll shiver. If too hot, he'll pant."

"Good thing I sprang for the heated kennel," Grandma said.

Mom glared at her mother, while Dr. Raintree fiddled with his wineglass. He cleared his throat and said, "Perhaps now would be a good time to take a look at Mr. Mallard. Girls, would you help me carry my equipment from the car?"

The opportunity I've been looking for! I'll get the vet outside, tell him something that'll scare him away from Mom, and Voila! A disappearing animal doctor will go...poof!

21

Veterinary House Call

"So, is Mr. Mallard doing better?" Haylee asked after Dr. Raintree looked inside Mr. Mallard's beak and felt for any nodes of significance.

They were out in the dog run with Grandma and Misty, where Dr. Raintree was weighing, feeling and examining Mr. Mallard.

"He looks pretty good to me." Dr. Raintree rose from where he'd been hunkering down with the duck. "You're taking wonderful care of him, Haylee and Marjorie. It was ingenious to set up the dog run."

Grandma preened a bit from his praise.

"Since we're all done here," he said, "if you don't mind, I'll go see if Elizabeth could use a hand in the kitchen."

"How thoughtful of you to check on Mr. Mallard for us. You really must stay for dessert."

So long as Grandma was with them, Mom and the vet wouldn't be alone. Knowing Grandma, though, she'd make up an excuse to leave. And that didn't suit Haylee at all.

"We should go in, too," Haylee said to Misty. "It's chilly out here."

"Oh, my gosh, Haylee, look!" Misty exclaimed. "Another-heart-shaped crystal!"

Haylee spun around and sure enough, there on the ground, near the end of the dog run was a rose quartz identical to the others.

"All right, this is getting more than just creepy," Haylee said, as she grabbed the stone.

"At first, I thought it was a secret admirer, but we have to be more realistic. Maybe your grandmother is the culprit." Said Misty.

Shaking her head, Haylee reasoned, "The timing doesn't always fit. Believe it or not, I thought maybe you were the one leaving them."

"Me?" Misty giggled. "That's funny, I wouldn't be able to keep a secret like this. I'm too transparent. That's what my mom says, anyway."

Haylee shivered. "It just freaks me out, how much whoever's doing this knows about my habits and my whereabouts. Come on. Let's go inside."

"Here, take it," said Misty, handing over the latest crystal.

Haylee dropped it in her pocket and went through the back door, with Misty on her heels. The first thing they heard was her mother saying, "homemade apple pie à la mode. Would you like a cup of coffee to go with it?"

The girls meandered into the kitchen.

Of course, Grandma was nowhere to be seen. As Haylee had suspected, Grandma had conveniently disappeared, leaving the vet and Mom alone together.

"I can't resist ice cream," Dr. Raintree said. "And I wouldn't mind the coffee, either."

"Oh, hi, girls," Mom said when she saw them. "I didn't hear you come in. Why don't you two go up to Haylee's room for a little while?"

"What about Michaela?" Haylee asked. "And where's Grandma?"

"Michaela is upstairs on her phone, of course. What else would she be doing? And Grandma said she had some reading to do. "Now, go on. I'm sure you'd rather hang out upstairs than with us old folks." Mom pleaded.

"Speak for yourself, Elizabeth," Dr. Raintree joked, showing off his gleaming white teeth.

My Dad should buy stock in whatever toothpaste Dr. Raintree uses, 'cause his teeth sparkle even in dimmed lighting. But how gross is his teasing with Mom. Not just teasing. Oh, my gosh, they were actually flirting!! Gross! Gross! Gross! Seriously, I heard kids mention how important flirting is in dating, but I never was sure what it would sound or look like! Ewww!

There was nothing Haylee could do. She had to go upstairs because Mom had said so.

Misty was tugging on her arm, pulling her out of the kitchen.

"Wait, Misty," Haylee whispered through clenched teeth. She had one more idea.

"Hey, Mom, you want me to light a fire in the fireplace?" Haylee winked at Misty. "It's pretty chilly in the living room."

"No, thanks, honey. You two go ahead upstairs. Misty's here to hang out with you."

"Come on, Haylee," Misty said. Both realized they could not weasel a way to stay downstairs with Mom and Dr. Raintree. Haylee couldn't think of any other reason to linger, so she followed Misty up the stairs.

As they reached the top of the stairs, Misty spun around with her finger to her lips. Haylee grinned. Another reason Misty was her best friend.

They'd been thinking the same thing all along. Although they couldn't see Mom and Dr. Raintree, they could hear everything.

Mom was leading him to the living room. By the sound of it, they were sitting together on the sofa with their dessert and coffee.

"I have to say, Elizabeth, that roast was really divine. And so is this pie. If I keep eating like this, I'll end up weighing four hundred pounds."

Mom laughed, a schoolgirl giggle.

"I can't imagine that," she cooed.

Disgusting!

Nodding, Elizabeth suggested, "Haylee had a good idea. Perhaps a fire would be nice. Let me light one."

"No, you relax. I'll take care of it," he said gallantly. "I've lit many a fire in my time."

Mom and Dr. Raintree laughed.

Misty raised her eyebrows at Haylee. Haylee just put her face in her hands, as she stifled an urge to giggle. The girls could hear them gathering kindling and matches. Soon they caught a whiff of wood smoke.

Haley motioned to Misty, she thought her mother and Dr. Raintree sat again on the sofa and were finishing dessert.

"Your daughters are lovely, Elizabeth," said Dr. Raintree. "Of course, I met Haylee before, but it was nice to meet Michaela, too. You've done a wonderful job with them."

Haylee rolled her eyes.

"Well, thank you. That means a lot to me. Still, I worry, because Dan and I fought so much. I have no doubt our constant arguing scarred the girls." Sighing she added, "To be honest, I know I did most of the screaming. How I wish I had curbed my tongue more often, because, in looking back, I think it would have forced Dan to talk more. Instead, he could just put the blame on me for our fighting. My impulsivity for arguing enabled him to avoid any disclosure or show of vulnerability."

Elizabeth paused and looked sideward. "Now, it seems like all Michaela cares about is fitting in with her peers. She seems to find the in-road to fitting in with peers so easily. But Haylee ... she turns everything inward. She won't say what she feels. I wish I knew how to help her."

Misty eyed her friend. She reached out a hand for Haylee to take, but Haylee ignored the gesture. Instead, Haylee turned her face to the wall so Misty wouldn't see her tears. Haylee's tears felt red hot on her cheeks. Mom must've confided in Dr. Raintree a lot. Haylee was embarrassed by what Mom had said about her. And once again, she was being compared to Michaela.

She couldn't even look at Misty. But her friend seemed to understand. She leaned close to Haylee, rolled her eyes, and mouthed, *"Parents."*

"You know, I don't have any children of my own," Dr. Raintree admitted. "So, I'm no expert, but I'd say your girls are human. They have talents and flaws just like the rest of us. They're individuals. There's no need for them to be perfect. And I just know you can't 'fix' them into perfection. And that's good that you can't, as you'd think they were boring robots if you did."

Leaning forward, Elizabeth joked, "Now you sound like my mother!"

Dr. Raintree chuckled. "Your mother's a hoot. I like her."

"She likes you, too," Mom said.

"Yes, I know," Dr. Raintree murmured.

"If she only knew," Mom said, and they both laughed.

Haylee put her index finger inside her mouth.

Misty threw her hand over her mouth to stop blurting into laughter.

Setting his fork and plate down on the coffee table, Dr. Raintree said, "I'd say we put on a pretty good show tonight, wouldn't you think?"

"That we did! Although I must say, I'm still unhappy about taking on another pet, let alone a duck who must somehow reside with an eager *bird dog!* We needed Mr. Mallard like we needed a hole in the head."

Turning his torso toward her, Dr. Raintree said, "How can you say that, Elizabeth? Mr. Mallard likes you." His voice lowered to a murmur. "Almost as much as I do."

Haylee shook her head. Misty patted Haylee's back.

Silence for a moment, and then Haylee and her co-hort heard kissing.

Haylee looked at Misty. Both girls' eyes widened.

"You tempt me, you really do," said Elizabeth.

"Good," Dr. Raintree replied. "Are we still on for lunch tomorrow?"

"Yes," she said. "I look forward to it."

"Me, too." Dr. Raintree said softly. "I wish I could stay."

"I wish you could, too," Mom said. "For now, just kiss me good-bye."

"My pleasure," Dr. Raintree whispered.

"Oh, Jeremy!"

Haylee had heard as much as she could stomach. She took Misty by the arm, and they tiptoed to her room.

Serious intervention was called for. What remedy existed for a divorcing mother who thinks dating so soon after separating is a wise choice? Determined, Haylee used Google to identify possible intercessions for radical brain washing.

22

A New Way of Thinking

Haylee traipsed into the house after play practice, still hurt from the words her mother had said to Dr. Raintree where, once again, in being compared to her sister, Haylee came up short.

That morning, she hadn't said one word to Mom at breakfast. Eye contact wasn't usual anyway for Haylee, but how could she, after what she'd heard the night before? Mom was dating Dr. Raintree, and worse, keeping it hidden from her daughters.

Funny, a firm rule under Elizabeth's domain is that punishment is made worse when not only is there a rule-break, like coming home late, but punishment is exponentially added when there is a lie to cover up the rebellion.

Hmmmm, spat Haylee! What's the phrase? What is sauce for the goose is good for the gander? An apt caution given the avian comparison, too!

And today, Mom was meeting Dr. Raintree for lunch. From what Haylee overheard last night, the pattern of lying about where she was going and what she was doing was a frequent occurrence.

It had been impossible for Haylee to concentrate all day. Classes had dragged on ad nauseum and the choices for food at lunchtime were horrible. As much as she normally enjoyed play practice, even that held little appeal. Haylee was relieved to get out of school and away from peers.

But now that she was home, she wished she was still at school. Eventually Mom would come home from work, and that meant Haylee would have to face her again.

Of course, Barney wagged his tail, glad to have Haylee home. He danced around her legs the way he always did when she came in the door. One thing about Barney—he made Haylee feel known, welcomed, and most of all, loved.

Today, though, she was too down in the dumps to consider Barney's big doggy grin and wagging tail as a happy-to-see-you greeting. Today, she felt sure the only reason Barney carried on the way he did was because he wanted to go for a walk. He didn't really care about *her*.

Just like Dad.

And just like Mom, too. If Mom cared, she wouldn't have lied, and she wouldn't have wasted time on dating! Mothers are not meant to date. Dating was for young, single people.

Putting her backpack on the peg handle of the water bench, Haylee grabbed Barney's leash. Briefly, she wondered where Grandma was. Usually, Grandma arrived home at this time of day. Even more peculiar, Michaela should have been home by now, too. But the house loomed quiet. Haylee didn't even hear Mr. Mallard flapping around in the mudroom.

"Come on, Barney," she said, once she'd hooked his leash on his leather collar. "I don't feel like going around the block today. We'll just go out to the backyard."

Barney seemed content enough with that plan. But when Haylee slipped out the back door, she stopped cold. There she was. Mom ... out in the dog run with Mr. Mallard. Not just that, she was hunkered down on her hands and knees, arranging plant growth around a plastic kiddie pool.

"Hi, Haylee," Mom called out. "I looked up duck habitats online today, so I could get a better idea of the best way to set up Mr. Mallard's new home. I left work early and stopped at the store. Of course, I can't plant all the recommended things until the real spring weather, but it'll be nice to give him a real pond then. I also got this special water bottle for him, so he can drink, and the water won't ever spill. How does his new home look so far? Do you think he'll be happy here?"

Squawk! Mr. Mallard chimed.

Mom chuckled and stood up. "I think he's telling us he approves," she said, brushing her hands to get rid of the remnants of sod.

Haylee couldn't believe it. Mom was not scowling. She wasn't complaining either. Quite the contrary. But she wasn't just grinning, instead her eyes had a gleam, and her cheeks were rosy. Haylee thought the change in her mother's face could be because she'd been outside in the cold for a while, but Haylee didn't think so.

Mom was clearly giddy over her accomplishment. Maybe Mr. Mallard offered side benefits Haylee hadn't considered. Haylee didn't know what to say. As it turned out, she didn't have to say anything, since at that moment, Michaela entered through the gate. Haylee could tell her sister felt just as stunned as Haylee seeing their mother content in Mr. Mallard's dog run.

"Mom!" Michaela stomped her foot. "What have you done? You've gone over to the enemy camp!"

"Actually, honey, I'm having fun. Would you like to help?"

The expression on Michaela's face couldn't have been more horrified. Mom burst out in a loud guffaw.

"Oh, my god!" Michaela wailed with fists on her hips. "Come on, Haylee, let's get out of here!"

Haylee was about to say she couldn't go in, because Barney hadn't done his business yet. Barney must have read her mind, because just then he lifted his leg. In fact, Barney lifted his leg high as though he was saluting Mr. Mallard's new bachelor pad. Yep, Barney was celebrating the occasion directly on the corner of the kennel run.

"Barney!" Mom giggled.

"I'm going inside," Michaela announced with her head shaking in disgust. "I want nothing to do with any of you right now."

"Come on, Barney," Haylee said in resignation. She then called out to her sister, "Michaela, I'll have you know Mr. Mallard is a duck, not a goose. Ducks squawk while geese honk," she said pulling Barney's leash away from the kennel. "Maybe if you wanted to learn more about him, since he is living with us until he's healed, you might feel more generous about him by showing interest in learning about his species," she said. Thrilled that Barney was less resistant to leaving the kennel run to go back into the house, Haylee encouraged him with a cooing tone so that he gladly followed her, right on Michaela's heels.

Once in the kitchen, Haylee handed her sister a glass of water. Michaela gulped it to slake her thirst.

Sliding the dishwasher open, Michaela said, "I don't know what's gotten into Mom, but at least that dumb duck won't be in the house as much." Pivoting toward her sister, she smirked, "I'm for anything that keeps that smelly bird away from me and my things."

Nodding, Hayley added, "I'm for anything that keeps Mom from thinking she can date while she's still married to our dad. You know, their divorce isn't yet final!"

Jaw open, Michaela pleaded, "Oh, Miss Haylee, please assure me, you don't have any sliver of hope that Mom and Dad will get back together. 'Cause honey that ship sailed when we left Chicago and drove all the way to Salem!"

Haylee's lip trembled, so she bit the inside of her cheek to stop the desire to cry.

Michaela peered at Haylee with concern. "Haylee, Dr. Raintree just came for dinner last night. Nothing will come of it..." Michaela snapped.

Haylee didn't wait to hear anymore. She ran upstairs to her room.

Once in her room with door closed, Haylee lay on her bed and stared up at the ceiling fan. To distract herself away from sadness, she imagined what Salem looked like in 1692 when the witch trials occurred.

Maybe there was something to that. Maybe if Mom had lived back then, the townsfolk might have thought her mother was a witch. After all, Haylee heard her mother cackle over her hard work on the kennel run. Haylee read how the pilgrims were suspicious over whether neighbors were pious or not.

Haylee pictured her mother in a tiny cell with a floor moldy from water that lacked drainage and walls so unforgiving that a prisoner couldn't stand upright. The only reprieve from such a dungeon was when guards led the accused to a scaffold built for a masked henchman who would put a noose around her neck.

And Haylee imagined her mother's demise as being Dr. Raintree's fault, because he would have served as the Spectral Evidence who'd bewitched Elizabeth.

Considering her visualization of life in Salem five centuries ago, Haylee knew what to do.

She got on her laptop and googled Dr. Raintree's name. Surely, she could find something about him online that wasn't good, something incriminating in his history, something she could use to dissuade her mother from liking him. Haylee didn't get that far. Interrupting her investigation was Grandma yelling out to her from down the hallway.

"Yoohoo, Haylee? Are you home?"

For a second, Haylee contemplated pretending not to hear. But she couldn't just ignore her grandmother.

Shutting down her laptop, Haylee trudged around the corner and found Grandma sitting on the bed with Michaela's dress across her lap. Fabric and piles of rhinestones were strewn across the bedspread within easy reach. In Grandma's hands were a needle and thread, and on one of her fingers, a thimble.

Peering through her reading glasses, Grandma beamed, "Michaela's either going to believe I'm her Fairy Godmother, or she'll never speak to me again." Holding up the dress for Haylee to see, Grandma asked, "What do you think? I know what I think, but I'm not a teenager, to be sure," she said giggling. "Be honest. What's your impression so far?"

Haylee looked at the fabric and rhinestones Grandma had sewn onto the bodice. Haylee thought the rhinestones looked like lightening bugs on a warm, summer night. Despite the darkness of her mood, Haylee had to admit, she loved it.

"Grandma, it's gorgeous!" she replied. "You're like Rumpelstiltskin, spinning straw into gold."

"That's sweet of you to say," Grandma said with a big smile. "Of course, Michaela and your mother will be the true test. Come and sit with me. Let's talk. I need a break. My arthritis is killing me."

Haylee didn't want to sit and talk. She wanted to go to her room and follow through with her plan to dig up dirt on Dr. Raintree. But Grandma was moving all sewing materials out of the way and then she pat the bed for Haley to sit.

Haylee plopped down.

"Speaking of Rumpelstiltskin, how did rehearsal go today?"

With one leg bent at the knee while the other leg dangled off the quilt, Haylee mumbled, "It was okay."

"Just, okay?" Grandma prompted. "That doesn't sound like the cheerful Haylee I know."

Haylee shrugged.

"Did I tell you my sponsor is knitting another Afghan? She knits one every time a new grandchild is born."

This reminded Haylee of the old lady she'd met on the bus when she'd first explored Cape Ann and discovered the cave.

"I think the grandchildren's births are just an excuse, though," Grandma went on. "She says knitting relaxes her and helps keep her hands out of the cookie jar, if you know what I mean. Do you know, ever since I went into recovery, I've craved sweets. Strange, isn't it?"

"Are you tempted to drink again, Grandma?" Haylee asked concerned.

Grandma chuckled. "All the time. Do you know the Old Testament, in the book of Genesis, where God tells Adam to name all the animals so he would have dominion over them? It's the same with thoughts and feelings. If you fail to name them, you can't conquer them, and that failure leads to turbulence. Sometimes, the turbulence hurts the drinker, but other times, it hurts those the drinker most cares about!"

Haylee wasn't sure she understood what Grandma meant. "Okay," she said.

Grandma paused. "So, I guess I'm learning through this recovery it's important that I admit to craving. In prior relapses, I now know I resisted talking about my yearnings for a drink. So, I need your honest opinion about my worry, because my sponsor asked me if I was second-guessing my decision to bring Mr. Mallard home."

Haylee was shocked! Edging closer on the bed, Haylee asked, "Are you? I mean, you bought the dog run and the water bottle. We went shopping for seeds, worms, and plants for food, too," Haylee reminded her.

"At first, I wasn't uncertain, but now, I don't know. I think perhaps Mr. Mallard is like a good luck charm. Even his pooping on Michaela's gown is turning out to be a good thing. The gown will end up more stunning than it was before. And look at your mother. I can't believe she took off work early and came home to work on the dog run for Mr. Mallard. She's changing. She's smiling again."

"She's smiling because of Dr. Raintree," Haylee mumbled.

"Yes, I'm sure that's part of it, dear," Grandma said. "My sponsor, who is a very wise lady, reminded me that I've had five relapses, and how easy it can be to fall into another. She reminded me 'sober' doesn't mean 'recovered.' Grandma said with her hands folded over her sewing.

"I must remember that highs and lows in mood fluctuations can cause impulsive choices." Grandma stood up and massaged her right hip. "I must learn to examine my feelings and my motives in my choices. I need to accept unresolved feelings for what they are. I think that's what I'm trying to do." However, Grandma had a puzzled look that made the lines on her forehead more pronounced.

When finished with rubbing her hip, she cautioned, "Haylee, you could try a little harder to understand your mom.

Not giving Haylee time to counter, Grandma explained, "I've worried about my decision to bring Mr. Mallard into our home. And so has your mother. What if Mr. Mallard doesn't heal completely, or worse, sickens and dies, what would that loss do to you girls? Especially after the death of your grandfather, and now, weathering your parents' divorce." She sat down on her vanity chair with her back to the vanity mirror.

"Are you saying Mom didn't tell us about dating Dr. Raintree because she didn't want us to get hurt?" Haylee asked.

"What I'm saying, dear one, is that even those who have the best intentions at heart, sometimes make mistakes. What's most important is being able to admit it and move forward with an idea as to how not to repeat the bad choice."

Grandma looked up while resuming her sewing, hoping Haylee would ask more questions.

Instead, Haylee sighed and retreated to her room.

Grandma gave her a lot to think about.

23

Best—Laid Plans

"I'll hang on to them for you," Misty offered. "We'll keep them in my locker."

"Good idea," Haylee said and handed the bag of crystals over to her friend. She wasn't sure why she'd decided to bring the stones to school, but Misty thought it was as good a plan as any, since so far, none had been discovered in school. Misty stuffed the bag into the back corner of her locker and covered it with books.

"If my locker gets broken into, hopefully the thief won't find the bag. Instead, the infiltrator will likely be spellbound by my air fresheners and my organizers for notebooks. Mrs. Piggle Wiggle never had a mystery this intriguing.

Misty uttered an uproarious laugh, and Haylee shushed her friend as she too giggled over Misty's comment. Now they had just enough time between classes for Haylee to hurry to her locker and get the book she needed for third period, computer science. It was her favorite class not because she liked the subject, but because Misty, Josh, and Brandon were also in the class, the only one the four of them shared.

She and Misty slipped through the classroom door right as the bell rang. They scurried to their seats, but not without scrutiny. Brandon watched them with interest, his expression curious. Haylee noticed that Josh was also staring at them.

The teacher, Mr. Ramsey, cleared his throat. "Good of you to join us, ladies."

The rest of the class burst into murmuring, indicating their lateness was a source of gossip.

Haylee could feel her face redden. She wished she could disappear. Skulking low in her seat, she opened her book and hoped everybody would stop looking at her.

"Let's get started," Mr. Ramsey said, waltzing over to close the classroom door.

Within ten minutes, someone knocked on the door. Haylee could see through the door's window that standing outside the classroom were the guidance counselor, Mrs. Lockwood, and the principal, Mr. McGillicuddy.

How weird. Why would two school authority figures intrude computer science class?

"Excuse me, class," Mr. Ramsey said, tapping the ruler on his desk. "While I'm gone, I want you to read the next section on systems information. I will expect you to be able to answer any question I may have as soon as I return."

He opened the door and went out in the hallway with Mrs. Lockwood and Mr. McGillicuddy.

Breaking into whispers, everyone wondered why both the principal and guidance counselor needed to talk to Mr. Ramsey. It was safe to say Mr. Ramsey surpassed all the other teachers with his monotone and dreary story telling of computers "back in the day" prior to families owning their own laptop or tablet.

Brandon leaned over in his chair, his head bent close to Misty's ear. "Maybe they've come to ask Mr. Ramsey to chaperone the prom?" he whispered.

Misty rolled her eyes. "They wouldn't interrupt class for that," she reasoned.

A couple of minutes later, Mr. Ramsey returned to class with Mr. McGillicuddy and Mrs. Lockwood.

Though the other students were staring down at their books, Haylee knew they were only pretending to read. Everybody was too curious. Invaded by curious energy that reminded her of lightning strikes, Haylee felt the hair on her forearms stand straight up. Eyeing the adults without being obvious, she saw by the expressions that whatever news they were about to share wasn't good. Mrs. Lockwood's smile was full of pity and looked as forced as a wax replica of a pilgrim stuck in Pillory.

Bending down by Misty's desk, Mrs. Lockwood spoke in a low, soothing tone.

"Misty, honey, please collect your things and come with us."

Veering and looking for help from her friends, Misty was behaving in a way that made it clear, she had no idea why she was being selected to leave class. Haylee could read exactly what Misty was thinking.

What did I do wrong?

Gathering her book, notebooks, and colored pens, Misty walked out with the adults. Everyone in class broke again into loud whispers.

Chewing the inside of her cheek, Haley wondered if someone had discovered the crystals and assumed Misty had stolen items that didn't belong to her.

Waves of guilt lapped over Haylee's stomach. Thoughts revving, Haylee wondered if the stones could be valuable and maybe that's why the school was taking control.

Once again, I ruin everything.

Mr. Ramsey barked, "All right, class, let's get back to work!"

As if she would be able to concentrate now.

Scenario after scenario circulated through Haylee's head like the spin cycle in a washing machine. Their washer at home sometimes stopped when items in the washer became unbalanced. Finally, class ended.

To get to her next class, Haylee should have veered right once she got to the break in the hallway. Instead, she turned left and headed straight for the school office.

But she was too late. As Haylee rushed in, she saw Misty's father standing there in his business suit, looming over Misty. Mrs. Lockwood held open the exit door.

Haylee called out, "Misty!"

Misty ignored Haylee. She refused eye contact.

24

What Is a Good Friend?

Haylee endured the next class, wondering the entire time where Misty's dad had taken her, and whether she'd be back in time for lunch.

Sadly, Misty failed to return in time for lunch. Waiting at their table in the cafeteria as she always did, Haylee eventually opened the lunch bag she'd brought from home.

It felt like everyone was staring at Haylee. Not only that, but the other kids were whispering behind their hands, covering their mouths so Haylee couldn't even read lips.

Without Misty, Haylee felt alone, and somehow, she also felt betrayed. Ever since they'd all gotten parts in the play, Josh and Brandon had been sharing a lunch table with her and Misty. But today the boys sat where they used to, with other friends, on the opposite side of the cafeteria. They were the only people in the whole school who hadn't looked at Haylee. They didn't so much as glance in her direction.

Haylee didn't know what was going on, but she didn't like it. She was relieved when lunch was over, and it was time to return to class. Heading out of the cafeteria, she made a beeline for her locker so she could collect books and notebooks she needed for the rest of the school day.

Grabbing her books from the high shelf in her locker, her head halfway inside, she stopped what she was doing when someone behind her said, "Have you heard?"

Haylee knew the voice before she turned around.

Danielle and her minion, Carly stood blocking Haylee from dodging what they were about to say. Haylee shook her head.

"Funny, you're her best friend, yet you seem to be the last to find out," Danielle said with feigned pity.

Carly stood there with a fake smile that showed her horse teeth.

Pausing, Danielle announced, "Misty's mother died. Even worse, she committed suicide."

The floor beneath Haylee's feet shifted. She grappled for the cold metal door of her locker to keep steady.

Haylee knew she said something, but she didn't know if she said it aloud. Hearing a roaring sound in her ears, Haylee thought maybe there were waves coming after her, like she was drowning. Then her vision bounced from three dimensions to flat and small.

I wonder if this is what it feels like to have a stroke.

"My mom texted me during third period," Danielle chimed haughtily. "She heard it from a neighbor. I can't see how a mother could possibly do that. I mean how selfish could she be?"

Haylee couldn't find her voice. She could barely breathe.

Danielle examined her perfectly polished nails. "I wonder who will take Misty's part in the play," she sneered. "I mean she can't possibly make it to rehearsals, not with this crisis going on in her life."

Now Haylee knew why she disliked Danielle as much as she did. She was just plain mean, and Haylee wasn't about to listen to her any longer. Slamming her locker door, she snapped, "I don't believe a single word you've said!"

"Ha!" Danielle sputtered. "You'll see!" Danielle tried to pat Haylee's cheek, but Haylee dodged her efforts by ducking and turning her back to Danielle and Carly.

Both flounced off down the hallway. Their giggles echoed until they turned the corner.

Frozen, Haylee didn't know what to do or where to turn. She needed to know the truth. Guilt flooded her recall. She remembered Misty talking about how weird her mother was acting and how dismissive Haylee must have seemed.

Within minutes, Haylee heard two teachers confirming the news that Misty's mother died by hanging herself.

Haylee could barely get through her classes. During afternoon announcements over the loudspeaker, the principal informed everyone, play rehearsal was cancelled for the day.

The notice that rehearsal was cancelled was the final confirmation Haylee needed. It was true. She couldn't imagine another reason for practice to be cancelled.

Haylee berated herself.

I should have asked more questions the other day. I am such a bad friend. I'm as self-absorbed as my father!

She didn't take the bus home, knowing she would be facing a bunch of kids staring at her. Instead, she ran the whole way home, bursting through the front door and rushed straight into Grandma's arms, sobbing with deep inhales that made her shiver and gasp for more air.

Grabbing the tissue box on an end table in the living room, Grandma cooed as she handed Haylee several.

"I'm so sorry, honey. I just heard from the neighbors down the street. So, I called your mother as soon as I heard the terrible news. She's on her way home from work, and she said to tell you she loves you." Grandma rubbed full circles with her hand on Haylee's back.

For a long time, Grandma held Haylee, right there in the foyer. Grandma held her tight, and she repeated over and over, "It's okay, sweetie." But Haylee knew it wasn't okay.

She didn't know what to do. She wanted to see Misty but knew she wouldn't know what to say to her friend, or how to act. She felt stupid and so helpless.

Even Barney knew something was wrong. He didn't dance around the way he normally did. He just sat there leaning against Haylee's leg.

Grandma finally convinced Haylee to come to the kitchen.

Pulling out a stool by the island, Haylee sat down while Grandma brought her oatmeal cookies and orange juice, Haylee's favorite snack. But Haylee couldn't swallow a thing. So, she used the cookies to brush at crumbs on her plate.

Staring downward, Haylee asked, "Should I go see her, Grandma? I don't know what to say." Grabbing more tissues, Haylee blew her nose.

"The best advice I can give you, honey, is to tell you, sometimes words are ineffective, especially when it comes to death," Grandma said. "I can't tell you what to say, but I can tell you what *not* to say. When you talk to Misty, don't tell her you know how she feels, or that she'll feel better in time. More important than what you say is your willingness to listen. Remember, Misty may not know what to say either, so you may be listening to absolute silence. But silence is preferable to empty words without any heart."

Grandma wiped the counter and took Haylee's plate to the sink. She put her arm around Haylee.

"You know, most people talk too much, because it gives them a false sense of control. But you've never done that, Haylee. Perhaps you're the best friend Misty could have right now, because you know words can't fix everything." Leaning with her arms on the island, Grandma reasoned, "Think about it. Your neurodivergence may be an asset, since you will give Misty the time to figure out what she needs and how to convey her needs."

A Divorce in Salem

Breaking the rest of her cookies into pieces, Haylee giggled as her grandmother rushed with another plate under Haylee's placemat. Haylee then tried to put her cookies back together. It was odd that a few missing chunks could make it so hard to do.

That's what her friendship with Misty felt like right now. Misty's mother's death had caused their friendship to fracture. And now, no matter what Haylee did, she wasn't sure their friendship could ever be the same again.

Looking up at Grandma, Haylee asked, "Do you think I should call her, or just go over to her house?"

"I suspect Misty and her dad are in the middle of making decisions about funeral arrangements tonight. A visit tonight might be viewed as an intrusion. What I would do is text her. Simply let her know how much you love her, that you're available whenever she feels like talking. Then after dinner, you and I can make some soup and pot pie for Misty and her dad. Most likely they'll be too busy to cook for themselves. You can deliver tomorrow whatever we make."

"That's a good idea. I'll text her right now," Haylee said. "I don't think Misty or her dad ever cooked any of the meals. Misty's mother did all of that for them."

Tearing up, Haylee thought she should have asked more about what Misty learned from her mother. I know she borrowed her mother's talent for meal and table decorating, but all I ever did was talk about me the whole time! I just assumed if she wanted to talk more, she would.

"Just remember, Haylee, Misty may not be available to chat with you right now. Accept what she can or cannot do. She will see from your lack of reaction, you're respecting her needs instead of foisting your own wishes onto her.

Haylee nodded. A feeling of sadness washed over her. There were so many potential pitfalls and regrets over how she behaved.

Haylee realized her grandma had a lot of great things to share, and Haylee struggled to reconcile how Grandma could be so wonderful today when she used to allow alcohol to steal so much from her mother. Haylee wondered if Misty felt similar about her mother. Maybe Misty's mother was lost the last few weeks.

Did Misty need more but knew she wasn't going to get more? Did she have to accept crumbs of contact rather than real connection? Haylee wondered if needs were going unmet all the way around from generation to generation. Haylee knew from her mother's stories that her grandmother wasn't happily married, and that unhappiness played a big role in thinking alcohol could numb her grandmother's pain. So, she wondered if Misty's mother ached as well, and once again, Misty, like Haylee's mother, couldn't engage or connect, so she used perfection as her way of avoiding the pain.

Haylee feared falling into similar traps even if she chose something completely different to self-soothe. Haylee saw many thieves out there maneuvering to grab adults. Smiling as she viewed herself as Athena, Haylee envisioned battling a future Tiffany; slashing any passivity she might tweak in her own thoughts of not speaking up for fear of making waves; wrestling the likes of alcohol, cigarettes, and drugs. Imagining herself using Aikido across her opponent's own weight was the only way to wage triumph over obsessions of all sorts; and finally, the ultimate slayer of all dragons: She would use charm to undo any possible Medusa or Pandora who dared to hijack her creative thinking. Haylee wanted better for herself and for her relationships.

Exhausted, Haylee chose not to eat the pizza Grandma had delivered for dinner. She wasn't hungry, anyway. Gathering courage, Haylee stared at her phone.

What should I say? Hey, I heard your mother committed suicide? Shaking her head, Haylee knew that was too harsh.

Instead, she opened her phone and went straight to Misty's contact. She thumbed, "Just wanting you to know, I am here. I hope you're okay."

Sighing, Haylee realized the only thing she wanted was her sketchpad. For once she didn't plan what she was going to draw before lifting her charcoal. Her heart simply directed her hand to pick up the charcoal and let the tool guide her hand across the page. Off-setting dark, rough strokes with light, gentle ones, Haylee's hands moved rhythmically. White space became light from the sun. Soon enough, the orb of an eye poked through the blank canvas. Strokes moved around the orb to show stress and sadness, some light gray lines, others heavy, almost onyx. Strands of hair covered the other eye, though not completely. It could still see.

Where have I seen this face before?

Around the face, she drew baskets and a candle on a silver holder. Beside it was a book, like a photo album, and all around the album, a ring of silver emerged.

Peering at what she'd created, Haylee gasped.

She had drawn an ode to Misty's mother.

25

You Can't Make Someone Love You?

The next day brought vivid sunshine; Haylee thought it was deeply wrong to have such a beautiful, balmy day.

Like the sun had betrayed Misty's mother.

Grandma packed the pot pie and carrot ginger soup inside a woven basket for Haylee to carry, and Mom placed a sympathy card on top.

"In your time of sorrow …"

It wasn't far to Misty's house, and though the basket felt heavy, Haylee was sure she could handle it.

"Are you sure you don't want me to drive you over?" asked Mom. "I can take you to school after, that way you won't have to worry about being late."

"No, thanks, Mom," Haylee said. "Walking over will help me think of what to say. And I don't care if I'm late to school."

Mom chuckled. "That's not a surprise."

Haylee chose to ignore her mother's sarcasm and grabbed her coat, just as Michaela waltzed down the stairs.

"I'm going with you," her sister said. There was no point in refusing. If anything, Haylee was relieved to not be going alone.

Down the block along the cobblestones they went, side by side, walking quietly. Haylee was careful with the basket. She didn't want anything to spill. At the same time, she was trying to think of the right words to say once they got there. Misty's house was just ahead when Haylee finally broke the silence.

I don't know what to say to Misty," she said.

Michaela nodded. "Me neither. Maybe something like, 'We made this for you, and then hand over the basket. They won't really remember what we say, and they'll appreciate the food. At least that's what Grandma says."

Haylee sighed. It dawned on her as they turned up the walkway that Misty's mother would never again be out there pulling weeds from around the Hostas, or arranging flowers in the pots, or adding things like Christmas lights and candles.

It felt like all the magic had vanished from Misty's house. Because Haylee's hands were full, Michaela rang the bell. They heard footsteps coming, but there was a long pause before the door opened.

Finally, standing in front of them, looming in the open doorway, was Mr. Bishop. He stood in silence. Although dressed, he didn't look the way he usually did in his business suit. Today, he wasn't wearing a jacket, and his shirt and pants were wrinkled. Not only were his clothes sloppy, but his hair was tousled, and dark stubble traced his jawline.

Mr. Bishop looked at Haylee and Michaela as though he'd practiced lines from a script ahead of time.

"Misty won't be going to school today," he said, and moved to shut the door.

"I didn't think she would," Haylee said softly. "We just wanted to give this to you. It's potpie and carrot ginger soup, and some baked goods. My Grandma made them." She lifted the oven basket hoping he would accept its contents.

"Misty doesn't want to see anyone," Mr. Bishop said, as if he hadn't heard a word Haylee had just said. He waved away the basket.

Haylee sighed with relief when Michaela spoke up.

"We don't want to intrude, sir, but Misty is a good friend of ours. We just wanted to know how she's doing, and to see if there's anything we can do."

Haylee again lifted the basket, hoping Mr. Bishop would take it, but he didn't. She thought maybe he hadn't noticed it, so she lifted the basket higher.

"Tell them to go away!" Misty's voice screeched from somewhere beyond the door. "We don't want their pity!"

"I'm sorry if this is a bad time, Mr. Bishop," Michaela said. "We'll go but we'd still like you to take the basket."

Mr. Bishop didn't say anything. He didn't take the basket. He just closed the door.

Michaela grabbed Haylee's elbow, and, for once, Haylee was glad to surrender to her sister's lead.

Haylee and her sister left the basket on the step and started running. They ran for a block before slowing.

Michaela bellowed, "I can't believe how rude he was! All we were doing was dropping off some food for them."

Haylee didn't know what to say. And even if she had, she wouldn't have been able to make any words come out. Her throat was clogged. She bit her lip to stop more rivers of tears. She tried to concentrate by putting one foot in front of the other to distract herself from utter desperation.

She just wanted to be home again, to crawl under her covers and to shut the world out. People always wondered why she didn't say much. Suddenly Haylee felt absolute clarity on the subject. Haylee didn't talk because the world became unsafe whenever you had words at your disposal.

By the time they got home, Mom had already left for work, but Grandma was sitting in the kitchen on a stool.

"How did it go?" she called out to them. "I'm surprised you're back so soon."

When Grandma caught sight of both girls' expressions, she jumped up and put her arms around Haylee and Michaela. Shaking her head, Grandma cried, "Aw, girls, you two wash up, dry your eyes, and I'll make us all a hot cup of tea."

In the half-bath, Haylee and Michaela splashed cold water on their faces, blew their noses, and headed back to the kitchen. It didn't take long for the teapot to whistle and soon Grandma had made their tea, and they were settled at the table together.

"Now, tell me," Grandma urged, "what happened?"

Michaela spoke first. "Haylee explained to Mr. Bishop that we had food for them. Grandma, I'm glad I was there as a witness, or I would have assumed Haylee offended them somehow. But she didn't! Everything Haylee said was the right thing to say, but Mr. Bishop didn't listen to her. Instead, he scared us, didn't he, Haylee?"

Haylee nodded and ducked her face closer to the steaming mug, so Grandma wouldn't see the new tears clouding her eyes.

Michaela continued. "Grandma, Misty's dad was *so* cruel. He just ignored Haylee. If he's always like that, it's no wonder Mrs. Bishop killed herself."

Grandma cut in, "Michaela! That's a terrible thing to say, and it's not appropriate. None of us know how....we'll react when someone close to us dies. Making judgments in situations like this doesn't help. Instead, you need to find compassion for his pain. What he's going through must be awful." She brought the cup of tea to her lips and suggested, "You must be understanding. He was probably so beside himself, he didn't realize he was being rude."

Haylee took a deep breath, hoping to stifle the sobs that threatened to burst forth.

"What really hurt is what Misty said, Grandma," "Misty knew we were there. And she shouted for us to go away."

Grandma handed Haylee a napkin to wipe her tears and blow her nose.

"Oh, honey. Like I said, grief makes people do and say things they never would say otherwise. There's no telling what Misty was thinking, but it could be that maybe she resents you for still having a mother when she doesn't."

Grandma realized she wasn't helping. Instead, she was just making both of her granddaughters feel guilty. Setting her teacup down, she said, "What I do know, darlings, is that you don't have anything to feel bad about. You tried to be a friend and that's all you could do. At this point, the best advice I have is to encourage you both to lay low for a few days. Misty's wounds are raw right now. Let her have a chance to grieve, and then you can reach out to her again. If she barks at you a second time, then retreat again until she chooses to come to you. Or not. But I think she'll come around eventually."

"Hey! What about the play?" Michaela asked.

"I don't know," Haylee sniffled. "We were supposed to have rehearsal after school today."

"While you were out, the director called and said rehearsal will be canceled for the rest of the week," said Grandma. "It won't begin again until Monday. She hopes Misty will come back after the funeral."

Michaela inquired, "Do you think she'll quit the entire play? Remember, her mother didn't want her to perform as the witch."

"I suspect the director is aware of that," Grandma said nodding. Clearing her throat, Grandma added, "I think the director is hoping this tragedy won't change Misty's mind about what she wants to do."

"Oh, it makes sense now," said Haylee. "Danielle and Carly came to my locker and suggested Danielle would replace me as the Princess! I didn't understand at the time what she meant. Now I get it. Danielle assumed I would be moved from the Princess role to the

Wicked Witch role if Misty no longer participated, because of trying to honor her mother's wishes. How diabolical can someone be?" Haylee suddenly found herself yawning from exhaustion.

"I don't even want to think about the play," Haylee murmured. "Grandma, can I stay home from school today?"

Grandma was silent, then finally she said, "Yes, dear. I think it'll be okay. I'll call the school and let them know."

"Well, I'm going," Michaela said. "I'd better go now, or I'll be marked tardy."

Grandma said something about driving Michaela to school, but Haylee didn't really listen. She took her cup to the kitchen sink, then called for Barney. Together, they trudged up the stairs to her room. Her refuge, where no one could hurt or abandon her.

She lay on her bed and patted the mattress to invite Barney up.

He leapt up, wagging his tail with pride. He seemed to realize Haylee's mood, because he quieted and settled next to her rather than hunkering at the foot of her bed. Ever loyal Barney, he didn't even circle five times, which always messed up her extra blankets. Instead, he curled up next to her back and snuggled close. Haylee closed her eyes. Surrounded by Barney's warmth, memories of the cave came to mind.

Perhaps it was time for her next visit to Stage Fort park. She only hoped it would afford the escape she sought, and not bring on any more despair.

26

'Cause Ya Gotta Have Friends

Bang. Bang. Bang.

Haylee squeezed her eyes shut and tried to ignore the noise.

Bang. Bang. Bang.

Awake now, she recognized the sound for what it was. Someone was knocking on her bedroom door.

"Haylee," Mom called. "You need to get up and get in the shower. You have to go to school."

Haylee didn't want to go. She'd slept most of the day before and through the night, so she shouldn't have been tired, but somehow, she still ached with fatigue.

"You can't stay home another day," Mom said, as if she'd read Haylee's thoughts. "Grandma was worried because you didn't eat dinner last night, so she made a big breakfast this morning. Talk about a treat on a school morning. So, get up, take your shower, and come down."

"Mom?" Haylee called.

Until then, Mom hadn't opened the door. But she did now, and peered in.

"Yes, honey?"

"What if kids ask me questions about Misty? What should I say?" Haylee asked. "I haven't talked to her, so I don't know anything."

"Then that's what you say: 'I don't know anything,' and quickly walk away. Don't hang around to see if they're okay with your answer," Mom said. "The more you avoid the things you dread, the greater your fear becomes. Which is why you need to go to school."

Haylee rubbed her eyes. "What happened to Barney?" The last she remembered he was curled up in bed with her.

"We had to let him out to do his business since Sleeping Beauty would not yet awake." Haylee's mom smiled and shut the door.

Haylee nodded, and somehow got up and dragged herself to the shower, where she took longer than usual. Haylee believed water from a shower nozzle held magical power, offering the receiver insights otherwise lying dormant. She had read about Avalon and watched Brigadoon, and both suggested certain imaginings came forward through water and in their due time.

Dressed in a white blouse with a rounded collar, a blue tartan skirt, and dark blue knee socks, Haylee hoped no one would notice her care to her appearance. She pulled a yellow ribbed sweater over top and grabbed a pair of loafers from her closet. She remembered Dr. Raintree had pennies in his, so she found a couple of new, shiny ones from the change from her last trip to Casselman's Hardware and carefully slipped them into the slots in her loafers.

Next, Haylee fixed her hair by winding a high ponytail on top of her head. Normally she didn't do much with "the beast" other than brushing it and letting it air—dry, but today she gathered the sides up and secured them with decorative bobbly pins. Finally, she wound a yellow scarf around the high ponytail.

The aroma of bacon drifted up from the kitchen.

Haylee rushed downstairs and through the hall to discover Grandma at the stove with Barney at her feet. He clearly swooned over the smell of bacon, too.

"Smells good, Grandma," Haylee said, as she settled on her stool.

Grandma turned around. "Oh, my! Haylee, don't you look wonderful! Let me take a picture."

Haylee rolled her eyes as Grandma grabbed her cell phone off the counter. Michaela was much more adept with her phone than Grandma; it took her forever even to find the camera icon.

"Oh, here we go. Smile pretty!" Grandma clicked the button.

With picture taking done, Grandma got down to the business of serving breakfast. She brought Haylee a tall glass of orange juice. A few seconds later, she delivered a plate piled high with scrambled eggs, rye toast, cottage cheese, and bacon strips.

Haylee was not a fan of cottage cheese. She must have made a face because Grandma used the spatula for emphasis and said, "Cottage cheese and scrambled eggs were meant to go together. Try it. You'll see."

Haylee forced a smile and gulped some orange juice. A piece of bacon was next. But she didn't finish it. Instead, she dropped the leftover piece for Barney to grab. He seemed quite pleased with the unexpected treat.

"Grandma?" Haylee murmured, "I'm nervous about what to say when kids ask me about Misty, or, even more stressful, her mom? Mom says I should just say 'I don't know.' But what if that's not good enough? What if the kids keep asking?"

"You tell them Misty is helping her father make funeral arrangements," Grandma said. "Even though you haven't spoken with Misty, we know this is what's going on. So you'll be giving kids an answer without lying."

That was a better option than Mom's, but Haylee doubted it would be any easier using Grandma's suggestion.

Mulling over both ideas, Haylee moved her fork around the scrambled eggs and cottage cheese, then decided to slather butter on the toast.

Woof! Woof! Barney barked as he lifted his head. The snout lift was his signal to Haylee any leftovers should go to him and would be much appreciated.

"This isn't bacon," Haylee told him, biting off a corner.

Squawk! cried Mr. Mallard from the mudroom.

Haylee hadn't seen the duck at all yesterday, and it felt weird.

"Patience, Mr. Mallard." Grandma chuckled. "I'll see to you after Haylee goes to school."

Haylee finished her toast, stared at the rest of the food on her plate, and decided she'd better get it over with. Loading her fork with scrambled eggs as well as a dollop of cottage cheese, she urged,

'Courage, girl!'

Tentatively, she closed her eyes and took a small bite. The two textures, hot and cold, married in her mouth and slid down her throat.

"Grandma!" Haylee blurted. "This *is* good!"

Grandma shook her spatula and grinned. "I didn't survive sixty-four years without learning the art of culinary combinations, young lady."

Thrilled by the taste, Haylee downed the rest of her food, and oddly felt better. Energized.

"Thanks, Grandma," she said. Picking up her plate, she started for the sink.

"I'll get that for you, dear. You'll miss the bus if you don't get going."

Minutes later, wearing her pea coat with backpack slung over her shoulder, Haylee headed outside. Seeing her breath, Haylee realized the temperature was much lower. The surprise in temperature drop forced Haylee to acknowledge the confidence she'd felt eating breakfast in the kitchen withered like some of the daffodils lining the sidewalks.

She remembered how two days ago in the cafeteria, Brandon and Josh had ignored her. When she spotted Brandon at the bus stop, she didn't know what she should say. She didn't know whether she should try to talk to him anyway, but how would she react if he ignored her attempt to talk? Doubt surged from her stomach and slid like a chute in a silo. Gastric acid raced to the back of her throat.

As it turned out, she didn't have to do anything.

Brandon shuffled over to her, and though he didn't look at her, he mumbled, "Hey, Haylee."

"Hey," Haylee echoed.

Brandon kicked at a loose stone on the sidewalk and murmured, "It's so strange, what happened. I tried to call Misty, but it went to voicemail. I didn't know what to say, so I didn't leave a message."

It was a relief to know Haylee wasn't the only one Misty was avoiding. But she also felt bad for Brandon. She understood his confusion, so she suggested, "I think Misty just isn't ready to talk yet. When I tried, she wouldn't see me either. I think if my mother died, I wouldn't want to talk to anybody for a while, either."

"Yeah, but we can't just do nothing. If we don't try, then Misty will think none of us care," he said. He swung his backpack closer to his neck rather than nearer to his shoulder.

Haylee thought that was an astute thing for Brandon to say. Never before had she considered Brandon an astute kind of guy.

"My grandmother suggested I wait a few days," Haylee said. "I think maybe she's right."

Brandon stuffed his hands into the pockets of his football jacket.

"Misty likes you, Haylee. You're her best friend. I've heard her say that," he said. Pointing with his hand in his jacket pocket toward Haylee, he explained, "You probably don't know this, but before you came to John Proctor, she always hung around Danielle. But Danielle was mean to her. Even so, Misty kept going back for more. I didn't even know Misty that well, but I saw the way Danielle treated her, and it made me mad."

Haylee was even more stunned by comments from Brandon than she'd been before, not because of what he'd said, exactly, but because he'd been so observant. She couldn't believe he, of all people, noticed others' behaviors like that.

"Hey!" Josh hollered, waving as he lumbered across the street toward them.

Brandon acknowledged Josh but looked right back at Haylee. Apparently, Brandon had more he wished to convey.

"You know," Brandon added, "you're the reason I auditioned for the play. When I heard Misty was auditioning, I figured, of course she would. She likes being on-stage. You know I'm a jock. I play football; I am not an actor. But then, when I heard you were auditioning, I changed my mind. You're so shy and quiet, and you're new, too, and I thought, if you could do it, maybe I shouldn't be so chicken then."

Haylee was floored by the notion she, Haylee, had been an influence! And an influence on a jock! Literally, she had to compel her mouth to shut.

Brandon chuckled. "And you know what's the coolest thing about it? I've made new friends. Cool ones. People I really like hanging out with. You. Misty, and a few others."

"Me, too," Josh chimed in. "I too wouldn't have auditioned if it weren't for you, Haylee. And then, look what you did for me at my house. You got my father not to be mad at me that I not only tried out but got the leading male role. You were why my dad didn't disown me. You've been a good friend. You and Misty both. I feel bad that Brandon and I used to tease you on the bus."

Haylee lowered her head, hoping neither boy would notice tears pooling in her eyes. If they did, she hoped they would chalk it up to the chilly temperature.

Fortunately, at that moment, the bus pulled up to the curb.

"You go first, Haylee," Josh said.

She appreciated that, not only because it was sort of a gentlemanly thing to do, but also because it gave her a chance to swallow a few times and compose herself.

She settled in a seat by herself, figuring Josh and Brandon would sit together in the seat behind her, like they usually did.

Instead, Josh plopped down right beside her, and Brandon flopped down in the seat across the aisle.

"Maybe we should go see Misty together?" Josh suggested.

"You guys can go," Haylee told him. "I'm going to wait a couple days."

"Please, Haylee," Brandon said. "Please. It wouldn't be the same if you're not with us. The four of us are like a team. If one of us is missing, it's not the same energy. We have to go together. We are two pairs of oxen, yoked together."

They all burst out laughing.

Haylee had never felt as though she'd belonged before. She would have described herself as Misty's tagalong, the same way Brandon described Misty with Danielle. But if what Brandon and Josh were saying was sincere, they didn't think of her that way. Not at all. They considered her part of the team. *Their* team.

For the first time in her life, Haylee had friends—friends who liked her for who she was.

"Okay," she said. "We'll go together."

And she smiled, even though she couldn't shake the feeling of doom that hovered across her chest. As warm as Brandon's sentiment was, Haylee felt an eerie dread.

27

Another Win for Michaela

Taking the bus home from school that afternoon, Haylee chewed on the sides of her fingers near to bleeding. She, Brandon, and Josh were supposed to visit Misty, but Haylee didn't think it was a good idea. Not yet anyway. As Grandma had said, Misty needed time to absorb the shock of her mother's death.

While Haylee desperately hoped Misty wouldn't be angry any longer, she had a feeling that wouldn't be the case. The whole thing left her torn between wanting to do the right thing for Misty and disappointing her friends, Josh and Brandon.

Fortunately, the boys spent most of the bus ride joking about something that had happened to Josh in gym class. He'd intercepted a pass from the football team's quarterback, someone neither Josh nor Brandon liked. They both thought the star football player was stuck-up. So, Josh's maneuver to block the jock's pass led to much laughter and jubilation between them, as it had made the guy look less athletic, downright inept.

It wasn't until the three of them were on the last leg of their journey, that Josh turned to Haylee. "I'm not trying to ignore you," he said.

As he'd done that morning, Josh had once again sat next to her on the bus with Brandon across the aisle. Haylee was happy when Josh leaned back and placed an arm over the seat behind her.

"It's okay," she muttered.

"Maybe we should figure out what we're gonna say when we get to Misty's?" Brandon suggested. "The only thing I know to say is that we've been thinking about her," Josh said. "What do you think, Haylee?"

"I don't know," Haylee contemplated. "I'm still worried that if all three of us go, she might feel like we're ganging up on her."

"How could she think that?" exclaimed Brandon. "We're just making sure she knows we care."

Haylee wanted to tell them again how upset Misty had been when she and Michaela had gone over with the food for Misty and her father. And she wanted to warn them about Mr. Bishop's rudeness, too, but she'd already mentioned that. There didn't seem to be any point in repeating herself. Brandon was determined, and so was Josh.

"What if Haylee's right, though?" Josh chimed in. "What if Misty doesn't want to see us? What do we say then?"

"I don't know," Brandon mumbled.

"Well, I've heard my mom say to her friends, 'Give me a call when you feel better,'" Josh said. "So, I'll say that. Except I'll say, 'Send me a text when you feel better.'"

"I wasn't nervous before, but now you're making me twitchy," Brandon said.

Biting her lip to keep from laughing, Haylee thought Brandon's wording was hysterical.

Apparently, Josh thought it was funny as well, because he snickered. "We can't have our bro feelin' twitchy."

Since he'd laughed, Haylee let a few chuckles escape, too.

Waves of guilt flooded Haylee in her belly. Immediately, she thought it awful she could giggle and enjoy her friendships when her best friend just lost her mother.

The bus lurched to a stop and all three of the friends piled off.

The smell of chimney smoke hit Haylee right away. It grew stronger as they made their way down the block toward Misty's house, but nothing billowed from Misty's chimney. Whoever had a fire burning, it wasn't from the Bishop's.

But smoke wasn't what now drew Haylee's attention.

There, on the curb, in front of Misty's house, were several trash cans filled to overflowing. As they approached, Haylee lifted one can and recognized the contents.

Misty's mother's decorations were put out on the curb as though they never mattered.

"How could they toss out her things so soon?" Haylee blurted before she could stop herself.

Beside her, Josh shrugged and shook his head.

"That's just creepy!" agreed Brandon. "What's the rush?"

"Something's weird about Misty's dad," Haylee said softly. Maybe this had something to do with Misty yelling the way she had. But she couldn't say that to Josh and Brandon. She didn't know quite how to explain it.

"Let's get this over with," Josh muttered.

Brandon led the way, Josh following behind, and Haylee brought up the rear. By the time Brandon rang the bell, they were all on the porch.

Haylee held her breath, hearing footsteps coming toward the door.

Misty cracked the door ajar, just enough to peer through with one eye.

"Hey, Misty," said Brandon.

To Haylee, he sounded overly jovial.

Misty didn't say anything.

Brandon, glancing at Josh and Haylee, said, "We don't want to bother you. We just wanted you to know we're thinking about you, and we've missed you at school. It's not the same without you there to joke around with."

"Joking is the furthest thing from my mind," Misty snapped.

"Yeah," Brandon replied, regretting his words. "I can only imagine."

"Misty, if you want, I can bring home your social studies assignments, and give you copies of my notes," Josh said. He fidgeted like he did at the bus stop sometimes, except there were no little pebbles to kick on Misty's porch.

"There's no need," Misty said. "My dad has all that coming directly from the teachers. Is that all you wanted?"

None of them knew what to say. They just stood there quietly.

Misty seemed to notice Haylee for the first time. "I thought I told you to leave me alone," she said roughly.

"Geez, Misty," Brandon said. "We were just trying to be nice. Sorry if you think we're intruding."

"Well, you are," Misty said coldly, and shut the door.

Josh yelled loudly enough that Misty was sure to hear on the other side of the front door, "Text me when you're feeling up to it!"

Haylee wasn't about to stay on that porch for one more second. She ran down the stairs and bolted away.

Behind her, she could hear Brandon and Josh trying to catch up, so she increased her pace. She wasn't running, but she was speed-walking.

Haylee didn't want to cry in front of them, but no matter how much she tried, she couldn't stop the perpetual stream of tears. That's when she felt Josh grab her hand.

"Hey, Haylee," he said, squeezing. "I wish I knew the right thing to say, but I don't."

Looking at Josh was a mistake. A torrential downpour slipped down her cheeks.

"I ... I don't know ... what ... I ... did ... to make her hate me so much," she hiccupped.

Josh gripped her hand so firmly, Haylee had no choice but to stop walking when he did.

"*You* didn't do anything wrong. None of us did. We don't deserve her spite. I think all we can do is forgive her, and like you said before, give her space." Josh leaned close, put his arms around her, and brushed her lips with his.

This was the last thing Haylee expected, even though she'd kissed him once before. Like that other time, Haylee savored the softness of his mouth, and the way her head felt a little bit dizzy when he pulled away.

When she looked over at Brandon, she saw him kicking at the loose pebbles in the street.

"Please don't cry, Haylee," Josh begged. "We'll stick together. That's all we can do. We'll be her friends again when she's ready."

Haylee used the sleeve of her coat to wipe her face. "How are we going to get through the play without her?"

"Well, we could pretend she really *did* turn into the Wicked Witch," Brandon said. "At least for the time being."

That made Josh chuckle, so Haylee did, too.

"Thanks, you guys," she said, when she could find her voice again. "Thank you for being my friends. And for trying to make me feel better. I appreciate it."

"You make us feel better, too," Josh affirmed.

"That's what friends are for," Brandon said.

"We'll walk you home," Josh offered, and so the three chose the quickest path through several backyards and an alley.

Haylee found herself both baffled and comforted by these two boys—her friends—walking on either side of her the whole way up Essex Street. They didn't stop until she was standing on the stoop in front of her door.

"Bye, Haylee," said Josh.

"See you later," said Brandon.

"Thanks, guys," said Haylee, and she pushed the door open.

Greeted with the smell of onions sautéing in the kitchen, Haylee knew her Grandma was cooking.

"Is that you, Haylee?" Grandma called out. "Dinner will be ready in ten minutes. We're eating light tonight. Hamburgers, fries, and a garden salad."

"That's okay, Grandma," Haylee called back. "I um .. I ate at Brandon's house, so I'm not hungry. I have homework, so I'm going to my room." Both things were lies, but Haylee knew if she went to the kitchen, Grandma would take one look at her and know something was wrong. Mom would see right through her, too.

"Oh, dear," Grandma said, coming around the corner and wiping her hands on her apron.

Haylee pretended she was busy hanging up her coat, so she wouldn't have to look Grandma in the eye.

"Do you have enough time to run out back and check on Mr. Mallard? I'm afraid I got busy and haven't had a chance. I'm getting worried about him. He's been out there alone all day." Grandma uttered her request with a smile, as she wiped her hands on her apron of spring flowers.

"Sure, Grandma, I can do that." Haylee grabbed her coat again and flipped it around her shoulders, slinking by so Grandma wouldn't get a good look at her face.

On the back porch, she grabbed the scooper and a bag of duck feed. Next, she headed to the heated kennel.

Squawk! hailed Mr. Mallard as he poked his head out and waddled toward her. Haylee couldn't help but smile. The silly duck seemed to realize that she was a friend, a friend who cared about him.

She stooped down and reached out tentatively. Mr. Mallard didn't stop her from rubbing his neck. In fact, he waddled even closer and then plopped his head on her shin.

"Do you like that?" she asked.

The way he nudged her with his beak was a perfect answer.

"Okay, enough petting," Haylee told him. "We need to scoop your droppings so you can waddle around and not get dirty. Then I'll take care of your food and water."

While she spoke, she did each consideration. Soon enough, Mr. Mallard sank his entire bill into the fresh bowl of water, and Haylee giggled.

Kneeling near the duck to stroke his neck, she said, "You're lucky. You understand what's expected from your friends. I don't know what to do to fix my mess. I only know the friendship with my best friend is broken."

Squawk! Squawk!

Haylee stayed with him for a few more minutes. She would have stayed longer if she hadn't gotten so chilled by the early spring air.

As she slipped out of the kennel, she spied another rose quartz crystal. How she'd missed it when she came outside, she didn't know, but there it was, plain as day, in the grass.

Stuffing it into her pocket, Haylee ran to the porch stairs. Wondering if she'd be able to sneak past Grandma again without being seen, Haylee peered in the back door.

She didn't need to come through all the way to hear Michaela bellowing. Apparently, her sister had come in through the front while Haylee had been with Mr. Mallard. And Mom was home as well. They were both in the kitchen with Grandma.

"Mom, isn't it fantastic?" Michaela asked. "Dad's coming the day of prom. He'll get to see my dress and meet Jason!"

Haylee knew this was the plan, and so did Michaela, but the way her sister made it sound, she'd just talked to Dad on the phone. Either that, or he'd texted her.

It had been a long time since Haylee had heard from Dad.

I wonder if this time he asked about me.

Haylee crept closer and right away saw the nerve jumping in her mother's cheek. Nerve dancing meant Mom was clearly upset about this development. The only thing Haylee could think to do was plop down on a chair and lean over, pretending to tie her shoes.

"What time will he be here?" Grandma asked. "Did he mention where he will be staying?"

"I didn't think to ask." Michaela frowned, but the expression quickly flipped. "This will be the greatest day of my life! I can't wait to tell Jason! I'm going to text him right now."

"Wait a minute, dear," Mom said. "Did your dad say whether he would be bringing ... anyone?"

Michaela rolled her eyes. "Mom, you know he broke up with Tiffany, remember?" Michaela placed both fists on her hips. "Do you know what your problem is? You want Haylee and me to think the worst of Dad. But I'm not going to. He's my father."

Lunging forward, Mom glared and said firmly, "Michaela! Don't you dare speak to me that way!"

Grandma knew her daughter and granddaughter were triggered for different reasons. She grabbed Elizabeth by her elbow. "Now, Elizabeth, I need your help with Michaela's dress. I'd like you to look at the finishing touches I put on the dress today."

Mom yanked her arm out of Grandma's grasp. "I'm certain it's fine. Michaela, don't you dare walk away from me. Ouch! Mom, what are you doing?"

This time, when Grandma took hold of Mom's arm, she got her right above the elbow where the nerves are sensitive. Haylee could see Grandma's grip was fierce. There was no way Mom would get away since Grandma dragged her off.

"Oh, Haylee, I didn't see you come in," Michaela said. "Did you hear? Dad will be here Saturday. I can't wait."

"Did he ... did he ask about me?" Haylee stammered.

"Well, no," Michaela said. She seemed to catch herself and quickly added, "He was at work. He had several patients, and he didn't have a lot of time." Then she lowered her voice and said, "Check it out. Grandma's gonna give Mom a what-for for not Spilling the Tea sooner. Ha!"

Haylee couldn't think about anything other than the fact that her dad didn't even ask about her. It felt like the walls of the kitchen were folding inward. Stifling. Smothering. Biting her lip, she told Michaela, "I have homework. I'm going upstairs."

But the retreat to her room didn't afford her the quiet and privacy she craved. Grandma was lecturing Mom, and their voices were far louder than whispers.

"I don't get it," Mom yelled. "Can't you see what an upheaval his pop-in custodial time will be for the girls? He thinks he can just text his daughters, without telling me? My therapist said parents aren't supposed to use the kids as messengers. Dan and I talked about this, and he agreed. So, help me, if he disappoints those girls any more than he has already, I'll ... "

Mom didn't finish her threat. But it didn't matter. Haylee resisted the urge to barge in there and scream.

"What about your snipes at Dad? Don't you think those hurt us? What about *your* boyfriend? Why would you think we'd be on board with that upheaval?"

Haylee lay on her bed looking up at the ceiling fan.

"Elizabeth," Grandma said, "you'd best watch your tone when you speak of Dan or his behavior. Your body language as well as your tone suggest you wish to lunge at him in anger. It's no wonder he avoids you and communicates his plans to the girls instead."

"Great! You're taking his side again," Mom snapped. "I suppose you think his outreach to Michaela was an awesome idea."

Grandma paused. "Elizabeth, you know that Dan stopped seeing Tiffany, yet you still bring her into the conversation. Need I remind you that you're seeing Jeremy?

Go Grandma!

"I applaud you for seeking a therapist to help you and Dan learn to co-parent, and also, to help you find your way, and learn more about who you are and where you want to be in the future.

But I encourage you to go for a walk, listen to music or try something else you love whenever you feel the urge to scratch Dan's eyes out, especially when the urge hits you and your girls are within their ear range. And whatever you do, do not blame your daughter when she has been used as a messenger. Smile and reach out to Dan yourself to get details of his itinerary. You can even invite him to have dinner with us and Jeremy. You can show the girls it's a new chapter!"

"You think I've been a terrible mother," Mom whimpered.

"Of course not," Grandma said calmly. "Honey, you are behaving like a mother tigress protecting her cubs. I get it. I do. But you have girls whose five senses are keener than yours. They're young, so they pick up on everything. Mark my words, they absorb your rage."

Grandma held her daughter's face in the cup of her hands.

"When they figure out, you're the parent who is angry, the girls will point the finger at you as being at fault, not only for the divorce, but also for your inability to get along afterwards. They will assume that means Dan is the victim!" Grandma chuckled. "But if you let the girls figure things out for themselves without adding intense emotion into each situation, they'll be able to see things from other perspectives and vantage points."

"God, Mom, how often I forget you're a recovering alcoholic. Your wisdom never fails to piss me off," Elizabeth replied. At least her voice wasn't raised this time.

"Honey, I'm wise because I'm a drunk. Recovery meant I finally dared to look up," Grandma said. "People who struggle with addiction see everything, which is why we crave escape in the first place."

"Okay. Try harder to say as little as possible. Do me a favor, though. Don't make one of your killer roasts—Dan doesn't deserve one."

Haylee went to her bedroom door and closed it quietly.

She's heard enough today. She'd heard way more than enough.

28

The Walls Are Closing In

Grandma was showing Mom the finished alterations to Michaela's gown. She dragged the garment bag from her closet, unzipped it, and carefully removed the dress. Haylee stood outside Grandma's bedroom, as she too wished to see her grandmother's work.

Elizabeth gasped. "Oh, Mother, it's exquisite! What a beautiful, professional job you've done!"

Both Grandma and Mom were teary-eyed. Grandma used her hanky to blow her nose, then shoved it into her apron pocket.

"I hope she likes it," Grandma said. "I've worked on it every day. See how the rhinestones and crystals pick up the light?"

"Let's not show it to Michaela until tomorrow. I want her to be surprised. I know she'll feel like a princess," Mom declared. Putting her hand out toward the dress, Mom asked, "How do you think she should do her hair?"

Smiling, Grandma walked over to her vanity and picked up a small, jeweled box.

"I thought we could ask the stylist to put her hair up, with wavy tendrils brushing the nape of her neck. And look at what else I got," she said, opening the box. "You put them throughout the hair. Each rhinestone coil catches the light. See how they coil around the tresses? Grandma held up a coil of thin wire, threaded on the ends were rhinestones. The coil makes certain each tress holds the rhinestone in place, offering different prisms from when light refracts."

"Oh, Mom, these are beautiful!"

Grandma urged, "We can't forget to take lots of pictures. I'll use my phone, too. That camera feature sure is handy."

Mom chuckled and kissed Grandma's cheek.

"I'll be down in a few minutes," Grandma said. "Dinner's ready. I just want to put the dress and hair coils away."

Haylee quickly tiptoed back to her room and closed the door. Lying on her bed, she stared at the ceiling and willed herself not to cry. Why, oh why, was eavesdropping a possible, frequent trait of neurodivergence? Rivers of tears flowed despite her resistance, and Haylee couldn't decide whether they were flooding down her cheeks because of Misty's rejection, or her dad's.

All Hayley knew, her father hadn't asked about her AGAIN.

Dad didn't care about her because she wasn't anything like Michaela—pretty or social, able to get good grades or have her sister's sense of style. Haylee wasn't someone Dad could be proud of. Instead, she was labeled complicated, stubborn, and prone to misread social cues.

The divorce had offered him a convenient excuse to distance himself further from his messy, difficult child. The child who, no matter how she tried, would never be good enough.

How could anyone be expected to love someone who is neurodivergent?

"Dinner!" Grandma called from the bottom of the stairs.

The doorbell rang, and Haylee heard her mother welcoming Dr. Raintree.

Not again.

As if everything else wasn't bad enough.

Haylee didn't want her mother dating Dr. Raintree. Wasn't it enough that she had to watch her father betray her mother; move states away; go to a new school; meet new kids; lose the city she had adored; find treasures in the Commonwealth of Massachusetts; discover a best friend, and, of yeah, lose that very best friend. Listing the changes, the upheavals made Haylee exhausted. But obviously, Mom and Michaela glided through change effortlessly.

Why couldn't her mother wait until Haylee was in college, or at the very least, no longer living at home? That way Haylee could coordinate her visits back home to avoid him, or have her mother come and visit her at college without Dr. Raintree.

From her room, Michaela shouted, "Be right down!"

A moment later Michaela pounded on Haylee's door. "You in there? C'mon. It's dinnertime."

Haylee scrambled off her bed. "I'll be down in a minute," she yelled to Michaela, hoping her sister wouldn't barge in.

For once, Michaela didn't and respected her boundary. Haylee needed to get to the bathroom and splash cold water on her eyes. The last thing she wanted was for Dr. Raintree to see she'd been crying.

Still in the bathroom, Haylee heard Michaela's chipper voice.

"Hey, Dr. Raintree."

"It's okay to call me Jeremy," he said. "Dr. Raintree' sounds kind of stuffy, don't you think?"

Haylee took one last look in the mirror before heading down the stairs. She did her best to sound as bright and friendly as Michaela.

"Hey," she said.

"Hi, Haylee. Good to see you," he said, just as Mom took his coat in exchange for a glass of wine.

He didn't tell me *to call him Jeremy.*

"From now on, *Jeremy*," Mom teased, "you can hang your coat up yourself. No standing on ceremony here." Then she leaned in close and kissed him on the cheek.

Haylee turned away so no one would see her repulsion.

She wondered what Mom would say when she told her everything, she'd dug up online about Dr. Raintree. What Haylee needed now was a plan on how to reveal it.

29
She'll Either Ignore You, or She'll Bite

Fans of Mass Hysteria history and witchcraft believe Salem is at its best in autumn. So, Haylee had been told. Every year, schools delivered busloads of children of all ages to walk the downtown cobbled streets, meander through the shops on Pickering Wharf, and visit its museums.

This year, however, schools and municipal authorities scheduled a day for students of all ages to enjoy all that Salem offers on the day before prom. The celebration-packed weekend was why Salem schoolchildren had been given a field trip day that Friday.

Haylee believed she alone knew a secret: Salem is at her finest in spring. Window boxes adorned houses and store fronts with ferns, hydrangeas, baby's breath, tulips, daffodils, lilacs, and peonies. Red bellied woodpecker, goldfinches, blue jays and song sparrows woke the town with cheerful tunes. The town of Salem became busy and alive with hope and endeavor in spring.

Haylee's school began their fieldtrip in the afternoon, to stagger the overload of bus parking. Haylee saw how shopkeepers had decorated their windows with children and teens in mind. Storefronts sported chocolate witches, marshmallow figures in pillories, candy chocolate rabbits, yellow peeps, and chocolate footballs in colorful foils as decoration in window fronts. Tarot card and palm readers stood outside the shops to make the most of the onslaught of young people meandering about.

Knowing it would be Misty's first day back after her mother's death, Haylee got to the bus stop early. She'd followed advice from both Grandma and Mom, so she hadn't contacted Misty again, especially after their second encounter made it clear Misty was done with a friendship with Haylee.

But on this auspicious day, she would have no choice but to face Miss Stalemate.

Of course, Haylee longed for Misty to greet her warmly, as she'd always done in the past. She didn't know what would happen today. She didn't know whether she should say hello first, or let Misty make the first move.

Just as she was deciding to go with a conservative, but friendly, "Hey, Misty," Josh and Brandon arrived. Haylee sighed with relief they'd gotten there before Misty. Their presence, and support, would make things easier. Or so she hoped.

"Isn't it awesome we have a field trip today? What a great way to end the week," Brandon said. He pulled cash out of his pocket, smiling. "Check it out. I saved thirty bucks just for this occasion."

"Cool! You can buy me an aura reading," Josh teased.

Haylee giggled.

As usual, when Danielle arrived, she stood on the other side of the light pole, draped in yellow, pink, and blue ribbons for the festivities. Danielle ignored the three of them and acted as if Haylee, Josh, and Brandon were too far beneath her to warrant acknowledgment.

Perhaps because Haylee was staring at Danielle, she failed to notice Misty's arrival. And she wouldn't have if it weren't for Josh bumping her with his elbow in warning.

Both Josh and Brandon seemed as uncomfortable as Haylee. Brandon kicked pebbles, while Josh stuffed his hands in his pockets and stared at Haylee like he was afraid to look in any other direction.

Misty approached, her steps slowing, though she didn't fully stop. "Hey, guys. How are ya?"

"We're good. How're you?" Brandon stopped kicking pebbles.

"Great, thanks," Misty replied. Still moving, Misty brushed by Josh. She put her hand on his arm and spoke in a lowered tone, "Josh, I hope to see you later on the field trip."

Then without another word, she sauntered toward the light pole and said, "Hey, Danielle. What's up?"

"Phew!" Brandon whispered, so only Haylee and Josh would hear. "At least she seems to be talking to us again."

Haylee was taken aback. Hadn't he noticed that Misty had completely snubbed Haylee? She wanted to scream at Brandon:

"Are you deaf?"

Luckily, Josh spoke before she could open her mouth.

"Uh, ... Brandon, didn't you see what I saw? Misty's talking to *Danielle*. Not Haylee."

As much as Haylee appreciated Josh being observant, his pity was just as mortifying. The only thing she could think to do was turn to wait for the bus and pretend she was indifferent to all of it—all of *them*.

Thankfully, it wasn't long before the bus arrived. They boarded, and Josh took the empty place by Haylee. She turned her head and stared out the window, but this didn't stop her from noticing Josh's arm stealing across the seat and behind her.

She couldn't stay mad at Josh, no matter how hard she tried.

A Divorce in Salem

As usual, Danielle chose a seat as far away from them as possible. Haylee assumed Misty would sit next to Danielle, her new BFF, but that's not what happened. Instead, Misty came up the aisle and stopped right in front of them.

"Hey, Brandon, slide over, will ya?" she said.

"Sure," he mumbled.

The bus lurched forward as Misty observed, "Isn't it awesome? My first day back and it's a field trip."

"Yeah, only half a day of boring classes," Brandon said laughing. "You'll hang with us during the field trip, won't you, Misty?"

"Of course," Misty said. "You're two of my best friends."

Haylee could feel Josh looking in her direction, but she refused to turn her head from the window.

"Well, I'm hangin' with Haylee," Josh said.

"Where do you and Brandon want to go first, Josh?" Misty asked, as if she hadn't heard his comment.

"I wanna hit the Monster Museum," Brandon said. "That place is really cool. It'll be a great place for the four of us to start."

It was just as bad that Brandon was now forcing Haylee into the picture.

"Sounds good to me," Josh said.

Turning with arm extended, Misty suggested, "After the field trip, would you guys like to come over, so we can practice our lines? If not this afternoon, how 'bout this weekend sometime? What do you think, Brandon? Josh, will you be able to?"

"Sure. I could do this afternoon and this weekend. You don't have anything else going this weekend, do you, Josh?" Brandon asked.

"No, I don't have any plans," Josh said, looking at Brandon as though he must be losing his mind, since Josh never spoke about "plans." He and Brandon were either at practices or they hanged out together.

For a moment, they rode in silence.

Josh broke the tension when he asked, "Misty, are you purposely not including Haylee?"

Haylee spun and thumped his arm.

Misty didn't look at either of them. Instead, she spat with an eerie, toothy smile, "Haylee doesn't have to be glued to my hip, tagging along with everything I do, does she?"

Nobody said anything after that.

As the bus reached school, the usual bottleneck in the aisle developed. Fumes in the air reeked of oil. Haylee imagined the bus was commiserating with Misty to add further insult to her torture.

Brandon and Misty got off first, laughing and acting like nothing was different or unusual. Josh clambered down next, but he stopped and waited for Haylee. The two walked together to the main entrance.

On the steps, Josh said, "I'll meet you right here before we leave for the field trip, okay?"

"Okay," Haylee said.

"See ya later. Keep your chin up," Josh said.

"Thanks," Haylee told him. "I owe you."

"No, you don't," he said with a smirk, "But if you insist, you can do my algebra homework."

Haylee smiled. All the way to her locker, she kept thinking of what he'd said like a mantra to self-soothe from injury.

Keep your chin up. Keep your chin up.

Despite the effort, by the time she got to her locker, she changed it to: *Don't cry. Don't cry.* Further insult occurred in first period.

Their desks were right next to each other, yet when Haylee entered the classroom, Misty was already seated. She didn't even look in Haylee's direction when Haylee sat down.

Instead, Misty spoke to Carly on the opposite side of her.

"As much as I hate to admit it—and you know I hate school—it's good to be back," Misty said. "I missed you guys."

"We missed you, too," Carly responded. "I'm really sorry about your mom. I'm sure your friends were there for you, though. That's so cool."

"Huh?" said Misty, sounding confused.

"Your friends, Haylee, Brandon, and Josh," Carly reminded. "The four of you are always together, so I just thought ... "

"Oh, Brandon and Josh were really sweet," Misty interrupted. "They came over." She paused, and said, "You know, Carly, we should hang out more. I'll text you. Maybe we can get together this weekend."

"Yeah, we could do that," Carly said. "Danielle's coming over to my house to help my sister get ready for prom tomorrow. You could come too if you want." She swiped her phone to access her calendar.

"Great," Misty said. "I'll do that."

Haylee didn't want to hear any more games. Listening to Misty talking with Carly had hammered the final nail in the coffin. Misty didn't consider Haylee a friend any longer.

At the end of class, Haylee left as quickly as she could. She didn't want to hear the new BFFs chatting again about their plans for the weekend.

It just so happened however that Danielle was in Haylee's next class. Normally, Danielle didn't pay any attention to her, but today, she breezed in and came right over to Haylee's desk.

"Carly told me Misty's coming over to her house this weekend. She's hanging with us now," Danielle said.

As Haylee wondered how someone so pretty could act so callous, it dawned on her, she knew exactly what Danielle was trying to do. It was like she was Cruella de Vil, and Haylee was a vulnerable Dalmatian puppy.

"So, what happened between you two?" asked Danielle.

"I have no idea what you're talking about," Haylee retorted.

"Brittany says you and Misty aren't friends anymore." Danielle smirked. Danielle's expression reminded Haylee of a horse-toothed sneer like the ones in silent movie melodramas.

Haylee refused to bite. Instead, she busied herself with opening her textbook and pulling out her homework. "Well, anyway, I'm sure you'll straighten everything out by the time we have dress rehearsal. In the meantime, I hope you have someone else to confide in. It sucks when you don't have a best friend anymore."

With that, Danielle flung her ponytail over her shoulder and flounced toward her desk. Haylee noticed when Danielle sat down, she realized Danielle had a snag in her sweater. Haylee couldn't help but smile as she watched Danielle try to hide the sweater pill.

30

Feeling Trapped

French was the last class of Haylee's abridged school day. The teacher, Mrs. Boatman, was a rounded, short woman with dyed, shiny black hair. She reeked of perpetual perm solution. Underneath the jet-black, shoe-polish color, Haylee could see much of Mrs. Boatman's scalp. Fascinating, Haylee could see Mrs. Boatman was going bald.

Regardless of the visual and olfactory distractions, Haylee enjoyed her class, because the teacher wove French history, cooking, travel, art, and music into each lesson, and did so while speaking French the entire time.

When Haylee first arrived in Salem and had toured John Proctor High, she'd overheard Mrs. Boatman speaking French to a class. The rapid sounds and stresses of the language felt overwhelming to Haylee's ears. Upon discovering she needed to take the class, Haylee believed she'd flunk. However, after a few days, once she'd relaxed and absorbed the rhythm, Haylee discovered that speaking French was a talent that had lain dormant within her.

The problem again centered on seating. What had seemed perfect at the beginning of the year now held Haylee prisoner. She sat in the third row between Brandon and Misty.

Making certain she got to the room before they did, Haylee looked neither left nor right. She grabbed her textbook and homework from her backpack and concentrated on the map of France hanging on the wall in front of her.

Donegal, the boy who sat in front of Haylee, showed up next. He sat down, but immediately turned around in his seat and said, "I heard you and Misty had a fight and you're not friends anymore."

Haylee didn't like Donegal ever since his insistence on staring at her drawings. She didn't know why he did this, but it unnerved her.

She decided not to say anything this time as he loomed over her artwork. Thankfully there wasn't enough time for him to say more, because right then, Brandon and Misty waltzed in.

Haylee didn't look at either of them, but she felt Misty's eyes bore into her. The glance was brief, as Misty let out a horrible fake cackle, and put her hand on Brandon's arm.

"I can't wait till this afternoon, Brandon. I always have so much fun with you. You're not dull, like some people I know."

Donegal's eyes bulged. It was like he was trying to goad Haylee into flinging back some nasty comment. Luckily, she knew what Misty was doing, and that the stinging words were meant for her. But what was she supposed to say? Haylee ignored both.

When her manipulation to goad Haylee failed to manifest into yelling, Misty quickly took her seat and Brandon his. Their positions meant Haylee was sandwiched between them.

"Misty, we're hanging with Josh and Haylee on the field trip, too," Brandon said. "Right, Haylee?"

At least Brandon hadn't looked straight through her like she'd become invisible.

Misty spoke up before Haylee could respond.

A Divorce in Salem

"I already told you, Brandon, we're meeting Danielle and Carly at Crow Haven Corner to have our tarot cards read. Too many at one time would just overcrowd the store."

"Aww, Haylee's not invited," Donegal mocked.

Haylee cleared her throat. "It doesn't matter. I already have plans with Josh."

"Why would Josh stay with you when he can be with Danielle and Carly?" Donegal asked. Donegal had a habit of acting as though he was an organic part of any overheard conversation.

Misty laughed. "Of course, Josh will come with us. He's not a complete fool. Oh, but will that ruin your plans, Haylee? I guess you'll be a little lost without him."

Haylee was done.

She grabbed her backpack and shoved her homework and textbook inside. Rising out of her seat, she then tromped up the aisle.

Behind her, Brandon pleaded, "Misty, what's your problem?" Then he called out, "Haylee, where are you going?"

Haylee didn't answer. She didn't yell and she didn't cry. She didn't wait to hear Mrs. Boatman's daily greeting,

"*Bonjour, mes* élèves. *Comment t'allez—vous?*"

Haylee vanished from the classroom. She sprinted through the hallways, grabbed her coat from her locker, and then raced to the main entrance of school.

Once free, Haylee let her feet fly along the sidewalks, through the streets, across the cobblestones, past shops, factories, statues, and houses. With no plan in mind, she hurried down La Fayette Avenue and onto Pickering Wharf. The whole time, she allowed only one image to prevail in her mind.

Grandma.

Haylee pictured her grandmother's welcoming, enfolding arms. She belonged to someone who understood her.

The only problem with Haylee's plan was, Grandma wouldn't be home yet. The realization came about the same time as the stitch in her side required her to slow down and surrender to the pain. The ache and pang in her side only served to remind her of the day she walked in on her father kissing Tiffany, Dad's 'dental hygienist'. Another excellent reason to stop running.

Exhausted, Haylee realized she was three doors down from Crow Haven Corner—the same place Misty, Danielle, and Carly intended to go for tarot card readings that afternoon.

Because of the crowd out front, Haylee thought of her father's office and realized the store offered a side door unrecognizable to most customers. She quietly entered the darkly painted shop through a similar side door. Inhaling, Haylee's nose picked up the scents of incense, spices, and herbs from Crow Haven Corner's Garden behind the shop.

Seeing her, the young cashier with fiery red hair asked, "Would you like a tarot reading?"

"How much is it?" Haylee only had so much money with her.

"Normally a half—hour reading would cost forty-five dollars, but Mary Ann is offering a special fifteen-dollar discount today," the cashier said.

Haylee had enough for a reading. She retrieved the bills from her pocket and said, "Yes, please."

The cashier took the money and said, "Mary Ann is with another client now, but you'll be next. You can look around while you wait. What's your name, so I can jot it in the ledger for her?"

"I'm Haylee, spelled H-A-Y-L-E-E."

While she waited for her turn, Haylee browsed the glass encased shelves around her, filled with jeweled swords, dowsers, essential oils, and bangles. The colors and prisms of light intrigued her, but what attracted her even more were the books.

Haylee adored books. They never disappointed the way people did. Because she couldn't resist, she retrieved several to explore their contents. "Haylee?"

Haylee spun around. The woman was older with long gray hair. Her outfit was a simple peasant blouse and gypsy skirt but layered with numerous brightly colored scarves. The ensemble reminded Haylee of new-age fairy magic, and she liked it.

There was something else about the lady, though. Haylee didn't know what it was. She looked strangely familiar. Haylee couldn't remember where she'd seen her before. Maybe that was why ...

"How did you know my name?" Haylee blurted.

The magic lady chuckled. "I'm good, but not that good. Your name is next in the ledger. I'm Mary Ann. Come on back, and I'll do your reading."

Haylee followed Mary Ann through strings of beads attached to the lintel of the doorway. Ushering, magic lady led Haylee into a darkened area, lit solely by candles. An intricately carved wooden chair with a red velvet upholstery stood in the back. Sitting in the Victorian chair, Mary Ann gestured for Haylee to take her seat in the not-as-regal chair across from her. In the center of the table lay a deck of colorful cards.

Mary Ann stared into Haylee's eyes, her gaze so intense, Haylee usually would look away, but something urged her to confront the stare by drawing her eyes to MaryAnn's generously applied lipstick. The technique of averting her eyes to the mouth was another trait of neurodivergence. The locking of eyes downward afforded Hayley to appear polite without making herself uncomfortable. Instead, she forced herself not to look away.

Seconds seemed like minutes. Hayley shifted her hip in the chair. Finally, Mary Ann spoke.

"I need for you to think of three questions you'd like to ask. And while you're thinking, I'd like you to shuffle the cards and cut the deck."

Haylee obeyed.

After the first shuffle, Mary Ann asked her to shuffle again. And then a third time.

When Haylee finished, Mary Ann inhaled and instructed, "Now, choose any four cards, and lay them on the table in front of you, facedown. I will turn them over."

Haylee chose her cards with care, making certain she didn't just pick from the upper part of the deck.

Once the cards were fanned out, MaryAnn considered each one. Flipping the first card, she said, "This is the Hermit. It means you're a loner, a person who prefers to be by herself, and you don't trust many people."

"That's true," Haylee murmured.

The second card revealed the Queen of Hearts. Mary Ann explained, "There is someone watching out for you who cares about you very much. She is a woman of great mystery and wisdom."

"It must be my grandmother," Haylee said.

Mary Ann's eyes lowered. "No, I don't think this is your grandmother. Perhaps the other cards will reveal more about who she is."

Inhaling through her nose and exhaling through her mouth, MaryAnn closed her eyes for what Haylee guessed was her tool for concentrating.

"Ah," she murmured, "the Nine of Swords. This tells me you are in an argument with someone—someone who has hurt you deeply. This person is behaving as though she hates you, and she's blaming you for something."

Under the table, Haylee's toes curled in her shoes. "For what?" she asked. "I don't understand what I did wrong."

"Is it possible she knows you would ask such a question?" Mary Ann's long, polished, fiery-orange fingernail pointed to the card.

"I ... how would she know that?" Haylee whispered.

Mary Ann peered into Haylee's eyes with an even more intense gaze.

"If this person can get you to believe *you* did something wrong, then perhaps she doesn't have to ask the question of herself."

"Oh," gasped Haylee. "Her mother died, you see. She committed suicide."

Mary Ann did the inhale—exhale thing again and bent closer to the cards. The behavior made Haylee think MaryAnn could listen to the card selection even prior to her turning over the card.

"Perhaps she's asking the same question of herself because she thinks *she's* done something wrong. She's wondering what she could have done, or did she say something that triggered her mother. Questions, that ironically make her the star in her mother's death. I call it the ego's Capital, small 'i'.

Perhaps she's searching, through history and time, could she have done anything to prevent her mother's death? You and I both know she didn't do anything to make her mother choose suicide, just as you haven't done anything to intentionally hurt your friend."

Haylee leaned forward over the table, too.

"Do the cards say anything else?"

"Choose another card, please," Mary Ann said, resting her arms on the sides of her lush, velvet Victorian throne.

Haylee did so, this time from near the bottom of the deck.

Mary Ann turned it over. For a moment, she said nothing. She just stared at the card.

"What does it mean?" Haylee asked.

Mary Ann reached over and took Haylee's hand. "Dear girl," she said, "this is the Hangman. Often, it is interpreted as being bad. But it does not always imply doom. You must choose another card. The two together will better determine what this card is trying to tell us."

The card Haylee picked next was the Five of Swords.

Mary Ann breathed in and out, and said, "This tells us you'll soon walk into a difficult experience. You may even feel lost somehow."

A pause entered as though it were a person coming into the space between Haley and the Tarot Reader.

Not being able to tolerate silence anymore, Hayley begged, "Can you tell me more?"

"That I cannot do," Mary Ann said. "The only thing I can do is warn you to be careful, especially of missteps."

After that, Mary Ann collected all the cards together and made the deck neat and tidy.

"Is there a way to prevent taking these missteps?" asked Haylee.

Mary Ann closed her eyes and laid one hand on the cards and the other hand over her heart.

"That is a wise question, Haylee. Remember the benefit of a reading is to help a person make shrewd decisions, choices with the reading in mind."

Haylee fidgeted. "But how can I do that if I don't know what the misstep will be or even when it will occur?"

"Pay attention to the choices you make over the next several days. Watch your words, especially around your friend, so that you don't anger her further. She is wounded, Haylee, and wounded people often act aggressively. The ricochet of pain only serves to make, what is, already raw and gaping, fester further. Make certain you step carefully. Now is not the time to take risks."

Mary Ann let go of Haylee's hand.

That was it. The reading was over.

Haylee grabbed her backpack and stood up.

"Thank you. I appreciate the advice, and I will be careful. May I ask one more question?"

"You may," Mary Ann smiled.

"I feel like I've met you before. Even your voice is familiar," said Haylee.

Mary Ann laughed. "I'm told that often. I believe it's the star alignment. Keep in touch. I'd love to hear how you and your friend are doing."

Outside the store of Crow Haven Corner, Haylee thought of everything the reading had offered. She wanted to be able to give Misty the benefit of the doubt. Misty was dealing with enormous grief, and on top of the loss, Haylee realized Misty's father wasn't very empathetic.

But the things Mary Ann had said about wounded people also reminded Haylee that she'd been wounded, too. Wounded by her father when he contacted Michaela and didn't even bother to ask about her; wounded by a relocation when both parents were taught transitions were difficult for Haylee's neurodivergence; and wounded by a sister who viewed Haylee as a pest. Haylee argued with herself, she hadn't taken out her hurts on Michaela, Mom, or Grandma, or even Misty. At least Haylee didn't use victimhood as an excuse to vent and perpetuate wounding.

What Misty was doing—unleashing Pandora's box of venom on Haylee—was not fair, and it was wrong. Haylee sat on a bench by a sugar maple tree to give her legs a rest for a few minutes. Still obsessing over Misty, Haylee thought what Misty was doing was not going to bring her mother back. If she kept up her snobby attitude of feeling entitled to isolate Haylee from friendship again, she'd worked so hard to attain. Misty would soon learn Misty's image would end up tarnished like neglected silver. Peers witnessing her maltreatment would not trust Misty for the knowledge she tried to divide one friend from another.

Haylee knew she didn't have time to linger any further, and she knew her thoughts were serving to make her more upset than she already was. Besides, if she stayed, she just might run into Misty, Danielle, and Carly. By now, the last class had ended, and the buses would soon arrive.

Quickly, she rose from the iron bench and walked on, this time stepping carefully, and doing her best to avoid cobblestones. Cobblestones weren't an issue in Chicago. Haylee missed Chicago for that reason alone. But Hayley asked herself if she was venting her own hurt feelings by blaming Salem for the way Misty was displacing her grief and morphing the loss into anger on Haylee.

Concentrating on each step, Haylee failed to notice what was going on around her. A noise alerted her, people were approaching. When she looked up, there, not more than half a block away, were Misty and her entourage as well as Brandon and Josh trailing behind.

Until that moment, Haylee had forgotten she'd promised to meet Josh at the school entrance.

Suddenly, it felt like bricks were lain on her chest, making it hard to breathe. She hadn't been there where she said she'd be. Haylee had broken her promise to Josh, the one person who consistently offered her kindness and courtesy.

Haylee stopped, hoping they wouldn't notice her. But of course, they did. There was no way to avoid them, as they were heading straight toward her.

"Salem always turns out the best witches," Danielle said chortling. "Oh sorry, it's only Haylee Higgins."

Misty burst out laughing, and so did Carly.

Haylee bit her lip.

Silently, she repeated to herself,

Misty's coming from a wounded place. Misty's coming from a wounded place. If I forgive her, I am released from resentment. If I forgive her, I am released from resentment.

The only thing she could think to do was to walk, so that's what she did, right past them, and right into Brandon and Josh.

"Hey, Haylee," Brandon said. "You went AWOL."

Haylee kept her eyes downward so she wouldn't have to look at either of them. Josh was silent. She assumed his silence meant he was mad.

"Hey," she said anyway.

Josh still didn't say anything.

Their exchange gave Misty a chance to veer back. She sauntered up to Brandon and hooked her arm through his.

"Brandon, Josh, come on. Let's hit the pirate museum" instead of the Tarot reading. It's way too crowded right now."

"That place?" Danielle sneered. "That's so sixth—grade."

"Yeah, it's boring," Carly agreed.

"Where do you suggest, Danielle?" Brandon asked.

"I say we go to the Dungeon Museum, where they imprisoned the witches. I've heard it's haunted," Danielle said.

"Great idea," Carly chirped.

"All right, let's go," Misty announced. "C'mon, Brandon, Josh. Danielle's right, the Dungeon Museum is the coolest."

With that, Misty tried to coax Danielle and Carly to follow, but when they didn't, she surrendered and stood with the two girls and continued to listen.

Brandon followed the girls, but Josh didn't. He just stood there with his hands in his pockets.

Gathering his courage, Josh looked at Haylee and said, "I waited for you. When you didn't come, I ran all over the school looking for you. I almost missed the bus."

"You didn't have to do that," Haylee snapped.

She'd had enough of Danielle and Misty. She didn't need Josh to scold her on top of it, even if she *was* the one who'd broken the promise.

"No, I guess I didn't," Josh said.

"What's this?" Misty said. "Josh, haven't you figured out by now how immature Haylee is?"

Josh spun around.

"Misty, what's your problem? If you don't want to be friends with Haylee anymore, fine. Just leave her alone."

"C'mon, Josh," Brandon coaxed. "Dude, people are staring at you."

"So?" Josh retorted. "Let them."

"Aw, isn't that sweet." Misty batted her lashes and cackled. "Josh has a crush on Haylee. He wants to be her real Prince Charming. Maybe he needs to read a romance—for—-dummies manual."

Danielle guffawed. So did Carly.

Brandon grew irate. "God, Misty, you can be such a ..."

"Witch?" Josh finished.

"Who needs you?" Misty scoffed. "C'mon, Danielle, Carly, let's get away from the nerds. Salem just isn't the classy town it used to be."

They took off and didn't look back.

Brandon remained with Josh and Haylee.

"We know what she really is, and it's not a witch," Josh said. He shuffled gravel under his shoe.

"Maybe," Brandon defended. "Remember, her mother just died. I think something's really wrong, and we don't know what that is." He started to walk but then immediately stopped. "I think we should talk to Haylee's grandma. She always has good advice."

Haylee shuffled her feet. "My grandma's not home. You guys can go with them if you want. I gotta go home and let Barney out."

"I'm sorry I gave you a hard time in front of them," Josh said. "I shouldn't have done that. It's just—Brandon said you ran out of French class, so I was worried."

"It's okay," Haylee replied. "I'm sorry, too. I was upset and forgot that I'd promised to meet you."

"I just don't understand why Misty is suddenly so close with Danielle now. If anyone's a witch, it's that one."

"Well, listen, I'll talk to you guys later," Haylee said, moving away. She offered a half wave, the best she could do. "I gotta go."

"We could come with you," Josh called out.

"Yeah, you sure you don't want company?" Brandon added.

"No, thanks!"

Haylee didn't look back.

Haylee thought she had to put all 'Misty stuff' out of her thoughts and focus on what the fortune teller told her during the reading.

Right now, I need to watch my step.

31

The Need For A Plan

Normally when Haylee got home from school, she was eager for a snack. Not today. Not when her stomach lurched and felt as hard as one of Michaela's field hockey pucks.

Facing a problem so vast there didn't seem to be any way to solve it, left Haylee despondent. She lost her father to divorce and her best friend for … she didn't even know why she lost Misty.

Ever since her parents' separation, Haylee had grappled with the idea of collecting memories of her dad. But each memory she recalled left her with an image so distorted, she wasn't sure anymore if she had it right. Would she recognize him when he came to visit? Right now, she couldn't even remember the sound of his voice.

Maybe that will happen with Misty, too.

She only hoped it wouldn't take as long, so she could forget about her.

As usual, the minute she came through the door, Barney started barking, panting and circling her legs.

"You can't wait for your walk, can you, boy?" she said, going to grab his leash from the hook in the kitchen.

As soon as the lead was attached, Barney darted for the back door.

"You just want to see your buddy, Mr. Mallard."

Barney's tail whipped to and fro. Normally the sweet dog's antics made her laugh, but she couldn't do that today, either.

Soon they were outside and on their way up the sidewalk.

"Now that it's getting warmer, you're going to help me plan when I can get to the cave. I know I'll feel better when I'm in that place. I just need to figure out how to get away from here. It'll have to be when nobody would notice."

Barney sniffed a fire hydrant with particular interest.

"I've got it!" Haylee exclaimed. "I'll go as soon as Dad arrives. Everyone will be so busy oohing and ahhing over Michaela's gown, they won't see me leave."

Barney looked up and wagged his tail.

"Never fear, Barney," Haylee scratched under his ear. "I have my headlamp, picaxe, and flashlight for exploring the cave floor. I'll bring extra clothes, just in case. I'll make sandwiches, too and will bring some cheese and crackers. I'll fill a thermos with water, too."

Resolved, Haylee felt better than she had in days.

They finished his walk a few minutes later by circling the block. Navigating the gate that led into the backyard, Haylee scurried over to the bench under the tree to make certain her cave supplies were as she'd left them.

They were.

Upon further thought, she decided to move them to the garage in case Mom or Grandma decided to do any spring gardening and came looking inside the bench for garden tools.

Squawk! Mr. Mallard said as they passed his kennel.

Woof! said Barney, tugging on his leash.

"Sorry, Barney, no time to visit Mr. Mallard today," Haylee told him.

"There you are!" Grandma said as soon as Haylee stepped inside.

She must have gotten home while Haylee and Barney were on their walk.

Already at the sink, Grandma was prepping dinner. "How was the field trip?"

"Fine," Haylee lied.

Grandma opened a drawer and took out a paring knife. "Well, I have some news," she said. "Seems your father will be here tomorrow at three o'clock. He said he wants to get here early, so he'll have plenty of time to take pictures of your sister in her gown."

"Oh." Haylee grabbed a magazine from the counter and thumbed through it.

"So, tell me, Haylee," Grandma asked, as she plucked an onion from the hanging metal basket. "You haven't said much about seeing your father. Aren't you excited?"

Haylee shrugged. "It's no big deal. If he comes, he comes. Makes no difference to me one way or the other."

Grandma peeled the onion with skilled hands.

"Well, that's a cosmopolitan attitude," she said. Her eyes focused above her glasses.

Haylee didn't know what Grandma meant by that. She shrugged again. "I'll go check on Mr. Mallard."

Upon hearing this, Barney darted to the back door and wagged his tail.

"Sorry, Barney," Haylee murmured. "I think you'd better stay here this time."

All it took for Mr. Mallard to come waddling over was hearing the kennel gate. But Haylee didn't go through it right away. She couldn't, because there in the grass lay another heart-shaped crystal.

This time, Haylee didn't pick it up. She didn't look around either, but she did say aloud,

"Whoever you are, I'm not afraid of you. You're not funny, and you're not scary. You mean nothing to me."

No reply, but she didn't expect one.

It didn't take long to fill Mr. Mallard's water dispenser and dump a scoop of food in his bowl. Grandma had filled up the kiddie pool, so now the duck swam in a pond of his very own. The last thing Haylee needed to do was replace Mr. Mallard's bedding. Once those chores were finished, she took a moment to stroke Mr. Mallard's shiny, green neck.

Squawk! said Mr. Mallard. Just as she clicked the kennel gate shut, an owl hooted overhead. She heard something rustling in the bushes—a squirrel, maybe? It wasn't fully dark yet, but it was getting there. A shiver whispered down Haylee's spine.

She stared at the crystal, long enough for the rock to become blurred by her stare. Haylee raised her chin and waltzed right on by.

32

The Princess Who Happens to Be Your Sister

Sunshine peeked through Haylee's curtains. Rubbing her eyes, she plopped her head back down on her pillow and murmured, "Just a few more minutes…"
It was not to be.
Outside her door, Michaela said loudly, "Isn't it the most glorious of days?
Haylee grabbed her pillow and pulled it over her head.
"Wake up, sleepy head!" Michaela barged in, flinging the door open wide.
"Go away," shouted Haylee into her pillow.
"But it's such a beautiful day, and it's Saturday," Michaela said. "You love Saturdays." Michaela zoomed into her room and loomed over Haylee. Pushing on her shoulder, Haylee said,
"Hey—did somebody overdose on cranky pills?"

"I'm going to use aikido moves on you if you don't stop," Haylee warned. She didn't need to look out from beneath her pillow to know Michaela was rolling her eyes.

"Oh, so you're a dog now, are you?" Michaela giggled. "Don't forget, Dad will be here at three o'clock," said Michaela. "I want to be finished with my hair, nails, and makeup before he gets here." She marched out, leaving the door wide open behind her.

What a pain in the butt!

Haylee would have preferred to spend the day with her friends, Misty, Josh, and Brandon. They could rehearse lines, or just wander around Salem together. That would have been a perfect day.

Except she couldn't do that because, oh, right, Misty wasn't her friend anymore.

Haylee threw off blankets and got up. She went through the motions of making her bed, then ambled downstairs.

Before she reached the bottom of the steps, she heard Mom and Grandma chatting in the kitchen, talking about eggs and milk for making French toast.

Haylee shuffled in and went to the cabinets to get cereal and a bowl to put it in.

"Haylee, honey, Jeremy will be here around noon," Mom said, looking up from her newspaper.

"Oh," mumbled Haylee. She settled on her usual stool, the one where she could be the first to see who else would enter the kitchen.

"Wouldn't you rather have French toast?" Grandma asked. "That's what I'm making for your mother and Michaela."

"No, thanks, Grandma. Cereal's fine," Haylee told her.

"Are you feeling ill, dear?" asked Grandma.

Haylee shook her head.

"Is everything okay?" Mom's newspaper crinkled.

"Geez," Haylee snapped. "Can't a person eat breakfast in peace?"

The room got quiet.

Haylee noticed her mother's narrowed eyes and the slight shake of Grandma's head—Grandma was telling Mom not to scold her yet. For that, Haylee felt grateful. She also adored Barney for sauntering over to beg for food. Stealthily, Haylee slid him a corn flake, and then another.

"Hand me the obituary section, if you don't mind, Liz," Grandma said. "I like to make sure my name's not mentioned."

Haylee smiled, though she tried to hide it.

"You know Grandma and I will be busy today, helping Michaela get ready," Mom said. "You're welcome to help, too."

"That's okay," Haylee murmured.

"You might have other plans? I shouldn't have assumed," Mom said.

Haylee swallowed a mouthful.

No, she shouldn't have assumed, but at least she'd noticed that she does and admitted it. In the scheme of things, it didn't much matter what Mom and Grandma thought, not when Haylee had an important mission ahead of her.

Of course, she couldn't say what her true plans were. To do so would ruin everything. What she needed to do was make sure Mom and Grandma weren't on to her.

"I have to walk Barney and take care of Mr. Mallard. I also have homework, and I'd like to work on some drawings."

"Oh, what are you drawing?" Grandma asked curiously.

This was why it wasn't good to lie, Haylee mused, because once you started, you had to keep covering the first lie with others. It was a vicious, perpetuating cycle.

Truthfully, Haylee had no plans to draw. In fact, ever since the row with Misty had begun, Haylee's normal inspiration seemed to have vanished. She didn't even *feel* like drawing, which was just odd.

To placate Mom and Grandma, Haylee said, "I'm not sure. Maybe some scenes from the play."

"That's a great idea," Mom said. "Those drawings could be useful. I'm sure your drama coach will want to use them for advertising."

"Mom! I don't draw for other people. My drawings are for my eyes alone."

"Haylee, I don't know why you're so testy today," Grandma scolded. "But talking back to your mother is unacceptable. You already bit her head off once this morning, and I let it slide. I won't this time."

Haylee stared down into her almost empty bowl. She felt the familiar sting behind her eyes and the lump paying rent in her throat. It was a big one—big enough to make it difficult for her voice to work right.

"I ... I'm sorry," she managed.

Speaking was a mistake. Her voice was operating like a dam overwhelmed by her tears. Soon streams turned to rivers of salty tears gushing down her cheeks. The only thing she could do was keep her head down, so Mom and Grandma wouldn't notice.

"It's okay, honey," Mom said gently. "Won't you tell us why you're so upset? Is it because of Misty?"

"I d-d-don't know wh-what to do," Haylee choked. "Misty h-hates me, and I d-d-don't know why. I don't know h-how to f-fix it."

"Time for a cup of tea," Grandma said, and she got up to set the kettle on the stove.

"Yes, a cup of tea is in order" Mom agreed. "We've got three generations of women here, and if we put our heads together, we can come up with a good solution. But we need lots of tea to stimulate our mental resources."

"It's no use, Mom," she sniffled. "Even Josh and Brandon tried to stick up for me, but even their input didn't budge her animosity. Misty still hates me."

Mom handed over a napkin so Haylee could blow her nose.

Nodding her head and pulling out her designated stool, Mom sat next to Haylee. She smoothed Haylee's hair off her shoulder. "Do you know, something similar happened to me when I was your age. My friend's name was Susan Malone. Mom, do you remember her?"

"Of course, I do," Grandma said. She poured hot water into each teacup, dealt three tea bags, and loaded cups to Mom and Haylee as she talked. The sugar and honey sat in front of them. Shaking her head, Grandma recalled,

"She gave your mother such a hard time." Out of the blue, Susan decided she didn't like your mom anymore, and she said a lot of nasty, mean stuff. Your mom cried and cried. I felt awful for her. The same way I ache for you."

"W—wh—at did you do?" asked Haylee.

Mom sighed after she sipped and when she wasn't satisfied with the taste, she poured more honey into her cup.

"I wasn't as strong as you, Haylee. I couldn't eat or sleep. Do you know, I literally groveled to that girl? She had so much power over me."

"Teen-aged girls, your age, figure out words have as much, if not greater power to wound than physical abuse, and some use that power to be quite cruel," Grandma said as she poured more hot water into their mugs.

"Boy, is that ever true!" agreed Mom.

"But why?" whimpered Haylee. "Why do people have to be so mean? I don't get it."

Grandma said, "Bullies are usually kids who feel they have no control in other areas of their lives. It could be something as simple as a bossy sibling or a demanding parent, or the problem could be more severe like actual abuse. The bottom line is, something has hurt them, and the only way they can make themselves feel better is by making others feel as bad as they do."

"Grandma's right," Mom said adding another full cup of hot water from the kettle. "I know it's not easy to understand, Haylee. Someday, though, it will all make sense to you. You'll see everything clearly. You'll look back on this time and realize it helped you become a stronger person."

Haylee didn't know about that, but at least the lump in her throat was shrinking, and her tears were slowing.

"Can I tell you something weird?" she asked.

"Of course," Grandma said leaning toward Haylee across the kitchen island.

"Sure, honey," Mom said at the same time.

"When Brandon, Josh, and I went to Misty's the other day, we saw Mrs. Bishop's decorations and stuff in their trash cans. Can you believe it? Mr. Bishop had already put them out for trash day."

"Ohhh," Mom murmured. "That's so sad. Especially for Misty."

Nodding, Grandma said, "Misty's hurt is what is called 'the walking wounded." Now, I don't think she'll be like this permanently ... hopefully. Think of how it is in nature. Let's say, a mother bear is strolling through the woods with her cubs." Grandma pushed aside her mug informing Haylee, Grandma thought what she was saying was more important than her tea. Mom was watching and listening intensely, too.

"Imagine now, one of her cubs spots a wolf pup whimpering. The bear cub thinks he's met a new friend to play with, so he wants to rush over to meet the wolf pup. Imagine the bear cub's shock when his mama bear swipes him back toward the Mama bear, even snarling at him when he motions toward the wolf pup again." Grandma put her mug in the sink, explaining, "I'll put them in the dishwasher after our chat, because this is important." Grandma said.

Both Mom and Haylee sat on the edge of their seats.

"Why would the mama bear be so mean? Doesn't she love her cubs?" asked Haylee. She sipped her tea without lemon, sugar or honey.

"Hayley, she swipes at the bear cub to warn the cub, and she is not trying to hurt it. She wants the bear cub to understand. Analyzing why a wolf pup is wounded could put her bear cub in jeopardy, because when it is wounded, it can lash out for fear of being hurt more if the bear cub used his paw with sharp talons to get to know him.

Hayley shook her head. "So, what are you saying? You think Misty is like the wounded wolf pup?" she asked.

"Exactly, Haylee. We do not know what Misty is thinking or feeling right now. So, to engage her when she is so raw isn't going to help you and it isn't going to help her. Think about it. Even on an airplane, we're told as adults to put the oxygen mask on ourselves first before trying to put one on a child.

It is important, Haylee, that you take care of you, so that if Misty ever returns to a stable state, you'll be able to listen to what all she was going through. Don't waste that energy on setting you up for further rejection, just like the Mama bear warns the bear cub that now is not the time to try to make friends with the wolf pup." Grandma squeezed lemon into her tea.

"It may seem cruel how the Mama bear teaches her cubs, but she knows there is a time for approaching, and a time to back away. Right now, you need to back away from Misty, and the retreat doesn't mean you've given up on the friendship. But you're anxiety is right, too. You don't know if she'll ever be your friend again." Grandma said.

Mom had tears in her eyes.

"Thank you, Mom," she said.

It didn't matter whether Misty ever came to her senses. She was going to the cave later. There, she could figure out a real solution. She was certain the cave would offer its own wisdom.

"I'm sorry I snapped," Haylee murmured.

"We know, dear," Grandma said.

"It's okay, honey," Mom said.

Haylee got up to take her mug to the sink just as Mr. Mallard let out a loud squawk from outside the mudroom in the kennel Mom made for him. It reminded Haylee of something else—something of dire importance she hadn't told anyone yet.

She turned around and said, "I have something else to tell you. Something I must warn you about."

"What's that?" Mom asked.

Haylee cleared her throat.

"I looked up Dr. Raintree online and discovered something terrible. He's not the great veterinarian you think he is. He was sued."

"Sued for what?" Grandma asked.

"Because of the ducks in the pond."

Mom smiled, and Grandma chuckled.

"Why are you laughing? It's not funny," Haylee said.

"We're laughing, honey, because we already know all about it." Mom said.

"You do?" Haylee said. "Then, Mom, please tell me why you are still dating him?"

"Perhaps you misunderstood the details of the lawsuit," Mom said. "Jeremy fought to *preserve* the pond for the ducks and geese."

"I don't understand."

"It was a pretty complicated suit," Grandma said, "but it goes something like this: The local township wanted to keep the ducks and geese from defecating around the pond. The township's solution was to poison them, so they couldn't reproduce. Our Dr. Raintree proposed a green solution, one that wouldn't harm the fowl, but at the same time, would limit how many geese would come to the pond, so the townspeople would be happy, and the birds would be able to thrive."

"Wow. I guess I really got that wrong." Said Haylee. She fiddled with a label on the honey jar. "I keep messing up." Haylee slapped her forehead in disgust.

"You're not messing up," said Mom. "You're a normal teenage girl, with some really hard stuff happening in your life right now. It's only natural that you're stressed over me dating, and that you wanted to know more about Jeremy." Mom put her arm around Haylee, and

Haylee bristled from her gesture of affection. "Haylee, I like Jeremy. I really do. But it's important to both of us that you and Michaela feel comfortable about our relationship. That's one of the reasons we decided not to tell you about it at first—"

"You aren't even divorced yet, Mom," Haylee cut in.

Haylee saw her mother glance toward Grandma for help.

"Your mother deserves to be—" Grandma started.

Haylee interrupted her, too.

"I don't want to talk about it anymore. I have homework to do. I'll be in my room."

She raced up the stairs and slammed her bedroom door.

At her desk, she grabbed her backpack and scrounged around for a notebook and pen. Her assignment was to write an essay about the Salem witch trials. Haylee wrote about Reverend Parris who, before he became a minister, operated as a rumrunner out of Barbados. He moved to Salem and, despite his lack of credentials from a credited seminary, became a minister in Salem village.

Somehow when she pictured Reverend Parris in her mind, Haylee pictured him as the spitting image of Dr. Raintree.

As Haylee finished her paper, the doorbell rang. A glance at her cell phone told her it was already near noon. She couldn't believe she'd been working on the paper for so long.

Downstairs she heard Mom open the door.

It was Dr. Raintree. Haylee had no desire to see him, but Michaela was down there, being all jokey with him. Dr. Raintree teased her right back. This was the only reason Haylee headed downstairs.

As soon as he saw her rounding the corner Dr. Raintree said,

"Haylee! How's Salem's best duck savior?"

Haylee could have done without the comment. She wanted to come up with a reason to make him leave, but she couldn't think of any.

"I'm fine," she mumbled. "And so is Mr. Mallard."

"I can't wait to see how well he's doing," Dr. Raintree said. "I'll go check on him as soon as we have a slice of your mother's awesome pie."

Apparently while Haylee was upstairs writing her essay, Mom had been baking. She'd made him an apple pie.

"Smells good, Mom," Michaela gushed. "I shouldn't eat any though. If I do, I won't be able to fit into my dress."

Mom and Grandma laughed, and so did Dr. Raintree.

Haylee didn't. She'd had enough. She wanted no part of this.

"Way to go 'fam,' reinforcing poor body image," she said. "I need to take Barney for his walk."

Her plan was to go for a nice long walk, long enough that when she got back, Dr. Raintree would already be gone. Surely, he would leave before Dad arrived at three o'clock.

Before she closed the door, Haylee heard Mom ask, "Are we still on for dinner tonight at Tavern on the Green?"

"Yep," Dr. Raintree replied. "We have reservations for eight o'clock."

The air outside was chilly for a spring day.

Haylee set a brisk pace and Barney didn't seem to mind at all. At least at first. As soon as they rounded a corner to a street they didn't normally travel on, Barney's nose took control. He stopped and sniffed and stopped and sniffed. The last odor of particular interest occurred in the middle of a bed of pansies.

Whatever was in them really had his attention. No matter how hard Haylee tugged on the leash, Barney wouldn't budge.

"Come on, Barney!" she ordered, still yanking.

Barney returned suddenly. Haylee was thrown completely off balance. Her feet went right out from under her, and she landed with a huff in the street.

"Barney!" she yelled.

Eagerly, Barney circled around, licking her face.

"Stop it!" Haylee bellowed. Barney was slobbering all over her.

Falling didn't hurt, but landing in the street felt like another failure, just like her inability to understand her best friend, her father and even her mother.

"Oh, Barney," she whimpered. "Why am I such a dunce? Why can't I do anything right?"

Barney kept licking. His mission was even more important now that he had salty tears to lap up.

Haylee wrapped her arms around his neck for a good long hug.

"I think you understand me better than anyone. So, here's the plan. We'll take our time on this walk. As soon as we get home, I'll check the garage to make sure everything I need is in my backpack. Then I'll go make sandwiches. If anyone wonders why I'm making so many, I'll tell them I'm meeting Josh and Brandon. They eat like lumberjacks. Then, when everyone's distracted with Michaela's fashion show, I'll sneak out the back door."

With that, Haylee got to her feet.

A breeze whooshed through, causing the "beast"—her ghastly, bushy hair—-to whip around her face. She made a mental note to bring enough hair ties and a bandana to keep her hair under control and so that it not be an attraction magnet for the bats.

But she worried. Had she thought of everything else? Did she have enough clothes to keep her warm? Enough blankets to make a comfortable bed? Enough food and water to sustain her?

The wind whistled. Strangely enough, she felt calm, a calm that enveloped her.

"Yes," she said aloud. Giggling, she realized, "Barney you were my misstep. So, yes, I'm ready."

33

Timing Is Everything

When Haylee and Barney returned from their walk, the first thing Haylee noticed was Dr. Raintree's car was no longer parked in the driveway.

Haylee caught herself smiling.

She still had an hour before Dad arrived.

Upstairs, Mom and Grandma were helping Michaela primp and preen, so Haylee slid into her bedroom. She spent a little time drawing the cave—the place where no one could ruin her privacy, the place that would save her from this awful world. Haylee knew drawing the cave would put her right there, right now, and if she could feel all aspects of the cave experience, she'd remember what all she needed to pack.

She couldn't wait to sneak away.

Absorbed in her artwork, she forgot to pay attention to the clock. When finally she checked her phone, it was almost three p.m. The bewitching hour.

Dad would descend on her home any minute.

Hearing voices downstairs, Haylee wondered ... it couldn't be Dad ... not yet, could it?

If Dad is here, why wouldn't anyone call me? It's one thing to practice invisibility, but geez, what a family to ignore me each and every time!

Haylee ran downstairs and through the hall. She swept around the corner into the kitchen and stopped so fast, she almost tripped over her own feet.

A man stood there with Mom and Grandma. He looked sort of like Dad, but then again, he did not. At Christmastime, he'd been slimmer. Here, before her eyes, stood a stranger, an alien from another country.

The face she remembered looked distorted. The bone structure protruded and cartilage in this man's nose made an angular swoop to the indent above his lips.

That wasn't the only odd thing, though. She recognized his clothes, but they didn't look the same. The shirt was not his typical oxford cloth. This one hung loose on his arms and billowed around the waist, so that the bottom of the shirt draped over his cinched belt. Even his trousers sagged.

He must have heard her shoes clomping, because he spun around and said, "Haylee!"

Haylee couldn't look at him. Instead, she stared toward the archway leading from the kitchen to the living room.

"Hey," she murmured.

He moved then, crossing the short distance between them.

Haylee backed up. She felt a surge of repulsion as he placed his hands on her shoulders. Feeling trapped, she cringed, as he leaned closer and wrapped his arms around her. Haylee froze like an opossum.

"I think you've grown an inch or two," he said, smiling. "You look bigger."

And you look smaller. So very different. How could I ever think you'd protect me?

A Divorce in Salem

Haylee couldn't speak. All she could think was that it was good she had a plan—a plan that would take her away from this eeriness. She hoped the opportunity to head out would come soon, like yesterday in time travel.

"It's good to see you, kiddo," he murmured, his voice softer this time, as if the words intended for her ears would offer a special closeness.

How DARE you? You've got some nerve acting as though everything is okay simply because you came to see Michaela.

"Have you met my dog, Barney? We have a pet duck, too. His name is Mr. Mallard." She offered the name, as she pet briskly her dog, Barney.

Haylee knew she sounded stupid. Of course, he knew they had a dog. Barney was right there, in plain view, lying in front of the mudroom door, his favorite spot since Mr. Mallard had become part of the household. She just figured it was the only safe thing to say.

"A pet duck? Really?" He chuckled. "I think—"

Gliding in, Michaela interrupted with, "Daddy!"

All eyes turned, and everyone gasped.

Michaela looked like a model in a magazine. The rhinestones Grandma had sewn onto the gown picked up the ceiling light and shimmered as she moved. Her long dark tresses were swooped up in the back and curls draped like a curtain around the nape of her neck. Rhinestones in her hair also glimmered. Everything about Michaela was perfection—the dress, hair, makeup, and shoes. She truly looked like an exotic princess.

"Oh, my goodness." Dad said. "My ... little girl." Michaela wasn't awkward in the embrace that followed. She held on tight, and Dad gave her a squeeze.

"Be careful, Daddy," Michaela chortled, "you'll wrinkle me."

That made Dad laugh, as he pulled back.

Grandma chuckled, and although Mom was smiling, her eyes were misty.

"How do I look?" Michaela asked, as she spun around. "Do you like it?"

"You're lovely, sweetheart," Dad said. "Truly lovely. You look so grown up. But you know you're gorgeous no matter what you wear. I'm just so thankful to be here, to see you again."

Mom cleared her throat. "Shall we go in the living room and take pictures? The fireplace will make a much better backdrop than kitchen cabinets."

"Yes, let's do," Grandma agreed, snatching her cell phone off the counter.

They all left the kitchen, including Haylee, though she dragged behind. She didn't go all the way into the living room. She just stood in the archway and watched as Michaela preened and posed. Her sister turned sideways. She threw her head back. She put a hand on the mantel for one shot. For some, she smiled. For other shots, she appeared sober, looking as grownup as possible. For one photo, she put her lips together and pouted, as if she were about to be kissed.

This expression reminded Haylee of Mr. Mallard. Duck lips. Maybe Michaela thought she looked sexy that way, but Haylee thought she looked kind of dumb.

Memory of her father kissing Tiffany made Haylee want to escape immediately.

All the adults were taking pictures, fawning over Michaela. They gushed and laughed. They were all having a great time, belonging, bonding, connecting.

Haylee remained on the sidelines. Amid the commotion, she heard the doorbell ring.

"Oh! It's got to be Jason!" Michaela shrieked. "Wait! Let me go upstairs. I want him to see me coming down the stairs!"

"Hurry up, go on," Mom said, and shooed her off.

Haylee watched her mother walk toward the door, passing Haylee without so much as a glance.

No one even noticed her.

It was time.

Haylee quietly went to the kitchen. She retrieved her backpack from the mudroom and tiptoed to the kitchen to grab four sandwiches from the refrigerator she'd made earlier that morning. From the cabinet, she groped until she located five power bars, even though she didn't particularly like them. She found cheese and peanut butter crackers and took them as well. Finally, she gathered five juice boxes and her thermos of water.

Backpack full, ever so quietly, Haylee slipped through the back door closing it behind her without a sound.

34

Getting There Is Easy, Staying There Is

The moon hung low in a mauve-colored sky. The scents of freshly mowed lawns blended with outdoor barbecues. Such peace rendered it a perfect time for Haylee's sojourn.

Quickly, but stealthily, Haylee rushed to the garage, unzipped her backpack, and gathered the rest of her loot.

It didn't take long to suit up in her khaki jacket, she'd already stored in the corner of the garage for this purpose. She put rope she'd bought at the hardware store in the deepest right pocket. Her backpack already bulged from the tools she'd pack—pickaxe, screwdriver and shirts and sweatpants, for layering. Despite the warmth of spring, the cave would be cold. A quick peek out the garage door window assured her that no one in the house had noticed her disappearance. Oddly enough, for all the excitement inside, from the outside, the house appeared still and calm.

She checked the positioning of her backpack one last time to balance the weight, pushed her hair out of the way, and took off.

A Divorce in Salem

Striding along in the crisp, cool evening, she imagined herself as the Huck Finn of New England—adventurous, hopeful, and daring. She even contemplated whistling, because Huck Finn seemed like the type of chap who would whistle. In the end, Haylee decided whistling might not be the best idea, since she didn't want anyone to notice her.

It didn't take long to get to the bus stop, and her timing couldn't have been better. The bus appeared over the hill and made its way toward Haylee. Within a minute, she had boarded and handed over the $2.50 fare from her pocket.

"You look dressed for camping." The bus driver smiled. She knew him, of course, because she'd been on his bus before. He was always friendly, and she liked the way his wiry gray hair sprouted over his large ears.

"It's for my science project," Haylee lied.

"In my day, we just read our books and took tests," he said. "You're lucky you get to have fun with your studies."

"I am lucky," Haylee said.

Looking around, Haylee noticed there were only ten or so people on the bus, and most of them were staring down at their phones. She lumbered along with her backpack to an empty seat about midway down the aisle and settled in.

The bus took much longer than a regular car to go the same distance. Haylee chewed the skin around her fingernails. She had no choice but to take the bus; she could never walk all the way to Stage Fort Park, especially with a 30-pound backpack strapped over and around her chest and abdomen.

Haylee noticed the driver periodically glancing at her in his rearview mirror.

As soon as the driver announced, "Gloucester," Haylee stood and hefted her backpack over her shoulders. Waiting until it was her turn to disembark, she then headed up the aisle.

"Young lady," the bus driver said as she passed, "how are you getting home?"

"My mom's meeting me after she gets off her shift. She's a nurse."

"Oh. Okay then," he said. "Have fun but be careful out there."

"I will," Haylee said, smiling.

She had every intention of doing just that.

On the sidewalk, Haylee redistributed the weight of her bundle as she watched the bus pull away. As she marched off, she felt a new appreciation for hikers who bore sixty-pound backpacks up and down dusty, rocky, mountain trails. All the stuff she'd brought turned out to be overwhelmingly heavy. Nevertheless, she resolved she could do it.

The cave waited for her.

She wondered if her sister had left yet for prom and if she was having a good time. Even though Haylee was mad at Michaela, she still hoped her sister knew she really *did* look like a princess. Jason better treat Michaela like royalty.

Of course, Haylee wouldn't be there when the dance was over, and Michaela returned. She wouldn't get to hear Michaela's stories of everything that happened. No tales of the other couples—who fought, who made up, who danced the most, who didn't get asked to dance as much as they wanted, or even who danced terribly.

It seemed strange to Haylee that she was wondering about these things. She was having some fleeting regrets. She realized she would miss Michaela.

No, she insisted, she wouldn't. She couldn't.

She didn't want to see all the pictures everyone had taken. She didn't want to see Dr. Raintree come to pick up Mom for their fancy night out at Tavern on the Green. And she most definitely didn't want to spend time with her father—her skinny father who thought of Haylee as a postscript. That is, if he thought of her at all.

Soon enough, the gazebo appeared at the entrance to the park just ahead. The Victorian structure invited tourists with its icicle lights dangling from gingerbread molding. On the other side of the main entrance, the paved pathway loomed ahead showing off the Massachusetts Bay Colony Rock.

Haylee donned her headlamp and maneuvered her backpack across her shoulders. Following the dirt and stone pathway leading to the top of the boulder, she inched slowly between stones. Finally, she managed to descend the other side of the massive rock by lowering one leg first, then dropping the other leg as well.

Several iron cannons from the Civil War overlooked the cove. Haylee walked by them, noticing as she went her timing couldn't have been better. The tide was low, so she would have no trouble making it to the cave's entrance.

Once just below it, though, Haylee saw the mouth of the cave appeared higher than she had remembered. Still, she forged her way onward. Would the wonderful, peaceful cave welcome her, she wondered, or would it belch her out in rejection just like her father and Misty?

35

Rationing

Haylee knew she needed to enter the cave within minutes of ebb tide and make her way into the belly of the cavern before neap tide filled the entrance. Haylee knew neap tide was the time of least difference between high and low tide where intense waters would consume all paths leading from the entrance.

The floor of the entranceway crunched and sloshed beneath her boots, and it smelled like rotten eggs. The odor emanated from sulfur compounds. In her research, Haylee learned this cave was a *littoral* cave, since it had been created from limestone and seawater that took thousands of years to form.

Despite layers of clothes, her backpack chafed her shoulders, yet she continued onward, each step resounding against the earthen walls.

Bats descended, swooping down to assess her as an intruder. Upon determining she posed no threat, they flapped away, only to land, turn upside down by their sticky paws, and hang from craggy rocks and mossy spots. It seemed like that, anyway. She told herself this to keep her fear of bats at bay. She tried to aim her headlamp in a downward direction, so as not to disrupt the bats' natural dark habitat.

Hayley trudged on, one foot in front of the other, until she arrived at the spot where the pathways forked.

"Sorry, little bats," she murmured.

Pointing her headlamp to help her decide which way to go, Haylee noticed both cavern pathways looked similar. She couldn't see far enough into either to figure out how deep they went.

Haylee's stomach growled. "I can't eat now. I have a job to do."

She really couldn't eat anyway, because her mouth tasted like metal. This, she figured, was caused by the lack of sunlight combined with seawater on the walls. She surmised the metal taste must mean the neap tide couldn't reach this far into the cave, or the sea water would have covered up the decaying material, and so, she assumed she was in a safe place for now.

Inching along the far wall of the left pathway, Haylee found herself moving downward, then turning left again. Here the smells changed a little, though it still reeked of sulfur. The metallic taste dissipated.

Looking around, she spied a shelf above her head. Crystal-like stalactites hung from it. Haylee gasped at their beauty.

It was as good a place as any to settle down and eat. She dropped her backpack to the ground. Sifting through the contents, she rummaged for one of the ham and cheese sandwiches she'd made. She'd done a nice job with these. They even included lettuce, tomato, and pickles, and she'd doused them with mustard. Most sandwiches Haylee made had to be dry, but ham and cheese with mustard sang to her tummy.

"Eureka!" she bellowed, loving the way the cave echoed back to her.

Normally, she preferred eating sandwiches with potato chips, but in this remote atmosphere, Haylee decided it would be better to eat as little as possible to preserve her rations. Instead, she opted to scarf down only half the sandwich and save the rest for later.

While taking in her surroundings, Haylee wondered who from her family would be the first to notice her disappearance.

"Probably Grandma," she said aloud. "Grandma notices everything and misses nothing."

A pang of guilt hit. She knew Mom would be worried. Unfortunately, there wasn't much Haylee could do about it. Getting away to regroup—to make the headaches of friendship, schoolwork, her sister, her parents' divorce, Mom dating again, and the strained relationship with Dad—was necessary for Haylee. It was the only way she would be able to survive the mess her life had become.

The funny thing was that back in Chicago, before she had a friend, she hadn't been lonely. Misty was her first real friend. Now that she'd experienced true friendship, Misty's loss left her feeling not just lonely, but adrift and isolated.

Misty's rejection only confirmed something Haylee had already figured out. Dad's reappearance proved it, along with Mom's fawning over Michaela, though Mom was better at hiding it.

Haylee was defective, and not just because of her neurodivergence. No, her defectiveness went deeper than that. This was a whole package kind of deal. Everyone else in the world offered something that Haylee didn't have. She was the one lacking. She was unapproachable, untouchable, unfriendly. Haylee was repulsive, the opposite of the filings of a magnet. Haylee was unlovable and repelled those she loved.

Lifting her head, Haylee shouted into the cave as loud as she could, "Lacking! I am lacking!"

The sound bounced off the walls and came back.

Lacking... lacking... lacking...

The cave confirmed it.

Silent and still, she remained on the floor of the cave as tears bubbled up and tumbled over. The little brown bats swooped to see her and fluttered away. Even they determined she wasn't worth their attention.

36

Here's Your Misstep

At some point, Haylee cried herself to sleep, though not for long. She awoke feeling chilled, and hungry, even though she'd eaten. Worse yet, the metallic taste had returned.

It was best not to stay where she was. She needed to move on, to find a better spot to claim and make a home base.

Haylee stood up and hoisted the backpack onto her shoulders. Edging carefully along the cave walls with her fingers splayed, she crept farther into the darkened depths. At least here, the floor felt less soggy and made it easier to maneuver. Her boots weren't getting sucked down, and that meant she didn't have to yank her feet up with each step.

Though she didn't want to disturb the bats any more than necessary, curiosity caused her to look up. Above her, the ceiling appeared lower than at the mouth of the cave, but it was still at least twenty feet high. Way too high to worry about.

Of course, her light challenged the bats. Several whirled down. "Sorry, guys," Haylee told them.

With just a few paces, Haylee noticed formations of stalagmites—mineral deposits that rose up from the ground—and stalactites—the ones that rained down from the ceiling. This time, as she craned her neck around to see better, she didn't worry about the bats. The stalagmites and stalactites were entirely too fascinating. It made no sense to her that most people didn't appreciate all the mysterious beauty the cave offered as well as the not-yet-identified scientific discoveries hidden in its contents.

Then and there, Haylee decided she would live in the cave forever. She would live free of hurt, disappointment and rejection.

Excited to see more, she let go of the wall and hastened her pace. The deeper she went the better.

Moving as briskly as possible, she took a step and her foot landed on ... nothing. The floor wasn't there anymore!

Haylee threw out her arms to grab onto something, anything, but she was too far into the center of the pathway to grip the wall. She couldn't reach it. It all happened so quickly. In an instant, Haylee plummeted.

She tried to grab at rocks protruding from the steep declining ground, but either the stones came off in her hands or her grip wasn't strong enough. She just kept sliding and rolling. Small rocks and pebbles pelted her. Her coat snagged on something and ripped, not just one sleeve, but the other as well. Once the coat tore, the fabric of her layered shirts underneath disintegrated. Her elbow, raw to the skin, burned as it scraped against hard-packed dirt and rock. Her pants didn't fare any better, snagging and tearing as she tumbled on. A jagged edge of rock slammed into her knee, or maybe her knee slammed into the rock. She didn't know anymore.

All she could do was yelp and shriek from pain and fear as she continued to go down, down, down, like a cartwheeling jackhammer.

And then, just when she didn't think her slide would ever end, she banged hard into something solid.

Everything stopped. Even the scattering racket of accompanying pebbles died out. All was silent and still.

This wasn't good.

Haylee heard sobbing. It was coming from her. She couldn't help it. Everything hurt. Her hands, her arms, her sides. But nothing was as bad as the searing pain in her knee.

Somehow, she hadn't lost her headlamp in the fall.

She craned her neck and felt thick goo. She knew it was blood, Blood gushing from her leg. Her pants were soaked with it. But the nasty cut on her knee wasn't the only thing wrong. Something else was too. Something underneath wasn't where it used to be. It hurt. It hurt so much.

"Help!" she cried. "Oh, help! Mom! Grandma!"

Oh, help! Mom! Grandma! Echoed above her head and captured in the walls of the cave.

Now what was she going to do?

Haylee swiped at her eyes and tried to hold back the sobs.

She needed to think, not panic. She needed to put something on her knee to stop the bleeding. And once she'd done that, she could try to figure out a way to climb out again.

She looked upward, up the long slope. The top of the incline was so far away. Haylee knew she couldn't tell how far it was to the top. The only thing above her was an endless disjointed tunnel of blackness.

37

There's No Place Like Home

No, please, no!" Haylee whimpered aloud. Her headlamp was growing dimmer and dimmer. The battery was dying.

Soon total darkness would descend.

Haylee didn't know how long she'd been lying in this pit of darkness. Time had passed since her terrible fall, but down here, there was no way to tell day from night. She had no phone, no watch, nothing to gauge time by. Communication and time were things she hadn't thought of before taking off on her sojourn.

And despite her tarot card reading, Haylee had never imagined something like this. She had taken a literal misstep and look where she'd ended up.

Three times so far, she'd tried to stand, and three times she had failed. The pain in her knee screamed at each attempt. When she tried to sleep, the burning in her leg kept her awake. Exhaustion eventually won over pain, and she had drifted off to sleep.

Now she was awake again, and the light from the headlamp was growing dimmer. Haylee had resituated herself, using the backpack to cushion her knee. Because her leg was elevated, the pain was a smidgeon less excruciating. Her backpack worked as padding for her back and butt. The padding afforded the damp of the ground not to seep through her coat as much—at least, she hoped that was the case. She'd put on extra layers of clothing and was using an extra pair of sweatpants as a pillow. She was glad she'd brought the blanket. Even so, the longer she lay there, the colder she became. For a while her teeth chattered. After she ate part of her third sandwich, the chattering stopped. Of her food supplies, all that remained, other than a sandwich and a half, were two packs of cheese and crackers and three power bars.

Her supply of liquids was faring worse. Haylee had already finished the water in her thermos. She'd drunk all of it, because she'd yelled, "Help!" So many times, the cries made her vocal cords hoarse. She slaked her thirst to keep her throat from being so scratchy. Of the juice boxes, only two remained.

The headlamp was growing dimmer with each passing minute.

"Don't cry, Haylee," she told herself aloud. If she cried, her tears would use up more of her body's water and cause her to dehydrate faster. She'd already cried enough.

Haylee didn't close her eyes, since she knew her only source of light was waning. Across from her, close enough to reach out and touch, was a craggy, mossy wall of rock. Haylee had stared at it so long; she knew every crevice by heart. Haylee counted the tiny balls of moss to keep her mind from deteriorating. The first time she counted one-hundred-seventeen, the second time one-hundred-thirty-two, but the third time only eighty-four. The lowest number she believed was because her light was disappearing.

Haylee was tired of looking at the wall. Instead, she started to picture the yellow clapboard house on Essex Street.

She saw Grandma turning around at the stove with her great big grin that lit up her face when Haylee came in from school or a walk.

She saw her mom, in the kitchen, looking up from the paper; sitting in the living room, with the remote in hand, unable to decide what to watch; and Haylee saw her mom sitting on the bed beside Haylee, tracing circles on her back with a warm hand and saying softly, "Everything will be okay, honey. Mommy loves you."

More images came to her: Michaela making a face because she thought Haylee ate like a lumberjack; Michaela chattering on and on about boys and friends and her perfect clothes; Michaela walking to and from Misty's house the morning they brought the basket of food, and Michaela telling Grandma, "Haylee did everything right."

Michaela wasn't always awful.

Haylee saw all four of them around the table carving pumpkins. Mom was hiding her eyes when she revealed what she'd done; Grandma hailing, "Not too bad if I say so myself." And Michaela bellowing, "Ewww! I made a Halloween oblong!"

Of course, no dreams of home would be complete without Barney. Not only did Haylee picture him, but she could also feel him—the softness of his fur under her fingers, the heavy warmth of his body when he slept on her bed. She saw the happy faces he made when she snuck him tidbits from the table and heard his woofing because he felt the need to express his excitement about his walk.

She thought of Mr. Mallard, too. She listened to his squawks and watched him waddle around his kennel, tail wiggling. If she ever made it home, never again would she complain about filling his water dispenser or his food trough. She wouldn't mind cleaning his kennel or replacing his bedding. Ducks weren't exactly neat creatures, but they were wonderful pets. She loved Mr. Mallard. She just hoped she would see him again.

She pictured being at play rehearsal with Josh and Brandon and Mrs. Esty. She thought of bus stop chatter and all the silly notes that got passed during class. She remembered the way Josh sat beside her on the bus, the way he'd stood up for her in town in front of Danielle and Misty, the way he'd kissed her on the lips, and not just once.

Josh didn't think I was lacking. Josh thinks I am loveable!

And then there was Misty. Someday, Haylee hoped, their friendship would be repaired. If not, though, it would be okay. She wouldn't press Misty. She would do as Grandma had suggested and give Misty time to grieve.

Then there was Dr. Raintree with the shiny pennies in his shoes. Haylee copied him, more than once, by putting pennies in her loafers. He was nice to Mr. Mallard, and he was nice to Mom. If she had the opportunity, she would tell him she was sorry for not giving him a chance. She would tell Mom that if she wanted to date Dr. Raintree, it would be okay with her. She would apologize for thinking mean thoughts of him, and mean thoughts of Mom, too.

And her father ... her poor skinny dad. He loved Michaela more than her, and that was okay. Haylee wouldn't begrudge him the closeness he shared with Michaela. She would be content to be the second daughter, the one not as close. And she would try to do better and not test his patience like she used to do in Chicago, with his stained-glass, Frank Lloyd Wright panel that sat on his coffee table. She wouldn't draw in front of him as much, because he didn't like that either. She would be a better daughter all the way around.

She would be a better daughter, granddaughter, sister, and friend, so long as she could go home again.

Why, oh why, had she run away? Why had she not listened to the IEP panel who warned her running away, skipping school, and eavesdropping were all traits of her neurodivergence that posed safety as well as interpersonal problems? Why had she not listened that all of them were clever ways she avoided others knowing her?

Why had she thought the cave would bring solace? There was no peace here. The cave offered only cold, hardness, and dampness.

The only things here were fear, isolation, and loneliness. All things Haylee brought to the cave, because they were things Haylee hadn't admitted to.

All she wanted... the only thing she wanted—was to be home again.

Dimmer.

Dimmer.

Darkness.

38

I Think I can! I Think I can!

Haylee slept again, though for how long, she couldn't say. The darkness was so pure and black, she couldn't even see her fingers in front of her face.

She'd felt swamped in it for far too long. Her food stash was depleted. So were her juice boxes.

The realization that no one would find her down here came at the same time as her need to find sunlight. She could no longer lay here waiting. If she ever wanted to be home again, she needed to get there on her own. No matter how much it hurt.

The pitch black made it difficult to get her bearings, but she could tell the difference between up and down. Up was the direction she needed to go. She stayed on her rump but kept a hand above her head to feel for outcroppings of rock and depressions in the cave floor. Inch by agonizing inch, she hauled herself up and up and up.

Once again, tears flowed. This time they weren't from missing her family, or from the predicament she found herself in. This time, she cried from the agony of moving. She cried with stoic determination. She cried until she panted and grunted with exertion and had to stop.

For a while she rested. But not too long. Then she got to it again.

It worked best if she pushed off with her good leg, and then picked up the bad leg with her hands.

Another inch. Another inch. Another inch.

Rest.

Another inch. Another inch. Another inch.

Rest.

So, became the pattern. And though she could see nothing, she was sure that any second now, light would spill down on her, because she was far enough up the slope for it to filter back into the depths of the cave.

She imagined what would happen when she reached the top. She would have to hug the wall. No more of this casual walking through the center. She would hug the wall until she came to the fork.

But how could she walk? There would be no way to do that and hug the wall too. The best she could do would be to continue along on her rump. Inch by inch by ... *whoa!*

The heel of her boot slipped on loose pebbles.

"No!" Haylee screamed. The rock wouldn't hold her. The slope was too steep. Down, down, down she slid. The only thing she could do was cover her head with her arms to protect it and let herself fall.

The thump as she landed cut through her knee, and this time, when she screamed, it was just that—a loud, bloodcurdling wail. She didn't need to feel around with her hands to find the backpack she'd left behind, or to know she'd fallen right back to the shelf where she'd been before.

She knew then that she would die down here.

There would be no getting out on her own. No one would find her. Eventually she'd starve to death.

When she died, who would come to her funeral? Mom and Dad and Grandma would be there, of course, but what about Michaela? What about Dr. Raintree? What about Josh and Brandon? Would Misty come?

Misty wouldn't come. Of course, she wouldn't.

Except there could be no funeral because nobody would ever find her body.

"Stop it!" she yelled into the blackness. "Stop feeling sorry for yourself!"

Lowering her voice, she went on, "If you're going to die, you're going to die. Heaven is supposed to be a nice place, a really nice place. Maybe instead of wallowing and being scared, I should think about what life in Heaven will be like. And maybe ... maybe I should pray."

So that's what Haylee decided to do. She remembered Grandma saying to begin every prayer with gratitude.

"Thank you, God," she said aloud, "for being there for my family, for taking care of Michaela and Mom and Grandma and Dad. Thank you for watching out for my friends, Josh and Brandon and Misty. Thank you for giving me family and for giving me friends. I didn't have friends in Chicago, but I do in Salem. Thank you for my parents and thank you for letting my mom find Dr. Raintree, because he makes her smile again.

Thank you for bringing my dad to see us, and for his being so happy to be with Michaela. Thank you for healing Grandma from her alcoholism, and for her friends in AA meetings. Thank you for Barney. He is such a good dog. And thank you for Mr. Mallard, because he's really special. Thank you for letting me get the part of Princess in the play and showing me that I could do it. And thank you for giving me art and letting me draw. I love to draw, but you probably already know that."

According to Grandma, Haylee was also supposed to remember how powerful God was. He could do anything. He could move mountains. If he wanted to, he could lift the rocks away, like he had parted the water in the Red Sea.

"Dear God," she said, "I don't know what will happen to me. But whatever it is, I promise, whether I live again on Earth, or in Heaven, I will be a good girl. I won't be angry or spiteful. I won't get jealous or act crabby. I won't ever talk back to Mom, and if I'm in Heaven I won't ever talk back to You. Dear God, the only prayer I have is please help me be a better me.

39

The Holy Grail Is Not Meant to Be Found

"Help!" cried Haylee. "Oh, help!"

Her cries bounced off the walls of black dampness and returned. No other voice. Haylee shouted again with more force, and another echo rebounded. Swooping wings flapped as the bats clicked from the noise intrusion. Hurling the backpack above her head, again and again, Haylee inched upward on her elbows. Her tongue felt thick, like it was coated in fur. It seemed like forever since she'd last sipped water or juice. At least hurling the backpack and moving a little bit warded off the chill prevailing through every bit of her.

She knew if she didn't find her way out, and soon, she would die.

Despite the endless throbbing pain in her knee, Haylee kept thrusting the backpack forward and counting while she did it. Ten throws, then sixty counts of rest. Ten more throws and again sixty counts of rest. The effort exhausted her, but she didn't quit.

"One, two, three!" she called and tossed the bag upward. This time, as she scrunched upwards after it on her elbows, she felt something odd.

Unlike the craggy rock, this was smooth. It wasn't rock. It was wood. Her hands smoothed along the rectangular panel and around to the corners. It was a box, that much she could tell by feeling it. Much of the object was buried in sediment, so she had to dig.

She dug for a while but eventually gave up. Her fingers were frozen and the grime under her nails tore the skin and made her hands sting. The box was just too big to dig out.

Even so, Haylee decided she wouldn't give up, just like she wouldn't give up on getting out of this awful dark dungeon.

For a while she rested, and then she repeated her efforts.

Fatigue overwhelmed her.

She was parched. And hungry.

In so much pain.

And so very, very cold.

40

How The Mind Wanders When Death Is Near

The sound of a trickle, like the bathtub faucet left running, brought Haylee's head up with a start.

"Oh, no!" she murmured, as droplets turned to a stream raining down upon her. "Oh, no!"

Was this the neap tide coming in?

Haylee didn't know how long she'd been stuck in the tunnel, but it felt like days had gone by. Not once since she'd been down in this abyss had she thought about the tides, perhaps because until now, she hadn't made much progress in trying to leave.

She should have remembered water ebbed and flowed because everything around her felt so damp. The rocks, the dirt, even the wooden box she'd uncovered.

"Help!" she cried, for what felt like the millionth time.

By now, her voice was little more than a squeak, reminding her how weak she'd become. She didn't just *feel* weak. She was sick, too. Her head ached; her stomach felt like a hardened bowling ball.

Sometimes she even felt like she would throw up, though this made no sense, since she hadn't eaten for so long.

During these times she felt the worst, Haylee let herself get carried away with memories. The aroma from Grandma's cooking; Josh, Brandon, and Misty being silly in the hallways of John Proctor; Sneaking into Michaela's room late at night; The two sisters crawling into Michaela's bed together, huddled under blankets with a flashlight, so they could giggle and commiserate about parents, kids at school, and dreams of whom they hoped to become.

The memory of flashlight gatherings under mounds of blankets came from Chicago, back when she and her sister were both much younger. They hadn't had a night like that for a long time. It was funny how Haylee couldn't remember anymore what exactly they giggled about, only the general topics. Haylee realized she couldn't recall specifics, because specifics weren't important. They saw the other as a mirror, and the mirror felt incredible.

Suddenly, Haylee was jolted from her reverie by more water. Not just a trickle this time, but an ice-cold wave, gushing over her. It doused her completely from head to toe and didn't stop. It got in her nose and mouth and made her cough and sputter. It was like a gale-force-wind, so strong it threatened to carry her away.

All she could do was squeeze her eyes shut, cling to the rocks, and pray soon it would stop.

"Oh, please," she whimpered. "*Please...*"

But the deluge refused to slow down let alone stop.

41

Jonah Exits the Whale

This way, to the left.

Over here, ... look!

Was she dreaming, or just hearing things?

If she was dreaming, Haylee didn't want to wake up. She felt so tired and grimy, and when she slept, she didn't feel the pain. She could dream of good things, of home, of Grandma, Mom and Dad, and Michaela, and of Barney and Mr. Mallard, and forget that she was stuck in a hole. Dying.

"Dr. Higgins, go back, we've got this."

"No, dammit!" a man cursed. "I can't just wait back there. I told you already, I'm coming with you!"

"It's not safe," a different voice said.

"She's my daughter!" the man bellowed.

Then, even more loudly, he shouted, "HAYLEE! HAYLEE! BABY GIRL! ARE YOU IN HERE?"

Haylee didn't just open her eyes. She sat up. Above her—far above her—light flickered. She'd been in the pitch black for so long. And that man, the one who shouted her name was ... *Dad!*

"Dad ... Daddy ..." Haylee cried.

Her throat was clogged and felt so scratchy. Her tongue, swollen from dehydration, wouldn't allow her to manipulate sound. It was hard to form words. But she tried again.

"Daddy!"

"Shhh! ... Stop—I think, I heard something," someone said. It was a different voice, not Daddy's.

"Daddy!" Haylee called out again.

"Oh my god, that's her. Haylee, baby!" Daddy yelled. "Haylee!"

"Haylee, we're trying to find you. Can you call out again?" the other voice said.

The lights above flickered and danced. They were close, so very close.

"I'm here," Haylee called out as loudly as she could. "I fell in the hole and can't get out."

"Here. Look," someone above said. "Looks like this is where she fell through."

"Dr. Higgins, what are you doing? Stop!"

Someone else—a female voice—ordered,

"You can't go down there!"

"She's my daughter," Daddy said, sounding hoarse, like he was choking. "I'm going."

"Look, I understand you're upset, but we don't know how far down she is. We don't know how narrow the gorge is or what we'll find once we get in there. The last thing we need is for you to get stuck, too, or worse, fall farther than she did. These cracks in the rock can go on for hundreds of feet. Let us do our job. We know what we're doing."

"Get her out. Please, get her out," Daddy said. "Please, hurry," he begged.

"Haylee," another voice hollered down. "My name's Jack, and I'm here with the Cape Ann Rescue Squad. We want you to stay right where you are. We're coming to get you."

"Oh, thank you, thank you," Haylee whispered, knowing they wouldn't hear. "I'm not gonna die down here."

Someone else—the lady—yelled down,

"Haylee, are you hurt anywhere?"

"My knee," Haylee called back. "Something's wrong with my knee."

With that news, they started buzzing with all sorts of ideas about ropes and equipment. They suggested a fiberglass sled to hoist down to her. When they got to her, they would put her in the sled to haul her out. Someone dropped a long cord down with a light at the end of it. So bright, it blinded Haylee a little bit, but she didn't mind.

"Okay, kiddo, this is Jack again," he called out. "April and I are rappelling down. Do you have something to cover your head? We'll try not to dislodge any loose gravel on the way, but some may fall on you. Okay?"

"Okay," Haylee rasped. She put her backpack over her head like an umbrella. The only thing wrong with this was she wouldn't be able to see them coming.

But she could hear. They spoke the whole time, sometimes to each other, but mostly to her.

Jack came first, with April right behind him.

The best part came when she heard Jack say "I see her Five yards out."

The next thing she knew, another man in an orange jumpsuit, with ropes around his body and legs, plopped down right in front of her. He gave Haylee a big smile, his grin revealing gleaming white teeth shining through a thick, dark beard.

"Hi, kiddo, I'm Jack. How would you like to get outta here?"

Too fatigued and weak to speak, Haylee nodded.

Jack grabbed the end of the sled and maneuvered it close. Here, the tunnel narrowed, so he slipped off to the side and made space for April. She was pretty and young with milk chocolate skin. She too beamed a wide smile toward Haylee.

"I see why you fell, Haylee. It's steep and slippery down here," April said. "First things first. I'm gonna give you some water on a sponge. And then we'll get your leg stabilized and get you into the sled. Okay?"

Haylee nodded again.

Nothing had ever felt as refreshing as the sponge April pressed to her lips. Little droplets seeped into her mouth and made the rawness in her throat beg for more.

"We'll give you more as soon as we're out of here, okay?" April soothed. "Now, let's see about that knee."

It hurt when April put the splint on, and Haylee's eyes smarted.

"I'm sorry, sweetie," she said. "I'm being as gentle as I can."

Haylee already knew that. These were nice people. Good people.

"Is my dad up there?" Haylee asked. "And my mom?"

"They are. Your sister's here, and your grandma, and a whole slew of your Grandma's biker friends. Some of your friends are up there, too."

Grandma has biker friends?

Haylee thought maybe she'd heard April wrong, but she didn't question it. Instead, she asked, "How did you know where to find me?"

"Your drawings," April said. "Your mom and grandma found the pictures you drew of this cave in your desk and gave them to the police. Your friend Misty told the cops you'd talked about coming here to explore this cave."

"Misty?" Haylee murmured.

"Yes. She said you're her best friend, and she wanted to do everything she could to help find you. There are two boys outside too, who are also worried about you. I think one of them said his name was Josh. Is he your boyfriend?"

A Divorce in Salem

April was teasing, of course. Josh wasn't Haylee's boyfriend. She didn't have a boyfriend, but she supposed if she did, she would want him to be Josh.

It took both Jack and April's efforts to get Haylee into the sled, and though she tried not to, she couldn't help but scream from the pain.

Once she was positioned in the sled and covered with a funny foil blanket around her, Haylee realized it wasn't so bad. She was warmer, and she felt safe. Buckled tightly, Haylee saw April made certain Haylee wouldn't slip or slide out of the smooth fiberglass sled.

"Okay, time to go," Jack said.

"Wait," Haylee stopped them. "The box. There's a box down here, sort of buried. Do you see it?"

"I do. But we'll worry about the box later. First, we need to take care of you," Jack said.

It was just like being on a ride at an amusement park.

Jack gave instructions to other members of the rescue team, up top, about hoisting the ropes, while he and April stayed as close on either side of her as they could. They each kept a hand on the sled to hold it steady. But at one point, the tunnel narrowed significantly enough that they had to let go. The sled swirled left and right, and then again before Jack caught it and stopped the spin.

And finally, they slipped Haylee through the top of the cave right near the fork in the pathways.

Haylee noticed several people decked out in orange jumpsuits like April and Jack. But they weren't the only people there. Before she even saw him, she heard his voice.

"Haylee, baby, it's Daddy. I'm right here, sweetheart. I'm right here. You're gonna be okay. You're gonna be just fine."

He *was* right there, beside the sled, peering down at her.

"Hi," Haylee murmured.

Daddy swiped his eyes with his sleeve, but it didn't do much good. More tears spilled over, and he swiped them, too.

"Okay, Dr. Higgins, let us through. The ambulance is waiting," Jack said.

"I'm right behind you, baby girl," Daddy said. "Mommy's by the ambulance."

"Do I have to go to the hospital?" Haylee asked. "Can't I just go home?"

April chuckled. "First, we must get you warmed up and hydrated, and the doctors will want to get an X-ray of that knee. But you'll be home before you know it."

"Will you stay with me, Daddy?" Haylee asked.

"I'm not leaving you, baby. Not for a very long time," Dad said.

They went through the cave, the entire entourage of orange-clad people, with Haylee strapped into the sled right in the middle. As they reached the entrance, Haylee could see a crowd. The dunes were as packed with people as the school auditorium on assembly day. Most of them, Haylee didn't recognize. There was even one man with a huge camera on his shoulder, and next to him, a lady holding a microphone.

"Haylee!" Mom shrieked.

Suddenly, like Dad, Mom was right beside her.

"Oh, honey," Mom said. She was crying, too. So were Grandma and Michaela.

"Haylee," Michaela sobbed. "Oh, Haylee."

Dr. Raintree was there, too.

"Hurray! Hurray!" the crowd began to chant.

Amid all the shouts and hollers, they carried Haylee to the ambulance. Men in white suits opened the rear doors. Just as they hauled the sled up, Haylee spied Josh and Brandon, and right there beside them stood Misty. All three of them looked worried. They didn't chant like the rest of the people.

But the cheerleaders continued shouting. Among them was a bunch of rough-looking men, mostly with long gray beards and tattoos, all wearing leather jackets with emblem patches on their sleeves and chests. Parked near the Massachusetts Bay Colony Rock, along with several police cars, was an array of at least a dozen motorcycles.

"I'm going in the ambulance with her," Haylee heard Mom say.

"We'll be right behind you. We'll meet you at the hospital," Dr. Raintree said.

Once safely inside, Haylee looked around the unfamiliarity inside the ambulance, as they unbuckled her from the sled. She was captivated, looking at all the compartments and equipment. But when they picked her up and put her on the gurney, she realized much effort, although looking chaotic, was because they were extra careful of her knee.

As soon as Haylee's hand was freed from under the buckles and plastic blanket, Mom grabbed it. Here in the daylight, Haylee saw how dirty her hand was. She knew Mom wouldn't be pleased to see her fingers, mud-caked and grimy. Mom didn't like dirt, not at all, yet she squeezed Haylee's hand and didn't seem bothered in the least by how dirty her hands were.

"All right, Haylee, we're gonna put the sirens on," one of the men in white said. "They can be loud, so be prepared. And we need to start an IV. It might prick a little."

"Okay," Haylee said.

The prick did hurt, but it was nothing compared to what she had endured in the cave.

Haylee gazed at Mom who, like Dad, was wiping her eyes. "I wish I could hold you," Mom murmured.

Haylee smiled.

For once, she couldn't have agreed more with her mother. Physical affection could be a wonderful thing.

42

There's No Place like...a Hospital?

By the next day, Haylee felt energized. Although she still couldn't wait to get home, the hospital offered her a private room with a nice view of the grounds, and a sky that she didn't have to get out of bed to see.

Both Mom and Dad stayed the night, sleeping side by side in recliners right there in her room. Having them close by helped a lot. Not once had she heard them snap at each other. In fact, they were getting along so well, a few times she even heard them teasing each other and laughing.

Of course, Haylee also overheard the doctor talking to them. The doctor listed dehydration as well as hypothermia as her issues at intake. It didn't take long, though for her to feel better what with the fluid from the IV hydrating her, balancing her electrolytes, and the heated blankets warming her.

But her knee was another issue. It was not only fractured, but she'd also experienced a tear of the anterior cruciate ligament—"ACL," they called it. This meant Haylee needed surgery. After she recovered

A Divorce in Salem

from the fracture, she would need physical therapy. As for the surgery, the date would be scheduled as soon as the doctors said she was well enough. At least now, with the way the nurses had bandaged and propped her leg, it barely hurt.

So far today, Haylee had had numerous visitors. The first, early that morning, was Chief O'Malley, from the police force. He had asked Haylee why she'd decided to run away.

"It was a bunch of stuff," Haylee admitted.

It was kind of embarrassing to say these things in front of Mom, Dad, Grandma, and Michaela, but Haylee knew better than to not answer a police officer.

"My friend Misty wasn't speaking to me, and I thought she hated me. I thought my dad didn't love me, because he only seemed excited to see Michaela when he came to visit, and I thought my mom wouldn't care about me anymore because she has a new boyfriend, Dr. Raintree. Plus, I thought Michaela wanted a different sister."

"Do you still think those things?" Chief O'Malley wanted to know.

"No," Haylee said. "I realized when I was stranded in the cave, my thinking was warped. When I was rescued, Michaela told me she loves me, and so did Mom and Grandma and Dad. They all said they were sorry. They didn't realize I'd felt the way that I did. They told me if they had known, they would have told me how wrong I was. The only person I haven't talked to yet is Misty."

"Well," Chief O'Malley said, "if it weren't for your friend, we wouldn't have found you. Your mom and grandma found the pictures you drew of the cave, but they weren't sure of the significance until Misty filled them in. She told me she's sorry for the way she treated you, and that you're the best friend she ever had. I don't know if she's planning to visit, but I'm sure when you next see her, she'll tell you the same thing."

Haylee didn't know what to say.

Chief O'Malley continued. "Next time you decide to take flight, don't. Okay, kiddo?"

"I'll never do anything like that again," Haylee said. "I learned my lesson."

He stayed for a few more minutes talking to Mom and Dad, and then told her,

"Get well," and left.

As soon as Chief O'Malley had departed, Dad came over and sat on the bed.

"Haylee, sweetheart, I'm so sorry I made you feel that way. It was my mistake and my fault. I want you to know I love both you and Michaela. I can't say I love you both the same, because you're both so unique. But I love you *because* you're both so different. I wouldn't have it any other way. You're both my girls, and you always will be."

"I know," Haylee said. She believed him, not because of his words, but because of the way he'd reacted when he knew she was in the in the cave—the way he'd ignored the pleadings of the rescue team to not descend further for safety reasons, and the way he'd cried when they found her. Haylee had never seen Dad cry like that before, not even for Michaela.

"Do you know," Dad continued, "you and I are a lot alike? Your mother reminded me of this last night. And she's right."

Haylee blinked. She didn't expect this.

After he cleared his throat, he said,

"You're quiet like me. You like sciences like me. You struggle to understand people. And you draw like I did when I was your age."

"I didn't know you used to draw," Haylee said, as she pressed the button to raise the head of the bed.

"All the time. Think about how much we both love that stained glass panel."

In the past, thinking of how upset Dad used to get when she dared to touch his favorite showpiece would have upset her. But now, she just giggled, and Dad laughed.

Haylee asked, "Do you have any drawings from when you were a kid, Dad? I'd love to see them."

"As a matter of fact, I do. They're in the attic at home," he said. Cradling her hand, he promised, "Next time I see you, I'll give them to you."

Turning her head to look out the window, Haylee said,

"Dad, when I was in the cave and so afraid, I remembered lots of things to take my mind off dying. One of the things was when it snowed bad that one year. I was little then. I was playing outside, and you came out to take the trash to the curb. Afterwards, you got the sled and dragged me around the yard until it was dark. And we kept on going. It was just you and me, in the dark, in the snow. I was so happy."

Dad wiped tears from his cheek. "I remember that, too, Haylee. You were four years old. It's one my favorite memories of us."

Haylee grinned, and Dad leaned over to kiss her cheek.

"You know, I must go back to Chicago soon. But don't worry, honey, I won't ever stay away for such a long time again. I missed you girls way too much."

"Do you promise?" Haylee asked.

"You don't think for a minute I would miss that play of yours, do you? You're the Princess—the lead role!" he said.

Haylee had already been told by her mother the performance date had been postponed. This decision, made by the school faculty as well as the school board, was unanimous. They rescheduled the performances for the following fall.

"So, my princess," Dad said, "I want you to do me a favor. Be nice to your mom, do your chores, and your homework, and never ever go off by yourself like that again."

Haylee nodded. "I'll keep my promise, if you keep yours."

"You've got yourself a deal, kiddo," Dad said.

Another visitor appeared, a reporter. Haylee recognized her as the lady who had been holding the microphone and standing by the ambulance. The same guy with the giant camera was with her again, too. They interviewed Mom and Dad, and then asked Haylee how she was feeling.

"Much better," Haylee said. "I can't wait to go home."

They laughed but didn't stay long after that.

After the reporter and cameraman departed, Jack and April came with Grandma and Michaela in tow. They wanted to see how Haylee was doing after their rescue.

Haylee and her parents thanked them for everything—the careful way they'd taken care of her, putting her on the sled, smiling and talking to her to keep her distracted from the pain.

Beaming, April said, "We want to show you something. Jack's gonna go get it. He'll be right back."

Jack left the room, and when he returned after a few minutes, he carried a box. Not just any box. Haylee recognized it right away. Because of how dark it had been in the cave, she'd never really gotten a good look at it, but she remembered running her hands over it plenty of times. It was the box that had been buried in the cave gorge. It wasn't covered with dirt anymore. They must have cleaned it up.

"We decided to go back down and retrieve this thing," Jack said. "You'll never guess what you uncovered, Haylee."

Setting the box carefully on the bed, Jack opened the lid. It was so old, the hinges creaked. But that's not what made Haylee gasp.

Inside were old coins—lots of them, both silver and gold. The precious metals in the coins made the box incredibly heavy.

"We're going to take this to the Peabody Museum to be evaluated, but Haylee, the coins in here have to be centuries old," he said

A Divorce in Salem

with eyes widened. "Believe it or not, I think you stumbled on a pirate's treasure."

Haylee's mouth dropped open. "Really?"

The entire room buzzed with comments as well as gasps, oohing and ahhing.

As Jack retrieved the box, he wished Haylee a speedy recovery.

"The whole town is grateful, Haylee, because we've known pirates as well as privateers, the government sanctioned pirates, gossiped about hidden treasure, but you've proved the rumors are true. So, thank you for your contribution to history."

After they all left, Haylee couldn't get the pirate treasure out of her mind.

It reminded her of something else.

"Mom, Dad, Grandma?" she murmured, "I need to tell you something. A secret I've been keeping."

The three of them surrounded the bed and Mom said, "You know you can tell us anything. You don't ever need to keep secrets again."

Haylee fidgeted.

"What is it, Hayley?" Grandma asked. She patted Haylee's hand to encourage her to fess up.

Turning her head toward the door, Haylee whispered, "Someone has been leaving me rose quartz crystals. They're all shaped like hearts. I've been finding them everywhere I go, but mostly in our backyard, by Mr. Mallard's kennel. Misty thinks I have a secret admirer, but I think she's wrong. I don't know what to do about them, because I don't know who's stalking me."

"You have no idea who's leaving them?" Mom asked yanking her head toward Haylee's father.

Grandma chuckled. "I'm pretty sure I know who the culprit is."

"Who?" Haylee, Mom, Dad, and Michaela asked at the same time.

"My sponsor," Grandma snickered. "I've told her all about you girls. And Haylee, she's taken a special interest in you. She told me that you remind her of herself when she was your age."

"But I never met her, so why would she leave me crystals?" Haylee asked.

"Ah, but you have met her, more than once. Do you know she knits blankets for her grandchildren? She has so many grandchildren she can't remember which colors she's given to which child."

"The lady who sat beside me on the bus is your sponsor?" Haylee blurted.

"She's also a fortune—teller at Crow Haven Corner," Grandma went on. "She goes by the name, Mary Ann."

"Oh! No wonder she understood me so well," Haylee said.

Everybody laughed at that, even Michaela.

"How's the little lady?" said a deep voice from the door.

They all looked up to see who'd come.

Six gray-headed men were standing there, all of them decked out in jeans and leather jackets with emblem patches sewn on.

One had chains dangling from his belt loops. He sauntered in first, saying, "I hope it's okay for us to visit. Just wanted to see how our girl is doing?"

It took Haylee a second to realize he meant her.

But how could they refer to her that way when she'd never met them before?

"Haylee," Grandma said. "These are my friends from the meetings I go to. I'm the only woman there. It's a funny story. I was beyond upset over a silly argument I had with your mother, and I didn't want to drink. So, I looked up where a meeting was near me. When I got there, I realized it was a meeting for biker's!" But honestly, they all were so nice, they invited me out to breakfast afterwards. I've been going ever since.

The bikers and everyone in the room nodded and chuckled.

Mom said, "Haylee, these guys had a significant hand in your rescue. They've explored the trails and the cove of Stage Fort Park, so they were familiar with the entrance to the cave. They were able to show the police and the Cape Ann Rescue Squad where it was."

"Thank you," Haylee told them.

"All that matters to us is that you're hale and hearty again," the guy with the chains said. "You gave us quite a fright, you know."

Grandma explained. "I was so upset when you disappeared—we all were—I called my friends, and they held an impromptu meeting at Brigida's Breakfast All Day Diner. Ever since, they've been working along with the rest of us. They were the ones who made missing person posters and hung them everywhere. I guess you haven't seen any of them yet, but they placed them all over town and then some, thanks to these guys."

"Yes, we owe you guys in a huge way," Dad said. "Not only for the posters and your search efforts, but also for your wise counsel. You calmed all of us down a time or two."

Haylee felt overwhelmed by the attention, but soon the bikers had everybody laughing. Haylee noticed Grandma eyeing one man and she wondered if he and Grandma were more than just meeting buddies. But it wasn't her place to ask, so she kept her mouth shut. Like everything else, she figured, in the right time, all would be revealed.

The men stayed until the nurse came in with Haylee's lunch tray. Since she'd been in the hospital, she'd eaten plenty, even some special snacks and goodies snuck in by Grandma and Michaela. She hadn't refused a bite, and it would be no different now.

Haylee said good-bye to the bikers and took up her fork.

As they were leaving, Dr. Raintree sauntered in.

"Hi, Haylee. How's my favorite duck parent?"

Haylee giggled. She missed Mr. Mallard. And she really missed Barney. As she'd vowed in the cave, never again would she begrudge taking Barney for walks or cleaning up Mr. Mallard's poop in the kennel.

"After Haylee's finished her lunch, how 'bout the rest of us grab a bite in the cafeteria, while she's resting?" Dad suggested.

Haylee's eyes widened. Dad having lunch with Mom and Dr. Raintree? He didn't sound mad, or jealous, or anything bad. She watched as the two men shook hands. They'd been friendly like this right after her rescue, and even though she felt bleary headed, she'd noticed the dramatic change in comportment.

It was a good surprise, for once. A very good one. It meant she was allowed to like Dr. Raintree, too.

Once she'd stuffed her belly full, Haylee thanked everyone for the visit. As they headed to the cafeteria for their lunch, she lay back in her bed and closed her eyes.

Maybe all the excitement of the morning had been too much for her, because her eyelids were heavy. It was good timing for a nap. Oh, it was glorious to be in a nice soft bed, even if it wasn't hers. It was so much better than the hard, cold, damp earth of the cave.

She drifted off for a while, but something woke her. She didn't know what it was at first. A couple blinks and she saw she had more company.

Not only that; they'd brought gifts.

"Hi, Haylee," Brandon chirped, thrusting a cuddly teddy bear at her. "This is for you. How are you feeling?"

"Better, thanks. And thanks for the bear." Hugging the bear, Haylee made a wide grin.

"We were worried," he said.

"And scared," Misty chimed. She stepped forward, holding out a big box of chocolates. "I don't know if you're allowed to have these, but I hope so."

"I'm allowed. Thanks," Haylee murmured.

Despite everything she'd heard about how much Misty had helped with her rescue from the cave, Haylee still felt leery. She couldn't help expecting Misty to spout out something mean.

But she didn't spout anything.

"I'm so sorry, Haylee," Misty said softly, "For the way I treated you. I was just mad because of what my mom did. I don't know what I was thinking. As soon as I heard you were missing, I realized what a fool I'd been. You're the best friend I ever had. You listen to me, and you care about me, and I threw it all away. I just hope someday you'll be able to forgive me."

"I heard how you helped the police and the rescue squad figure out where I was," Haylee told her. She sat up and fluffed her pillow for better support. "Thank you for that."

Misty had tears in her eyes. "Thanks, Haylee. If I ever get stupid again, make sure you call me on it, and remind me that we're best friends. I want us to be best friends forever."

"Okay," Haylee said smiling, "I'll remind you."

"Hey, Haylee," Josh murmured.

He was holding a vase filled with red roses. She swore his face was pinker than normal.

"I hope you like roses. I wasn't sure ..."

"Nobody has ever given me roses before," Haylee said shyly. "They're beautiful. Can you put them here, on the table beside me, so I can look at them all the time?"

Josh stepped close to the bed to do as she asked.

Haylee thought he was going to turn around and step away again, but he didn't. Instead, he leaned over and brushed his lips against hers.

Haylee didn't know whether to chalk up her sudden lightheadedness to her ordeal, or the kiss.

He didn't give her a chance to blink herself back into focus. Settling on the bed beside her, Josh took her hand, and said softly,

"I was so scared when you went missing. I couldn't sleep. I couldn't eat. Brandon laughed at me, but I even cried. And it made me realize something. You're special to me. I ... I really like you. I'd be honored if you'd consider being my girlfriend."

"What's this?" came a bellow.

Josh stood up abruptly.

Haylee gulped.

It was Dad.

"Don't you think you're a little young for that, young man?"

Dad's narrowed eyes were boring into Josh.

"Daddy!" Haylee tried to intervene.

"What are your intentions, young man?" Dad demanded.

"I ...uh, I ... ummm ..." Josh stammered. "Sorry, sir, I don't have any intentions, except ...uh, ... it's just I really care about your daughter. That's all."

"Daddy, please!" Haylee screeched.

"Well," Dad said, suddenly breaking into a crooked grin. "That makes two of us." His eyes narrowed again. "So long as you keep those intentions honorable."

"I will, sir. I swear," Josh said.

"Good," Dad said. "All right, then. I'll give you a few minutes to visit and I'll be back. No funny business!"

Haylee rolled her eyes as Dad strolled out of the room.

"I thought he was gonna kill you!" Brandon snickered.

"Me, too!" Misty giggled.

"Yeah," Josh plopped back down on Haylee's bed. When he turned to her, though, he was smiling. "I think your dad likes me."

"I think so, too," Haylee said. "And ... so do I. Yes, Josh, I'd be honored to be your girlfriend."

Haylee's friends stayed for a little while and made plans to return the next day to rehearse their lines together. Having them with her again, joking around and laughing, making plans—the camaraderie was just like it used to be. Her problems couldn't have turned out better.

Except it was better, because now Josh was more than a friend.

Josh gave her a final kiss farewell, and no sooner had her friends walked out than her dad strode in.

Haylee figured he'd been right outside the door, eavesdropping the whole time.

Kind of like she was always doing.

Maybe Dad was right. We are a lot alike.

"How's my princess?" he asked.

"When can I go home?" Haylee asked.

"Soon," he said, chuckling. "For now, how 'bout I move you to the window. I'll roll the IV for you. There's something you gotta see."

Haylee was curious.

Her dad ordered her to close her eyes until he told her to open them. Moving the chair for visitors parallel to the bed, he gathered Haylee in his arms and carefully placed her in the seat. He rolled her IV over and positioned it behind the chair. Then he maneuvered Haylee and her IV close to the window.

"Okay, baby girl, open your eyes," Dad instructed.

Down below, in the parking lot right outside the hospital, was a row of Harley—Davidson motorcycles. Haylee recognized most of the riders as the men who'd visited earlier.

But they weren't the only ones.

Grandma was with them.

Grandma—clad in jeans and a leather jacket was hefting a leg over one of the bikes. As if she knew they were watching, she looked up at the building and waved.

Haylee and her father cackled.

Then, Grandma hit the throttle and rode off into the sunset with the rest of the pack.

Acknowledgments

My pathway to this novel is not a straight line, yet the journey is one I am so grateful to have dared to scale. As a Christmas gift, my husband gave me a year's subscription to Year of the Book. Demi Stevens, owner of Year of the Book, provided tutorials every other week for three hours each month for an entire year. She has helped thousands of would-be enthusiasts organize their thoughts and efforts so most become published authors. Her lessons and example are indelible imprints on my mind, and this book would never have manifested without her encouragement and expertise.

I also wish to thank Steve Eisner who presides over When Words Count, a writer's dream of a retreat as well as a digital contest. His offerings of literary agents, publishers, writers, and marketing agents also provided so much wisdom and inside knowledge on how the literary world works and looks for in a budding novelist. His atmosphere is collegial so entrants and experts in their fields celebrate together when one special novel rises to the top of the contest. The real blessing is that more than two-thirds of the would-be authors become published. I am one of the lucky entrants who, although I did not 'win,' I became published anyway.

I also would like to thank my parents who engaged in a contentious divorce when, at the time, neither Oprah nor Dr. Phil existed. Truly, I learned what not to do from them. I so hope in Heaven they are at peace and can feel proud of their children. Their vitriol taught me feelings are neither positive nor negative, but when intense, can provoke the worst of reactions.

I wish to thank my ex-husband who had the courage to end our marriage of twenty-three years, as it was the first divorce in his family line. I learned from him, holding on for the sake of a vow, yet not putting effort in the couple-ship is toxic and can bring as much harm to children as a divorce of intense animosity.

Most of all, I wish to thank my husband and our seven children (my three daughters, his two sons, his two daughters, as well as his five grandchildren). We have weathered much, but all are wonderful people with amazing talents. Yes, indeed, I struck gold when I went pan handling for a better way to navigate life, when the one I thought I had, disintegrated. Thanks to all the people mentioned, as I learned disappointment does not end a story. All that is required is a willingness to try anew, anew with better efforts. And so, the magic continues ...

About The Author

Laurie S. Pittman knows divorce in a three-dimensional way.

Forget the 30 years of experience, prior to her retirement where she worked as a licensed psychologist helping families navigate the throes of divorce. Instead, her empathy for parents and children runs deep. At the age of five, she and her older sister witnessed their parents struggle through a perpetuating, toxic dogfight that lasted for decades. Ever recalling how bitter her parents' divorce was, Laurie longed to break the fourth generation of marriage failure. Adding salt to old wounds, Laurie learned in her late forties, the father of her three beautiful daughters wished to divorce her after twenty-three years of marriage. The request shattered her hopes of breaking the fourth generation of separated/divorced parenting.

Instead, Laurie would now be a parent navigating the grief process, financial fears and confused/hurt children. Ultimately, Laurie learned an important truth that divorce ends a marriage but, the family unit can remain intact if adults can put the focus on the children, so that the children are not used as pawns for manipulating or even venting the unfinished business of muddied feelings.

Laurie's prior writing experience is her dissertation, "Attachment Issues, Self-Esteem, and Sense of Symbolic Immortality: Are Their Differences between Couples Not in Treatment vs. Couples in Marriage Therapy?" UMI Dissertation Services from ProQuest Company; September 15, 2007: Union Institute & University, Cincinnati, Ohio.

Laurie was a guest speaker at the International Symposium in Caja Marca, Peru, and she won the local pageant, Miss Cumberland Valley, of the Miss America Pageant in 1980 and won Miss Congeniality in the Miss Pennsylvania Pageant. She also won the Gould Award for Acting in 1979 as well as the Winfield-Davidson Walkley Prize for Forensic Declamation in 1977 while attending Dickinson College for her undergraduate degree. She also was interviewed for a radio program about drug and alcohol issues for loved ones who love a problem drinker in 1994.

Laurie holds a Bachelor's Degree (1980) in Political Science and Dramatic Literature from Dickinson College; a Master's Degree (1993) in Clinical Psychology from Millersville University; and a Ph.D. of Philosophy with a concentration in Clinical Psychology (2008) from Union Institute & University, Cincinnati, Ohio. Laurie resides in East Berlin, Pennsylvania where she enjoys the bucolic scenery as well as woodsy animals, geese and ducks.